AMY
AMONG THE
SERIAL KILLERS

AMY
AMONG THE
SERIAL KILLERS

A NOVEL

Jincy Willett

ST. MARTIN'S PRESS
NEW YORK

First published in the United States by St. Martin's Press, an imprint of St. Martin's Publishing Group

AMY AMONG THE SERIAL KILLERS. Copyright © 2022 by Jincy Willett. All rights reserved. Printed in the United States of America. For information, address St. Martin's Publishing Group, 120 Broadway, New York, NY 10271.

www.stmartins.com

Library of Congress Cataloging-in-Publication Data

Names: Willett, Jincy, author.
Title: Amy among the serial killers : a novel / Jincy Willett.
Description: First edition. | New York : St. Martin's Press, 2022. | Series: Amy Gallup ; 3
Identifiers: LCCN 2022005968 | ISBN 9781250275141 (hardcover) | ISBN 9781250275158 (ebook)
Subjects: LCGFT: Novels.
Classification: LCC PS3573.I4455 A78 2022 | DDC 813/.54—dc23/eng/20220224
LC record available at https://lccn.loc.gov/2022005968

Our books may be purchased in bulk for promotional, educational, or business use. Please contact your local bookseller or the Macmillan Corporate and Premium Sales Department at 1-800-221-7945, extension 5442, or by email at MacmillanSpecialMarkets@macmillan.com.

First Edition: 2022

10 9 8 7 6 5 4 3 2 1

To Tess Link,
whose fault this is

AMY
AMONG THE
SERIAL KILLERS

Writing is no trouble: you just jot down ideas as they occur to you. The jotting is simplicity itself—it is the occurring which is difficult.

—*Stephen Leacock*

The fact is that all of us have only one personality, and we wring it out like a dish towel. You are what you are.

—*S. J. Perelman*

CHAPTER ONE

Carla

Friday, March 5

Carla Karolak was positive she had ADHD. "I've got ADHD," she told her therapist. "That's why I'm blocked. I need distraction! Nothing ever happens here!"

Carla's therapist, Toonie Garabedian, sighed. "Last week your whole problem was pseudobulbar affect."

"I have that also."

Toonie was checking her damn phone messages again. She wasn't even trying to do this secretly. "Look," she said, not making anything close to eye contact with Carla, "if you're just going to keep on self-diagnosing, you don't need me. Carla, everybody doesn't have ADHD. You know what your problem is, and it's not ADHD."

Carla gazed out the window, far out and down at the pounding La Jolla surf. Toonie was harping on the cremains again. Carla was beginning to dislike Toonie. No, she was beginning to admit that she'd always disliked her. "They're just ashes," she said, "and I'll deal with them when I have a day to waste carting them up to

L.A. And after I do that, I'll still be blocked. They're not magical cinders."

"Not by themselves, no, but, as we've discussed, they've been made *magical,* as you put it—and that's so significant; listen to yourself!—by your mother's demands about them and your own refusal to comply. I mean, look." Toonie gestured toward the urn, which squatted in a corner, unsuccessfully obscured by a potted fern.

Ever since Ma died, Toonie had been nagging Carla to deal with her ashes. Toonie was certain Carla's writer's block was caused by profound guilt, which was as stupid an idea as this stupid urn, a 3-D printout in the shape of the stupid hat Carla had worn for the stupid Nutty and Corny ad campaign when she was thirteen years old. Ma had insisted on this actual urn in her will. She must have ordered it from some custom 3-D tchotchke outfit: The thing was a huge blocky acorn spray-painted dull gold, and they'd misspelled "Corny" with a K, but Ma had died before it arrived so she never knew how awful it was.

Or maybe she had. Maybe that was the point. Carla was supposed to trudge north to the Hollywood Forever Cemetery bearing the Acorn of Broken Dreams, a symbol of her mother's crushing disappointment in her only child, and scatter the ashes in the Abbey of the Psalms Mausoleum, where Judy Garland was entombed.

Carla had never once looked at the ashes. This was a small triumph of will, as the lid was ill fitting and tended to pop off whenever she tried to move it. "Toonie, it hasn't even been three years since she died. I'll deal with it when I get the chance. Meanwhile—"

"Listen to yourself! Not *even* three years! Deal with it before another year runs out. Make a point of it. Set a calendar date. You'll be amazed at the difference it makes."

"Deal," Carla said, just to shut her up. "Meanwhile—"

Toonie made a big production out of looking at her watch.

"Meanwhile I have this *problem.* You *do* see the big fat irony?

I'm not even an agent, and I've gotten forty-two people, forty-two, started on a writing career. Eleven of them have agents. Four are published already. And here I sit, blocked for all time."

Toonie sifted through her notebook, an expensive leather thing she always carried with her. Carla doubted the notes had anything to do with her patients.

Did therapists take lessons in rudeness? Was Carla boring her? "How's your meetaphobia book coming along?" Carla knew it wasn't "meetaphobia," but she didn't give a damn about Toonie's stupid book. She should never have agreed to pay the woman in trade. If Carla were a regular paying patient, she could just quit therapy, which was obviously what she needed to do.

"Symposimania." Toonie brightened, snapping back to the present. "I had to coin the word myself! And it's coming along brilliantly, thanks to you and the Point." Toonie was working on a pop-science book-length anecdote-crammed exposé of "Meeting Addiction," an epidemic which she claimed was endangering the mental health of hundreds of thousands of managers. Carla wasn't sure what a manager even was. "I'm still fiddling with a working title. Right now it's between *Don't Take That Meeting* and *Meet the I*. I think *Meet the I* is better. What do you think?"

"What is *Meet the Eye* supposed to mean?"

"Isn't it obvious? You have to meet yourself before you can meaningfully meet a roomful of people. Carla, don't you know that?"

"But what does that have to do with—you mean you have to look at your face in a mirror or something?"

Toonie drew a large envelope out of her bag. "I got the headshots this morning. Want to see?"

No, but Carla looked at them anyway and pronounced them amazing, which they weren't. For some reason Toonie was leaning against a jacaranda and hugging herself. She looked conspiratorially into the camera, glasses off, her wiry black hair exploding from an updo at least twenty years too young for her. The overall effect was that she had a terrific secret, but it was making her stomach hurt. Carla almost asked her if the headshot wasn't a little premature, since the book was half finished and she didn't have a publisher, but let it go. "Look," she said, "could we get back to my writer's block?"

"Time's up. I've got to get back to work."

"You are at work now, aren't you? Isn't this your work too?"

Toonie smiled, as though Carla were an adorable brat. "Fifty minutes is fifty minutes. We'll do this again on Thursday, regular time. Meanwhile, don't forget your exercises."

Before Carla could object, or even say so long, Toonie scooted out of the office, no doubt on her way back down to her warren, the farthest cell out in the western wing. Carla stared after her. She'd have to do something with the damn Acorn before their next session, and then she'd terminate their stupid contract.

Carla's house, the Birdhouse, was so named because, when viewed from the bluffs above, its long, sweeping, symmetrical wings gave it an avian outline. Both wings were filled with writing cells, each opening only to a corridor that ran the length of the wing. Carla's quarters were the central tower, consisting of four round rooms stacked on top of each other, each narrowing in circumference. The very top room was her office, and it was here that she had been meeting twice a month with Toonie. Otherwise, she spent most of her time with her friend and assistant, Tiffany Zuniga.

Carla grabbed the Acorn, descended one floor down to Tiffany's office, and popped her head in to ask what was up. Tiffany was feverishly pedaling her desk bike while doing something with an online spreadsheet. "What's up," she said, "is two applicants from Coronado and one from, get this, Topeka. Also, I'm pretty sure Garabedian's been smuggling her iPad into her cell. What do you want to do about it?"

"What do you mean 'pretty sure'? We can't search her bag."

"She stopped in on her way to see you, and her satchel was playing a tune. Silly woman isn't even bright enough to mute the thing." Carla rifled through the file cabinet, looking for Garabedian's lease. "Don't worry about it," Tiffany said. "I'll take care of her when the time comes."

"You shouldn't have to. I should be the one to do it."

"You're the one who makes the rules. You're just shit at enforcing them. That's my job."

Do you enjoy it? Carla wanted to ask. How do you handle making them hand over the cell keys and pointing them toward the door, not to be darkened again until after a three-month penance? Sometimes they cried. Well, once. Mrs. Stotch, who had claimed to be compiling ancestral research, carried on so much that Carla had relented, which is why Tiffany did enforcer detail now.

Tiffany stopped pedaling and looked Carla over. "You're still not writing, are you?"

"What do you think?"

"Garabedian's useless. Terminate the contract. She won't mind—she's got plenty of money. Want me to do it? Cut her loose and I won't narc her for the iPad."

"I've got ADHD."

Tiffany laughed. "See, that's textbook malpractice. Last week it was pseudobulbar affect, which is the silliest thing I ever heard of."

"Those aren't her ideas, they're mine; she's not even paying attention. But that has to be what's wrong with me. Why else am I the only one here not writing anything?"

"Remember what Amy used to tell us? If you don't have anything to say, give up."

"Now you're making it worse."

Carla missed Amy so much.

"I told you, do a serial killer. They're still hot. You can crank out one of those while you figure out what you really want to write." The phone rang. Tiffany picked it up, listened for a moment, yelled "FUCK YOU!" and hung up.

"One day," said Carla, "you're going to do that to a real human being."

"That was a real human being who wanted me to take a brief survey about home security." Tiffany put her laptop to sleep, grabbed her sweater, and stood to leave. "Seriously, do a serial killer. It'll write itself."

"Big whoop."

Tiffany fluttered her fingers toward Carla and left for the day. Carla opened the bottom file cabinet drawer and shoved the Acorn behind a ream of printer paper. The lid popped off. "Button it, Ma," said Carla, jamming it back on.

Carla Karolak didn't want to do a serial killer. She wanted to write a memoir. She was a natural for it, what with a predatory mother who had pimped her out as a child actor, forcing her to flog local car washes, taco stands, and car lots, and later to appear in national ads for junk food. The zenith of her showbiz career was when she became the spokes-tot for Nutty's Joint, a family fun zone franchise that had been big in the '90s before being crushed by Chuck E. Cheese. Corny made Ma a boatload of money, enough to buy the La Jolla house outright, enough, when invested, to set them both up for life. Ma had imagined it was only the beginning. She had been wrong about that. Ma was gone now, sort of. Her vengeful spirit swanned about the Birdhouse they had shared, hissing at Carla to eat less, you can never be too thin, and hustle, hustle, hustle. *You're only as good as your last gig, Carla.*

Well, her last gig had been going strong for three years now. She had transformed half the house into Inspiration Point, where writers and writers-to-be could, for a substantial fee, rent windowless cubicles for three-month increments. She had marketed it first as a writer's retreat, but really it was more a cross between a factory and a rehab facility. Renters signed a lease and committed to a minimum of four hours a day, five days a week. If they ever failed to show up and bolt themselves into their cubicles, they forfeited the rest of the rent. They could bring laptops, but Carla did not supply WiFi, and anybody caught using cell phone service to access the internet was banned for three months, which is what Tiffany wanted to do to Toonie Garabedian.

Inspiration Point was a money machine. Within two years, four of her renters had gotten book contracts, and one of them, Misha Bernard, who was already well-known, had made a huge splash with a series of erotic thrillers, the Aztec Moon Chronicles. All this occasioned a lot of sniping from the more traditional writer's retreat industry: Critics asked where the inspiration was, given the absence of supportive fellowship, rustic solitude, yoga classes, spa treatments, and artfully wrapped writing prompts on pillows, and sniped about the wretched boiler room vibe of those cramped and joyless cells.

Writing Industrialists sniped because Carla's boiler room was costing them customers.

So the gig was great, but since starting it up, Carla herself had yet to finish a thing she wrote. She'd given up on poetry, romance, and mystery. Everything she began remained unfinished, withering and slinking off in the middle chapters, in what Amy, her old writing teacher, called the Bog of Despond. And the truth was, although she knew better than anyone that what writers needed was four walls and iron discipline, she had yet to use a cell successfully herself. The walls, the spartan desk, and worst of all the un-Wi-Fied laptop terrified her. She needed distraction. She could not work without chaos. And now she couldn't write at all, even while juggling multiple online role-playing games in front of the TV with *L&O SVU* blaring, which had long ago—when Carla was thriving in Amy's workshops—worked like magic.

Carla hadn't spoken with Amy or even seen her for almost three years. When Ma died Amy had written with condolences, a real letter that Carla never threw away. One time later Carla called her but just got a recording. She knew Amy was probably out, and would have picked up the phone otherwise, but Carla never tried again, because Amy wasn't teaching anymore. Amy was writing, and Carla knew she shouldn't be bothering her. Anyway, Carla was a businesswoman now; she didn't need to keep leaning on Amy.

Determined to give her own writing a try before closing down for the day, she grabbed her laptop and headed down to the wings. It was Friday; most clients were gone for the day, and she had a passkey card to all the cells so she could use whichever one appealed to her. She started down the west wing. Each cell had its renter's nameplate slid into a holder on the door: She strolled past Ricky Buzza, Simonetta Colodny, the Herman Twins (who did everything together), the redoubtable Harry B., and, on impulse swiped her way into the cell of a local pediatric dentist, Manny Singh.

Carla routinely used her renters' cells and didn't worry about intruding since they were almost always bare when not in use, and furnished only by writers and their laptops otherwise, so it wasn't as if she was trespassing on private space, but now she was brought up short by what looked like a family picture propped up on Manny's desk. Six kids, three of each, flanked a pretty woman in a burgundy pantsuit, all smiling right at Manny, so proud that he was going to write the story of their family. Or maybe he was the one working on a Raj serial killer whodunit. No matter, they were proud and happy, and Carla scurried back out and locked the door.

She kept on, past Dr. Surtees, Sophia Rosales, John X. Cousins, past all five McPhails (Tiffany was convinced that four of these cells were for forced homework, but there was no rule against that), and on and on, finally arriving at Toonie Garabedian's cell. The Doc hadn't gone home yet, plus Tiffany was so right—she had to be fooling around with her iPad. Carla stood at the door and listened. Toonie's playlist was apparently all about meetings. A Bing Crosby song (Ma had been crazy about Crosby), "Fancy Meeting You Here," was just ending, followed now by some shrill R&B chorus telling women not to be late for "a meeting in my bedroom." Carla wanted to turn back and try the other wing, but something about the music gave her a What Would Tiffany Do? shove, and without further thought she raised her keycard to swipe into Toonie's cell, but the door wasn't even locked.

Carla stood in the doorway, looking toward Toonie but not really at her, formulating her next words. *I'm sorry to interrupt, but . . .* That wouldn't do, because she wasn't sorry, or at least she shouldn't have been, because music was a no-no. *Toonie, you know you're not supposed to bring online devices in here.* No, she should apologize first, because she was, after all, barging in. "Toonie," she said, looking not toward her but at her—well, at the back of her head, because Toonie wasn't turning around. Her laptop was closed, her iPad propped on a stand in front of her, and on it the stunning Retina display image of a mollusk. Or a penis. Definitely a penis. Carla reached out to put her hand on Toonie's shoulder but hesitated because Toonie was looking at a giant penis and not turning around at the sound of Carla's voice, which was just not the behavior of a normal human being. And it smelled bad in here, like Toonie had had an accident.

When she was ready, Carla walked around Toonie so she could look at her face. Then she called the police.

CHAPTER TWO

Carla

Carla could not stop looking. Toonie's face was the color of eggplant, her eyelids were swollen almost shut, and her pink tongue ballooned from her lips. Something had been drawn and tied so tight around her neck that it was invisible, buried deep in her flesh. Carla didn't feel anything, and then she did, but it wasn't fear, it was wonder. That a person who had just been in her office, fluttering around, ignoring her, stuffing a notebook into her handbag, waving goodbye, walking down stairs and through corridors, staring at a penis, that a person could just disappear like that, leaving behind a Halloween mask and an embarrassing smell. And that music, someone was singing *I see that you're hyper, let's take it upstairs. Hey girl! Let's have a meeting,* and Carla started to turn off the damn iPad, but then thought about fingerprints and DNA, and she was afraid to even turn down the sound, she could go find some gloves, but where.

Now she could feel fear, just in general, not for her own life, just fear that something like this could happen to a person, that the world was such a place, and without thinking she took out her phone and called Amy Gallup.

It rang just once, and then to Carla's amazement Amy answered with her actual voice, not the recording, and she said, "I know who you are. I know where you live. If you call me again, I will hunt you down and kill you." Then she hung up.

Carla stared at her phone. Now she felt wonder, fear, and crushing sadness. When it rang again, it was Amy.

"Carla? I'm so so sorry! I didn't even look at my damn caller ID!"

"You aren't mad at me?"

"I had no idea it was you! I would never—"

"Something terrible has happened," said Carla.

"What? Can you turn down that music?"

"Something terrible!" Carla shouted. She kept shouting it.

CHAPTER THREE

Amy

When Amy pulled up to the Birdhouse, Carla was sitting in the grass out front. She'd lost a lot of weight since Amy had last seen her; she looked downright gaunt. People in paper suits were just beginning to garland house and lawn with crime scene tape. Among them was a fortyish man in a sport jacket who looked familiar to Amy. Lottie was wrestling with the belt to her canine car seat, because if Amy left her in the car she'd go nuts. "This is a crime scene," she told Lottie as she put her on the leash. "Behave yourself."

Carla was trying to rise to greet her but clearly could not summon the strength. "Wait," Amy said. "I'll get a chair."

She pulled a chair over and sat down beside Carla. The grass was already damp in the early evening air. "Sorry about the dog," she said. "I can't leave her in my yard at night. She's little, and coyotes could jump the fence."

"You have two dogs now?"

Amy shook her head. "Alphonse died last year."

"Oh no! Oh, I'm so sorry!" Carla burst into tears, her sobs sudden and jagged. "You loved that basset so much!"

"Yes, I did. Carla, who is Toonie?"

Carla couldn't stop crying. Whoever Toonie was, Carla didn't seem to be crying for her, and she wouldn't stop until Amy handed her the dog. Lottie sat still and sniffed avidly at the buttons on Carla's blouse.

"Carla, who is Toonie?"

After a time Carla got ahold of herself and started to explain who Toonie was and the state in which she had been found. Uniformed police milled about the yard, some walking around the house, others apparently waiting for something, and then an ambulance pulled up. "No rush," somebody said, and somebody else laughed. That fortyish man emerged from the front door and walked up to Carla and Amy. He introduced himself to Carla and asked if she could answer a few questions.

"Have we met?" Amy shaded her eyes against the glare of what seemed like a hundred high-powered flashlights. "Aren't you Sergeant—"

"Lieutenant, ma'am. Lieutenant Kowalcimi. Yes, I think we did." He squatted beside them. "Couple of years ago. You had that trouble with a student."

"And here we are again," said Amy.

Kowalcimi asked Carla how many people were in the Birdhouse. She just stared up at him, her face gleaming wet.

"Carla," said Amy. "Do you know if you were alone in the house, with Toonie? Or are there other people working there now?"

"Nobody in the west wing. Tiffany went home. Nobody was there but Toonie." Carla wiped her eyes with her sleeve. "I don't know about the east wing. It's Friday evening. I think most of them are home on Friday evenings. I don't know. Tiffany could tell you. If you look at the computer in Tiffany's office, there's a way you can check on it. I don't know how to do it." She started to zone out again; she was looking down at Lottie, her expression forlorn and, to Amy, remarkably young, considering that by now she had to be in her thirties.

Carla's phone was in the grass beside her, and Amy picked it up and found Tiffany Zuniga's number in her contacts. "I think Tiffany works here," she said. Glancing first at Kowalcimi, who nodded, she dialed Tiffany, who answered after the first ring and twenty minutes later drove up. Amy hadn't seen Tiffany or Carla or any of the old writing group for three years. Tiffany's blond hair was loose and messy, as though she'd been sleeping fitfully in a rocking hammock. Amy wondered if she still lived with her father.

Tiffany knelt before Carla and cupped her face in her hands. "How are you doing?"

"They want to know if anybody's in the east wing and I don't know how to do that." She was crying again. "I was going to fire Toonie! I was going to tell her off! I was so mad at her! Everybody I hate dies!"

Tiffany and Amy exchanged glances. "If that were so," Amy said, "the world would be a better place."

"You didn't hate her," Tiffany said. "You just didn't like her. Nobody did."

Kowalcimi cleared his throat, startling Tiffany.

"Don't I know you?" she asked, and Amy introduced him. Tiffany stood up. "You're a lieutenant now! Look," she said to Kowalcimi, "Carla doesn't hate anybody. Dr. Garabedian was a client here and also Carla's therapist, but that's as far as the relationship went. Do you want me to check the computer now? If anybody's still here in the cells, or if they were here earlier tonight, I can tell you, and I can tell you when. Everybody uses keycards. The cards leave an audit trail."

"Cells?" Kowalcimi looked entranced. "You call them cells?" The two walked away into the house, Tiffany bringing him up to speed in a most efficient way about the workings of the Birdhouse.

After a time, Amy spoke. "You call them cells? Carla, that *is* brilliant." The last time Amy had been here, Carla had just started up Inspiration Point, which Amy wasn't able to think of unpunctuated—Inspiration Point!—and while the sterile cubicles that had lined the walls of the great round living room had, in fact, looked the opposite of inviting, they weren't dungeons. "Do they have bars on the doors?"

Carla sighed. "I don't remember who started calling them cells. It wasn't me. Amy, I keep seeing her face."

"That will stop eventually," Amy said. There was no point in talking to Carla right now. She needed to steady herself. "Stay here. Take care of Lottie. She'll want to come with me, so don't let go of the leash, no matter what she does. I'll be right back." Amy didn't wait for an acknowledgment or look back as she made her way through the tape. She had to know what was going on.

The interior of the large round living room had yet again been completely overhauled. In earlier times, Carla had Disneyfied it into a mini-Adventureland with hulking jungle plants, rattan furniture, bamboo sconces, mandrill-themed wallpaper, and a bridged lagoon. This was shortly after her nightmare mother, a creature straight from *The Gashlycrumb Tinies,* had quit the premises she had shared with her daughter and gone back to Philadelphia. Later, another incarnation of the Point!, bone white everywhere with those cubicles and severe, angular furniture entirely free of curves, had a Tomorrowland vibe. Amy had wondered at the time if this meant Carla was growing up at last, however slowly.

Now, curved sofas and sectionals in pale greens and blues lined walls on which paintings, or perhaps prints, were hung at regular intervals, each a portrait of some sort. The western section was floor-to-ceiling glass, framing surf and sand in the daytime and now, out there in the dark, the sidelights of small boats and party ships in the bay. So Carla must have grown up—it was a room for adults, tastefully appointed in a way that made Amy nostalgic for the wicker monstrosities and man-eating vines of yesteryear.

Then she looked at the room's center and there was this enormous dollhouse, a three-story Colonial that must have been four feet high. It sat on what looked like a converted pool table. Beneath the green baize–covered surface emerged the cellar. Amy could not resist bending down and pulling a tiny chain that lit the space up, but dimly, like a real cellar light. The walls were fashioned to look like concrete, with cracks and holes here and there, and a workbench running the length of one wall. Attached to it was a tiny vise. Miniature hand tools hung from a miniature pegboard. Everything in this room was real, three-dimensional; the only painted-on feature was a minuscule centipede crawling from one of the holes in the wall.

Amy longed to study the room further and then explore the rest of the dollhouse, which was phenomenal. Here was the child Carla, not yet extinguished. And what a beautiful installation for would-be writers. Each detail stimulated the imagination and awakened old memories and dreams, like an enchanted smoke alarm. In each of these rooms were a thousand stories. Carla was a human Muse. Amy hadn't wanted to play since she was twelve years old, but she wanted to now.

Well, there might be time for that later. Hearing low voices from above, she climbed the stairs, past the second floor, which contained one large bedroom and a bath, and on to an office on the next floor. Tiffany and Kowalcimi were hunched over a computer screen. "You can see," said Tiffany, "that nobody's here. The cells are empty."

"What about the audit trail? Can you show me what it looked like an hour ago?"

Amy watched as the screen changed, showing both wings, each with two lit-up rooms. Tiffany changed the screen. "Okay, east wing. So Misha B. was still here an hour ago, but she left at 8:17. Looks like . . . wow, Syl Reyes checked in! I thought he'd given up. Checked in at 8:15, left two minutes later. That's Syl for you. He's paid more in fines than anybody else here."

"What about the west wing?"

Tiffany hit a couple of keys. "Voila. So there's Toonie, checking in at 8:30. The only other one is . . ."

"Manoj Singh," read Kowalcimi. "Look. He checked in at 8:55 and out a minute later. That's interesting."

"No it's not." Carla stood in the doorway holding Lottie, who spotted Amy and began to scream like a hound on helium. Lottie was a pleasant little dog except for her piercing shriek of joy whenever Amy went out of sight and then returned, whether within thirty seconds or after an absence of days, which had happened only once, but still the result was equally earsplitting whatever the interval. She always sounded like she'd been hit by a car.

"Apologies," said Amy, taking the dog from Carla, which quieted her down.

"Manny wasn't here," said Carla. "That was me. I went into his cell and then out again."

"Why?" asked Kowalcimi and Tiffany at once.

"I don't know. I was just looking for a place to— Look, it doesn't matter, Manny wasn't here. Plus he's a really, really nice man, a family man—"

"I'd like to see your security camera footage," said Kowalcimi.

"Okay," said Tiffany, "but it's just outdoor-and-driveway stuff. We don't have cameras in the house. Carla didn't want them."

"They creep me out," said Carla.

The cameras clearly showed Syl Reyes, who had put on midsection weight since Amy had last seen him but was still wearing gym gear, leaving and driving away ten minutes before Toonie, according to the audit trail, had entered her cell. Close behind Syl was a tall woman in a beige fur-trimmed cape, whose car looked expensive.

"So that's Misha Bernard?" asked Amy. "She's the one who wrote that Aztec series excrescence?"

"Which is making her a steaming pile of money," said Tiffany. "You're right, they're awful."

"But how do you know it's an excrescence?" asked Carla. "You never read books like that."

There was little about Amy's habits and tastes that Carla didn't seem to know by heart. Sometimes Amy wondered if Carla was planning to write her hagiography. "Her agent hit me up for a blurb. I trust you people had nothing to do with that."

Carla and Tiffany both denied it, and Amy believed them. She'd probably been just one of hundreds of writers to be honored with advance proofs of thrilling erotic chronicles. The last blurb Amy had written was for *Caligula's Scalpel,* Ricky Buzza's first serial killer novel, and she'd done that only because she was fond of him. When she got the latest Bernard book, she dutifully read the first sentence and then dumped it. Amy copied the sentence into her Don't Do This list just in case she ever decided to teach again: "Coyolxauhqui regarded herself in the mirroring lake of Metzliapán, caressing her smooth shoulders, and wondering for the hundredth time if her lover Huitzilopochtli would ever be, like his namesake, an amatory adept."

"Assuming," Tiffany was saying, "that whoever killed Toonie came in the front door earlier today and hasn't been living in a secret compartment, I'm guessing you'll want the whole day's camera footage." She arranged for this with Kowalcimi, while Carla, Amy, and Lottie walked upstairs, Carla in the lead.

They stopped at the next floor, Carla's bedroom and bath. "I'm sorry," Carla said, pointing to the mess. As could plainly be seen through its open door, Carla's closet was half empty, and no wonder since the floor and all available surfaces were strewn with sloughed clothes. On her walls Carla had had taped posters of Nelson Mandela, Tom Hanks, and something called Meat Puppets, along with vintage motivational posters reminding her to "SAY IT WITH SNAP!" and "FIND YOUR GIFT, THEN GIVE IT AWAY." Judging by the brittle condition of the yellowing tape, most of these must have been up for decades.

"Carla," said Amy, "you shouldn't stay here alone tonight." Judging by the racket downstairs, the police might be hanging around for hours, but Carla still looked alarmingly disoriented. "Who would you like me to call?"

"I'll be all right," Carla said in a small voice. They watched Lottie roll around in a pile of sweatpants. "I love your dog," she said. "I'm so, so sorry about the basset."

"There are dogs, and there are people," said Amy. "A woman died here."

"She thought I couldn't write because of Ma's ashes. Does that make sense to you?"

Amy sighed. "Pack a small bag," she said. "You're coming home with me. For the night."

"Really?"

"I'll wait in the car." Amy left the room before Carla could pretend to try to talk her out of it. She had never had a houseguest, and she wasn't looking forward to having one now. She poked her head in Tiffany's office and let Kowalcimi know where Carla was going and how to get in touch with her; he just nodded, apparently distracted by whatever he was hearing on his cell phone.

Amy wanted to get back to the dollhouse but saved it for another day. Instead she waited outside her car, listening to the surf, watching the dog inspect all four tires. This was part of Lottie's ritual. She had a great nose—not as superb as the basset's, but still impressive. The two dogs used their gift for vastly different purposes. For Alphonse, scent trails had been Holmesian puzzles, intellectual fodder; he followed them only to feed his head. If there were emotional hounds, Alphonse had not been one of them. But for Lottie these trails were the high-voltage plots in her daily dramas. When they came back from a walk or a shopping trip, Amy could always tell if anyone had visited in their absence. Lottie's growls meant the UPS guy or the mail lady had been by; the pest control people would leave a worrying trail; and if Sophie, who had rescued the homeless dog from the mean streets of Escondido, had called, Lottie would pull on the leash in wild anticipation, only to be crushed to find she was no longer there. Lottie was a questing beast.

Carla's bag was, of course, enormous, but she said this was because she couldn't think straight. Since Lottie's dog seat was in the front, Carla had to sit in back. She was silent most of the way to Escondido, but as they took the Centre City Parkway exit she said, "When I was leaving I heard that Colostomy guy talking on the phone, and he was saying something about another one."

"Another what?"

"That's what I don't know."

"His name is Kowalcimi."

"But didn't you used to call him Sergeant Colos—"

"Only because I misunderstood him. He tends to swallow his words." Was Carla wired? Did she take down Amy's every word and keep a running log? "Carla, that was three years ago. You have an impressive memory."

"I only remember it because it was so funny."

"I wasn't trying to be funny. I don't make deliberate fun of people's names." Not to their faces anyway. "What did he say, exactly? About 'another one'?"

"'We got another one.' No. 'We maybe got another one.'"

Must be a banner night for homicides. Another day in paradise.

When they got home, Amy showed Carla her room, her ex's old man-cave—he had actually called it that—into which she'd moved the bed they had shared. "Can you sleep?" she asked. Carla said she had pills. "Can you sleep without pills?" Carla said she would try. "Do that," said Amy. "I'll put out some towels in the bath. I'm going to do some work now, unless you need anything."

"I won't. I'm so sorry you had to do this."

"I didn't have to. I wanted to." This was not exactly a lie. One wants to do the right thing.

Carla disappeared behind her door, then opened it a crack. "Amy? I don't know what's going to happen now."

"Can you imagine?"

"I can imagine all kinds of things. I can't stop imagining them. I keep seeing her face."

Amy opened the top drawer of her maple secretary, drew out a yellow legal pad and a pencil, and handed them to Carla. "So get writing," she said.

CHAPTER FOUR

Carla

Saturday, March 6

Carla had never been in this room. Whenever she'd come to Amy's house—which was only a handful of times over the course of the last ten years—the door had been closed. The others had thought it odd, since the house was so small to begin with. Once, when she'd carpooled here for a class, Tiffany, Ricky, and Harry B. had played a silly "What the Hell Is in There?" game all the way back to San Diego, and when Carla objected, they pointed out that Amy was always telling them to make lists, that lists were the lifeblood of fiction.

Nothing on the list, at least not the guesses Carla remembered, panned out. There was a closetful of old stuff, but not "Size eights from 1974"—just some winter coats that probably never got worn since it was never really winter here. Amy came from Maine, where they had winter. There wasn't a rack or an iron maiden, which hadn't made sense anyway since Amy didn't torture people, and there were no corpses of workshop students who had missed their deadlines. Really there wasn't much of anything—a double bed, an empty maple bureau, a rickety painted nightstand, a rug that belonged in a '50s bathroom. Books piled horizontally on shelves that looked like they came from Target. A cheap old stair stepper in a dusty corner. An unplugged television set. A wall clock shaped like an owl head, stopped, probably years ago, at 12:37.

There was nothing of Amy here. Disappointed, Carla started to undress for bed, then spotted what had to be a yearbook, high school or college, on its side beneath one of the book piles. This promised to be a trove. Carla nestled beneath the covers with *The Cranstonian*.

It was a high school yearbook from 1964, which must have been Amy's senior year. The endpapers were collages of newspaper headlines: BOLT STRIKES AGAIN. KENNEDY KILLED BY ASSASSIN'S BULLET. KNOW YOUR ZIP CODE. A RECORD YEAR FOR CIGARETTES. SCHOOL START SNAFU. She was dying to look at Amy's picture but put it off for dessert, instead scanning photos of other girls, many of them with hairstyles that made them look like water buffalo. She read what some of them had written on their pictures: "May the best of everything come your way." "I never really got to know you that well but I am sure you will have a wonderful life." "To a good kid, whom I have not really known all that long." "May you find success and happiness in all you do." "Never forget our great times in Santagata's class oops I wrote on your picture sorry I'm on the other page." But the picture was not of Amy, but of someone named Carol Ann Winkelman.

Well, this wasn't Amy's yearbook at all. It was Carol Ann Winkelman's, and who in the world was that? Cranston, as it turned out, wasn't even in Maine. And why had Amy kept this yearbook? Carla wondered if there were other yearbooks, collected for some weird purpose—the yearbooks of friends, or maybe enemies, except Amy was such a loner, and her only enemy, at least the only one Carla knew about, was doing twenty-five to life in Chino.

Suddenly too tired to get up and rummage through the books

or write anything in that yellow pad, Carla turned off the light, closed her eyes, and tried, in a writerly way, to imagine Carol Ann Winkelman. In seconds she was deep asleep. She woke up three times in the night, each from a different dream. Toonie was in none of them. The first was about her mother, who figured in most of Carla's nightmares, and in this one she was on a computer screen pointing and laughing, and Carla could turn the sound of her laugh down but couldn't turn off the picture. In the second, something was chasing her from cell to cell in the Birdhouse, but she woke up before it got her. The third was just a water buffalo at a riverbank, drinking clear, clean water. It looked up and said, "You are not alone." The voice was Amy's.

When she woke again the sun was out and something was scratching at her door. The dog, Lottie, because Carla heard Amy say, "Leave her alone. Come, Lottie, come," and the sound of the dog scampering off. Carla lay still for a while, waiting for the events of last night to overwhelm her but happy just to be here in this sunny room. She couldn't remember ever doing this, just lying still, alone in a morning bed, listening to the warm sounds of a stirring household. Ma had never let her come awake on her own. There was always a schedule, a class, an audition, another class, a job, and Punctuality was the Watchword of the True Professional. Breakfast at 7 sharp, exercise, tap dance, hair, the noon train to Penn Station, the limo to Burbank, whatever, she hated it all. And when she finally broke free, her mornings were empty. Better than before, but not like this. She would wake alone in the Birdhouse and celebrate, in a muted way, the absence of misery.

This was different. This was joy. She knew she couldn't stay for long, but she had this morning now, to remember.

Amy sat at her computer and waved Carla into the kitchen behind her. "There's coffee in the French press and cereal on top of the fridge."

Amy's kitchen was a wonderland. She kept green tea bags in a tea chest, freestanding on top of a shelf; her floor was covered in linoleum squares, so much cheaper than Carla's marbleized porcelain tile that Ma had insisted on, like she had insisted on the Best of Everything, and here was a perfectly nice floor, soft to stand on, that didn't scream "I'm Richer than Hell." Everything here was so homey: an old gas stove, a non–Viking refrigerator with no ice maker, dog food next to canned soup in wood cabinets painted yellow. Carla had been to the house before, of course, but never in the morning. In the morning light everything was new.

"You're going to want to read this," said Amy. She had the *Trib* page up on her screen.

The strangled body of a 55-year-old woman was found Friday night at a house in La Jolla, police said.

Police discovered the body of the woman after receiving a call from the owner of the property, Carla Karolak.

The woman was positively identified as Hatoon Garabedian, a psychologist associated with the Clairemont Center for Stress, Anxiety, and Eating Disorders. Her body was found in a rented office at 123 Kemper Place, which, in addition to being a private home, also serves as a retreat for local novelists.

The police said they were investigating the death as a homicide.

"Boy, nothing gets past those cops," said Carla. "And it's 'writers,' not 'local novelists,' for Pete's sake."

Amy's phone rang. "This is probably them," said Amy, picking up. "They'll want to talk to you." She listened for a moment, shook her head, and then said, in a voice made frighteningly deep, "Does your mother know what you're doing?" and hung up. "I hope that sounded like the voice of God," she said.

"Why?"

"I've been working on it."

Carla began to despair of ever understanding what was going on anywhere. Why was Amy trying to frighten the police? "Do you want me to call them? Is that it?"

"Kowalcimi's got my number. He'll call."

"Oh! So that wasn't them?"

"What?" Amy laughed and laughed. This was an occasion; Carla couldn't remember ever hearing her laugh, although she was often very funny herself. "I take it you don't have a landline?"

"Well, there's one in Tiffany's office, but I use the cell."

"Just about everybody does." The phone rang again. This time Amy checked the caller ID before picking up, answered the call, and handed the phone to Carla.

It was Lieutenant K. He wanted to interview her. "He wants to interview me," she said to Amy.

Amy took the phone from her. "Lieutenant? Does she have to come to you?" There was a long pause. Amy tucked the phone against her neck and told Carla that he'd be willing to meet her here, in Escondido, if that was all right.

"When?"

"He says this afternoon. If we could get Tiffany here, that would be helpful too."

As excited as Carla suddenly was at the prospect of staying here, at least for the day, she was puzzled. "Why doesn't he want me to go back to the Birdhouse?"

After hanging up, Amy explained that the crime scene people were still swarming all over the property, and the police said she had to stay away for at least another day. "He'll be here midday, so I suggest you give Tiffany a call to make arrangements. Eat something first."

Carla took coffee and a bowl of Special K into the backyard and sat in a rickety Adirondack chair. Lottie ran around the yard looking for something. Little reddish birds hopped around hanging feeders and drank from puddles in a raised garden, at the center of which stood that birdbath Amy had knocked herself out on two years before. Or was it three? The dog came up to her and presented her with a small squeaky ball. For a half hour she threw it, farther and farther out in a yard dense with fruit trees and weeds. Sometimes Lottie would disappear for minutes, and then there'd be a triumphant squeak from the underbrush, and she'd hurry back.

"She'll never stop," said Amy, pulling up a chair next to her. "She'll chase it until she's wobbly."

"I love your yard," said Carla. In the morning sun Carla could see Amy had aged some in the past years. Her cheeks were hollowing out and there were new lines around her mouth and eyes. Ma, who had called Amy "Miss Frizzle" and her writing class the "Magic Goddamn School Bus," used to say the only reason Amy didn't have wrinkles was because she was fat. Ma never liked any of Carla's friends, but she especially hated Amy. Amy was much thinner now; wrinkles both aged her face and defined its earlier shape. You could see the outlines of a much younger woman, a pretty one, a stranger. She had been young. Carla had never considered that.

"What I'm wondering is why Kowalcimi is coming to you," Amy said. "Why don't they ask you down to the station? Wherever that may be."

"I think they only do that if you're a person of interest."

Lottie, clearly winded, staggered up with the ball; Amy picked her up and handed her to Carla. "Just hold on to her for a few minutes and she'll settle down."

The dog grazed on Carla's bathrobe for flakes of Special K. "I never had a pet," Carla said. "Ma wouldn't allow animals in the house. Except this one time I had a chameleon for like five minutes. I was doing a circus gig and an acrobat gave it to me. I didn't tell Ma. I made it a secret home in a shoebox under my bed, but it got loose the next day and disappeared. I looked and looked and never found it."

"Did you leave the top off the box?"

"No! That's why I never could figure out how it happened. He must have poked the lid off and after he escaped it fell back down."

Amy was quiet for a while. "How often did your mother clean your room?"

"She didn't, not after I started making money, which was pretty early on. We had this housekeeper, Mrs. Schultz. Oma Schulteez, that's what she had me call her. I liked her a lot. She was a madman for spotless living, you never saw a speck of—Oh."

"I'll get you some juice."

"No, that's okay." Just like that, the Mystery of the Missing Chameleon was solved. Carla could feel herself clouding up and didn't want to. "Oma Schulteez was a nice lady. She'd have wanted to tell me about the chameleon. She must have shown my chameleon to Ma and Ma told her to put the box back empty and keep her mouth shut or she'd lose her job."

"Why? Why would your mother do such a thing?"

Carla looked at Amy. "You had to know Ma," she finally said. She sighed and stroked the top of Lottie's head, where the fur stood straight up in spikes like a round mohawk. "His name was Boffo."

After a long while, Amy rested her hand, just for a moment, on Carla's. She lifted it immediately, but Carla could still feel it, like a cool feather. Lottie licked the fingertips of her other hand. "I love your dog," she said.

"I know," said Amy.

It was odd, Carla thought, how she had refused to discuss Ma with Toonie, and here she was, gassing on about her with Amy. Of course, Amy had run into Ma more than once, so it wasn't like talking about a total stranger, but that wasn't it. Amy was interested in Ma; you could tell. Well, Ma had been a lot of things but never boring. And now it was such a relief to tell Amy these things. She was *sharing* Ma, which should have felt like sharing typhoid, except it wasn't, it was more like sharing a burden, as though maybe in time they could, between them, manage to lug Ma high into the mountains and leave her on some frozen peak.

After a late lunch, Tiffany drove up with Chuck Heston. Carla hadn't seen Chuck since Amy stopped teaching; Chuck was the only workshop member who hadn't rented a cell at the Point, not even once, and he'd drifted away without a word to anyone. Carla had especially missed him. He had been funny and kind, especially during the first class they took together when she'd brought in that pathetic suicide poem that half the class thought was about the tensile strength of rope and the rest were just grossed out.

His notes were the only ones she'd saved. *I hope this was just a thought experiment,* he said. *If it was, you're a writer! And if it wasn't, you still are, and a talented one, but maybe next you should try looking at the narrator from the outside. The ropes always break. Does this make her mad, or hopeful, or both? I'm looking forward to more from her.* She had memorized this.

"Amy, it's Chuck!" Carla was practically jumping up and down.

"He called me this morning when he read the news," said Amy.

Chuck hurried up the walk ahead of Tiffany and to Carla's amazement wrapped his arms around her and squeezed. "How's it going, kid?" he asked.

Carla leaned into him, which wasn't easy as he was half a head shorter, but the sensation of his embrace was intoxicating. Carla wasn't a hugger. She had not been hugged by a man for twenty-eight years, not since Cal Hoving, the Nutty's Joint Chief Squirrel, and he hadn't been wearing his squirrel outfit, and the effect had not been intoxicating. Chuck was saying something. "I missed you," he was saying.

"Why?" Carla meant, "Where have you been all this time?" but it came out wrong. Although she really did wonder why.

Amy brought them inside. Lottie greeted them, barking her head off.

"This is Lottie!" Carla said.

"I know Lottie." Chuck reached into his jeans pocket, pulled out a plastic baggie, knelt, and gave the dog a piece of cheese.

"How?" This time Carla and Tiffany spoke in unison.

"Chuck has been working with me," said Amy.

The silence that followed threatened to become both prolonged and uncomfortable, but Lieutenant Kowalcimi's sudden arrival cut it short. He emerged from a big black SUV carrying a leather binder with a broken zipper and was greeted at the front door by Amy's hysterical dog. Chuck picked Lottie up, instantly calming her. He was apparently the Lottie Whisperer. How often did he come here? What was his deal with Amy? Carla wasn't exactly jealous, but she really wanted to know.

Amy brought them all to the backyard, where there were enough chairs for everyone to sit. "Sorry," she said, "but I'm not set up for company indoors."

Kowalcimi handed Carla a sheaf of papers, on each of which was a black-and-white photo, and asked her if any of the faces were familiar.

"Is this a photo array?"

"Just some pictures." Kowalcimi smiled. "Watch a lot of cop shows, do you?"

Carla looked closely at each one. They were all male, dark-haired, and more or less young. "Who are they supposed to be?"

"They're not supposed to be anything. I just need to know if one of them rings a bell."

"Is one of these guys a suspect?" asked Chuck.

Kowalcimi ignored this and showed the pictures to Tiffany, who recognized none of them. "Do either of you," he said, looking at Carla and Tiffany in turn, "have any thoughts about what happened to Dr. Garabedian? Have you remembered anything about the day?"

Kowalcimi brought out a pencil and an old-fashioned steno pad, the kind Ma had used to list daily appointments. Carla hated those steno pads. He was looking at her with exaggerated intensity, as though assuring her that her thoughts were important to him; he reminded her just then of Dr. Matthieu, Ma's cancer surgeon, a man with zero social skills who had obviously taken a course in Displaying Empathy with Families. Matthieu had given Carla her mother's dire prognosis and then suddenly leaned in, staring, unblinking, placing a hand on Carla's knee, and said, "Now, do you have any questions?" and Carla had almost screamed because the guy was such a machine. It was like being cuddled by a robot. She liked this cop better than Matthieu, but he was playing her, and not very well.

Carla closed her eyes and focused on the day—her walk down the west wing, her brief stop in Manny's cell, the voice of Bing Crosby mellowing through Toonie's door. "I wasn't even going to bother her," she said, "but the music was so loud and I figured now was as good a time as any to have it out with her."

"What do you mean?" asked Kowalcimi. "Tell me more about that."

"She just wasn't a good therapist for me. I wonder if she was good for anybody. Toonie was all about her book. She was writing this thing, she was this big authority on symposimania for some reason. That's where people have too many meetings? And she was supposed to be my therapist, I let her have the cell in exchange for sessions, but she really wasn't focused, she kept just telling me 'You must do your grief work.'" Amy and Kowalcimi regarded her with identical expressions of mild concern. "Like grief, which I don't have anyway, was this huge *job*. Stuff like 'Recognize all the hopes and dreams you shared with your mother.' Really! Hopes and dreams! Stuff like 'Pretend this pillow is your mother.' I said, 'Look, does it have to be a pillow? Can we do it with a stapler?'"

"So you were angry with Dr. Garabedian? Were you particularly angry on Friday?"

"No, it wasn't a big deal! I wasn't mad! Just fed up. I was going to go in there and say, 'Toonie, I'd like to discontinue my—'"

"What did you notice when you opened the door? Tell me exactly." Kowalcimi held a pencil to his steno pad.

Carla tried very hard to remember everything, but there was nothing new. "Three things. Just three." Carla ticked them off on her fingers. "She was sitting there with her back to the door not moving, she smelled like poop, and she was staring at a penis. Which I thought was a geoduck, but it was definitely a penis."

Tiffany raised her hand. "Wait a minute, you thought a penis was a duck?"

"It's a not a duck, it's a mollusk."

"That's four things," said Chuck.

"No it's not," said Carla.

"Seriously," said Tiffany. "Where was it?"

"Where was what?"

"She was staring at a disembodied penis?"

"There was a photograph of male genitals on Garabedian's iPad," said Kowalcimi.

"It must have been a screen saver," Carla said. Chuck rolled his eyes. "Hey, they have screen savers for everything! Is it an important clue?"

"Certainly a clue to something," said Chuck.

"Not a screen saver," Kowalcimi said. "This was a Web page image. And she hadn't searched for it—the Web address was typed in. So she knew the address." He folded the steno pad and looked around the group. "Thoughts?"

Chuck said it was probably just the Doc being kinky. Tiffany rolled her eyes but offered no explanation. "Maybe she was going to use it for her book," said Carla, who now felt oddly protective of Toonie's reputation.

"How would that work?" asked Kowalcimi. This occasioned a free-for-all competition with Chuck, Tiffany, and eventually

Carla trying to come up with the silliest chapter titles, all variations on "Meet My Penis."

Amy stood up. She did not look amused. "Were the fingerprints on the iPad all Garabedian's?" she asked, and Kowalcimi said yes. "Well, if whoever killed her wore gloves, which would be the smart thing to do, couldn't that person have typed in the Web address? Why assume it was Garabedian herself? Does anyone want wine? I do." Amy went inside. Kowalcimi followed, pausing at the back door to thank the group and tell Carla that she could have her house back on Monday.

As Chuck and Tiffany squabbled about the iPad image, Tiffany arguing that Toonie was planning to make a point about the patriarchy of meetings and Chuck continuing to make dick jokes, Carla was imagining tomorrow, when she'd have to leave this place, which she so didn't want to. On the far garden wall two little fence lizards faced off doing push-ups, and Carla thought about Boffo and tried hard not to tear up. She was on the point of losing it when Amy came back with wine.

"He says," she said, pouring them each a glass, "that three other women have been murdered since Christmas. One in National City, one in Jamul, and two weeks ago one in Rancho Bernardo."

"So?" Tiffany was instantly outraged. "What else is new? Every single day, 4.6 women are murdered by their domestic—"

"They think these are connected?" Chuck asked. "They've been in the news, but nobody's saying anything about that."

"Because they don't want to start a panic," said Amy, "and anyway, they're not sure. But so far they can't find reasonable suspects for any of them, and now there's Garabedian, who makes four, and they're taking it seriously."

A serial killer! A serial killer in San Diego! Nobody said it, but everybody thought it, and after a while Tiffany reached out and touched Carla's shoulder. "There's your book," she said. The kitchen phone rang and Amy went back inside, not bothering to close the door. After a moment she spoke in that low register, her Voice of God. "Listen to me. Are you listening? YOU MUST CHANGE YOUR LIFE."

"Seriously," said Tiffany. "It'll write itself."

CHAPTER FIVE

Amy

Amy's house had filled up with people. Ricky Buzza had called Tiffany, or maybe the other way around, and then had gotten in touch with Syl Reyes, and of course Harry B. got in on it, and they'd all shown up an hour after Kowalcimi left. At one point Amy caught Tiffany giving driving directions to a complete stranger, a person named John X. Cousins.

"He's got a doctorate from UCSD. He's written a study of serial killers, and now he's researching for a second book, one for the pop market," Tiffany told her. "He's been with us for a year—everybody knows about him. He's planning to do one of those online Guru Classes, right from the Point! I'm sure he can help us out." Tiffany, generally critical of men, was clearly impressed with John X. Cousins.

Help out with what? "All right," said Amy, who didn't bother asking what a Guru Class was because already the afternoon was annoying enough, "but no more. My dog is going to lose her mind." Actually Lottie was thrilled—Ricky threw the squeaky ball for her nonstop—but Amy herself was not. She liked these people and had pleasant memories of working with them in workshops, but that part of her life was over. She was making enough money writing so she didn't have to do classes anymore, and while she wished them all well, they were, as far as she was concerned, on their own.

Chuck Heston was an exception. He'd done her POV opposite-sex exercise during the first class he took with her—writing an amusing, strikingly skilled paragraph about a woman whose boyfriend brings home a bird-eating spider—and then had submitted nothing else while faithfully attending each week and offering intelligent feedback on others' submissions. She'd assumed he wasn't interested in writing, so when last year he had tactfully contacted her with a novel manuscript, she had decided to glance through it before rejecting his request that she work with him one-on-one.

To her surprise, the novel had grown organically out of that old workshop exercise: The female narrator overcomes her arachnophobia through a behavior modification exercise, then becomes claustrophobic, then afraid of clowns, then terrified of bees, and so on. Chuck devoted a chapter to each exercise and replacement phobia. The novel shouldn't have worked, since there was little narrative pull (obviously she'd dump her boyfriend, and she'd come to some sort of understanding of the value of phobias), but it did because it was funny.

Amy had not wanted to help him polish the manuscript—this was book doctoring, a noxious practice to which she was opposed—but the pages had made her laugh, and so did Chuck. After a few months he set it down and started working on nonfiction. She enjoyed working with him on that just because it was a new experience for her.

"So, Amy, are you taking on new clients these days?" Ricky asked. He leaned in and said, in a lower voice, "I'm asking for the others, not for me."

"No." Why didn't they ask her directly? Was she an ogre? She shepherded them into the backyard, charged Carla with offering wine and tea, and when they were settled addressed them. "First of all, yes, Chuck is working with me on a project, and no, I'm not taking up workshopping or book surgery. I'm happy to see you all, but rather puzzled. Why are you here?"

Syl Reyes raised his hand.

"Don't do that, Syl."

"Okay, we're here to support Carla."

"In what sense?"

"There has been a grotesque act of homicidal violence in our sanctuary."

Amy whirled about, in slow motion because of her knees, but the voice was unfamiliar and stentorian, the sort of godlike voice she had been trying to cultivate to fend off telemarketers, so she might have admired it if she had known who this person was and what he was doing on her backsteps.

"I am John X. Cousins," he said. He looked nothing like Richard Burton.

It took Amy a second to understand why she had anticipated the resemblance: He had entered dramatically pronouncing a "violation of sanctuary," as though Inspiration Point! were Canterbury Cathedral, with Hatoon Garabedian as Thomas à Becket. John X. Cousins was bald and slender, with a salt-and-pepper chin patch and mustache circling a thin mouth that looked chronically downturned, as though everything disappointed him. The man inspired instant dislike, yet most of the group seemed to welcome his arrival. Now that John X. Cousins was here, they could really get started. Xerxes? Xavier? Way too old to be a Xander. He walked down the stairs, past Amy, and went straight to Carla.

"We *will* get through this," he said.

"Well, that's a load off my mind," said Chuck, sparing Amy the task of saying precisely the same thing. Perhaps they were spirit twins.

"Again," said Amy, "I would like to know why we're all here. I know why I'm here—I live here—and since Carla's home is a crime scene, I know why she's here. What do you plan to—"

Harry Blasbalg, Carla's lawyer for the Point!, spoke up. "I'm here to discuss possible legal liabilities."

Tiffany gasped. "Seriously, Harry? Carla could be on the hook for this? That's outrageous!"

"Not unless she actually killed the woman, but it's my job to make sure we're covered."

"Well, is she?"

"Yes."

John X. Cousins, glancing back, almost, at Amy and extending a languorous hand in her general direction, said, "If you'll permit me. I understand that this murder may be the work of a serial killer."

This was mischief. "The police say it's just one possibility," said Amy.

"Yet if it should be a serial, all Inspiration Point! writers should be prepared, for the sake of their own safety, to anticipate the killer's next moves."

Syl raised his hand again. "But wouldn't we have to do that anyway? Suppose it's just some jerk who hated this gal. We'd still have to keep an eye out—"

"According to the latest records," said Harry, "we've got thirty clients—"

"Twenty-nine now," said Tiffany.

"—and all of them have keycards. How well do we know these people?"

"A psychosexual sadist," said John X. Cousins, "is not well-known by anyone."

"Oh for god's sake," said Chuck and Amy in perfect unison.

"Except, of course, by his victims."

"I understand you're writing a book on this subject." Amy kept her voice level.

"True," he said. He didn't add "Dear Lady," but might as well have. "And you're thinking that these events might provide me with useful material, and you'd be right, but of course that is not why I'm here today."

"It's an ill wind," said Amy.

Carla, who had been silent through all this nonsense, cleared her throat. "I've never understood that expression. 'It's an ill wind that blows nobody any good.' Where's the ill wind?"

"It means," said Syl, "that her murder is a really bad thing."

"Yeah, but of course it is, why bother saying that at all? Nobody thinks it's a nice wind."

John X. Cousins opened his trap to explain this to the masses, but for once they ignored him, and the meeting turned into another free-for-all as Tiffany and Ricky tried to parse the sentence and only worsened Carla's confusion.

Ricky said, "It's a really ill wind. It's the illest of winds. No wind is as ill as this wind."

"Look, William Shakespeare was making the point that—"

"Not Shakespeare, Tiffany," said John X. Cousins, chuckling paternally. Why did they like this man? "Sir Walter Scott. And—"

"You're not helping," said Carla. "I know it's a really really ill wind. Everybody knows that. What's the point of saying it?"

"It's an ill wind *indeed*—" said Harry B.

"Skip it."

"Carla, look at me." Amy had to overcome a strong temptation to let this go on until people wore themselves out and went home. "An ill wind is misfortune. Right?"

"Of course it is."

"And most misfortunes are not universal. A stock market crash is bad for most but good for a few. A tornado is awful for the people it hits but good for home builders. Malpractice is terrible for patients and a boon for lawyers. Sorry, Harry."

"Okay, so what does that have to do with—"

"A misfortune that benefited absolutely nobody would be an ill wind indeed."

"Yes yes yes, it's this big fat metaphor. I hate metaphors, they just fog everything up."

John X. Cousins chuckled yet again. "You've just used a metaphor to describe metaphors! I had no idea this was possible. A meta-metaphor! Carla, you're a genius!"

Carla stood up. Amy couldn't remember seeing Carla angry, but she was angry now, and with John X. Cousins. "I wasn't trying to be cute! Toonie was horribly strangled, and that was a huge-ass ill wind, and it didn't blow anybody any good! Except you! Because you got cool new material out of it—lucky you! Oh. Wait." She turned to Amy, smiling, suddenly radiant. "I get it!"

In minutes, John X. Cousins swanned off, thanking Amy profusely, again without meeting her eyes, for graciously admitting him into her home, and promising the rest that he would keep in touch. The late afternoon sun came out just as the door closed behind him, the sort of happy coincidence that never happens in decent fiction, and Amy relaxed into an evening which was now inevitable.

More old workshoppers came by. Dr. Surtees, who by now had retired from cardiology, abandoned his quest to write medical thrillers, and become a health care columnist for the *Trib,* arrived, with colleague Kurt Robetussien in tow. Amy remembered Kurt R. as a promising writer but was not surprised to learn that he'd set that aside and was now in private practice as a geriatrician. And there was Pete Purvis, still living with his father and playing in a garage band, still writing children's books; he'd put in one three-month period at the Point! and was looking forward to doing it again when he could scrape up the fee.

These three spoke with Amy for a bit but were obviously here for Carla and for the company of their old gang. Syl went out for beer and more wine, pizza was ordered, and little was said about what had befallen Toonie Garabedian. They milled around Carla, comforting her with occasional discreet pats and smiles, while talking to one another, catching up.

This was herd behavior. Elephants, crows, dogs, apes, all had been observed consoling melancholic fellows in just this fashion. As Amy grew old, she found herself focusing often on humans as animals. She would sometimes see a face—a particularly handsome or beautiful face—and view it through a lens uncontaminated by the natural bias of her own species. This symmetrical arrangement, she would think—the large eyes, the full mouth, the cheekbones contoured just so—is considered attractive to other humans, and in this moment the face would not appear beautiful to her, its features ideal only according to some evolutionary whim. In such moments she felt like an alien observer.

Was this a sign of impending dementia? She thought not. She hoped not. Any writer of fiction should be an alien observer. Perhaps she had just come to that understanding late in life. She cradled her exhausted dog, who was played out for the first time in her young life, sipped merlot, and surveyed the herd. Carla and Chuck were laughing, Harry B. and Syl arguing, Ricky Buzza and Pete wandering, the two docs consulting, Tiffany pouting. Chuck raised his glass to her and smiled. In a while they would make noises about leaving and then all but Carla would go home. Amy tried to look forward to this and realized that she could not. Damn it, she thought. I've missed this.

CHAPTER SIX

Carla

Sunday, March 7

Sunday was sunny and quiet, a perfect early spring day Carla and Amy had all to themselves. Amy did get the occasional phone call, but not from anybody they knew, and by afternoon Carla was confident enough to answer these nuisance calls for her. She picked up the ringing phone and said, to some guy warning her that her privacy was at risk, "I KNOW! Isn't it WONDER-FUL?" He hung up.

"An interesting approach," said Amy. "It never occurred to me to engage with them."

"You never worked in show business. You gotta connect. Do that and you'll kill." Before lunchtime the phone rang twice more, which Amy said was just about average. One lady started to tell Carla about a fabulous opportunity to triple her savings, but Carla cut her off. "Look," she said, "I keep telling you people, I already have way too much money, money is the last thing I need, I don't want any more money, for the love of God LEAVE ME ALONE!" Amy was laughing in the other room.

Carla was throwing the ball for Lottie when the phone rang again. "Grandma?" The voice was young and trembling. "Grandma, I'm in terrible trouble."

"Who is this?"

"It's your grandson!"

The famous Grandparent Scam! Carla had heard about this one from Harry B. "You don't sound like yourself." Carla used her best Ma voice, sharp and crackling.

"I know, I got a bad cold, plus these guys are a bunch of thugs! They busted my nose! Grandma, you gotta help me!"

"Oh, son," said Carla, "what's happened to you?"

"I'm in Tijuana, Grandma. They've got me in a Mexican jail!"

"Whatever for, sweetheart?"

"I'm not gonna lie to you. I bought some . . . you know . . . marijuana . . . from this man on the street, and it was a setup, I'm so sorry, I was stupid, and I'll never ever—"

"How can I help, son?"

"I have a lawyer, and he says that if I pay them off, they'll let me go. They need five thousand dollars! And I don't have five cents!"

"How can I do that, son? Tell me. Tell me everything." She hung up. The phone rang again.

"Grandma, we got disconnected!"

"I'm so sorry, dear. I have so much trouble with these buttons—"

"No problem! Just—"

Carla hung up again. When he called back and spoke, she yelled into the phone, "Hello! Hello! Put my grandson on the phone right now! Hello!" for a full minute, then hung up. The fourth time, she picked up laughing. "Aren't I the silliest old thing? That time it wasn't my fault. My cat—Miss Kumquat, you remember Miss Kumquat!—she jumped up on—"

"Grandma, please listen carefully. Don't touch anything, just listen. You call my lawyer. I'll give you the number. You just call, and he'll explain what to do, and I'll come right home and pay you back as soon as I can. I love you so much, Grandma!" He gave her the number.

"You just hold on, honey," Carla said. "Just hold tight. Don't worry! I'm hanging up now."

Amy was standing in the doorway to her office, staring at her. "Who is that you're talking to?"

"My grandson's been kidnapped by the Federales." Carla looked at the phone number. "I better not call this so-called lawyer. It's not an 800 number. It might cost something."

"Be my guest," said Amy. She took a seat.

Carla was thrilled. "It's a Quebec City area code," she said, punching in the number.

"Carla," said Amy, "do you do this often?"

"Not really. This is a treat. I gave up my landline at the Birdhouse." After nine rings, a man who did not sound French or Canadian answered. "Law Offices of Miguel Escobar, state your business." A faint New Zealand accent; he reminded her just a bit of her last agent, Clyde Cogwell from Clyde. Clyde from Clyde had to be dead by now.

"Am I speaking to Miguel?"

"No, this is one of his associates."

"Well, I need to speak to Miguel Escobar."

"I can take care of your—"

"It has to be Miguel Escobar. It's a matter of life and death."

There was a phone drop and a long silence, then the guy came back, speaking in a higher pitch and with a crap Latin American accent. "This is Miguel Escobar."

"Oh thank the good lord! The Mexicans are holding my grandson hostage! I have to give you five thousand dollars! How do I do that?"

He took Carla through the process of wiring money. This involved several steps. "As soon as the wire goes through, I'll take care of the problem."

"Bless your heart! Now, what are the account and routing numbers of your bank?"

"You don't need that information, señora. Just follow the steps—"

"Mr. Escobar, Miguel, I *never* wire money. My husband, Ralph, god rest his soul, made me promise. 'Elsie,' Ralph would say to me, 'Western Union is Satan's handbasket.'"

"What? Look, it's perfectly safe—"

"No, absolutely not, Ralph would spin in his grave! Ralph was a *stickler.* All I have to do is have my bank transfer the money to yours. Just give me the numbers."

They argued for five minutes, Carla ratcheting up her desperate willingness to part with ever-increasing amounts of money to make the transfer worth his trouble. When she got it up to fifteen thousand, he caved and gave her the numbers. Carla told him to have a blessed day, hung up, and googled the routing number.

Amy started to stand up. "Carla, you're not going to—"

"Drain that account? File that under What Would Ma Do. Actually, she wouldn't, but she'd think about it. I'm just screwing around. So the kid is in Mexico, his lawyer got to Quebec by way of New Zealand, and the bank is in West Virginia."

"What do we do now?"

"Now, we wait."

Amy went back to her office, though she seemed reluctant to do so. Carla could not recall ever having interested Amy so much. Or at all, really. Amy liked her, but that was about it, except for now. The phone didn't ring for a half hour, and when it did, Carla didn't answer. She counted twenty rings before they gave up. They tried again, and then again. Amy and Carla ate grilled cheese sandwiches on the back patio, watching the birds, playing with Lottie, listening to the telephone ring. Eventually, midafternoon, Carla picked up. "Son, is that you? Are you free?"

"Grandma—"

"Praise the Lord!"

"No, Grandma, I'm still in jail! My lawyer says he didn't get the money from you. You have to wire it!"

"Now, you know I can't do that, honey. You remember what your Pampaw used to say!"

"Grandma, this is serious, there are bad people here!"

"Right!"

"'Right,' what?"

"That's just what he used to say!"

"Grandma—"

"He used to say, 'Elsie, there are bad people all around us, and some of them pretend to be your grandson and try to scam you out of five thousand dollars.'"

He said something under his breath.

"And you can tell that nice Mr. Escobar he might want to check his bank account." Carla hung up. "I don't think they'll call again."

Amy applauded. "Now you have to tell me how you learned to do that."

"Improv," said Carla. "Really the only part of my so-called showbiz life that ever did me any good. When we got out to L.A., I had to take tons of acting classes, and my favorite exercises—the only ones I enjoyed—were improvs. They said I was a natural. I really love it, and I never get a chance these days."

"It's a wonderful talent for a writer, too."

This had never occurred to Carla, although when Amy said it, it was instantly plausible. "How would I use it, exactly?"

"Well, you might just run through scenes in your head, making up situations, and then characters, bringing them together, seeing what happens—"

"And then writing them down!"

"Writing down what works, or what might work, yes. You never tried that?"

"No, but I will now!" This felt like an empty promise. Carla had given up on fiction; occasionally she put something up on her own

Web page, which no one ever visited, because why should they. Tiffany endlessly schooled her on "influencing," whatever that was, and why she should keep some sort of running tab on the number of people who looked at her blog. "You keep a blog, don't you?"

"Not religiously," said Amy. "I drop in every now and then. A blog is more of a diary, really, and I never was big on those."

"Why?"

"Too public."

"Don't people usually keep diaries hidden in drawers?"

"I suppose. Still, they're visible."

So are fiction manuscripts, Carla thought but didn't say. What was the difference?

They stayed put on the patio and threw the ball for a while. Then Amy said, "Carla? Do you mind if I ask you a personal question?"

"Of course not."

"Could you tell me about the dollhouse?"

When had Amy seen the dollhouse? Friday's events continued to recede from Carla's mind; she had clearer memories about that last conversation with Toonie than she did about finding her dead body; that event had been described so often that it wasn't a memory anymore. When she tried to recall it, it was a story, not an experience. Amy must have seen the dollhouse, but Carla had no idea how or when.

"Forgive me," said Amy. "It's not my business."

"No, it is! I want to tell you. I was just surprised for a minute." Where to start? "You sure you want to hear the whole thing?"

Amy nodded.

"Well. You know I came from Philadelphia? The house we lived in on Mawney Street . . . that's the dollhouse."

Amy nodded again, as though she already knew this.

"When I was five, I was already doing local commercials. By the time I was eight, Ma was taking me up to New York for lessons and gigs. I missed school a lot—she kept telling them I had mono or German measles or whatever—and I spent what seemed like days on the train, trying to catch up on homework. She'd let me do that after I'd run lines with her. When I could look out the window I liked the train rides, but I hated everything else. My father . . ."

"Yes?"

"I know, I never talk about him, it's like he was never there. But he was, sort of."

"You did talk about him once. You said he ran off with some—"

"Oh god, yes, I'm sorry. That wasn't true. It was what I used to tell people when they asked. That he ditched Ma and me and took off with a floozy. I wish he had, for his own sake.

"He was a food broker. He sold products to grocery stores, like the A&P before it closed, and Acme. You wouldn't recognize the names. He wasn't around much, at least not that I can remember. Most of the time when he was home, he was in the basement making stuff. He was really good with tools and wood. He liked to make birdhouses for purple martins. They were so beautiful. Ma didn't have any use for them, or for him. That's what she used to say, exactly. 'I've got no use for your father.' So it's not exactly a big mystery why he kept to himself."

Amy was looking at her with pity. "No, it wasn't like that. I liked him. He was nice to me. He made me things—like there was this marble game we'd play together. He'd get a shoebox and cut three doors in it—one small, one medium, one large—the lid would be the roof, and he'd set the box in front of the sofa in the living room, and we'd have a contest rolling marbles, trying to get them in the smallest door." Carla had totally forgotten about the shoebox game until just now. "I think really that we loved each other. We just didn't get much of a chance to show it. It doesn't make me sad to talk about him." What was odd, she realized, was that Toonie had never asked her about her father. Toonie sure was a crap psychiatrist.

"I have his feet," she said, and when she saw the look on Amy's face, she laughed. "In a box! Wanna see?? No, I don't, I mean, that's what Ma always said. 'You got your father's feet.' It wasn't a compliment. She wanted me to have slender feet, so I could be a foot model if the other stuff didn't pan out. 'You could never model clothes,' she'd say. 'You don't have the face for it.' So anyway, the dollhouse.

"On my ninth birthday, Ma threw this bogus party for me, and my father was there, and her sisters Agnes and Gertrude. No kids except my cousins, and I didn't really know them. Agnes and Gertrude weren't as bad as Ma, but they weren't nice either. She was always showing me off to them, because their kids weren't special. Lucky them. So she made this big announcement. She'd gotten us—us!—a great agent, and the agent was sure we'd make it big in Hollywood, so we were moving to L.A. Which was news to everybody. Including my father."

Carla closed her eyes. She could see the dining table loaded with Ma's best china and a punch bowl and a huge chocolate ice cream cake with letters on the top: *Bon Voyage Carla!!!* She could see all the faces looking at her; she could see that only Ma was smiling. The aunts were teed off, the cousins were bored, and her father looked at Carla with the saddest expression. And then he shook his head side to side, very slowly, and she knew this was just for her, and she knew what it meant. It meant he couldn't stop it.

"Once I got it through my head what 'moving' meant—that we were never coming back to this house—I just went crazy. Not right then, but later that night, and on to the next day and the next. I didn't throw a fit or anything. I just stopped talking and eating. I holed up in my room. Ma went nuts on about the third day. She and my father were yelling at each other—I'd never heard him raise his voice before—and she was making all kinds of threats. Ma never laid hands on me, and I knew she wouldn't do that now. To put your hands on a person, you have to have some kind of emotional connection with that person, and she wasn't connected to anybody, ever. Instead she threatened to have me committed. That's what they were yelling about. I didn't know what 'committed' meant, but it must have been bad enough to make him stand up to her.

"So this went on for a week. My father snuck food to me and I stayed put. Then a child psychiatrist, Dr. Mary, came to the house. I never knew her last name, but that's what everybody called her, Dr. Mary. She talked with me through the bedroom door, and when I let her in she sat next to me and said nothing. She was good-looking, sort of like Marlo Thomas, with this little smile and perky voice, and she introduced herself and then didn't say a word, for I don't know how long. She waited me out. It was kind of brilliant. Of course, I talked in the end, and once she got me talking she got me to answer questions, and it was basically all over. She kept asking *why. Why are you angry? Why don't you want to go to California?*

"Of course, the answer, duh, was that I hated Ma and once she got me out there I'd be alone with her forever, but I couldn't say that. I couldn't even form that thought in my head, it was so awful. So I came up with the house. I said I loved the house and didn't want to leave it because it was my home and I felt safe there. That wasn't exactly a lie, either. My house was old and huge with many rooms, and each room had a door you could shut. Not like the houses here.

"Cut to the chase, I gave up. Ma got us packed and ready in, it must have been, two or three days. I was just in this fog that whole time; I think maybe Dr. Mary gave me something to zone me out. Anyway, the morning we left, my father called me down to the basement. I knew he wasn't going with us, and I didn't blame him. I thought he called me down to say goodbye, and I suppose that was part of it, but he wanted to show me what he was working on. He had drawn up this amazing thing, what I know now was a blueprint. It was the outline of a house, our house. He was going to make a dollhouse for me and send it out to me in California. He talked about how big it would be, and what he would put in each room, and the materials he would use. He had never lied to me, so I knew he wasn't lying now, but what made him think Ma would let me have the dollhouse? He said she promised. He said you know she keeps her promises. And this was true: When Ma said that something was going to happen, it happened. Like now. I was going to L.A.

"And all the time he was telling me about the dollhouse I couldn't look at him. I was staring at this hole in the basement wall, it was a concrete wall and crumbly, and this centipede crawled partway out of the hole, it was huge and ugly, but I didn't look away. And then Ma called down from the top of the stairs, which meant she had been listening, which scared me to death for some reason, but she just said, 'You have my word, Carla. Now come up here. It's time.' And I came up, and he didn't, and we left for California."

They sat still for a long time and watched the light redden as the sun went down. Amy said, "Jesus, Carla."

"It's all right," said Carla, because it was. This was what Toonie never understood, that ancient history is just that, a story you tell yourself so often that it becomes a story.

"When did you get the dollhouse? How long did it take your father to finish it?"

"It took a year. When it came we were living in Tarzana, and it was so huge it came in a moving van."

When it got set up in the spare room and she unwrapped all the furniture and all the wonderful little things—the bedspread for her tiny bed, just like her old one, blue and gold, and the pictures and mirrors and her old rocking horse, and a backyard with purple martin houses and a gopher sticking his head up from the dirt, and a little shoebox in the living room in front of the sofa, everything so perfect—she wrote her father a three-page letter thanking him. She was going to mail it herself but Ma took it and said she would, and of course, a long time later, Carla found the unmailed letter in Ma's desk drawer.

Carla decided not to tell Amy that part, or about when her father died and Ma didn't tell her. A year almost after he died Aunt Gertrude called and Carla answered the phone, and that's when she found out. When Aunt Gertrude realized Ma hadn't told her she just said, "Typical."

"That dollhouse is still my favorite thing in the world," Carla said.

"And no wonder," said Amy. "Carla . . . how did your father know to draw in that centipede?"

"He didn't," said Carla.

Amy smiled, a little. "You drew it yourself."

Carla nodded. "Took me forever. I practiced on paper with black acrylic paint and a tiny brush, over and over, until I could get it just right."

Amy was still looking at her. Carla saw this out of the corner of her eye, but she didn't look back. There was a decrepit pink dog-house at the other end of the yard; Carla focused there and didn't blink. After a while, Amy handed Lottie to her and went in the house. "Dinner at seven," she said.

And breakfast in the morning, and maybe lunch if she was lucky, and then back to the Birdhouse. Carla sat studying the yard, taking in every little thing: the weeds, the orange tree, the bird-bath, the feeder birds, the shape of each flagstone, folding each into her memory so that, no matter what happened, she would always have them.

CHAPTER SEVEN

Amy

Monday, March 8

Amy watched from the front-room window as Chuck threw Carla's bag in the backseat of his car, and both Carla and Chuck turned to wave at her before getting in and backing out of the driveway. Chuck had been kind to volunteer for this duty. Amy had the house to herself again. This did not feel as good as it was supposed to.

Having Carla there had been a trial. Having to dress and undress with the door closed, feed someone other than herself, deal with Lottie, who, both mornings, had scratched at dawn at the spare-room door, all of these interruptions annoyed her, yet when Carla left she took something away, and Amy could not grasp what that was. Amy was incapable of loneliness, but now there was this vacuum, small but sturdy, a thing you could trip over.

She tried writing but found herself unable to quit scouring the local news for more information about the murder. There was nothing more on Garabedian, so she searched for the other murders, which had apparently started—assuming there was anything to start—last November. A prostitute had been strangled in National City, and another woman on Christmas Eve in Jamul. Both crimes had gotten little play in local media. Then a month ago, on Valentine's Day, a teacher in Rancho Bernardo had been murdered in her garage. This was a prominent story, though how she had been murdered was unclear; Amy wondered if this is when the police started shielding the public from panic-inducing details. And then came Toonie. Maybe one person really was responsible for all of it, but Amy was skeptical.

In her youth the only serial killers anyone knew about were Jack the Ripper and Albert DeSalvo, and they weren't even called that. The Boston Strangler may or may not have been Albert DeSalvo, may or may not have been one person, but he was, like Jack, a mythic creature, and this gave him outsized power over the imaginations of women in Southeastern New England. These days, he would barely register in the national consciousness. He probably wouldn't even qualify as a serial killer. Was he charismatic? Unusually handsome or spectacularly ugly? Had he taken trophies? Did he taunt the police and press with anagrams and rebuses? When Ted Bundy broke out of jail, he terrorized the nation and murdered three more women. After DeSalvo escaped from Bridgewater, he hung around a shoe store in Lynn, Massachusetts, waiting for the police. DeSalvo wasn't a *star*.

Amy had been visiting a distant cousin, Carol Ann Somebody—Winkelman—at Brown when news came about DeSalvo's escape. She'd met the cousin at a family gathering in Augusta; why she had taken her up on the offer of a Wild Ivy League Weekend was now a mystery to Amy, who had already been involved with Max, so surely she hadn't been looking for a date. She was languishing at a fraternity mixer when the news about the escaped strangler electrified the gathering, especially those girls who lived off campus and now faced the prospect of going out into the drunken midnight to find a ride. One of them, smashed and hysterical, was sobbing about winding up dead in a ravine. Carol Ann Winkelman lived in a yurt in the backyard of Spanish House, and Amy was not looking forward to sleeping on the damn ground and would happily have taken her chances with Albert DeSalvo if he'd been willing to drive her back to Augusta.

She had stopped going to the movies decades ago, but she did watch television, and you couldn't shuffle through screening choices on Netflix and Hulu without encountering serial murder, whether fictional or documented. As Tiffany said, these killers were hot. Amy's new agent, Robin Something, who had last year inherited Maxine's clients when she died, had actually pushed Amy to "write a serial killer." Amy had not deigned to respond to that suggestion.

Instead she was attempting to pump out enough short stuff to fill a new collection. Right now she had three finished stories but was stuck on the rest. If her new stuff had a theme, it was death. She found herself unable to write about sex, not that she had ever dwelled inordinately on that subject. Robin Something was uneasy about this focus, which was likely to appeal mostly to older readers. "Millennials aren't going to buy it." She had needed to define this term for Amy, who responded that when she was that young she thought death was a hot sketch. Robin Something didn't find this funny. In Amy's last email to Robin, she explained, as to a toddler, that any readers she still had were probably her age and thinking about death 24-7, and that if they weren't, they should be. Amy missed Maxine.

Now, post-sleepover, post-Toonie, Amy couldn't get murder out of her mind, even though she did not understand why people obsessed so much about murder and so little about accident.

Accident was infinitely more likely and equally scary. You can die because you turn left instead of right, because your front tire blows on the freeway, because you annoy an African bee, because you're beaned by a foul ball or a falling coconut, and your untimely death will not be mythologized. Just like a murder victim, you'll never finish that thought, that sentence, that cross-stitch, your universe will suddenly wink out, but your mourners will not have the comfort of a scapegoat. Of course, if your poor choices somehow contribute to the accident—if you're driving drunk or have consumed pods of laundry detergent on a bet—you'll be used as an object lesson, but you won't be a victim of anyone but your own dumb self.

Amy had once been menaced by a murderous student and a year later had knocked herself out on a birdbath. That accident had had a much more profound impact on her life. A positive one, all in all—it had gotten her writing again—but it could just as easily have ruined her. She rarely thought about that student now, who had killed two workshop members and assaulted her with a knife. The accident had been more traumatic.

Still, she had to admit that being assaulted was remarkable. People are interesting, Amy mused; birdbaths are not. A murder threat thrusts you into a role for which you are unprepared and, in most cases, unsuited: The hackneyed script is laid out for you, and there you are, onstage with an audience of one idiot. Murder is a lot of things, including absurd, but it has the advantage of design, of purpose. Accident is pointless. So that whereas murder is easy to deal with in fiction, accident is practically impossible. Because the writer is supposed to be in charge, nothing that happens in a story can be read as truly accidental.

Amy had a file drawer full of dead stories, some unfinished, most completed and abandoned, and fully a third involved fatal accidents interrupting a story line which had chugged along nicely until a point-of-view character was struck by lightning, choked on a cube of cheese, stumbled in front of a bus, or drowned in a hot tub, at which point the story necessarily ended. Most of these were duds, but for a while she had thought one was workable. A train story. Amy liked trains.

✳ ✳ ✳

A young woman riding coach from Los Angeles to New York, unable to sleep sitting up and terrorized by two screaming toddlers, takes refuge in the ladies' room and strikes up a conversation with a beautiful woman in her thirties. The woman is a shampoo model in TV commercials; she lives in L.A. and is taking the train to meet her rich lover at the top of the Chrysler Building; they do this every year on the same weekend. She is happily married with children and feels no guilt about this. The model is warm, intelligent, generous with her attention, and because she so freely shares her secret life with a stranger, the younger woman does the same, and, knowing they will never meet again, they spend the whole night and early morning trading intimate stories.

As soon as the dining car opens in the morning, they have waffles and coffee and watch tree limbs and furniture race down a swollen Johnstown river. They part at Penn Station with a tight embrace and no promises to keep in touch. The younger woman walks away in a gorgeous daze, enchanted with the magic of an encounter so rich and unfettered by history or obligation. She stands in the sunlight, at the corner of Eighth and Thirty-third, and enters into the most skilled epiphany Amy has ever written, which cuts off when she is struck in the head and killed by an airborne manhole cover.

"I get it," Maxine had said, "but this time you've gone too far. Nobody is going to laugh at this."

"It's not supposed to be funny."

"It's juvenile," Maxine said, which hurt Amy's feelings. After Max died, Maxine had been her best reader.

In the end, Amy shoved it in the file cabinet. The last time she'd taken a look at it, she'd seen what she'd refused to recognize before—that the manhole cover was a goddamn symbol. Amy loathed symbols and never used them intentionally. Of course they appeared in her fiction as they did everywhere in life, but they were not her responsibility. Still, the fact that she had no idea what the damn manhole cover symbolized didn't keep the story from making exactly the kind of sense she was trying to resist: *This is what happens to young girls who have epiphanies.* Well, no, it wasn't, but the hell with it.

After an hour staring at the blank screen, Amy gave up and did a search on John X. Cousins, the Serial Killer Whisperer. The Official Website of Renowned Writing Guru John X. Cousins featured him smirking seductively, not at the camera but at a book he was pretending to read, which just happened to be *Finnegans Wake.* If this had been a video rather than a still image, he would have glanced up, and exclaimed, "Oh, there you are!" in surprised delight. Floating about the image were clouds of inspiration: *Read to write! Write to be read! What's your story?! Dare to Fail!* At the top of the page were links to "Works," "Appearances," "News," and "Writing Guru to the Rescue" *(Coming* SOON!). The Works page featured links to articles in online magazines and journals and one book, *Lightborne Redux,* which was going to be published in six months but was available for preorder now at the reduced price of $24.95. Here was his pop serial killer study; the Web page was already decked out with windy blurbs about its scope and erudition, most from other SK authors, fictional and non.

There was only one blurb from a newspaper, *The Boston Globe:* "If you read only one book this year . . ." Amy now scoured Google and the *Globe* archives for the complete quote, which she hoped included the full sentence, as in ". . . for Christ's sake read anything but this," but could find nothing. How had Cousins' publicist allowed an ellipsis-throttled blurb to be featured on his page? For that matter, how had his agent let him get away with the title? Lightborne, Marlowe's nightmare executioner in *Edward II, was* a terrifying character, but hardly well-known, and "redux" was just stuffy.

For now, Amy avoided the Guru video but clicked on "Appearances," and there was a shot of the Birdhouse next to a photo of Cousins flanked by Carla and Tiffany. His arms were around them both, his hands perched upon their shoulders like white crabs, and below was the caption "Inspiration Point Guru" along with an invitation to join his classes and a smorgasbord of pay buttons. The degree of alarm this image set off impressed Amy. *Get your hands off her.* Not them; her. Tiffany could take care of herself.

Her old workshop group had been adopted, co-opted, seduced by this person, and what was that to her? Was she jealous now? There was a dismal thought. Hadn't she always told them they should seek other opinions? Hadn't she refused to be connected with Inspiration Point!? Yes, and she didn't regret it, but Carla . . . Carla deserved better. Amy couldn't dismiss the memory of Carla conning that grandmother scammer yesterday, the manic inventiveness that had seemed to come out of nowhere. Amy had for years known Carla well enough to worry about her, but there was so much more to her than she had imagined, layers upon layers, going all the way down to that cellar, that centipede.

After she and Lottie had walked the neighborhood and eaten supper, after a day in which the telephone did not ring once and Amy had failed to take advantage of that rare reprieve, after she had shut down her computer for the night, and after she had spent a half hour trying to sleep, she rose, made a cup of green tea, fired up the desktop, and began to write.

Megan Soames, a young blogger armed with an Ivy League degree in English Literature and an Iowa MFA, struggling to come up with a marketable premise for her first book, sets up a Serial Killer Association website. She is careful to disguise her own identity (Amy made a note to ask Tiffany and Ricky about IPs and whatnot) and starts out small with just a cover page inviting real honest-to-god serial killers to apply for membership and listing an email address set up just for the purpose. On the page are photos of Bundy, Gacy, Dahmer, Berkowitz, and some random guy she chooses after googling "photos of random guys." Gradually she adds pages. The first is a detailed explanation of who might qualify for official membership in the association (no lookie-loos or wannabes; three-corpse minimum; inventive, gag-inducing methods of murder and disposal).

When applications begin to come in, which they do within hours, she creates a *Storied Kills* page and invites the applicants to send her detailed descriptions of their deeds (five-hundred-word minimum), which, if they're sufficiently impressive, she will post after "curating." Of course she posts them all. Megan's hypothesis: While a few applicants may be actual unhinged wannabes, most will be smartasses, trolls, and clueless moralists. For a while this is true. Megan keeps a file of the most promising essays. Her nascent plan is to work the material into a quick and dirty pop culture exposé of America's fixation on serial killers. Much of the writing is hilarious: WurstNitemareBaddass brags of nineteen victims and describes his kills "like a lion grabbing it's pray and hiding there beasts and privet parts in my dead sisters jewelry box." As the membership swells, some of the new ones seem literate, five of them startlingly so, enough to make her a bit nervous. Two are literate in the Lecter style, free of misspellings and cliché, introspective, witty, rich with allusions to historical characters like de Sade and Gesualdo. They don't disturb her as much as the other three, who convey personae less erudite but impressively complex and self-consistent. All three link to grotesque unsolved crimes, all real; each describes his deeds in obsessive detail that is at once clumsily depicted and uniquely awful; each involves prolonged torture. One of them, RideUHrd, in his fourth post addresses Megan by her full name; the other two, Toucheee666 and HandymanKan, do so the following week. Then Handyman tells her he knows where she lives. Before she can stop them, the others contact him directly for this information. How this breach is possible Megan does not know. She shuts down the site, installs new locks, takes pills, can't sleep, and finally begs for help from a Web developer, who easily identifies all five.

Two are women and all of them have or are presently earning MFAs in creative writing. HandymanKan and one of the Lecters are, as a matter of fact, working on a quick and dirty pop culture exposé of America's fixation on serial killers. Undaunted, energized, Megan decides to shift the focus of her book: She will expose the internet culture that feeds on itself in an infinite loop, perhaps calling it "The Mobius Something" or "The Cyborg Centipede." Before she can decide on methodology and a working outline, she is tracked down and horribly slaughtered by WurstNitemareBaddass.

Of course Amy would never publish this silly thing—it was way too close to the book Chuck was working on now—but getting it down made her happy. Her last thought before sleeping was that maybe she'd send it off under a nom de plume, Otto B. Schott, to the Writing Guru.

CHAPTER EIGHT

Carla

Chuck accompanied her inside the Birdhouse and walked with her through both wings and all the rooms and didn't leave until she told him five times that she was okay. And she was. She waved down at him from her bedroom window as he walked to his car. He stood smiling up at her before driving away. What a sweet man. He had worried she'd be afraid to be alone there. She wasn't. She was too sad to feel anything else. Already Amy's home was receding to dollhouse stature, and for the first time in . . . the first time ever, really, she wished her father were alive to live here with her, and that they could build a second dollhouse together. If he were only here, she'd have the will to bury that stupid Acorn and get on with her so-called life.

Tiffany showed up late and shuffled papers around for a while. There wasn't much for her to do. Carla had decided to reopen the cells Wednesday, after a brief, tasteful hiatus—Toonie's funeral was tomorrow—and Tiffany had already phoned all twenty-nine writers and explained the situation. For the most part, she said, they hadn't seemed put off by the murder. "I explained that

Toonie's door wasn't locked, so all they have to do is—It wasn't locked, was it?"

Carla thought. "No, it wasn't."

"The good news is that only the McPhails are a little jumpy. Which is understandable because of the four kids, but I don't think we'll lose them. I gave them a free month." Tiffany said she planned to spend today and tomorrow straightening up her office. She said this without looking at Carla; she probably thought she should stay and keep her company.

"Go home," Carla said. "The office is spotless. I'll be fine."

Carla ate lunch and then wandered down to the Rotunda, which Tiffany always reminded her wasn't a rotunda because it didn't have a dome, but it was huge and round and light in the daytime, and it had the dollhouse. She needed the sunlight and the tiny surfers on the sparkling expanse of blue. She needed to spot some passing gray whales far out near the horizon, and she did, and she needed to see one breach, and she did. She stood at the great curved window for an hour, thinking about nothing.

This was an old trick she had picked up from Cal Hoving when she was twelve. Not that he had showed her how to do it. He had just made it necessary. Carla didn't think often about Cal Hoving, the Nutty's Squirrel perv who had not literally raped her anyway; he had just been handsy, and he said foul things to her under his garlic breath, and he had grabbed her once when she was alone in the funhouse. She liked to hide there even though it was gross and filthy, and Ma told her to stay out of it. "They never clean those things, they're lousy with germs," which was surely true, which meant Ma stayed out of it herself.

You entered through the round gaping mouth of a clown painted on whitewashed fencing, and inside were old-fashioned paintings of freaks like the Lagoon Boy and the Armless Violinist and the Spider Lady, who had four legs. There was a pretend guillotine with a pretend head in a basket, both so badly made that they weren't scary at all; there were skulls propped up on rickety barstools and so on. It was super cheesy. Behind the black drapes that showcased the skeleton with the top hat was an old record player and on it a 78-rpm record of cornet music and people laughing for no reason, and Carla knew how to turn it on full blast.

The Hall of Mirrors was just before the exit door and brighter than the rest of the funhouse interior, mainly because of cracks in the ceiling. Carla would take a stool from one of the skulls and place it up against a mirror, and sit against the curvy mirror and daydream. The laugh track always suited her fantasies, and Nobody, meaning Ma, could find her in there, but Hoving did. He didn't rape her, so it wasn't a big deal, but he did put his hand on her under her skirt and she stopped thinking, just cut it out like magic, though she could not stop hearing, but she focused on the laughing and let it cover what he was whispering and after a while he let go and went away.

She could have told Toonie about Hoving but didn't because Toonie would have been all over it like a cheap suit because Toonie was clueless. All that crap Toonie gave her when she refused to talk about her sex life, which was nonexistent but none of Toonie's damn business anyway, not to mention the damn urn and her "unacknowledged grief." Toonie did ask her once if Ma "haunted" the Birdhouse. She clearly didn't believe Carla when she said no, but it was the truth. In the pre-cell Birdhouse, Ma had haunted it when she and Carla had lived there in separate wings: Though they had lived disconnected lives, Ma had had an uncanny ability to pop out of a door like a poltergeist and ruin any project Carla was working on, especially if it involved Amy and the writers' group. But when Ma was gone, she was gone for good.

Now the place seemed even emptier than it had before the murder, which was okay. Carla was used to having it to herself when Tiffany went home. She would watch a ton of old movies. She would try to write. Sometimes she'd drive down to the water.

When the tide was low the tide pools on the reef stretched out some distance, their rocks green and slippery; she would take off her shoes and navigate barefoot, looking for starfish and octopuses, anemones and urchins. There was one spot where she could sit cross-legged and wet, fully absorbed in the secret civilization beneath the surface. Most of the pools were near-perfect circles, tiny moon craters, and each pool was its own little dollhouse furnished with barnacles and mussels, inhabited by the smallest crabs and octopuses, ugly creatures somehow made beautiful by seawater. The best time to study them was late afternoon. She would sit with the western sun at her back, so her shadow would vanish the sparkling surface of the water. More than once a passerby would warn that she shouldn't sit that way. They would singsong, "Never turn your back on the sea!" Made sense when you thought about it, rogue waves and all, but she always felt safe there.

So she would go down later today, but first she was going to write something. Anything. She didn't know where her laptop was, so she fished the yellow legal pad Amy had given her out of her suitcase, found a pencil in Tiffany's desk drawer, and sat down to write. All that happened was doodles, a series of Os smooshed together into a spring, and the spring lengthened and curved into a spiral, and at the center was another O. She was relaxing into this until she realized where the Os came from, which was Toonie. Tooooooooonie. Carla tried to feel something about Toonie but could not. She and Tiffany were going to the funeral tomorrow. Maybe she would feel something then.

Amy said that lists were the lifeblood of fiction. Make lists, she would say, and see where they take you. Carla had mentioned this once to John X. Cousins, who had just said, "Interesting." He had this way of nodding and smiling that meant, "You're so wrong but I won't bother arguing with you." "Interesting" meant "Bullshit." Meant "Typical." He had not yet let everybody in on what the lifeblood of fiction really was; apparently all would be revealed when his Guru video landed. Everybody, even Tiffany, liked John X. Cousins. Until yesterday Carla hadn't paid much attention to him one way or the other, but Amy obviously thought he was bad news, and that was good enough for Carla.

It took Carla fifteen minutes to achieve a list of five:

Murder
iPad
Ambulance
Yearbook
Lottie

This was no good, just a bunch of things she'd looked at recently, a Seuss list. *I saw an iPad and a penis and a black tongue, and to think that I saw them on Mulberry Street!* This is what always happened to her when she tried listing, she'd get all self-conscious and fakey. After an hour of this, during which she scratched out everything but *yearbook,* she tried a subconscious list. Amy said the subconscious, which was a man in a projection booth in her head, was really in charge anyway, at least of things like character names and random details and the best lines of dialogue and plot lines that suddenly came to you. Carla needed to hear from the projectionist in her head, and now she had an idea about how to do it.

Toonie had tried hypnosis therapy more than once. Carla hadn't been up for it for two reasons: She figured Toonie would just try to make her do something with the Grief Acorn, and she didn't believe in hypnosis anyway. She used to watch the carnies hypnotize people so they'd *bawk* like chickens, and of course those audience members were usually plants, although sometimes marks would get into it on their own, they were that dumb.

One time, Carla let her do it just to get it over with. Toonie showed her this corny old spiral video on her laptop and made her stare at it. Toonie's voice got breathy. She said stuff like *Breathe into the spiral* and *Fix your mind in between your eyebrows like a third eye and launch it on the shoreless sea of calm,* which was a neat trick because how did you launch a boat, let alone an eye, if there isn't a shore to launch it from? Carla was then supposed to sink into the warm whatever and walk down some spiral of steps into an enchanted cave where she would feel something fabulous. The whole business was soothing but stupid.

Now she tried it by herself, not for hypnosis but to simmer down, to stop trying so hard and let her subconscious do the listing. She stared at the Tooooonie spiral on her yellow notepad and imagined falling into the center, and the center getting bigger and bigger as she fell. She had to do this for some time before it sort of worked and her breath became slow and her eyes closed, but then she had to open them in order to grab the pencil, which blew off the trance. How could she write in a trance?

She spent a half hour figuring out how to use the mike on her cell phone, propped the phone up on a shelf next to her face so she could speak into it without holding it to her mouth, then did the spiral bit again. She breathed slower and slower, emptied her head, bathed in the warm whatever. She had stopped thinking, but not like with Cal Hoving, this was a pleasant thing, a choice. She closed her eyes. Every muscle in her neck and shoulders snuggled down. Every single muscle everywhere. She was weightless. The phone rang.

Not the cell phone, which she knocked off the shelf flailing for, but her landline. Jeremy from Pacific Fresh Air offered to clean her ducts for free and asked when was the best time for an appointment. Carla didn't answer right away—she was distracted by the light in her room, the color of deep sunset, and how could that be, and then she saw it was five o'clock and she'd been out cold for two hours. "WHEN HELL FREEZES THE HELL OVER, YOU GIANT BOOB," she said to Jeremy from Pacific Air, trying for Amy's Voice of God, and hung up, but she felt bad because whoever Jeremy was he probably didn't enjoy bothering people, probably hated himself for having to do it, probably lived in a rented room, and now she'd called him a giant boob. How did Amy and Tiffany yell at these people without feeling guilty?

She picked the cell phone off the floor and put the recording on playback, just in case hypnosis had worked and she'd populated her list through magical dictation. All she could hear was herself breathing. She fast-forwarded in five-minute increments, heard nothing but occasional faint snorting. She inspected the waveform thing on the app, which stretched on and on in a flat line—she hadn't even snored, for Pete's sake—until she saw spikes like mountain ranges, starting at minute 74. Excited, she fast-forwarded to listen. At first, just *shhhhhhhhhhhhhh*. A lot of *shhhhh,* like she was trying to calm somebody. Then more: *Nobody nobody nobody nobody home. Ohh-hhhhhhhh.* Then lots more *Sshhhhhhhhhh. Nobody home help me. Wrong wrong wrong help. Help me. Die. Help me die.* Then nothing. Another long flat line ending in Mount Everest spikes, a ringing phone, the clatter of the phone on the floor.

Great. Now she had her story idea: All alone, muttering gibberish, Nobody commits suicide.

Carla grabbed her car keys and a flashlight, drove to the Jack in the Box for a fajita pita, and parked on Coast Boulevard near the Hospitals Reef tide pools. It was low tide, and the pools at night were fantastic. She was going to get something pleasant out of this crummy day.

The park was almost deserted—she could see one family out on the pools, finishing up the afternoon. She sat down on the grass and waited them out, eating her dinner, watching the sun sink away. When she was a kid, the first time she saw the sun set on the Pacific she half-expected it to hiss. Of course she knew better by then, she knew that except in cartoons the sun did not literally sink into the sea, but already her life was a cartoon, sometimes funny, mostly not. Her mother was a Disney witch, Maleficent without the looks;

her agent looked like Mr. Burns and talked like Nasty Canasta. Friendly woodland creatures did not garland her with ribbons and lace, but the local birds were less standoffish than the ones back East, probably because in the subtropics they had to hang out where the water was, which meant putting up with people.

Now a huge seagull plopped down a few feet away and stared at her coldly. She tossed him a piece of chicken and a cube of tomato. A woman walking by in back of Carla told her to stop it. "The gulls are vicious here. They'll steal food right out of your hand. We don't want to encourage them!" Carla told her to mind her own beeswax, but not out loud. She waited until the woman was far away, then fed the vicious gull the rest of her pita.

Then she waited until the sky got dark, which happened fast in California; Amy always said that night dropped like a felled ox out here. She waited some more until that family departed, until there were no newsy passersby to warn her against going out there in the dark because anything could happen to you, and then she stood and stepped down past the closest little pools, far out to her favorite one, not a small circle but a large rectangle shaped like Pennsylvania. She sat down on the green rock cross-legged with her back to the sea.

You had to find just the right angle for the flashlight so the light wouldn't shoot back at you. There were sea hares and hermit crabs in snail shells. Barnacles, anemones, urchins in faded colors sectioned the pool into three rooms. One was small and lined with lobster shells, its only furniture a sea lemon shaped like a fainting couch. Next was a rec room or maybe a playground, cluttered with stones and shells. Tiny crabs skittered about the obstacles playing a complicated game. The biggest room of all had a great bat star, bright pink, in the exact center. This was the ballroom, and through and around it swam opaleyes and sculpins.

Every so often she changed the position of her flashlight, playing with angles and shapes.

The altered light source did not disturb her kingdom's inhabitants. Carla relaxed deeply without using nonsense spirals. She should have spent the whole day here. An octopus who had been disguising himself as a hassock rose and swept about, shadowing the rooms with waving tendrils, designing the interior.

All around her the air was velvet black. *Never turn your back on the sea.* Would the sea rise up and grab her? And would that be so bad? Carla bent down close to the pool, darkening it with her giant head. "Nobody," she whispered to the bat star. "Oh, Nobody?" The star did not move, or if it did, it moved too slowly for the human eye. "Yoo-hoo, Nobody, shhhhhhhh," she whispered. "Help me." The star pulsed a little. "Help me die," she whispered. The star waved just the tip of an arm.

This should have been more pleasing than it was. She had connected with this little world, which is what she supposed she was trying to do. She had whispered to the bat star without thinking first. Maybe the little man in the booth made her do it. And *that* should have pleased her, since she'd wasted so much time today trying to get him to help out. But something was off. Maybe the air—the temperature had dropped, and she wasn't wearing a coat. She had wanted to stay longer, but it was probably time to go home.

She walked back among the pools very slowly, at one point slipping and almost sliding into one, then crossed the grass strip toward her car. No moon tonight. She could make out Mars and Jupiter, but yellow streetlights washed out the stars. She drove around town looking for an errand to run, maybe groceries, but she didn't really need anything, so she headed uphill, and when she saw the Birdhouse everything changed.

Not the house. The house was the same: The lights had come on by themselves, both outside all around and in the Rotunda and way up through the offices and living quarters. Tiffany had programmed them to do that. There was nothing different about the house and Carla sat still behind the wheel of her parked car, which was locked and inhabited only by her, and she had never been more afraid.

No reason for it, which made it worse. She tried to calm herself, slow down her breathing, close her eyes, see the spiral, see the bat star waving, see Chuck, see Amy, fill her mind with everything good, and when that didn't work, she asked *What's wrong with me?* at first in her head and then out loud, but she could manage only a whisper. Then something about the whisper, the sound of it. The whisper was *off*. Carla knew about whispers from voice training. All whispers sounded pretty much alike. Except not exactly, because whispers have no tone but they do have pitch. She whispered, *What is wrong with me?* Carla's whisper pitch was *high*. She stared up at the top, at her office window. Now she whispered, *Help me*. She whispered, *Nobody nobody nobody nobody home*. And now the pitch was wrong. It was too high. It was too high for *Help me. Die.*

She could be misremembering. If she played back the audio on her cell phone, she'd find out. Her cell phone was in her office. Where she had slept for two hours, probably alone, probably all the whispers were her own, all she had to do was play them back, but her phone wasn't here, it was in there. She watched the windows for shadows. Eventually she stopped thinking but kept watch. She was a statue sitting watch. She did this until the sky began to light, and then she curled up tight in the backseat and slept.

CHAPTER NINE

Amy

Tuesday, March 9

Amy awoke the next morning, the day of Toonie's funeral, with no plan to attend the ceremony, yet after she fed and walked Lottie she found herself chasing down the internet obituary. It would be a graveside ceremony in Sorrento Valley. I could stand that, Amy thought. I can lurk around a grave site without explaining why I'm there. Now if only I knew the answer.

I'm going for Carla, she decided, as she headed south. A kind gesture showing solidarity, and then she could duck back to Escondido.

The cemetery was huge. For some reason she had thought it would be easy to spot a cluster of mourners, but there were at least five clusters scattered over the acreage, so that her bad knee was throbbing after she visited them all, and none of them were there for Toonie. She then spotted a chapeloid structure with a digital marquee. It said "Dignity Memorial Chapel," and underneath was a large picture of a middle-aged brunette woman leaning against a small jacaranda tree, and under the picture "Hatoon Garabedian,

Psy.D.," and under that details about her memorial service, which was now half over.

Amy entered and stood in the back, careful not to draw attention to herself. All the seats were taken, so good, the woman was mourned or at least missed. Amy studied the backs of heads and from her perspective could identify only Tiffany, Cousins, Chuck, and maybe Ricky. She couldn't spot Carla. In front of a closed coffin, there were other pictures of Toonie, a huge digital PowerPoint. The child Toonie, building a sand castle; the college graduate in gown and mortarboard; a thirtyish woman smiling gamely at something behind the camera.

Amy had not realized that slideshows were part of the modern death ritual. The images seemed designed to tell a story—here she is, brand-new, her whole life ahead of her, just think of that, and then elementary school, and then college, and then she got married, and then she wrote a book, and look, she wrote another one. If the impulse were narrative, by rights the last image would be of the poor woman's bloated face with her tongue poking out. On the left wall was a large nondigital sign that said "DIGNITY." In case you missed it, an identical sign was on the opposite wall.

Amy hadn't been to many funerals. Max's had been held in the college chapel, overflowing with students and faculty and friends; their presence there, the weight of all those people who loved him, remained in memory while the ritual itself did not. Her father's funeral was her first, when she was nineteen; she had been distraught and took in nothing. When her mother died, Amy had let a Bangor funeral director set up everything, and all she could recall of it was a hushed and simple ceremony in an old church. No snapshots had been involved in any of these ceremonies. Amy hated photographs. She didn't allow them in her own book jackets.

They had come to the moment where people could share their thoughts and memories of Toonie. There was some coughing and whispering, and then a bearded man in a denim jacket stood up and said he'd been married to Toonie for ten years. "We had our differences," he said, "and our divorce was not a friendly one. Still, I'm sorry this happened. Nobody deserves this." He sidled back to his seat. *Not even Toonie deserves to be strangled by a maniac.* The silence that followed should have been stunned but wasn't. Stunned silences are truly silent; people freeze and hold their breath. This audience shuffled and checked watches. Had anyone here actually cared about the woman? Then John X. Cousins stepped up and took the mike like a lounge singer.

"We are horrified and saddened beyond measure," the man said, "by the untimely death of this wonderful woman—healer, thinker, author—taken from us by a rapacious pervert to satisfy his own bestial desires."

Maddened by the need to dash up there and tackle him, Amy fled the Dignity Chapel and waited for the mourners to emerge. Cousins must have been the last to speak—how could anyone follow that?—because they came out within minutes. The first bunch seemed anything but subdued: They chattered about the murder and "the doctor" without using her name, so they had no ties with the deceased. The obit hadn't mentioned "family only"; these people were here for a thrill. A group in business dress searched their phones and headed to the parking lot. These had been the watch-checkers; they must be Toonie's colleagues.

The rest turned out to be Inspiration Pointers and police, including Kowalcimi. Was he there to scan the crowd? In real life, did gloating murderers really come to funerals? She watched him say a few words to Toonie's ex, who didn't seem worried by the exchange. Cousins and Tiffany emerged, strolling together like a couple, which perhaps they were, or else why were they so pointedly not holding hands? Chuck approached the three of them, looking at his phone.

"Where's Carla?" Amy asked him, because clearly she wasn't here.

"That's the question," said Chuck.

"Something's wrong," said Tiffany. "She was going to meet us here, we set it up yesterday. She's not answering."

Chuck stabbed at his phone. "No accidents between La Jolla and here, at least not twenty minutes ago," he said. How did he know that?

Tiffany tugged on Kowalcimi's elbow and told him they were worried about Carla, and why. Kowalcimi said he'd send a car around to the Birdhouse, but he didn't say when. He looked distracted.

Amy would have liked to stay and talk with him, but Tiffany, Cousins, and Chuck were already running across the grass to the parking lot. She got in her car and followed.

At the Birdhouse, Carla was sitting on the front steps, flanked by Tiffany, Cousins, and Chuck. Carla looked terrible—slumped, pale, hair plastered straight by morning rain. When she saw Amy, she did not brighten; she did not say hello. Amy had never seen Carla like this. Here was the girl who had once saved her life, picked up an empty wine bottle and brained the student about to murder her, then shrugged off the moment with no drama, as though decking homicidal old bats were just part of her daily routine—which, now that Amy thought of it, wasn't totally far-fetched. Not that she had ever bludgeoned her mother, but she surely must have imagined doing it more than once. Perhaps daily. Now she looked defeated. This wasn't Carla.

"We can't get her to tell us anything," said Chuck. "Should we take her somewhere? To the hospital?"

Amy stood before her. "Carla, are you injured?" She had to ask her three times before Carla shook her head, not meeting her eyes.

"I'm calling an ambulance," said Tiffany.

"What has happened to you?" Amy used her teaching voice. When Carla didn't respond, she said, louder, "I asked you a question."

"She needs a doctor." Tiffany looked at Amy reproachfully.

"She needs to stand up and walk."

"You're right," said Chuck, "she's frozen."

"Is the door unlocked? We can get her inside and—"

"No!" Carla's eyes were wild. "Not in there!"

Now they were getting somewhere. Whatever it was, it was in the house.

"Who's in the house, Carla?"

Carla mumbled something.

"Again," said Amy. "Who?"

"'What,'" Carla said. "It's 'what.'"

Cousins had already bolted for the door, followed by Chuck, and they let themselves in.

"Are they safe in there?" Tiffany asked.

Carla shut her eyes and laughed and laughed.

"Listen to me," said Amy. She sat down beside Carla and took her face in both hands. "I have never struck a human being in my life, but if you don't stop laughing, I'm going to slap you." Of course, she wouldn't; simply threatening to was bad enough.

Carla stopped laughing.

"Now, right now, tell me what has happened to you. I'm not kidding."

Tiffany ran inside. Amy turned back to Carla. "See that? You're letting people go in there. People you care about. Two of them anyway. This tells me that whatever it is, they're not in danger from it. Correct?"

Carla nodded.

"Good. Now, are you ready to talk?"

She was.

Carla told Amy a bizarre story about a day spent alone in the house trying to overcome for god's sake *writer's block,* putting herself in a trance somehow and recording her unconscious gibberings on an iPhone, and later realizing that hers wasn't the only voice on the recording. When Amy asked her to play the recording for her, Carla said she couldn't because it was inside the house.

"Then let's go in and listen to it. Maybe you're wrong."

Carla raised her head and, finally, looked straight at Amy. "Toonie used to ask me if Ma haunted the Birdhouse. No, I always said, no, that was ridiculous."

"Good for you."

"What if I'm wrong?"

Amy stood and took both Carla's hands in her own. "Come with me," she said, "and we'll find out."

They found Chuck and Tiffany in Tiffany's office, where nothing looked amiss. "We've been everywhere," said Tiffany. "Your office, the bedrooms, the living room, both wings. There's nobody here."

"Give me my cell phone," Carla said. "It's on the shelf behind your chair." Her face had some color now, and her voice was stronger.

Cousins appeared in the doorframe. "I checked again— nothing upstairs, nothing downstairs," he said.

Tiffany rummaged through the bookcase. "Where? Which shelf?"

"The middle one."

"There's nothing. Are you sure—"

Carla brushed past her and scoured the shelf, pushed books out of the way onto the floor, knelt and peered beneath the bottom shelf and the desk. When she stood and faced the three, she looked triumphant. "Someone's taken it," she said, and let out a great sigh of what looked like relief. Why was this good news? "So I'm not nuts. It's not a ghost."

"You ought to see somebody," said Tiffany.

"I am. I'm seeing you. Everything's okay."

"Why do you need the phone anyway?"

Amy watched Carla explain again about the night before:

the trance, the whispers. The story didn't make a lot more sense the second time around. That she had hypnotized herself—and this seemed to be the case—threw all her claims into question. Still, she seemed more herself now. "How do you know it's not a ghost?" Amy couldn't believe she was asking this question, but she was still worried about Carla's state of mind.

"Ghosts don't pick up stuff. Ghosts don't interact with the material world."

Amy opened her mouth, then shut it again. While Tiffany nagged her about seeing somebody, Chuck took out his phone.

"No," said Carla. "No doctors."

"I'm calling you," said Chuck.

The four stood still and in a few seconds heard the faraway honking of Canada geese. "Is that—"

"Yeah, I switched from barn owls last week."

"What?" said Amy.

"It's coming from downstairs," said Tiffany.

Yelling "The Rotunda!" Carla scampered downstairs.

The great round room was brilliant with noon light; even the dollhouse was lit to blinding. Amy was drawn there naturally, but the sound wasn't coming from the dollhouse: Carla's cell phone was honking from a chair beside the curving western windows. Everybody gathered around it, and Carla shut down the geese. Oh, these kids and their ringtones. Did they ever stop to imagine receiving a positive biopsy result heralded by crickets or howling gibbons? "Okay, listen to this," said Carla. Everybody listened. She kept fiddling with something but there was still no sound. Tiffany told her to turn it up. "No point," said Carla. "It's been erased." Again, she seemed pleased. Apparently ghosts couldn't erase recordings either.

"How sure are you that you didn't leave it down here?"

"Positive."

Amy tuned out while Cousins expressed deep concern for Carla's mental health and went on at length about the damaging consequences of stress and the rest chattered about what probably had happened or couldn't have happened and whether it was anything to worry about. She had a headache and no tolerance for the supernatural. Eventually they would come to the conclusion that should be obvious to any child, including Carla: that if she didn't leave the damn phone down here, another human being did, and that was awful news.

To quiet her temper she began to inspect the portraits on the walls; she had noticed them the last time she was in here, but from a remove. There were eight, of uniform size. Two were paintings, portraits of George Eliot and S. J. Perelman. Both portraits were unfamiliar, though their subjects of course were not. They looked like they had been painted by quasi-professionals, perhaps locals on commission. The rest were photographs, blown up to the same dimensions as the paintings and similarly framed. Here were Orwell, Cather, Mencken, and the Ediths Wharton and Sitwell, and Amy was pleasantly surprised at such an eclectic selection, until she came to the last one, the one with pride of place between the two curved windows.

How had they gotten this picture of her? Amy had not allowed a camera near her person since that Holly Something from the *Trib* interviewed her while she was concussed and non compos. This picture was less hideous than the one that had run in the paper, probably because this one was black and white. No, that wasn't it. Her recent age spurt had left the bones in her face more prominent, so her image wasn't actively doughy. The old dame in the photograph looked . . . interesting, intelligent, unknowable, three qualities to which she had always aspired. Still she was annoyed. In the shot she was standing at a table full of books but not looking at them, instead gazing with mild interest at something to her left. Now she recognized the venue—the secondhand store in the local public library, just about the only one she frequented these days.

"Sorry about that." Tiffany stood next to her. Carla and

Chuck were still going at it about the damn iPhone. "I told her you wouldn't like it, but she got so excited. You know Carla."

Amy just looked at her.

"She hired a private eye to take it."

"What??"

"She told him to be super discreet."

"A *private eye*??"

"Nice guy, actually. Grateful for the job. He said it was a pleasant change not to be digging up dirt on cheaters."

"How did he super discreetly find me in the library?"

"I guess he just hung out in his car at the end of your street until you went there. I don't know. It took a couple of weeks." Tiffany was trying to act contrite but obviously thought the whole thing was funny. "We just got this one last month."

Amy took a breath. "I'll get over it," she said. "Don't say anything to her." She would get over the invasion of privacy, since she had been snapped in a public place and not through venetian blinds in her bathrobe, but she would never get over being included in this pantheon of betters, writers all of whom she particularly admired, it was embarrassing, and with this thought she knew exactly how Carla had chosen the other eight. They were all *Amy's* literary heroes, and Carla had faithfully kept track. When all this blew over she would have to do something about it. Carla was not a stalker, not a threat, but being idolized was becoming a burden.

She walked over to Carla. "I'm going home," she said. "Lottie's been alone too long. Carla, you're not safe here. Pack your bag and come with me."

"See, I told you!" she said to Chuck, and then, to Amy's amazement, she turned her down. "I'd really, really love to but I have to stay here. It's my, you know, place of business, not to mention my home, and we're opening back up tomorrow."

"But what about—"

"I'm moving in," said Chuck. "I'll stay as long as she needs me."

Well, that was a pleasant surprise.

Tiffany said she'd be here every day, which she was anyway, and Chuck would be here at night, so Carla would never be by herself.

Her old writing group was turning into Scooby-Doo and Friends, off on an exciting mystery adventure. *To the Rotunda!* Pop culture had a way of seeping into your brain, which was okay when you were young, but there was only so much room in there. Amy had never once watched *Scooby-Doo*, yet Scooby and Shaggy had now taken up space in her head and no doubt evicted some of the Muses.

All the way home she gnawed on the Mystery of the Nomadic Phone. That Carla's account was reliable was now a working hypothesis, and Amy tried to work out what that meant. Whoever was in there with Carla last night had not done her real damage. Not physical anyway. It had been more of a trick, a prank, but a nasty one. Why whisper *Help me die*? Carla had feared this was her mother's shade, and no wonder: Toonie, for all her faults, was right about Carla's failure to confront the woman's death. No matter how terrible the memory, Carla defaulted to *That was then, it's over and done, no big deal.*

But if the trickster meant to trigger this response, he or she must have known a lot about Carla, and that was so disturbing. How well did Carla know all the people who rented those writing cells? Did Tiffany do background checks? Amy knew it couldn't be anyone in the old workshop gang. Of course except the one in Chino, but she was in there for life. Not life without parole, but parole wasn't possible until the woman was ninety-five. Amy was pretty sure this was still true, although she should probably check with Kowalcimi. Who, now that she thought of it, had not sent anybody around to the Birdhouse, which he'd promised to do, and she doubted he'd have forgotten. Something must have come up.

When she got home, Lottie was so mad that a generous meal

did not placate her, and Amy had to walk her after dark just to calm her down. The dog could hold a grudge. They walked uphill, slowly because of her knees and Lottie's intense interest in scent trails. They found a rabbit ear and the skull of a raven. They strolled past feral cats and Mrs. Bradstreet's aviary. Mrs. Bradstreet lived at the top of the hill and kept turkeys, chickens, pheasants, and a sulfur-crested cockatoo that sometimes exchanged pleasantries with Amy, but not tonight. On the way back down they encountered a coyote, at which Lottie lunged, barking wildly. "You have no idea," Amy said, watching the creature trot off without a backward glance, "what a prancing hors d'oeuvre you are."

She slept poorly, waking on the hour from dreams that evaporated as she tried to hold on to them, although one of them had definitely featured a raven. She tried counting Muses, just to see if she had in fact forgotten any. The Cs and Es were easy—Calliope and Clio, Erato and Euterpe—and Terpsichore and Polyhymnia made six. There were three more. Thalia, who was Comedy. So . . . what's her name, Tragedy, Melpomene. And Mnemosyne made nine! All was well with her mind, and she almost made it down to sleep and then remembered. Mnemosyne wasn't a Muse, she was the goddamn goddess of memory, she was the *mother* of the nine sisters, poor woman. "You're a riot," she said out loud to that little man in the projection booth. Lottie stirred and sighed. She'd look up the ninth Muse in the morning. Damn you, Scooby-Doo.

CHAPTER TEN

Carla

Wednesday, March 10

All the next morning Inspiration Pointers on their way to the cells besieged Tiffany and Carla, looking for inside info about the murder and gossiping about Toonie's private life, about which most of them knew nothing, although Rachel Herman had consulted her once about getting therapy for her twins. "She really wasn't interested," Rachel said. "I got the impression she was all about her book." Not one failed to ask whether Toonie's cell had been locked. "It was locked when Toonie swiped in, and it locked behind her, which it's supposed to do, and it can't come unlocked by itself, so you have nothing to worry about," Tiffany said, explaining that the audit trail, which had been set up strictly to make sure Pointers put in their allotted times, only tracked when they swiped in and out. By noon she was threatening to put all that on a sign and tape it on the front door, and once they understood the whole audit trail thing the Pointers seemed reassured and stopped bugging her.

"But Toonie's door wasn't locked when I went in," said Carla.

"So," Ricky said, "she must have let in whoever it was."

"I wonder why they find this reassuring." Harry B. had arrived midmorning, anxious to get on top of whatever legal liabilities might concern the Point. "If she let somebody in, doesn't that imply it's one of them?"

Tiffany pointed out, "Yes, she could have let in somebody, but she could also have gone to the john and left the door open and come back and confronted the guy already in her cell."

"Yeah," said Harry B., "but if it was a stranger, wouldn't the place have been messed up? Wouldn't she have been on her feet, fighting, knocking stuff over? Carla says she was just sitting there and nothing was out of place."

Carla noticed that Ricky Buzza had taken out his phone and placed it on the middle of Tiffany's desk, which was kind of weird, like they were all supposed to look at it, which for a minute they did. Ricky hadn't come to the Point for a while. *Caligula's Scalpel* was selling so well that he had bought himself a condo in Julian. He was working on a new book now—his first had ended with Caligula Hammersmith (formerly Denton) locked up in the "Bridgewater State Hospital for the Criminally Insane."

"Just a heads-up," Ricky said, pointing to his phone. "I'm recording everything because it's easier than taking notes. I'll erase later."

Alarmed, Harry B. asked Ricky if he was planning to do a true-crime thing about Toonie, and Ricky reassured him that he just took notes for general serial killer deets, and anyway *Caligula in Egypt*, his working title, would be pure fabrication. "He gets out of Bridgewater somehow and goes to Cairo to research ancient embalming methods. Or maybe Croatia; there's this archaeological museum in Zagreb. Anyway, the Egyptians used to remove the dead person's brain by sticking a hook through the guy's nostrils and yanking it out, and Caligula wants to do this, only not with dead people, and—"

"Rick," said Chuck, who had wandered into Carla's office with a box of doughnuts, "we're eating here."

"Toonie knew the guy was in her cell," said Tiffany, "and she trusted him, and he came up behind her and did it. That's the only thing that makes sense."

"Not necessarily." John X. Cousins was suddenly present, framed in the doorway, making a magazine cover out of himself. Tiffany seemed thrilled, and most of the others, to varying degrees, appeared to welcome his presence. Carla had by now decided that he was a pompous tool. He glided in and posed, again, in front of the box of doughnuts. "Carbs are a surprisingly effective way to ward off anxiety in the short term."

"Take two," said Chuck, shoving the box his way. Carla was beginning to love Chuck.

John X. Cousins slapped his flat midsection and announced that he was watching his weight. Then, all eyes upon him, he pulled a chair out from behind the file cabinet, turned it around, and straddled it. Why did guys do that? "I have news," he said.

Carla and Chuck glanced at each other at exactly the same time and with exactly the same underwhelmed expressions.

"It's definitely a serial killer. They're keeping this from the press for now because they don't want people to panic, but they're calling in the FBI."

"If they're keeping it under wraps," said Chuck, "how come you know about it?"

Cousins smiled. "I have a source." He paused, theatrically. "And there's more."

Everybody but Carla leaned in. Carla tuned them all out—she was getting really good at this—and drifted over to the potted Medusa she had picked out herself the day after Ma died and placed so that it bullied Ma's stupid Golden Acorn of Maternal Cremains into a shadowed corner.

She needed to get this gone; disrespecting it wasn't enough anymore. Toonie had been wrong about dealing with grief but getting rid of the ashes was definitely on, and now she thought she could do it. Maybe with Chuck? Should she ask him to accompany her to L.A.? While they were up there she could show him around. She could take him to all the places she'd lived, and the TV studios, and maybe the fairgrounds where she'd gigged in Pomona and Orange, and maybe another time they could hit the funky one in Victorville and she could show him where the funhouse used to be, the one with the laughing Austrians and the curving mirrors and Hoving the Perv. It had been torn down before the millennium. If it had still stood, she'd have already taken the Acorn up there and dumped the ashes all over the mirrors.

During the past year, starting with Ma's death, she had more than once fantasized about getting together with Amy and the two of them going up to the Hollywood Forever boneyard, and Amy would watch her sprinkle the ashes and would understand everything and say just the perfect words. Carla could never summon up the words themselves, but the scene, however imagined, was always what Amy would call "pastoral," the experience bonding in a way for which she had always yearned. When she'd stayed at Amy's house, which was only two days ago but now seemed a distant memory, she had even rehearsed asking Amy to do this. They could take Lottie, she would say, and visit Terry's grave. Terry, she would explain, played Toto.

But now, and she wasn't sure why, she felt suddenly grown up. This was kind of silly, given that she was thirty-five, but Ma had always called her a "late bloomer," which was lucky because "you can keep doing juveniles until you're twenty," juveniles being Ma's moneymaker. Carla hadn't begun to feel like a real adult until Ma moved back to Philadelphia and the Birdhouse became Carla's for good: In the two years that followed, Carla came up with Inspiration Point and, with Tiffany's help, became a real businessperson, though deep inside she still felt thirteen.

Today, for some reason, she was starting to bloom. She would always be grateful for Amy, but maybe she didn't need her anymore. Maybe for her writing if she ever got back to it, but not for her life. Amy was old and stern and a wonderful person, but Carla needed to surround herself with people her own age. Especially Chuck. Chuck was wonderful.

Last night he had sat up with her in the Rotunda and they'd looked out at the bay and talked for hours. Mostly he talked and she listened. She had never thought of him as married, but he *had* been, fresh out of college, and they had a baby and it died, and then they split up. His wife's name was Charmaine. And Chuck had been on his college wrestling team, and after the divorce when he turned thirty he started a walk across the country but only got as far as Truth or Consequences, New Mexico. He'd given up on writing fiction. "Fooling around with it was fun," he said, "and that was about it." His college major was civil engineering, and for six years he worked for an environmental consulting firm, but then he quit and went to work as part of a team investigating highway accidents for Caltrans. She was going to tell him her stories about showbiz and the circus but ended up just listening to him and watching his face.

Carla had never had a boyfriend. Until she was thirteen she was too busy working and fending off perverts, and then she gained seventy pounds to get free of the perverts and showbiz and Ma, and that worked great but left her on her own. And she didn't mind, because freedom was worth the cost. Especially the first ten years. She hadn't known what to do with herself—with her father gone there was no point in going back to Philadelphia, and though she had worked all her life she had never held down a job on her own, not really, and she had ended up sharing space here with Ma while they lived on her residuals and the money from their investments. But she'd confined Ma to what was now the east wing, so they seldom spoke, and she could still remember the pleasure she had taken from days unshadowed by purpose. She had lived mostly in her own head, relishing the solitude there.

Last night, watching Chuck, Carla realized that she had not yet had a life, never mind that it might be half over. Here he had already loved somebody enough to marry her, had lost her and lost a child, and had gone walkabout, for Pete's sake. He had seen and done so much, and when he said, "Enough about me! What about you?" she had been forced to improvise. He already knew about her child star antics, but he was asking what happened *next,* when she got out from under, and all she could come up with on the fly was getting a degree in oceanography from UC, which was a flat-out lie but at least she could BS about tide pools. Then he asked if there was anyone special in her life. He didn't put it that way, Chuck was way too cool for that, but that's what he meant. And as if!

She made up this thing about how she'd almost married Holman Bellavance but it hadn't worked out. Another huge lie, though she and HB *had* been lifeboat buddies on the Universal lot, so she could and did spin a tale about their childhood friendship (true) and how it inevitably turned to romance (bullshit; HB was probably gay, or at least the creeps who used him up thought so). They'd done some of the same commercials and shared space in a pilot, *The Big Voila*, which was supposed to feature the Hilarious, Hair-raising, Heartwarming misadventures of a family of professional mascots who moonlight as crime solvers. HB had ended up as the Demonic Child in a bunch of cheesy horror movies, and OD'd at sixteen. As kids they'd had a blast making fun of that pilot script, but when she heard about his death she was in the throes of her breakup with Ma and her first thought was *HB, free at last.* She didn't tell Chuck that, and she felt kind of guilty about it. And about lying about that bogus oceanography degree. The next time they were alone, she would tell him the truth.

And with that thought, the thought of lies, she suddenly recalled that moment at Amy's house when he showed up out of the blue and she learned that he was working with Amy on something, something neither of them felt like sharing with anybody else, something that shut her out, and she'd been so happy to see him that she'd let it just slide by and then forgotten about it. It just slipped right out of her mind.

But he *was* writing something! He was writing something with Amy and keeping it a secret, which she guessed he had a right to do, but he'd lied to her last night. "Not writing," he had said, "is a real hobby of mine." Why was he lying to her now? That hurt. A lot.

"Carla! Hello? Don't we know this woman?" From across the room Tiffany was waving both arms like she was signaling aircraft, and the rest were looking at Carla and waiting for her to say something. She didn't want to.

"What woman?"

"Donatella Ng! Her house is in Farms. She came here once to scout out the place, remember? I was going to rent her a cell but you didn't want to for some reason."

Carla remembered a tiny overmanicured person with a shop-lifted face who had made a big show out of her multimillion-dollar address and her close ties with a local Literary Agent to the Stars. "Yeah, she was that Botox princess, huge phony. What about her?"

"What about her is that she's missing."

"Sorry," Carla said, although she wasn't. "Why is that a big deal?"

John X. Cousins, backed up by Tiffany, Ricky, and Harry B., breathlessly explained that Donatella Ng's husband had reported her missing yesterday and the police were pretty sure something very bad had happened to her and what if it was the same guy, the guy who killed Toonie, and if it was, he was right here in La Jolla! Tiffany and Harry B. both claimed to be ultra-concerned about whether they had a duty to alert the Pointers, whom they had just reassured were in no real danger.

To Carla they seemed less worried than excited by the prospect of their very own homicidal maniac. They looked happy. Cousins especially. Except Chuck, who was looking at her funny. Suddenly she was overcome by a brand-new impulse, a mean one. "She's probably off getting dimpleplasty or she's run off with her gardener."

Tiffany looked confused. "No, Carla, listen, because all her stuff, her handbag and driver's license and phone and everything, is in her car, which they just found at the Aquarium."

"Whatever." Carla stood and walked to the open door. "I'm going to go write something," she said. "I've had an idea, how about that? I'm taking Toonie's cell."

All the way down and out to the top of the wing she went over and over what had just happened. The look on their faces when she said "Whatever." The look on Chuck's face. The hell with Donatella Ng. The hell with all of them. She was in bloom.

CHAPTER ELEVEN

Amy

Amy was sipping gingery green tea and glaring at a white computer screen when Lottie leaped to her perch at the living room picture window and started running back and forth on the couch back, barking wildly. It was early for the mail carrier, and Lottie was way too excited for that anyway. Now she was scrabbling at the window, which she only did when Chuck came, but it wasn't his day. Except there he was, looking apologetic.

"I tried to call," he said. "I kept getting deafening hundred-year-old band music."

"Oh, no, that was you?" She led him to the kitchen and prepared another pot of ginger buzz. "More than a hundred. I'm using the original Sousa recording of 'Stars and Stripes Forever.'"

"Feeling patriotic?"

"Yes! I am rebelling against the tyranny of my telephone. Yesterday I was menaced by colonoscopy enthusiasts. I often wonder what the Ediths would make of—"

"Carla's all messed up."

They went out back and sat down. Chuck threw the ball for

Lottie as he talked. "I thought she was all right, but today she did a one-eighty."

"Scared all over again?"

"No, that would at least make sense. Standoffish and flippant. Pissy. Cold."

"Carla? *Our* Carla?"

Chuck described in detail behavior that sounded nothing like Carla, who was an inherently kind soul. Apparently she had ridiculed Tiffany for worrying about the murders and just walked out on the group while they were trying to fill her in on the latest news. He explained about the missing Ng woman and Amy said maybe Carla was right to be unimpressed, people go missing all the time. "Yeah, but she's not missing anymore. You haven't heard?" It turned out that Donatella Ng had been located last night and early this morning.

"How can you be located over a period of time? Either you're located or you're not."

"Depends on the state you're in. They found her on the Mount Soledad bike trail, and near the tenth hole at Torrey Pines, and in front of the Yahoo's Taco place on Pearl."

"What?"

Chuck was looking at his phone. "And apparently just now at the Birch Aquarium. Jeez." He looked up at Amy. "Her right foot was in the seadragon tank."

"Ridiculous." Amy took the ball from Lottie and lobbed it into the lantanas above the raised garden. That would keep her busy for a while.

"Apparently some schoolchild spotted it. 'Ridiculous' isn't the word I'd use."

"Yes, but what is the point?"

"Of what?"

"Of all this elaborate nonsense? People kill each other. That's terrible enough, but this is just cheesy theater, and it must take so much *time,* so much *planning* and *effort.* I don't understand this kind of thing at all. It's like there's some new playbook."

"Psychopathy," said Chuck. "We can't understand these people because they're not like us. To a psychopath other people are just objects to play with."

"So this Ng woman is a Tinkertoy?"

"I think that's it. When you lack empathy—"

"I've read all about that. I'm not convinced. Not about *empathy.* If you truly can't imagine how other people feel, if you don't even invest other minds with emotion, then how can you enjoy tormenting them? If you have literally zero fellow feeling, then what gives their suffering value to you? Do you see what I mean? If you make somebody scream in fear and pain, but you can't imagine how they feel, then where's the joy? They're just windup toys! And anyway, that's not what's so annoying. If this is theater, then it's being done for the benefit of the audience. What's 'ridiculous' is that the audience doesn't walk out and demand their money back."

Lottie emerged from the underbrush with the yellow ball in her mouth and covered with dried leaves which Amy had to pick off by hand. "Her fur is like Velcro," Amy said.

"So now you're saying I'm wasting my time with the book?"

"No! I'm straight up asking for an explanation. This is what your book is about, isn't it? The fetishization of these killers and their deeds?"

Amy hadn't spent much time thinking about Chuck's work, a nonfiction book, not a novel, so she was basically acting as sounding board. What she'd read so far wasn't bad. He was not what he called 'John X-ing,' feeding off the public appetite for atrocious gore, nor was he planning to just show people how popular the stuff was, cataloging all the movies, bestsellers, and websites. Amy and Chuck both loathed that sort of thing, which stuck a mirror in front of readers who knew perfectly well what they were watching and reading but just enjoyed a fun preen. Instead Chuck was trying to understand why these creatures, real and fictional, were so popular. Why them, and why now? This had been his pitch to her, anyway.

"That was the idea." Chuck looked downcast. "I don't know. Mostly I seem to be throwing stuff out. I wasted two months on the SK groupies, got a ton of info about these women, the ones who wrote letters to them, the ones who married them, the one who got pregnant while the guy was on death row, and I ended up tossing all of it."

"Targets too easy?"

"No kidding. I don't want targets, and I don't want to treat people like freaks. I'm flailing. Anyway, that's not why I'm here."

Amy brought him green tea and watched him describe his long talk with Carla two nights ago, how much they'd learned about each other. She was pretty sure Carla had never even finished high school, let alone studied oceanography, but she kept that to herself. Carla might be in love, or at least falling toward it. Amy found herself hoping this was true and wanted to ask Chuck if he cared about the girl, but it wasn't her place. "I assume she didn't do a turnabout with you—just the others."

"No, that's just it, she gave me the dirtiest look before she flounced off."

"That is odd." Or maybe not. "Anyway, if you want me to read something new, let's do it—otherwise, I'd like to get back to my own work."

"And this morning she said I didn't need to keep staying there. That she was just fine by herself."

So Carla *was* in love. Amy sighed. "That's probably not very wise."

"Wise?? It's crazy! People are getting dismembered, and she's 'just fine' with staying in an enormous rambling house that everybody has a key to and that's been invaded by creeps, or one huge creep, at least twice. Look, I know it's asking a lot, but could you invite her back here? I'm sure she'd come."

"How about if I drive down there this afternoon and see what's going on."

Chuck looked hugely relieved. "What about your work?"

"I lied. I'm not working, unless staring at a blank page counts."

She sent him off and promised to see him in a couple of hours, at Carla's. "She's not going to throw you out before nightfall."

"She sure as hell isn't," he shouted as he drove away. His voice cracked a little, as though he were fourteen. Amy seldom concerned herself with the romantic lives of others, but Carla, she now had to admit, was special to her, and she admired Chuck, who, like Amy, had endured a crushing loss and emerged unshattered. No, he had lost a child; that must be worse than the death of a husband.

She spent a half hour wrestling with the start of yet another accident fiction. Amy normally had no trouble starting a story; it was the middle that killed—what one of the Ediths called "the Gobi Desert." Lately, though, she found herself sitting stone still in front of the monitor for long stretches of time, her mind as blank as the screen. She was developing a morbid fear of not finishing what she started.

Amy was at the eastern edge of old age and death was everpresent in her thoughts, though not yet in a frightening way. She found herself tidying up a lot, tossing out old clothes and mismatched plates and teacups, painting and otherwise sprucing up the inner and outer walls of her house, her penultimate resting place. Once every couple of months she brought to the Goodwill a cardboard box loaded with videotapes, kitchen gadgets, small appliances she had not used more than once, and uncracked hardbacks foisted upon her by blurb-seeking agents. Her impulse not to leave a mess was odd, since when she died she would also leave no survivors. Still, there it was, and she honored it.

Amy centered "Leaving a Mess" at the top of the blank page and double-spaced twice.

An old woman, Lucy, watches television at night when her eyesight is blurry from reading. She mostly watches old *CSI*s and true-crime reenactments, but one evening she chances upon a program about hoarders being buried alive. She sees another old woman living in spectacular squalor, surrounded by objects with which she refuses to part. She nests beyond mountains of Chinese take-out cartons, newspapers, dirty clothes, boxed dress shirts, glass bottles, bicycle parts, radios, pizza boxes, pizza, open bags of cat food, Hummel figurines, plastic Christmas trees, six mummified cats, and a three-quarter ton of *National Geographic*s. When asked about this or that hoarded object, the old woman explains its purpose in detail. The pizza, for example, is still edible if warmed in her microwave, which abides beneath an eight-foot mound of souvenir throw pillows. She is led protesting off-screen by a posse of TV people, disaffected daughters, therapists, and moonlighting crime scene technicians, all of whom stage-whisper about rat feces and stench. Lucy shuts off the program and inventories her house. Since she can easily move from room to room without displacing mounds of garbage, she must not be a hoarder. In fact, the rooms look neater than they did when she was younger. But she does have a lot of books. Every room contains bookcases, all overflowing, unshelved books piled in front of the shelved ones due to lack of space. She remembers a *CSI* where somebody was killed by falling bookcases, but this was not likely here, since none were freestanding. Still, she does not want to leave a mess. The following afternoon, seeking Goodwill donations, she begins with her reference books, starting with her great-grandfather's *Farmer's Almanac*s from 1847. She bundles these along with her husband's books on structural steel-work and carpentry and volumes K, M, N, and XYZ of the 1964 *World Book Encyclopedia*. Loading one box so fast fills her with optimism, but the task soon becomes daunting. For every book she lays to rest, she finds herself leafing through another, boxing it, changing her mind, taking it out, reading some more. How had she come into *The Moldavian Book of Root Medicines*? The hand-written inscription on the inside cover uses an alphabet unknown to her. She can remember noticing the book from time to time; it seems always to have stood there on the middle bottom shelf in the hall. Here is *A Short History of the World* by H. G. Wells: She does recall buying that secondhand since it was short and cheap and by H. G. Wells, but his history stopped with the formation of the League of Nations, which happened long before Lucy was born, so she hasn't yet got around to it. She shelves it between *Birds of the Northern Plains* and the *Physicians' Desk Reference* she bought when her husband was dying. Which is of course outdated and useless and would not again be opened but apparently functions as some sort of monument, or else she would be able to toss it out now. Frowning, she places it beside her on the floor. It becomes the foundation of a pile of other curiosities, books she should discard but can't quite. Orange sunset deepens to crimson all about as she explores shelf after shelf, book after book, and by moonlight the shelves are half empty with more than enough room for Shakespeare and Tolstoy and Lardner and Woolf and all the other respectables, and she sits amid stacks higher than her head, mountain ranges of etiquette manuals, idiot's guides, ghost stories, Yiddish folktales, biographies of Mary Astor, Horatio Nelson, Davy Crockett, and Petroleum V. Nasby, *How to Avoid Probate*, *A Girl of the Limberlost*, *Fun with Stunts*. Is she a hoarder? She thinks not. If anyone asked the purpose of keeping *The Wonderful World of Salt*, she would, unlike the crazy old woman on that show, have no answer. She finds this comforting. Rising, she surveys a mess of piles and boxes and admits that the whole project was ill-advised without a game plan; she'll return to it later. Sighing, she reshelves everything except for the oldest *Farmer's Almanac*, which she takes to bed. . . .

* * *

Amy stopped when she realized she could barely see the keys. It was promising, and she hated to leave it unfinished, but orange sunset had in fact arrived, crimsoned, and almost gone, and she was hours late for her promised visit. She googled Donatella Ng, who had indeed died horribly, apparently last night, at the hands of some human who imagined himself a mythic fiend. The cause of death was not yet pinpointed, and no wonder. Ng had been a patient intake specialist, whatever that was, married to a cardio-thoracic surgeon, and her body parts had begun to turn up twelve hours after he had reported her missing. Like most murder victims, she was universally adored, and no matter what room she entered, her smile lit it up like Broadway. If I am ever murdered, Amy thought, I will haunt anyone who says that about me.

When she looked up the Ngs in La Jolla, she saw that they lived about a quarter-mile from the Birdhouse. Was that supposed to be significant? How could such an over-the-top body disposal connect with what happened to Toonie Garabedian, whose equally unjust end had left a comparatively tidy tableau?

Still, Chuck was right about Carla's recent mood swings. Just two days ago she had in a few minutes done, as he would say, a complete one-eighty from terror that bordered on catatonia to bouncing exhilaration. *To the Rotunda!* And at the time Amy had tried to see this as striking evidence of Carla's default relentlessly upbeat temperament. But Chuck had been persuasive: Carla needed help. Amy put Lottie in the hated canine car seat and set off for La Jolla. Maybe on the way she would figure out what the hell old Lucy was up to with those damn books.

CHAPTER TWELVE

Carla

For an hour Carla sat in Toonie's old cell staring at the curled remnants of crime scene tape on a bare desktop. She'd left the others in such a rush that she hadn't brought her laptop or even a pad and pencil, and for a while that was okay since what she really needed to do was brainstorm.

Except brainstorming never worked for her. She'd taken at least twelve writing classes where they made her brainstorm and it hadn't worked once. And other classes where you spun a dial or cut tarot cards or shook dice or whatever to come up with characters and plot points. Of course, Amy didn't believe in any of that, which was the first reason Carla loved her classes. When Carla tried to brainstorm, her mind would go white as a picket fence. Of course, she could try hypnotizing herself again, that worked out so well the last time, ha ha, but she didn't have a spiral thingy to stare at anyway.

Then it came to her: improv. Amy had been impressed with her skills. This was something Carla could actually do. And she said something about using it for her writing. But how? *Start with what you know.* She needed a setting, a couple of characters, some props, a situation.

Setting: the Victorville Funhouse. She could still see it plainly, she could place herself right there now, no props required. Who is she? She is Cindy Horner, thirty-five, a divorcée with two children. No, she's married; it's a whole family of Horners. Why have they come to this decrepit sleazehole? The husband used to work here. He ran the cotton candy booth. No, he took tickets for the Wild Rat Roller Coaster and measured the kids to see if they were tall enough for the Rat. The youngest kid, who looks like Holman Bellavance, asks what *that* was like. He's bored but being polite. No, he's bored but afraid to show it, and his dad says it was fun until one of the cars came off. There was nobody in the car, which was good, except it landed on two people and killed them. No, there's only one child, and the mother, Willa, worked the funhouse, and she laughs and laughs when her husband tells the story. "Whole fair went belly-up," she says. "Lawsuit City." No, it's a daughter, not a son. Molly. Maybe Molly looks sort of like Holman Bellavance. And Molly doesn't know why they came here and she wants to leave, and the father does too, but the mother says, "Check this out," and kicks open the clown mouth door of the funhouse and drags them both inside. She is a big woman, big enough to knock down a door, and she has to stoop to not hit her head on the ceiling. She takes up the whole inside of the first room, and now she's bent so low that her forehead rests on the sawdust, her profile reaches halfway to the ceiling, and in Willa's enormous eye all Molly can see is herself, tall and thin, squat with a nose as wide as her chin, and Willa shoves Molly into the mirror maze then disappears and Carla can't find the way out. Her father isn't here. "I want out," she says, but there's no door and laughter everywhere. She tries to find the record player but can't and it's not the Austrians anyway, it's Willa laughing, and this isn't improv, it's a waking nightmare.

Carla got herself together, tiptoed out of the wing, out of the house, started her car, and headed north on the 5. She didn't know where she was going but she had to get out. At first she thought about driving to San Pedro and finding the old apartment, the first place they'd lived when they left Pennsylvania, but she wasn't sure she'd even recognize it, assuming it hadn't been torn down by now. So she took the I-5 to the I-15 and headed for Vegas because why not, why not visit old haunts. She hadn't been there since the last time she'd filmed a Nutty's Joint commercial. A hundred miles in she realized that the Vegas Nutty's Joint couldn't possibly be standing what with the whole company going, as Ma would say, belly-up, and she hated Vegas anyway. She wasn't thinking straight. She was about to turn around when she saw the sign for Victorville and she knew where she was. Roy Rogers Drive to Plaza and there was the Fair with the Carnival. Except it was closed, because it was only April and state fairs don't start until June and she was so stupid stupid stupid. Just miles of chain-link fencing and billboards of coming attractions, Hootie & the Blowfish, whoopee. Nothing like the place she knew. Hootie & the stupid Blowfish. And why had she wanted to come here? She must be losing her mind.

She turned around and headed south with nowhere to go. She was thirsty, so after a few miles she stopped at the Atomic Diner, a place she actually recognized from before. Ma had never stopped there, but Carla had wanted to because it was shaped like two train cars. Just another greasy spoon, Ma would say, "And you'll never stay thin if you eat that garbage."

Carla wasn't hungry but felt bad about just ordering a Coke, so she sat at the counter and asked for a Neutrino Burger and Comet Fries. All the seats and booths were red and the counter and tables dull turquoise. The linoleum floor was checkered black and white and had seen better days, but someone clearly bothered to scrub and mop, so the whole place shined. There was a stamped tin ceiling and old signs for Coca-Cola and a huge old clock on the wall behind the counter that said Atomic Clock. She would have loved this place when she was a kid. Even now it wasn't so bad. The place was almost full, probably of locals. In a corner booth two kids were arguing with their parents about salad.

Carla wondered why it had taken her so long to figure out how to break free of Ma. It had been so so easy. All she'd had to do was eat. Ma didn't keep junk food in the house and monitored every bite Carla ate and never figured out where she was getting the good stuff. She didn't know that the kids on the lot, the ones like Carla, the ones who'd never dreamed the dream in the first place, got candy and cookies and chips smuggled in from sympathetic extras and caterers. Or maybe the smugglers were mean-spirited, who knows, who cares. When the pounds started to show, Ma went crazy trying to stop it. She took her to quacks, got speed pills and watched Carla swallow them, except of course she didn't really, because she could *act* for Pete's sake and she just sucked them behind her back teeth and swallowed, Ma was so gullible. Turned out the woman who was brilliant at managing her daughter's showbiz career was a mark when it came to what the biz was all about. Illusion, you old witch. Ma would watch Carla bust through the seams on a dress that wardrobe had just altered and she'd wail and fret and Carla would cry on queue. "It must be my *glands,* Ma! I can't help my *glands*!!!" and Ma would bring in the specialists, an army of glandologists. One of them, Dr. Stookey, spent a long time listening to Ma's complaints and discussing inconclusive test results and then she (*she*—this was the only woman doctor Carla saw) got Ma out of the room to sign some stuff and leaned in to Carla and asked, in a low voice, "Are you worried about your weight? How do you feel about it?" and Carla said, to her own astonishment, "I feel just fine about it," and Dr. Stookey nodded and smiled and said, "All right, but be careful. You don't want to gain too much and ruin your health." Ma came back in and Dr. Stookey prescribed some vitamins and told her a bunch of BS about making sure Carla got enough sleep and exercise and Ma just shook her head and slammed out and Carla rejoiced for the whole rest of that day.

Carla had always planned to tell Ma how she pulled it off. "Remember Sherman Wuntz, the Thirteenth Squirrel with the big earlobes? And his uncle Marty the prop guy? Uncle Marty used to bring us Toll House cookies and Almond Joys by the pantload! Right under your nose, Ma!" But the day never came. When they shared space in the Birdhouse, Carla often rehearsed it, the whole scene, but she never got around to it; the time was never quite right. Now she looked down at her Neutrino Burger, its bun glossy with grease, and forced herself to take at least one bite. So the waitress, a nice lady who called her "honey," wouldn't think it was any fault of hers.

By the time she left the place the sun was low and she was all road-tripped out. The whole day had been a disaster. She was most of the way home, still on the 15, when she saw the signs for Escondido and at last knew where she had to go.

It was dark when she pulled up to Amy's house. The porch light was on but the house was dark and Lottie wasn't barking, so they had to both be out somewhere. That was okay. Carla parked so Amy would have room to get into the carport, then pushed her seat back and stretched out to wait. Maybe Amy would invite her to stay the night. Maybe not. It didn't matter. She felt so calm right here, right now, and, like Amy said, that's all we ever have. Right here, right now.

CHAPTER THIRTEEN

Amy

Wednesday evening

When Amy pulled into Carla's driveway the Rotunda was gleaming like a lighthouse beacon. Amy assumed Carla was in there, but when she and Lottie got inside, the big room was populated with what looked like everybody except Carla. Harry B., clad in a tan running suit—Amy figured he must own a rainbow assortment—was on his feet attempting to keep the crowd's attention, which was not easy given the posture of John X. Cousins, also upright, positioned in the exact center of the window overlooking the sparkling night sea. Their seated audience might have been watching a tennis match. Harry was saying something about an elephant; Cousins was shaking his head. "Madam!" he called out to Amy with elaborate delight. "You're just in time!"

Amy sat down next to the dollhouse and put Lottie on the chair beside her. "Where's Carla?" she asked the room. *Madam.*

"Not here," said John X. Cousins, "but I'm sure she's fine."

Amy spotted Tiffany on the other side of Dr. Surtees. "Just in time for what?" she whispered.

"He's got news about Toonie," Tiffany whispered back.

"Harry, please tell me where Carla is."

"She took off."

Tiffany spoke up. "We thought she was in Toonie's cell, but then Chuck saw that her Mini was gone. He went looking for her a couple of hours ago."

"Why are we sure," Amy asked, "that she's fine?"

Ricky Buzza said they weren't, at least not the people who knew her. "She's been acting kind of squirrelly."

A woman seated across the room closest to John X. Cousins laughed. When no one joined her, she fiddled with a gigantic squash blossom necklace that could have passed for a breastplate and said, "Well, let's face it, what else is new? She's not exactly—"

"Mrs. Colodny," said Tiffany, "you haven't been with us long enough to know Carla as well as we do. She's been upset ever since, you know—"

"Of course! I didn't mean—"

Amy was impressed by her old group's rising up in defense of their friend. Was this Colodny person the one with twins? No, that was somebody else. "Has Carla done this before? Just taken off?"

"It's not a usual thing with her," Harry said. "She mostly walks on the beach. But Chuck would have called us by now if something were wrong—"

"Ricky's been checking for accidents on the Caltrans map," said Tiffany.

"I'm sure we'll hear something soon," said Cousins, "and meanwhile—"

"Meanwhile, I'd like to get back to that elephant—"

"Misha!" sang Cousins. An impossibly elongated woman who looked like the love child of Tilda Swinton and Tim Gunn swept through the crowd and perched light as a hummingbird on the arm of Kurt Robetussien's chair. Dr. R. glanced up at her in alarm. Amy, who had no trouble remembering people whose fiction she'd read, wondered if he'd gotten married yet and whether he'd ever done anything with that oncology nurse novel. Did he still work the ER?

Anyway, here was the famous Misha Bernard, the Aztec Moonie who had no doubt earned more from her bestselling excrescences than Amy had from all her books combined. "John," said Misha Bernard, "tell us everything you can about these grotesque events. I'm sick with worry. Well—and curiosity! I'm sure we all are."

"You're just in time!" said John X. Cousins. "I was about to share what I've put together about the murders."

"Before you 'share,'" said Amy, "I'd like to hear from Harry. Otherwise I'll be too distracted by his elephant to benefit from your lecture."

"Thanks, Amy," said Harry B. "It's Edna Wentworth."

"What?"

"Edna."

"Ah."

"Do I know this Wentworth person?" asked Misha Bernard.

"Well, do you hang around Chino a lot?" Ricky got a dirty look from Tiffany.

"Edna Wentworth," said Harry, "for those of you who don't know"—he shot Cousins a look—"was a member of our writing group a few years ago. She murdered two of us and is serving twenty—"

"Yesyesyes," said John X. Cousins. "But she's locked up, and take it from me, she's no serial killer anyway."

"Of course she's locked up. But Edna is, or was, very . . . What's the word?"

Everyone who remembered Edna offered one.

"Furious!"

"Clever!"

"Sneaky!"

"Snarky!"

"Scary!"

"Baleful!"

"Who said 'baleful'?" asked Amy. Pete Purvis raised his hand. "Good one!"

Dr. Surtees cleared his throat. "Edna Wentworth could nurse a grudge like Florence Nightingale."

"And," said Harry, "*and* she's had a couple years to work on it. And yes, she's not out, I checked, but suppose she made friends with some wacko cellmate and that woman got released? And came down here to mess with us? I wouldn't put anything past Edna. She was one manipulative old dame."

"I get it!" said the Colodny woman. "The white elephant in the room!"

"Harry," said Ricky, "in all fairness, you just described the plot of at least sixteen movies."

"She's not a Serial," said Cousins.

Ricky snorted. "Because she only killed two? She was just getting started! She would have murdered us all!"

Amy was startled by a hand on her shoulder. She turned and Syl Reyes was there, leaning down to whisper. "This John X. guy is horseshit."

"I'm impressed," said Cousins. "She was obviously a murderous lady, but she had *motive.* She wasn't driven by the psychopathic need for celebrity."

"The hell she wasn't!" Dr. Surtees was on his feet. "She was crazy to get published!"

Cousins cocked his head. "Was she a psychosexual sadist?"

"For god's sake—"

"If we must call her names," said Amy, who couldn't stand it anymore, "I suppose you could say she's a monomaniac, although I don't know how that helps. The woman was a pretty good writer, not a great one but certainly publishable with a bit of luck—which, as we all know, is the essential ingredient—who had become terminally embittered by rejection. Some people paper their walls with rejection slips; Edna ate hers."

"She *did*? Good god. I didn't know that!"

"Sorry, Harry, it's a bad metaphor. They poisoned her metaphorically, and she took it out on us. Look, I don't think she's our elephant, but why must a serial killer be sex-crazed?"

"Yeah," said Syl. "Is there a rule book?"

"Are there bylaws?" Pete Purvis again, all grown up. Amy wondered if he was still writing stories for kids. He had a lot more wit than she'd given him credit for.

"I think you're missing the point." Misha Bernard extended a long arm toward Syl, smiling, touching his shoulder with a manicured finger. Syl stared at her wide-eyed, as though charmed by a cobra. Lottie barked wildly. She had been keeping her own counsel, but apparently she didn't care for the long pointy arm of Misha Bernard. Amy shushed her with a piece of cheese. "Serial killers are almost always men who gratify themselves sexually by exerting ultimate control over their victims," Misha went on. "The vengeful woman you describe had much less . . . lofty ambitions."

Pete said, "Hey, getting published is a pretty lofty ambition."

"Let's get back to Dr. Garabedian," said Cousins, clearly annoyed. "Strangulation is an intimate act, particularly when the murderer is facing the victim, witnessing her final agonies. The medical examiner has found that this was in fact the case—she was not strangled from behind. Add to that the fact that she was deliberately left as part of an obscene tableau, appearing to gaze directly at a photograph of an erect penis. There was a strong element of sexual sadism in this murder." Cousins looked up past the crowd. "Cindy? Are you ready?"

"Absolutely!" Good lord, here was Cindy Stokes. Amy hadn't thought about her once since the whole Edna debacle. The last she'd heard, Cindy was trying to get the Murder 24-7 network interested in the workshop crimes. Amy wouldn't have known about this if the TV people hadn't called her; she'd feigned senility and hung up; when they emailed her, she shut them down. What was Cindy Stokes doing here? Now, behind Cousins, white motorized shades descended from the ceiling until they covered the window, forming a screen on which, seconds later, as the houselights dimmed, appeared what looked like the beginning of some god-awful PowerPoint presentation. Which it was. The title: "SERIAL 101."

The first images were Venn diagrams depicting overlapping sets of murderous motives, acts, and people, and of course at the very center of each was the star, the serial killer, what Cousins called the SK. Each graphic would have been clear to a ten-year-old, but Cousins explained them anyway. Amy loathed Power-Point. Then came a screen with four circles, each representing one of the Four Categories of SK. "This is horseshit," said Syl again under his breath, and Ricky asked, "Is there going to be a quiz?" but the others were mostly quiet.

Cousins pointed to each in turn: The *Collector*. The *Fantasist*. The *Psychosexual Sadist*. The *Thrillist*. From his intonation, the third category was his favorite, probably because of all the syllables, but Amy could not be sure. Cousins offered multiple examples of each, all the old familiar faces, and went into detail about how this one killed for celebrity and this one for pleasure, and none of it was even remotely edifying. Or new. Amy doubted that anybody in this room, or in the whole of the United States, didn't know chapter and verse about BTK and the Happy Face Killer. People clueless about Picasso and Eleanor Roosevelt and Jonas Salk could recite in detail the lifetime achievements of Ted Bundy.

Amy was about to stand up and leave when that jacaranda snapshot of Toonie Garabedian appeared behind him, and the room sighed. Then her image shrank so that she could share the screen with three other women. Her image, a professional headshot, was the most polished. To her right was the grainy mug shot of a dejected young black woman. Couldn't he have located a family photo? Had he even tried? Cousins said her name was Patrisse Robinson, and that she was a prostitute killed in National City at the age of eighteen. Beneath her was the high school yearbook picture of Marisol Jimenez, who smiled into a future that did not involve being slaughtered in the parking lot of a Jamul casino. Finally, underneath Toonie was that Rancho Bernardo teacher grinning indulgently at whoever took the picture. Clearly the fates of the middle-class white women on the left had been required to excite the imaginations of Cousins and the press.

"By the way," he was saying, "the timing of the kills just *may* be significant. Patrisse Robinson was killed in late November, the day after Thanksgiving. Marisol Jimenez died on Christmas Eve, and Martha Jensen on Valentine's Day."

"Oh!" shouted Mrs. Colodny. "He's doing it on holidays!"

"Well, but then there's Dr. Garabedian. And Donatella Ng." On cue, the four images shrank again and poor Mrs. Ng's lovely face appeared in the center of the screen. "Dr. Garabedian died on March fourth, Mrs. Ng just four days later."

"And—we're on a roll!" said Ricky, holding up his cell phone. "The eighth of March is when Johan van Oldenbarnevelt was appointed chief legal adviser of the Netherlands. In 1586. And the fourth is . . . wait for it . . . Casimir Pulaski Day in Illinois! This year, anyway. It's always on the first Monday in March." Tiffany mouthed "Knock it off" at him, but most people laughed.

"Of course there are *private* holidays," chided John X. Cousins.

Syl said "Horseshit" again, this time out loud.

"By which I mean days—anniversaries, if you will—that commemorate some event in the past that started the killer on his road to—"

"Look," said Harry, "seriously, you're not telling us anything we either don't already know or couldn't find out by ourselves."

"Right," said Ricky. "The inciting event or stressor or whatever. On the fourth of March his mother forced him to eat a liverwurst sandwich. *Ergo.* On the eighth, a fifth-grade bully took a dump in his lunchbox. *Therefore.*"

"I thought the point was to persuade us that Toonie's death was connected with the others," said Harry. "You're not doing that."

"I'm getting there, Harry," said Cousins, who looked to be breaking a sweat. "And you're right that the timing alone doesn't prove anything one way or the other. So . . ." He snapped his fingers at Cindy and the victim photos were replaced by one giant word that extended the width of the screen: "TROPHIES."

"I'm outta here," muttered Syl, and he was. Amy glanced back longingly at the closing door.

"While it's too early to be able to say definitively whether trophies were taken from the first three victims, we have reason to believe this happened with Dr. Garabedian. Since so many of you are apparently well-versed in SK behavior, I'll try not to bore you." Cousins was getting huffy. "But it's worth noting that anything—*anything*—can function as a serial killer's trophy." Again he snapped his fingers as though summoning a waiter, and a list appeared in the shape of a stiletto.

DRIVER'S LICENSES
LIBRARY CARDS
FINGER BONES
CHESS PIECES
SCALP WIGS
CRAMPONS
GENITALS
EYEBALLS
JEWELRY
PANTIES
SALIVA
NOSES
HEADS
FACES
HAIR
EARS
FEET

"I see the makings," said Amy, who could have resisted the urge but decided not to, "of a challenging creative writing exercise."

"Write a story," said Pete, "that uses each of these words at least once."

"I was thinking smaller," said Amy. "A sentence."

Ricky was on it. "Eyeballing her lovely face, reveling in her auburn wealth of luxuriant hair, Dick Wadd furtively fumbled with his genitals, his finger bones electric with anticipation, all the while imagining the removal of her bejeweled . . ."

"Panties," said Pete, "while snot dripped from his nose onto the library card he'd so carefully placed on top of his—"

"The point," shouted Cousins, "is that Toonie's *thumb drive* is missing." He paused to let that electrifying fact sink in. The moment lengthened.

"I thought you were going to say 'thumb,'" said Mrs. Colodny, plainly disappointed.

"'Thumb' would be better," said Dr. Surtees, and the crowd seemed to agree.

"Also," said Kurt R., "what was the deal with crampons? How do you target people with crampons?"

Mrs. Colodny raised her hand. "What *are* crampons?" Amy began to warm to Mrs. Colodny.

Tiffany, usually defensive of John X. Cousins, looked exasperated, and not just with his rowdy audience. "Why do you think she had a thumb drive in the first place? I never saw her with one."

Misha Bernard rose and waved to Cousins. "John, this has been fascinating! I'm sure I'll see you tomorrow." She swept off. For a moment, Amy thought she had shown herself to be as disenchanted with the PowerPoint as most everyone else, but Cousins looked relieved. Bernard's announcement had implied that the lecture was concluded and had been a great success, which was false but let him off the hook, since he'd have had a tough time getting his audience back. "More to come," he promised with a game smile. "See you in a few!" Then he snapped one last time at Cindy Stokes, waved to the crowd, and followed Misha out the door.

Amy gathered herself to leave. "Tell me," she asked no one in particular, "does he do this often? Is this a regular thing, with the PowerPoint?"

Tiffany looked despondent. "It was supposed to be a special event."

"Is he really in close contact with the police? I can't imagine why they'd allow that."

"I don't know. He says he knows somebody on the inside."

For a while no one spoke. Cindy hadn't turned off the projector, or whatever it was, so the list of trophies remained, dominating their attention. "I hate that word," said Tiffany.

"Crampons?"

"Panties."

"I do too," said Amy.

All the way home she tried not to worry about Carla. She'd asked Tiffany to call her when they found her. All the way home she scanned both sides of the I-15 for breakdowns. Was this what it was like to have children? Probably, and how did people stand it, sending their little hostages to fortune out into an indifferent world? Maybe this was how the human mind came up with the strategy of denial. With this thought came Fred and Ginger.

It had been years since she'd thought about Fred and Ginger, dachshund littermates she and Max had inherited from one of his friends. After six years, Fred one day felt poorly and died right after they got him to the vet. Turned out he'd eaten a sock. Max and Amy, equally bereft, split sharply over what to do with the body. Amy wanted to take Fred home. "Why?" said Max. "The grave would have to be deep and it's ninety in the shade. Do you really need to do this?"

And Amy had said, no, *she* didn't need it, but Ginger did. Ginger had to understand that her brother was dead. Max just stared at her. "He was dying when we left the house. She was right there.

She knows." "No, she needs to face facts." And Max laughed and laughed and finally said, "You're talking about denial. Amy, dogs don't do denial. *People* do denial." And of course he was right. When they got home, Ginger never looked for Fred. Whatever the depth of her grief, it was private. As was Amy's, when Max had died. Amy and Max never did denial either. Nighttime drives always brought her back to him.

Chuck emerged from the car parked in the street in front of her house and waved at her as she slowed to turn up the driveway. He leaned in and whispered, "She's sound asleep." And she was, her Mini snuggled against the laurel hedge so Amy could get into the carport. Amy and Chuck had a time extracting her from the car. Carla mumbled something about being a bother but did not fully waken, and Chuck carried her up the steps and into the house. Lottie knew to behave herself and refrained from welcoming screams. There seemed to be an enchantment.

Amy showed Chuck the guest room, where Carla was stretched out and fast asleep, and fetched clean towels and sheets, then went to bed herself. She didn't ask how he'd found Carla here. She didn't ask if he wanted to stay the night, or point him toward the sofa. He could sleep where he thought best. She just told him to sleep well. And did herself, minutes later, with Lottie curled at her feet, and all their dreams were unremarkable.

CHAPTER FOURTEEN

Carla

Thursday, March 11

Sleeping Carla enjoyed a happy dream in which she was sitting in Amy's backyard talking to Carol Ann Winkelman and throwing the ball for Lottie and Carol Ann's basset hound. Awakening in Amy's actual guest room was almost as stunning as the presence of Chuck stretched out beside her. He slept on top of the bedspread, fully dressed and on his back. Morning light slanted across his face, and she could see stubble on his cheek and chin. Some of the tips were gray. She leaned close and inhaled; he smelled of soap and something else, a pleasant scent she couldn't name; she figured it must be his own. His eyes opened, inches from hers, and she remembered the funhouse nightmare with her mother's huge mirroring eye, but she could not see herself in this eye. She just saw him.

"Was I snoring?"

Carla shook her head.

He propped his head on his elbow. "Do you have any questions?"

"About what?"

"How you got here?"

"Let's not talk," said Carla.

Chuck blinked and pulled back a little; he looked at her warily. Had she said something wrong? "About yesterday. Let's not talk about yesterday." That seemed to calm him. "I just had a bad day is all."

"Your friends were worried. I was worried. Amy was worried enough to drive down to the Birdhouse, and you know how she hates to travel, and then you weren't even there. Where were you?"

"Why was she worried?"

"Because I told her she should be."

"Now I'm embarrassed." Actually she wasn't; actually she was pleased, but she knew she shouldn't let on. "What do you want to do now?"

On cue, Lottie, who must have heard them talking, scrabbled at the door, and Amy called out that there were clean towels in the bathroom.

"I'm going to take a shower," Chuck said.

Carla lay in bed listening to the water run. She was confused in a new way that was at once good and kind of scary. She was thirty-five years old and had never before shared a bed with a man. Her only boyfriends had been the fake ones set up by Ma and her agent, Clyde Cogwell from Clyde: Other aging child actors whose caregivers were desperate to keep them in the public eye, and of course by the time she was fifteen none of them wanted to pretend to date a fat girl, which was just peachy with her.

Carla could recall a life before the funhouse when she would have certain thoughts, sensations, fantasies, and in waking dreams imagine sexual fulfillment, although she didn't know that was what it was. The dreams involved guys like Kyle MacLachlan, actors she passed by on movie lots or saw on TV, and other men, too—not boys her age but men—and she knew instinctively that these dreams were intensely private, and she lived for them.

They made her working life, her life with Ma, bearable. They were her private island. In time she came to believe that one day she wouldn't need the island anymore, that her body would be touched and would touch and there would be great joy, and in the real world. She was patient; she could wait. And then Hoving in the funhouse, and that was the end of that.

She never told anyone about Hoving, especially not Toonie, who would just have wanted her to go on and on about it, even though it wasn't rape and it wasn't some big trauma. All she told Toonie was that she had tried sex and opted for celibacy. *But why,* Toonie had asked, *if it wasn't so terrible, why did you close and lock the door?* Toonie loved metaphors, what Amy called "tired metaphors," like that locked door one. She probably shoved a ton of them into her stupid book. *Why give up on life?* Well, she didn't give up on life, she just took herself out of that part of it. And it's not as though she did it on purpose. The fantasies just stopped, the private island sank beneath the waves. *What waves?*

Sex was the only topic Toonie really enjoyed talking about; even without knowing about the funhouse she was always at Carla about her "sexuality." When she'd say the word she'd take a tiny pause first, as though it were a foreign-language word and she didn't want to pronounce it wrong, and she'd make a production out of maintaining eye contact. To get Toonie off her back Carla had to come up with a lot of BS about wild teenage beach blanket orgies, and how she knew quite well what she was shutting the door on thank you so very much, until Toonie gave up and started nagging about grief and closure and the Golden Acorn of Maternal Cremains.

Now she listened to the shower running and thought about Chuck and tried to understand what was happening to her. She liked Chuck. A lot. But did she like him like *that*? Like she'd liked Kyle MacLachlan and Jimmy Smits? Like *that*? She pictured him now, naked in the shower. He was a little shorter than her, and stocky, and he had a wonderful face, crinkly eyes and a strong chin and his shoulders were broad, and his arms had muscles, his forearms at least, she'd seen them, so the rest of his body was probably . . . All alone, Carla blushed. Wasn't blushing something you did in front of other people? How could you be embarrassed all by yourself? The shower shut off, and after a while she heard him open the bathroom door and walk away toward the back of the house.

"Are you sure?" Amy was saying.

Amy and Chuck were in the backyard with Lottie, and Chuck was nodding yes, he was sure.

"Sure about what?" Carla sat on a bench and picked up Lottie's squeaky ball.

"Did you get breakfast?"

"I'm not hungry." The other two had stopped talking, as though Carla had interrupted something she wasn't supposed to hear, but the hell with that. "Sure about what?"

Chuck glanced at her sharply. "I'm abandoning this book I was working on."

"I thought you said you weren't writing anything. You told me you were through with writing." Carla almost asked why he had hidden it from her but stopped herself. She was trying to trust him. She needed to trust him.

"I was through writing *fiction.* Carla, what's the matter with you?"

"What do you mean?"

"I mean you're not yourself. Something's eating at you. How exactly have I ticked you off?"

Amy took the ball from Lottie, picked her up, and took her into the house. Carla was horrified. She'd made Amy mad, which was the last thing she ever wanted to do.

"No, you didn't," said Chuck.

"Didn't what?"

"You didn't offend her. She's just giving us some space."

"How did you know—how could you tell I was thinking that? How do you know why she—"

"I'm an observant guy." He stood up and reached out a hand to her. "Let's go for a walk."

Almost as if she knew they were going to walk, Amy came back out and handed them Lottie on a leash, and they set out under a cloudy sky. They made it almost to the top of the hill without speaking, just strolling and letting Lottie stop to inspect tires, coyote scat, and gopher holes. They paused at a chain-link fence with a pair of turkeys behind it. Chuck leaned close, and the birds stretched out their necks and gobbled at him. "Heritage, I think. Bourbon Reds."

"How do you know about that?"

"My wife had a thing about heritage turkeys. We never owned any, but she collected pictures of them."

"Do you miss her? I'm sorry! I shouldn't have asked that!"

"I miss that time. We were very young. I got her pregnant before we really knew each other, and then the baby was stillborn, and there was nothing left for us. We wished each other well. Last I heard, Charmaine was remarried and in D.C. She landed a job at the Museum of Natural History." Lottie noticed the turkeys and started to mouth off, so they started back down the hill. "And no, I don't know if she's had more kids."

Carla stared at him. "How did you know—"

"Here's the thing about your face: It's the most legible face I've ever seen. I'll bet you never got away with a lie in your entire life."

"Hey, I was an actor! I was paid to lie. Well, Ma was paid, but I was pretty good at it."

"Are you acting now? Do you act when you're not being paid?"

"Of course not. Well, sometimes, for fun. Actually, acting isn't exactly lying, not really. Even when I do improvs, I get into it. I'm not secretly thinking one thing and saying another thing." They walked without speaking, down past Amy's house and around and up the next hill, where the houses and lots were bigger. "Actually I lied a lot, but only to Ma. I had to."

A rabbit emerged from a stand of rosemary and scampered down the hill, exciting Lottie, who strained at the leash but not as if she really meant to catch it. The rabbit was as big as the dog.

"So," said Carla, "I've got this legible face."

"It's one of your charms."

She had charms. "If you're not going to write, what will you do?"

"I'm thinking of hiring myself out as a bodyguard."

Carla clapped her hands. "That's a great idea! I can pay you, and—"

"Carla. I was kidding."

"Oh."

"I'll do it for nothing."

They sat on the wall in front of Amy's house. Lottie sprang into her lap and settled there. After a long while, Carla said, "Would you like to know what I was doing yesterday? Where I went, and why, and all that?"

Chuck nodded.

"Okay, I'll tell you. But not now. But I will tell you when I'm ready. But not before."

"Okay."

"Is that okay?"

"That's okay." He put his arm around her, and it was light and strong and safe. "I don't have a handkerchief," he said.

"That's okay." Great tears had come out of nowhere, spilling down her face; she had no time to duck her head or hide behind her hands.

"Want me to find some Kleenex?"

Carla shook her head and held up Lottie. "I can just do this," she said, lifting up Lottie, closing her eyes, and wiping her face on the dog's curly white coat. "See?"

Chuck smiled. "Yes, you can. You can do anything."

❋ ❋ ❋

Amy was on the phone in the living room. "I have reached the limit," she said, her voice rising, "on the number of ways I can express my profound indifference to this offer. Have I made myself clear? Thank you." She hung up.

"Orphanage scam?" asked Carla. "Fake IRS refund? Another grandson in a Tijuana jail?"

"I wish," said Amy. "It was that Bernard woman. How did she get my number? Calling on behalf of John X., who is all bent out of shape because of last night's fiasco."

"Ooh! What happened?"

"If you'd been there," said Chuck, "you'd know."

"Come on!"

"And I wasn't there either, because I was out looking for you."

"Oh, right. But you'd tell me if you had been there."

"No, I wouldn't."

If Amy hadn't been right there in the room, Carla would have hit him with a sofa pillow.

"Bernard used the term 'pear-shaped' at least three times," said Amy.

"And that is annoying because . . ." Behind Amy's back, Chuck picked up Lottie's stuffed chew possum and lobbed it at Carla.

How and why was he doing this? It wasn't just her legible face. This was something more, something wonderful. They were *paired*.

"It's annoying because the woman is from Minneapolis, not London." The phone rang again. "Oh, look," she said, reading the caller ID, "it's me."

"What?"

"My own phone number. I'm calling me from my very own phone. Sometimes I amaze myself."

"If you will allow me," said Chuck, elaborately raising the receiver to his ear. He listened for a full minute and then said, "That sounds terrific! Is there a limit to how many I can order? Can I use my Discover Card? Wait—there's somebody at the door—be right back!"

Carla opened the front door, rang the bell, and ran back in. "Gotcha, Mr. Man!" she crowed. "Thought you'd gimme the slip!"

"Hey, hold on, you can't come in here!" Chuck yelled. "Who are you?"

"You know damn well who I am, you two-timing sonofa-bitch!"

"Oh my god! It's you!"

"No shit, Sherlock!"

"Oh my god! You've got a gun!"

Carla slammed the door hard.

"Oh my god! You shot me!"

Amy left them to it and disappeared into the kitchen. Their scene ended with Chuck fumbling with the receiver, dropping it twice, gasping that he was sorry but he had to dial 911, and hanging up. "Not bad," Carla told him, joining him on the floor. "Although *'Who are you?'* was kind of lame. You should have come up with a name. *'Olivia Stoopnagle! What are you doing here?'*" Chuck was still laughing. "*'Is that you, Roxanne LaTouche?'* There are whole worlds in a name," she said.

Amy came in with a teapot and cups and set the tray on the coffee table. "I'd offer you people something stronger, but I don't think you need it." She poured out the tea, which was green and super gingery. "Where did you hear that?" she asked. "'Whole worlds in a name'?"

Carla smiled. "Old Sally Gee. She was my best acting coach. She used to say—"

"Was her name Old Sally Gee?"

"That's what she called herself. She came up from vaudeville. She was about a million years old and really sharp."

"You have to tell me about her sometime," said Chuck.

"Well," Amy said, "it was brilliant advice. I wish I'd thought of it."

"So," said Carla. "Misha Bernard called you."

"And pretended she wasn't calling on behalf of John X. 'He'd never forgive me if he knew about this conversation—he's your number one fan.'"

"Ewww," said Carla and Chuck in unison.

"She went on about his deep appreciation for the Point and everybody connected it, especially me, its founder and inspiration, which is not true, and how he was more than willing to back off if I wanted to take over the reins. 'The reins'!"

"That would be so cool!!!"

"It would not be cool. Carla, in what sense does this human have 'the reins'?"

"Only in the sense that he's renting space and ramping up this stupid Guru Class bullshit, which I thought was just going to be an online thing, but now Tiffany says he's 'willing' to hold classes at the Birdhouse if we want him to. But the Point belongs to me—he's not running it."

"You absolutely sure?" asked Chuck. "You're not the most detail-oriented—"

"I'm absolutely sure that Harry B.'s all over John X.—can we just call him 'X'?—like a cheap suit. He can't stand the guy. We're Harry's client, you know. We can trust Harry B."

"Agreed," said Amy. "Anyway, when I tried to end the conversation, the woman complained that I had sabotaged his serial killer act."

"She actually said that?"

"No, but that's what she meant. 'I'm sure it wasn't intentional, but your very presence distracted his audience.' I showed up only because I was looking for you, and I stayed only in order to ask if anybody knew where you'd gone to, and I did not sabotage his ludicrous PowerPoint nonsense. I may have made one or two unenthusiastic remarks, but Harry was the one complaining. Syl Reyes huffed and puffed and walked out in the middle of the damn thing."

"Oh, god, I wish I'd been there."

Chuck gave Carla a dirty look and addressed Amy. "I'm guessing you wouldn't have had to say a word. All you have to do is show up and they're yours."

"That does not make me happy."

They all sipped their tea. Carla could barely get it down—the ginger almost burned her throat. "This is delicious," she said.

"Oh, and there are two girls missing."

"What?"

"From Torrey Pines High. According to Misha Bernard, X is apparently beside himself with concern. Somehow I doubt that. He must be thrilled. There is something so unseemly about that man."

"How long have they been gone?"

"I don't know, I cut her off. "

"You know," said Chuck, "I'm very skeptical that X has a mole in the police department, or that, if he does know somebody, the guy is dependable."

"She said something about 'red flags' and 'triggers' and 'high alert.' I probably should have let her go on, but I was just fed up. Look, Carla, what do you want to do?"

"About what?"

"Where do you want to stay? You're welcome here. Are you truly safe in your home right now? I'm not as convinced as you were about that business the other day with your cell phone."

Carla and Chuck looked at each other for a long minute. "She'll be fine," he said. "I'll stay with her."

"How about your day job?" asked Amy. "You're an accident investigator. Don't you have to visit the scenes of accidents?"

"I used to, but not so much now. Most of the work I can do online. It won't be a problem."

"Thank you so much for the invitation, but I'll be fine." Carla was surprised at her willingness to turn it down, at her lack of sorrow for the missed opportunity; at her eagerness to go back home.

They said their goodbyes, and Chuck drove off first, since his car was blocking hers. Carla turned to wave at Amy, who stood in her doorway, holding Lottie. Her expression was kind of grave. Not exactly unhappy, but serious. She almost looked like she was posing for a picture. She seemed a little small, as though she had lost an inch or two overnight, which couldn't be right, and her thick white hair was a halo in the noontime sun, and Carla wanted this picture so badly that she stood still long enough to frame it in her memory. And then she drove away toward whatever was going to happen now.

CHAPTER FIFTEEN

Amy

Amy walked back into a house that felt empty for the first time in two years, since the day Alphonse died. That had been an awful day; this one was not awful, but the two had this emptiness in common. The very next morning after he died she had gone out and found Lottie at the local shelter, and that little dog was and continued to be a great comfort, but now she thought it must have been this emptiness rather than grief that propelled her. Amy prided herself on never having to deal with loneliness. Her house could hardly be empty with her in it, or at least so she had always assumed. She missed Max, she missed Alphonse, and if she lived long enough she would miss Lottie, but missing them was an acknowledgment of loss, not loneliness. What she was feeling now was lonely. This was unpleasant.

She was happy for Carla embarking on what might be her first romance. She was confident that Chuck could watch out for her. She did not *miss* them, but still there was this longing, longing for no discernible object. What did she want?

She sat down at her desk, opened up a Word file, centered "The

Empty House" at the top of the page, and waited. Nothing happened, and until something would, she fell to googling.

Two local murders dominated the online San Diego news, where there was no mention of missing high school girls. Toonie Garabedian was now linked with Donatella Ng, but only in the sense that "now two senseless murders have cast a pall over the sunny seaside community of" whatever. There was no hint of a connection, neither in the stories nor in the reader comments.

On a whim she hunted up Harry B.'s number and called him. "Do you have a minute to give me your opinion on something?" He did. "What do you think about John X.—"

"John X. Fugazy!"

"What?"

"Phonus Balonus!"

"Agreed, but—"

"Three-dollar bill!"

"Truer words," she said, "but I'm a little concerned about—"

"His 'in' with the PD? Bullpucky. Doesn't exist. If he knows anybody in the PD, it's probably a janitor. They can't stand him over there."

"Do *you* have an in with the PD?"

"I used to practice criminal law, so a lot of them know me. Kowalcimi wasn't my biggest fan back in the day, we were at opposite ends a few times, but he's friendly enough now when I run into him. He's a good guy. He likes you, by the way."

"In what sense?"

"He admired the way you handled that business with Edna."

"Why? I handled it by almost getting myself killed."

"Yeah, but you were very low-key about the whole thing. He hates drama."

Amy said maybe the man was in the wrong line of business.

"Speaking of Edna," said Harry.

"I wasn't."

"I could arrange for you to go up there and talk to her."

Amy almost hung up the phone. "Harry. She has nothing to do with anything. She doesn't have tentacles."

"I'll go with you. We'll make a day of it."

"We were talking about Cousins."

Harry was silent for a beat. "We still are. Do you remember how he acted last night when I brought up Edna?"

"He kept steering you off the topic so he could get to his ludicrous list of crampon trophies."

"Judging from his behavior, how well-acquainted would you say he was with Edna's case?"

Amy had to think. "He said she wasn't a 'Serial.' He patronized her as a 'murderous lady.' He must have read about her in the paper or online, or probably Tiffany or somebody told him about her. Why?"

"He's visited Edna five times in the past year."

"You're kidding. How do you—"

"I know people."

"What are they doing?"

"That I don't know. Just that he spends a couple of hours each time. What do you think about that?"

"Harry, I'm getting a headache."

"Just think about it. Get back to me if you change your mind. Chino is lovely this time of year."

"Bye, Harry."

"Think about it."

Amy hadn't given Edna Wentworth one thought for at least a year. According to all the crime reenactment shows, being violently attacked was supposed to induce PTSD and no doubt it usually did, but for whatever reason Amy never dreamed about the attack, at least not to her recollection, and she felt no less safe now than she had before Edna came at her with a knife. True, she was occasionally haunted by the two people Edna had killed. She'd been in charge of that workshop; had she been more observant she might have prevented their deaths, and during occasional sleepless nights she'd try to imagine how. But Edna herself was a closed book.

X, though, was not, and against her will Amy wondered what he was up to in Chino. Edna had been a member of the group that eventually formed Carla's Inspiration Point!, which was a moneymaker. Was he planning to use Edna somehow to undermine Carla and take over the business? Amy had no head for that sort of thing. She would have to ask Harry about it, but not now.

Again she gazed at the empty "The Empty House" page. Nothing.

Just to clear her head, she decided to mouse around in someone else's life. Sometimes she searched out the names of old public school friends, distant relatives, Max's colleagues, former workshop members. The internet was a writer's wonderland. Yes, you could waste hours there, but the longer you lived, the more you could learn about how people turned out, and that could help with the construction of fictional characters. Because she had kept pretty much to herself since childhood, there wasn't a huge number of search strings available to her, but there were enough. For some reason she remembered more grade school classmates than she did those in high school; she could recall the names of men she had dated in college, but not much else about them.

She decided to look in on some old favorites. She typed "Carol Ann Winkelman," whom she had last seen at that Boston Strangler Panic weekend at Brown. But Winkelman had just died; mourners were encouraged to give to the American Cancer Society. So she looked up Bart LaFon. Bart LaFon was a kid from her high school accelerated classes who had one time in biology class while they were dissecting frogs made her laugh so hard she cried, by crooning "Anesthesia" to the tune of "Anastasia" from an Ingrid Bergman movie. Since there wasn't a slew of Bartholomew LaFons, she always found him with ease. He'd gotten a degree from Bard and achieved modest success as a dancer on Broadway; he'd been a gay rights advocate since Stonewall; he had married at sixty, and the two of them were raising his husband's grandchild. He was having a good life.

Now she dropped in on him, and there he was, gone. Killed six months back in a pedestrian traffic accident. Damn it. She had planned to look up Martine Slocum, the third-grade redhead who used to write poems for every occasion, including Arbor Day (which was "nicer than Pearl Harbor Day"). But she no longer had the heart for it, preferring to believe that at least someone besides herself was still alive. So, no more Boomers.

John X. had a Wikipedia page even briefer than her own, just one paragraph (in which he was referred to as "nationally re-nowned facilitator for the Slingshot Writing Workshop") listing a degree in communication from SNHU and mentioning a doc-toral thesis on serial killers (no title, which was odd), as well as the Lightborne thing he was presently working on. She went back to his official Web page and there found nothing about the thesis, which Tiffany said he'd earned at UCSD. Amy spent forty-five minutes trying to track it down. There was no record of a USCD thesis for John X. Cousins. The man was a fraud. Maybe she'd bring this up with Tiffany and the rest, and maybe not. As obnox-ious as Cousins was, he really wasn't her business.

"Empty House." Not "*The* Empty House." This revision took fifteen minutes.

Amy had never once searched online for Carla Karolak and now wondered why. She'd known her for over ten years: Carla had signed up for Amy's first California extension workshop and had been a fixture in all of them. Once, when a workshop was canceled because only four people signed up, she burst into tears, thus terrorizing Amy into agreeing to one-on-one work with her. In the early years Amy felt stalked, but she eventually passed through denial, anger, bargaining (pointing Carla toward other workshops, which worked in the sense that she took them, but only in addition to Amy's), and depression, arriving at last at acceptance. And then came the class with Edna. Amy had definitely moved beyond acceptance; she cared about Carla now.

She googled Carla Karolak. At the top of the first page was a Wikipedia link to "Carla Cameron (born Carla Karolak November 3, 1985, in Philadelphia, to Willa Massengill (mother) and Hal Karolak (father)." There were pages and pages with mentions of Carla Cameron.

She had expected hits on "Child stars: Where are they now?" sites, but she was stunned by the number—three—of websites devoted solely to her. One of these was the work of Carla's mother, who must have hired somebody to put together "Little Carla C.: The MegaStar Who Might Have Been." The biographical section highlighted Carla's storybook childhood in Philadelphia and the tireless labors of her loving mother, sacrificing domestic bliss to satisfy her wonderchild's driving ambitions.

Too disgusted to read further, Amy checked out the second site, which turned out to be either pitiful or alarming, or perhaps both. "Carla: My Lost Love" was a multipage valentine assembled by somebody identifying himself as "4Ever Yr Guy," probably a middle-aged sad sack living in a granny flat. The prose was semi-literate, the images, pasted from old commercials and TV shows, captioned uninformatively ("Here she is, nine yrs old in her sloth custom!"), and there were hundreds of site visitors ("All comments welcome!"), most of whom made vicious fun of the guy as well as of the child in those pictures. The handful of Carla-loving commenters had to be 4Ever Yr Guy himself, since the same words were misspelled in each comment. Amy hoped Carla never came here.

The third site was a gold mine, meticulously assembled by somebody named Harriet Cogwell. Amy looked her up; she worked for an L.A. talent agency. Maybe this had been Carla's agency, but that wouldn't explain why they'd maintain a site for somebody who hadn't worked for twenty years. On the site were links to hundreds of videos, some of them old sitcoms and TV dramas, one of them commercials. One section was devoted to her years with Nutty's Joint. The stills and videos had few captions and no descriptions—the images spoke for themselves.

There were blurry snippets and outtakes from those sitcoms and dramas. Carla was nine years old when she came to L.A., but in the oldest of these she looked closer to seven. She was used mostly to ask questions. *Why don't I get to play with Cornpuffy? Why can't I wear lipstick too? Does Mommy have eyes in the back of her head? Why do I have to go to bed first? When will I get my very own talking pig? Are you God?* For the last one she was dying in a hospital bed, addressing a gruff physician who turned toward the camera to display his tears. Which seemed real to Amy, and no wonder. Carla was brilliant, making dreck believable as long as she was in the scene. She inhabited each character fully. She was never cute, fetching, or adorable; she was not a tot but a complicated child set down in a simplistic and unjust world.

The commercial video was fifteen minutes of Carla hawking everything—chocolate gum, appleicious oatmeal, grahamcrammed cookies, fun finger forks, the Victorville Funhouse, Laugh Zones, Martian pencil boxes, Cheezy Chews, battery-operated barrettes. In each commercial her smile was never forced. Whatever the product, she regarded it as though she'd never seen anything so splendid. The Nutty's Joint collection was carefully curated, taking the viewer from the earliest days of the franchise, with amateurish yet amusing presentations, to the slick, migraine-inducing musical numbers that Amy remembered rushing to turn off whenever they came on, which at the time seemed hourly. Carla had an impressively brassy singing voice, better than Nutty's, with whom she sang interminable duets about who was the world's biggest nut. *I am! No, I am!* In the last few, she had begun to put on weight. Her acorn costume now reached from knee to neck, and they'd used contouring makeup to disguise the new plumpness of her face. If the franchise hadn't already been in trouble by this time, they'd surely have fired her.

Carla was extraordinarily talented. Should Amy have realized that? She had always seen Carla as a basket of needs, an annoyingly likeable girl with more "issues" than charms; she had never before really taken her in. She wondered now if she had ever taken anybody in, except Max. You are, he used to tell her, wonderfully well-defended. She had not heard that as criticism.

"Empty House."

Nope.

—Maybe Lucy, the old book hoarder! She'd never finished that one.

"Leaving a Mess"

. . . Lucy goes to bed with the October 1847 *Farmer's Almanac* and starts to read.

Amy searched fruitlessly online for text from the 1847 *Almanacs*.

. . . Lucy goes to bed with a collection of classic ghost stories and starts to read. She settles in with an old English one set on the windswept moors. Nine-year-old twin sisters share a room containing a locked teakwood armoire with a missing key, and they spend idle hours alternately trying to pick the lock and outdo each other with predictions about its grisly contents. One of them goes mad and murders the other. In another story, a widow is haunted by her husband's shade, which keeps popping up in his favorite armchair, on the front lawn viewed through her picture window, at her bedside in the dead of night. Lucy shuts the book. Lucy would not care what was in that armoire even if it were right here beside her and her house had a history of homicidal lunacy. She cannot imagine malevolence, or for that matter benevolence, attaching to a physical object, nor can she imagine being spooked by visions of dead people. How would she respond if she turned on her left side and found her husband stretched out beside her, his head inches from hers on the pillow? She tries a thought experiment. There he is, his hair is mussed, he's wearing his favorite L.L. Bean pajamas. She can see his fine gray hair and starched striped pajamas, but his face is wholly obscured by fog. In *words,* she can describe each feature in detail, and she tries this now, but no matter how exhaustive her description, his face remains hidden from her. His image, such as it is, is neither frightening nor reassuring, and when she blinks it away, it leaves nothing behind. Lucy can recall his *voice,* hear it clear in her inner ear whenever she likes, which is often, but the *sight* of him began to evaporate almost immediately upon his death. If there are ghosts, which of course there are not, they must feed on visual memory. How shallow of them! With that thought she sleeps, and, as sometimes happens, she does not wake up. After her grandnephew has flown in to deal with the settling of her estate, he stands alone in her house, having completed almost all the necessary preparation for sale. His great-aunt was a hermit; her body lay undiscovered for weeks, and he'd had to hire professionals to deal with what was evidently a mess, but none of that remains. As her only heir he has claimed the best pieces of furniture for himself and dealt with the rest, so that nothing is left but these large bookcases, eight of them, each shelf so tightly packed that books need to be pried loose. A conscientious man, a family man, he takes a moment now to summon up some memorial reflection, some childhood memory of her, but all he can recall is her face in the family albums, and he never really knew that woman, let alone the old one who died here. He wanders through the empty house, its bare walls and floors hollowing the sounds of his footsteps, trying to work up energy to pore through a thousand books to see which are worth keeping. Sighing, he begins. He carries in Goodwill boxes and starts packing one with useless reference books, setting aside the occasional curiosity, like the ancient *Farmer's Almanac*s. He fills that box in good time; he should be able to finish up today.

But as he proceeds, the pile of keepers grows, topples, so he has to make a second pile, and then a third. Some books he sets aside because they look valuable, but most for reasons that are unclear to him. Why did she keep a Moldavian study of root medicines? Why doesn't he want to give it up now? What is he going to do with a biography of Mary Astor? The day lengthens, the sunlight deepens through uncurtained windows, the bookcases slowly surrender their burden, some of the boxes fill, but the keepers pile up around him, he won't finish today, he may never finish at all, and with this thought he stands and walks around to clear his head, and now he hears that his footsteps are no longer hollow. The house is no longer empty. He summons the will to pack up those mountains of keepers and empty the house; he knows he can and must do this. But before he does, he stands among the books and remembers her.

CHAPTER SIXTEEN

Carla

March 15 through May 5

The missing high school girls weren't murdered but grounded, having run off and spent the night partying on the beach at PB. That they had been missing at all had never, despite the efforts of X, become a matter of public knowledge, and Carla learned about it only because Ricky still had friends at the *Union-Tribune*. "Cousins kept bugging the *U-T* staff," Ricky said, "trying to gin up excitement about the 'Next Serial Killer Victim,' but they didn't bite." How X knew about the missing girls in the first place was a mystery. Not a particularly interesting one, though.

Over the next few days Carla didn't see X, and when she asked Tiffany what he was up to, Tiffany didn't know and looked put out. Carla felt bad for Tiffany, who now seemed the remaining holdout in the X camp, among the old workshop group anyway. Carla thought Tiffany had kind of a thing for him, even though he was at least fifteen years older. When she'd first met Tiffany back in Amy's class, she'd been the girl most guys noticed, Ricky especially. Now, not so much. Which was weird because she was really pretty and carried herself, as Ma would say, like the Queen of the May.

But Carla didn't have much time to worry about Tiffany or anybody else because she and Chuck were so busy with each other. He worked for Caltrans every weekday, sometimes on his laptop, and sometimes on the road—it was raining a lot more than usual, and there were tons of bad accidents on the 5 and 15. She wondered how he felt and what he saw, but she never asked. He'd tell her if he wanted her to know. She was pretty sure the dead and injured were gone by the time he got there, but still.

She started thinking a lot about her father, which she hadn't done for years. Something about having Chuck here. She never interrupted him when he was working, and that was because she knew better, and that reminded her of her dad. He had never scolded her for bothering him, but she grew up with this idea about the sanctity of men and work. Or maybe sanctuary. Maybe that was it. Maybe she knew that when he was alone in his little office in the attic, or puttering around in the cellar, he experienced some form of peace.

When Chuck wasn't working, he was with her. They spent hours at the tide pools during the day, and then she took him there one night and showed him the one shaped like Pennsylvania. They sat together with their backs to the sea and shone their flashlights into the rooms, which were different from the last time she had been there. The lobster-shell room was carpeted with seagrass and the sea lemon had been replaced by a blue anemone; in front of it a pincushion sea urchin munched on a shard of kelp. "See," said Carla, "this is the dining room now."

In the rec room next door, crabs were still jousting as though they'd been at it since Carla last watched them, but the next room, the great ballroom, had changed dramatically. Barnacles and anemones lined the walls, and in the center of the room, in place of the pink bat star—where had it gone?—a rectangle of white barnacles rose through the surface of the water, their tips pointing to the stars like skyscrapers. Around that structure danced two amazing creatures she had read about but never seen until now— Spanish shawls, sporting saffron-colored mohawks, their bodies bright magenta. They paraded around the spire and stopped now and then to sip from an anemone.

"So this is the ballroom?" asked Chuck.

"Not anymore," she said. "Now it's the Rotunda."

"I get it," he said. "There's the dollhouse."

On the first Sunday evening in April, a month after Toonie's murder, Chuck kissed her. They had gotten into a habit of meeting in the kitchen just before bedtime: She'd heat up milk for hot chocolate and they'd talk about the day, or sometimes about other stuff like why he stopped writing that nonfiction book and what it had been like to walk all the way from San Diego to Truth or Consequences. They didn't talk about the murders—there hadn't been any more since Donatella Ng—although they often joked about X. One night after he washed up the mugs he stood drying his hands on the dish towel and folding it much more neatly than necessary and he said, "I'd like to kiss you now."

Carla was caught so far off-guard she laughed. She almost said something stupid like "Thanks for sharing" or "No kidding" but stopped herself. He wasn't kidding. He was waiting and she didn't know what to say.

He cleared his throat; he was looking at her with this odd mix of kindness and confusion. "I'm asking," he said. "You can say no."

She couldn't say anything. She felt . . . not frozen but *stopped,* like a clock.

He nodded. "Hey, kid, no worries. Good night. See you in—"

"How?" *How?* What was wrong with her?

"How what?"

"Who knows? I don't know. Don't pay any attention to—"

"How would I kiss you?"

Carla burst out laughing. "See, I've got pseudobulbar affect, it just pops out every now and—"

"I was thinking of doing it like this." Chuck cupped her head in his warm, gentle hands and kissed her, just like that, just like it was the most normal and beautiful thing. She leaned in and breathed him through his shirt. She couldn't look at him right now.

"Are you all right?"

Carla nodded.

He uncupped her head and ruffled her hair. "I'm going to bed now."

Carla looked up at him. "Do it again," she said.

He did.

After a time he asked, "Should we stop?"

"For now," she said.

Carla had heard the expression "walking on air"—had even trained to seem to do this when the script called for it—but she had never experienced it before. It was a real physical thing: She felt like a helium balloon. All the way to her bedroom, her feet never once touched the floor.

After that night they kissed a lot, at least once a day, but that was all. He seemed to understand this was all she had right now. When she was alone, she was having feelings about him that she recognized as sexual—sensations she had not experienced since she was twelve years old. They frightened her. For the first time ever, she missed Toonie Garabedian. Finally she was ready to talk about this, and she couldn't. At night, waiting for sleep, she began rehearsing the way she would tell him about everything, the perv Hoving and everything, like she used to rehearse telling Amy, but she always fell asleep midway through. Still, there was no rush; he made that plain.

They spent less and less time at the Birdhouse. Tiffany ran the place—collected the money, dealt with complaints, which didn't usually crop up anyway—and Carla had for the moment given up on writing. They went to the Zoo at least once a week and hung out a lot at jazz clubs. Chuck loved jazz. Carla hated it and didn't pretend not to, but she did pretend to be interested. After a couple of weeks she started not to hate it, and by Cinco de Mayo they were regulars at Rosie's and Dizzy's and the Turf. She still didn't enjoy the music itself all that much, but watching the musicians listen to one another was exciting. It was like her old improv classes, where you were constantly reminded to be present in the moment, except these people didn't need reminding.

She tried to explain the difference to Chuck. "I think it's ego. Ego has everything to do with acting. I don't mean it's all there is, but you have to want people looking and listening to you. You have to need it, to be the center, all eyes upon you. These people"—she pointed at the trio playing "Blackbird"—"they need us here to pay the rent, and they enjoy performing, but if they could do it all by themselves they'd be just as happy. They're so *happy*." The bass player dropped in a snippet of melody from a different song, "Bird on the Wire," and just like that the keyboard guy picked it up and tossed it back and they batted it around, smiling. "Look at that. If I could just do that."

"If you could just do that, what?"

"I don't know." She drained her Diet Coke. He was looking at her the way he always did—as though she were a person of value. He almost made her believe it. "You can't kiss me in here. It wouldn't be seemly."

Chuck laughed. "That's an Amy word."

"Yes, it is."

"Do you miss it? Acting?"

"I don't know. I miss the improvs, I guess. I never got paid for them, but I loved doing them in class. I was pretty good at it. You know, Amy says I could use what I know about improvs in my writing, but I'm not sure how that would work."

Chuck listened for a while. He said the keyboard guy was playing the melody upside down and it fit anyway, which was crazy. "How about teaching it? Could you do that?"

"You mean teach how to do improvs? I suppose so, but why

would anybody go for that? Picture Syl Reyes playing 'What's in the Box.'"

"You could teach something like 'Improvs for Writers.' Or 'Dialogue through Improv.'"

"Where? UC Extension? Dream on."

"At the Point. You could offer it for an extra fee."

Carla sat back. "What are you suggesting? I'm no teacher. I'm not a writer, either. That's my whole problem. I've got no business—"

"You're an actor who's trying to write and it's making you miserable. Am I wrong? I'm just suggesting you take what you have and see how it might connect with writing. Maybe it will, maybe not, but I'll bet a lot of the Pointers would sign up."

"You're insane." This idea confused her. She began to imagine connecting what she knew about improvs to the writing of dialogue; she could probably come up with a bunch of cool exercises to loosen people up, silly ones, like the ones she used to do for Old Sally Gee. What she couldn't imagine was being a teacher. A teacher was like Amy, an authority. Carla wasn't even her own authority, let alone anybody else's.

"I couldn't do it alone. I can get up in front of crowds and make a spectacle of myself, but I can't be *in charge*. Chuck, I know me. If I gave them an assignment, like 'Do Adverbs,' it'd sound like a lame suggestion, like 'Do Adverbs, if you feel like it.' Do you know what I mean? I'd need somebody to make them pay attention. Make them show up and do what I tell them."

Chuck grinned and waggled his eyebrows. "Wouldn't it be miraculous if you knew somebody who was willing to do that?"

"Are you serious?"

The band wrapped up "Blackbird" and asked for requests. Somebody yelled "Fly Me to the Moon," and the band pretended not to hear. Chuck raised his hand and shouted "Lean on Me." They heard him. So did Carla.

By the time they got back to the Birdhouse, Carla was revved. "I can do the classes in the Rotunda," she said. "It's perfect. I can use the dollhouse!" She grabbed his hand and pulled him into the room to show him.

Except it was all horrible. Somehow, sometime, somebody, either earlier that day or yesterday—she couldn't remember the last time she'd dropped in here—had taken it over. In the center of the Rotunda were TV cameras—*two* of the nasty things—and lighting and sound equipment, booms and mikes, and a huge hideous snarl of wires. Carla screamed, "What have they done with my dollhouse?"

"It's back here behind these screens." Chuck was standing on the far side of the room peering behind some Japanese-looking room dividers. "It's okay, they didn't hurt it."

The sofas and chairs had been moved all around, so that two chairs sat right in front of one of the big curved windows, sort of facing each other. And the two author portraits on either side had been replaced with full-length pictures of John X. Cousins and Misha Bernard.

"Amy's missing!!"

"What?"

"What have they done with Amy? They swiped her picture! I'm going to kill somebody."

Chuck rummaged behind the screens. "She's back here with Edith Sitwell. They're unharmed."

"Are you sure they didn't hurt the dollhouse?"

"I don't see anything wrong with it."

Carla ran back and looked through every room in the house. It was all in order. "I'm calling Tiffany." She took out her phone.

"Hey, it's almost midnight. You're right to be upset, but you can ask her tomorrow."

"No way."

"Doesn't she still live in her father's house? You're going to wake him up."

Tiffany answered. "Carla, what's up?" She sounded like she'd just run up a flight of stairs. "Are you all right?"

"I'm standing in the Rotunda. My Rotunda. What used to be my Rotunda. Which is now a television studio. Imagine my surprise."

"Carla, take a breath," said Tiffany. "I'd have told you about it but you haven't been around."

"Told me what?"

"John is using the space—"

"I can see that!"

"—for the Writing Guru series."

"The hell he is!"

"Not the whole series! Just the first couple of—"

"He can rent the space somewhere else."

"Yes, but that would cost a lot of money, and this space isn't being used at the moment."

"So what? The space belongs to me. Remember?"

"Look. Even if we wanted to clear it out tomorrow, we couldn't. You have to be reasonable, Carla. That's a lot of equipment, and we've hired—"

"Who is 'we'? Does Harry know about this? Because if he doesn't, he will tomorrow." Carla was furious but at the same time stunned by the sound of her own voice. She sounded like an adult woman. A seriously pissed-off adult woman.

"Carla? Carla, hold on just a minute. I'll be right back."

Tiffany must have closed her hand over the receiver because Carla could hear what sounded like a long and muffled conversation with her dad. Carla remembered now that he had some kind of serious heart condition. "You were right," she said to Chuck, "I shouldn't have called. Her dad's been in the hospital—"

"Carla," said Tiffany, "I can straighten the whole thing out—just—" There was the sound of a dropped phone and then Tiffany

whispering "Stop it!" and then, "Sorry about that. We can fix this."
She dropped the phone again and got back online, swearing and
giggling. "Listen, I'll call John first thing tomorrow and we'll figure
something out. Don't worry."

"I wasn't worried," said Carla. "I was ticked off. So you'll get
that stuff out of there? And put it back the way it was?"

"Promise," said Tiffany.

"Tell your dad I'm sorry."

"What? Dad's in the—I'll do that!"

Carla said goodbye and sank onto a hassock. "She must have a
great relationship with her dad."

"Why?"

"Because he's got a bad heart and here I woke him up in the
middle of the night and he was clowning around with her. He's
gotta be a real sport. They were even laughing."

Chuck was inspecting the cameras. "Have you met her father?"

"No, but I know a lot about him. Her mom left when she was a
kid, and he raised her. He's a big reader—a retired librarian. Now
I feel like a jerk. What is it?" Chuck looked preoccupied. "What
are you thinking?"

He kissed her on the forehead. "Nothing that can't wait. I've
got an early morning. Get some sleep. This will all work out."

She was so worked up, first about the idea of teaching, and then
by the gross stuff they'd done to the Rotunda, that she figured
she'd have a hard time sleeping. And she did, but not because of all
the excitement. She closed her eyes and lay still, thinking about her
old improvs, the best ones, and wondering which she'd try in the
first class, if there was a first class. Telephones were great props, she
could start there. She remembered a nice one she had done with
Holman Bellavance—they were the only kids in that class, and
they just wowed the adults. HB was supposed to be in a closet hiding from a serial killer and he dialed 411 by mistake instead of 911,
and Carla was a city directory robot. She couldn't remember much
of it—just HB whispering hysterically about serial murder and

Carla demanding the Syrian area code, and everyone was laughing, but HB and Carla were troupers, they didn't break up.

Not like Tiffany. Tiffany had been breaking up on the phone, laughing when she wasn't supposed to.

She hadn't been fooling around with her *dad*.

Carla almost went to Chuck's room, but he needed his rest, and anyway, he already knew. *Have you met her father?* Sometimes she wondered what he saw in her, really. She didn't doubt his feelings for her, but his patience might run out. How long would it take her to grow up? How could she be that naïve? She wasn't a kid anymore. Of course Tiffany was sleeping with X. Of course he was using her, and it had something to do with the Point, and tomorrow Carla would have to call Harry B.

She opened her laptop to look for the latest on X so when she talked to Harry she wouldn't sound totally clueless. She googled "John X. Cousins + La Jolla" and some news links appeared, but they all had "John X. Cousins" crossed out. Which would have been comforting, but the La Jolla news story was not. Two more women were missing.

CHAPTER SEVENTEEN

Amy

Friday, April 30

After a week of nagging Amy and a month of negotiations with the California corrections people, Harry secured an appointment with Edna Wentworth. He was so excited when he called Amy with the news. You couldn't just drop in at the California Institution for Women at Chino on a whim, he said: Amy had had to be *vetted*. She could have asked him what exactly that had entailed but decided not to.

She wanted to drive up alone, since Chino was only two hours north of Escondido so she wouldn't have to go anywhere near L.A. traffic, but Harry said he had to be there for procedure. His presence was required for some arcane required legal reason. "Besides," he said, "I know the ropes, and you don't." While Amy did not enjoy driving, she preferred it to being driven. She tried to remember the last time she'd been in a car with a man; there was an intimacy about that prospect that put her off. Harry was a nice guy, and he probably had entertaining stories to tell, but still she dreaded sharing the space.

It turned out she needn't have worried about social unease, because he drove like a maniac. All during the trip, which was supposed to take two hours but didn't come close, Harry careened through slower traffic on the 15 like an ambulance driver whose cargo had seconds to live, which Amy was afraid might well be the case. She finally lost control of herself and stomped on her non-existent passenger-side brake pedal as they zigged past a looming semi. "No sweat," he said. "I've got a Python"—he tapped on an ominous black appliance sitting on his dashboard—"and backup Ghost Watch."

"Harry," she said, "don't take this the wrong way, but if you don't slow down I'm going to make a citizen's arrest."

"You could do that," he said, slowing to an 80-mph crawl. "Technically you'd need to inform me that I'm under arrest, then give the reason for the arrest and express your authority for making the arrest. Also, unless it's absolutely necessary, you should avoid the use of force."

"I'll do my best."

"Because you could be subject to criminal charges such as assault and battery and false imprisonment."

"What is a Python?"

"You don't want to know."

As planned, they got to the sprawling prison facility an hour ahead of their appointment because there were forms to fill out and they had to be searched for contraband. "Don't worry," Harry said, as they approached an innocuous-looking building that reminded Amy of the Portland, Maine armory, except this was gray stone instead of red brick. "All you have to take off is your coat and shoes."

"My shoes?"

"Plus there's a metal detector. No biggie."

"You do this a lot?"

"Used to."

Amy had been moody ever since she let Harry browbeat her into this, but she had to admit to a certain curiosity about the place. The personnel behind the welcome counter seemed cheerful enough. Some of them wore jumpsuits. One of them called her "honey."

While Harry filled out forms and arranged for passes for them both, Amy read the visitor rules posted on the wall. There were thirty-two of them, a full third about forbidden attire. Camouflage was out of the question unless you were in the army. "Harry, why can't we wear forest green pants and tan shirts?"

"So you won't be confused with one of the inmates during a violent uprising."

They entered a long echoing hall furnished with round tables and chairs. Along the green walls were candy and soda machines and a few guards, all female, only one of them armed. Across the room, couples, friends, and families united around the tables. Some woman's little girl was having a birthday. Amy had anticipated a spectacle of human misery, but the scene was not appreciably sadder than one you'd see at a Denny's.

They'd been sitting silent for fifteen minutes when Amy said, "Harry, she's not going to show up. The only reason she agreed to the meeting was to mess with us. With me."

"It takes a while," Harry said. "She has to go through a bunch of stuff too. She's coming."

"Remember: *You* agreed to do the talking. I'm not going to say one word unless I have to. We said it all the night she tried to kill me."

"Waylon Jennings, right?"

"You're hilarious, Harry."

When Edna Wentworth entered the room, in forest green pants and a tan shirt, a young guard took her arm and escorted her to their table. The guard was attentive, respectful. Edna was somebody here.

She was also much older now, even though it had been only a few years since Amy'd last seen her. Edna was one of those granite women: strong, sharp, self-possessed. Now she owned her age, which must be at least eighty. Her white hair was clipped short; her glasses, prison-issue, were outsized for her face; and she moved with effort. Still, she had the same self-possession that had enabled her to visit mayhem on Amy's last workshop while maintaining the unquestioning trust of everyone. Including Amy. Especially Amy.

"Thank you, Corina," she said to the guard as she took her seat. "I'll be fine now." Corina smiled warmly at her and pointedly not at Harry and Amy, and left them.

Edna shook hands with Harry, then regarded Amy for a long minute. "You've lost weight," she said.

Amy, maintaining eye contact, said nothing.

"Are you still teaching?"

To continue saying nothing would be rude. "Not for some time."

"Let me guess. Not since our last class?"

Amy said nothing.

"So sorry about that." Edna grinned.

This grin was so abrupt, so extreme, that Amy blinked. That this woman had this easily provoked a visible physical response was infuriating. "Don't be," Amy said, her voice low. "The group is carrying on without me, and quite effectively, too. I have time now to write again."

"How wonderful, for all of us." The grin was wider. Edna had not lost her teeth. She probably had all thirty-two originals. Her canines looked like icicles.

"And how is *your* writing coming along, Edna?"

Harry gave Amy a look of mild confusion.

"I'm running a fiction workshop here. My third. There's a waiting list."

Of course she was. "What's it like? Are they productive? Are they learning from you?"

"They all have stories to tell. Unfortunately, it's mostly the same story. I don't know if they're learning anything, but they enjoy the attention. These women, most of them, grew up without much of that. I assign outside reading, by the way. You never did that. Why not?"

"I've never seen the point. Does it help them?"

"Probably not. They all want to write memoir."

Harry cleared his throat.

Amy ignored him. "What stories do you have them read?"

"Well, there was one of your recent ones, that bus plunge story in *The Paris Review*."

"You get *The Paris Review* here?"

"Secondhand copies, sure. They hated the story. They said it was garbage." No grin this time. Edna was, like most people, complicated. "Same thing with Updike and Munro and Cheever. They roll their eyes."

Amy thought a minute. "Try O. Henry. Try de Maupassant, 'The Necklace.' Dickens."

"Tried Dickens first. They whined that the words were too big."

"Make them read 'Captain Murderer.' It's short, gruesome, and funny. At the very least it will give them something to think about."

"'Captain Murderer,'" said Edna, wistfully. "I'm not sure the warden would let me. The title might alarm the censors. We have quite a few murderers here."

"Are there any in your class?"

"Just one." Again the jack-o'-lantern grin.

"Stop it." Amy was quickly furious. Here they'd been talking civilly, collegially, then the woman pulls this Hannibal Lecter baloney. "It's beneath you."

"You're right," said Edna, after a pause. "I guess you just bring out the worst in me."

"Ladies," said Harry.

Amy and Edna glared at Harry.

"Hey! Look, I like Old Home Week as much as the next guy, but we'll run out of time, and I'm here—we're here—to discuss one subject—"

"I already have a lawyer."

"That's not—"

"In fact, the Innocence Project is looking into my case." Edna had the grace to look uncomfortable. "I know it's ludicrous, but they're nice people and I don't have the heart to disabuse them. I have a soft spot for the young."

Did this mean Edna was penitent? Amy found that hard to believe.

"They visit me every couple of months. A breath of fresh air. Not a cliché. Literally. They smell of fresh air."

"Do we?"

"You need to get out more."

Why had Edna okayed this visit? Amy had assumed it was Harry's doing, that he'd tempted her somehow, maybe with a bump in privileges or some cell improvements. Amy had no idea how this sort of thing was done, but Harry would know. Edna was ignoring him, and Harry was getting peeved.

"I know people in the Project," said Harry. "Let me know if there's anything—"

Edna flicked a hand in his direction as though dismissing a footman. "I'll die in this place. You know it and I know it, and to be honest, I'm fine with it. There are certain . . . perks." She cast Amy a look, opaque in its meaning, but deliberate nonetheless.

Good for you, thought Amy. You're where you belong. Edna, even at her most baleful, had always been a full-fledged adult. "Edna, would you mind explaining why you agreed to—"

"John X. Cousins!" Harry's announcement was so loud that everyone in the hall, including the birthday child, turned toward their table.

He had Edna's attention now. She looked profoundly amused.

"Sorry!" Harry held his hands up, apologizing to the room. "Sorry, but we didn't come all the way up here just to shoot the breeze."

"We're not shooting anything," said Edna. "We're talking shop."

"Cousins has visited you multiple times—"

"Yes, and what's that to you? Surely you're not"—she stared at Amy—"*friends* with this man?"

"Hardly."

"We are concerned," said Harry, "that he might have certain designs on Inspiration Point."

"What in god's name is Inspiration Point? A mountaintop church? Is Amy establishing a cult?" Edna laughed. "Now there's a thought."

"Harry," said Amy, "obviously she has no idea about—"

"We can't be sure."

"I'm right here," said Edna, clearly enjoying herself.

"Harry, why don't we just ask Edna what the visits are for. If she wants to, she'll explain, and if not, it's really not our business anyway—"

"What happened to 'I'm not going to say one word'?"

"Vampires!" said Edna, to Harry. "I've been sitting here trying to remember the story you wrote for our class. It was about vampires in Central Park, wasn't it? Are you still writing, Harry? Still chasing the dream?"

"Edna, listen to me. Inspiration Point is a company conceived, created, and owned by Carla Karolak. Carla and her company are clients of mine. If you have access to the internet in the library here, and you should, you can look it up. It's very successful, which means the company is worth serious money. My concern today was that Cousins was hoping to use you in some way to grab the company for himself."

Edna heard him out, yawned, apologized for the yawn, and said, "I'm afraid that business dealings have never meant a thing to me. For all I know, you're right about his motives, but he hasn't mentioned this Inspiration outfit, and I don't see how I could possibly be of use to him."

Harry sighed and slapped his palms on the table. "Edna, forgive the intrusion. Amy, I'm sorry I dragged you up here. You were right, this was pointless."

Amy rested a calming hand on his arm. "Edna, what do you know about Cousins?"

"Pompous fool. Thinks he's going to get rich writing about people like me. Silly man has no idea how many other would-be millionaires have traipsed in here to talk to me, and not just me. There are quite a few celebrities in this place, you know. I killed only two people. I'm minor-league."

"Are you trusting him with your story?" asked Amy.

Harry leaned forward. "If you have any interest in getting out of here, the last thing you should do is share details of your crimes with this man."

"In the first place," said Edna, "as I've told you, I have no interest in leaving. And even if I did, I wouldn't share a *lifeboat* with this person. *He* is trusting *me*."

"To tell the truth?"

"Yes. I have spun him a cliché-ridden backstory that explains in lurid detail how I came to such a sorry pass. Orphaned at ten, raised by survivalists, lost the love of my life at Khe Sanh, labored for decades in a paper cup factory, all the while penning novel after novel, constantly honing my craft—"

"And he believes you?"

"The man believes in himself. He'll believe anything."

"So what you're saying," said Harry, "is that the focus isn't on the crimes themselves but on the, as you say, 'sorry pass'?"

"Well, he does ask a fair number of questions about some people. You, particularly." She nodded at Amy. "Also, that chubby creature who brained me with the wine bottle. Your number one fan. Who, I now learn, is a gifted business tycoon."

Amy sat up straight. "Carla? What does he want to know about Carla?"

"Everything I know about her history. Which is nothing. I was planning to make up a backstory for her, but he stopped asking about her a few weeks ago. He still asks about you." Again she gave Amy that guarded look.

"What do you mean?" asked Harry.

"He just tries to get me going about you. He has this idea that you and I are archenemies."

"I can't imagine why," said Amy.

Harry shook his head in frustration. "What the hell is he up to?"

"Also," said Edna. She stopped.

"Also what?"

Edna sighed. "It's embarrassing. He is apparently doing some TED Talk thing?"

"He wishes it was a TED Talk," said Harry. "It's a so-called master class in writing he plans to flog on the Web. Get a million followers. Become a media sensation. Vlad the Influencer."

"Whatever," said Edna. "He wants to interview me on that show. As a writer, I mean. An imprisoned writer."

"And you'd agree to this, why?" Amy pictured X and Edna sharing writing tips against a wall of rioting ferns.

"I've told him I might consider it if I can read something of my own. If I can be the only writer on that particular episode and he soft-pedals the 'imprisoned' part. If he backs off and just lets me read."

It never ends, thought Amy. "So you're not just teaching. You're still writing."

"Cousins started off by claiming he could get one of my stories published in some collection of 'inmate fiction.' I could 'headline' it! That was his first come-on. The man takes me for an idiot. As if that kind of publication would mean a damn thing to me."

Amy nodded. Cousins was a rotten judge of character, patronizing a woman like Edna Wentworth.

"I think I'm . . . I think I'm finally getting it right." Her eyes met Amy's. "You said I wrote polemics, not fiction."

"I did? That doesn't sound like me. I mean, I definitely thought it, but I wouldn't—"

"You said it the night I tried to kill you."

"Waylon Jennings," said Harry to Amy. "I'm telling you."

"You were right," said Edna. "You were dead-on. Anyway, I think I may have gotten past that. I don't have any more *messages*. The writing I'm doing here . . . it's different now. Or else I'm deluded. Which is certainly possible. I honestly don't know." Edna looked down at the table, up at the ceiling, everywhere but at Amy.

The three were silent for a long minute. Then Amy said, "Do you still have my address?"

Edna nodded, eyes closed.

"What?" said Harry.

"Feel free," said Amy.

"Feel free to what?" said Harry.

Edna slowly got to her feet. Amy stood too. They shook hands. "Thank you," said Edna.

"No need," said Amy.

Corina the Guard led her from the hall.

"What just happened?"

"Let's go home, Harry."

Halfway back home, Harry finally spoke. "Why does she have your address?"

"She might just have saved it, but anyway, I'm in the book."

"What book?"

"The phone book."

"There's no such thing as a phone book."

"The virtual phone book. The point is, anybody can find out where I live. I have a listed phone."

"Why?"

"Why not? I'm not an atomic spy. There's no such thing as privacy anymore, Harry. Whatever we once had, we gave it up after 9/11."

Ten miles on, he said, "So, you agreed to read her fiction? That's what you agreed to?"

"Yes."

"You're really going to do that? Like she's still in your workshop?"

"Well, technically, the workshop never finished, because of the, you know, sorry pass."

"So you figure you owe her one more critique? Is that it?"

"Maybe. Doesn't matter. By the way, thank you for not speeding. This is much more enjoyable than the ride up."

"Amy, do you believe what she told us about X? You don't think she's hiding something about him from us?"

"I believe her."

"I do too. So, as far as we know, all he's up to is the guru thing." Ten miles later, he said, "I'm still not convinced."

"At least he stopped asking her about Carla. That was the only bit that worried me."

"Yes. Don't you wonder why he stopped?"

"You have a suspicious mind, Harry."

So did Amy, but that night, waiting for sleep, she found herself thinking about Edna, as she had been. Edna's story, the one she had submitted to the workshop years ago, was entitled "The Good Woman." Amy remembered it vividly because it was one of the better student stories she had read. It failed when it turned preachy, but before that turn Edna had surgically dissected its title characters (there was more than one candidate), as well as its theme, in dialogue and description. Edna was a skilled writer and a serious person. How did she live with what she had done? Surely she would use it in her fiction, but how? We make up stories, Amy knew, to make sense of reality. Harry thought Amy a saint for agreeing to read it, but the truth was, she wanted to see what Edna had made of her life.

CHAPTER EIGHTEEN

Carla

Thursday, May 6

To give X and Tiffany time to clear out the Rotunda and put everything back where it belonged, Carla avoided going down there until late afternoon. She didn't want to have to deal with X. Or Tiffany, for that matter. She spent the time in Tiffany's office, looking through client files, scouring the internet for improv ideas, doodling on the legal pad on Tiffany's desk, and ignoring the Acorn of Cremains. She looked through drawers for pencils and erasers but carefully avoided opening folded-up papers and envelopes. Having guarded what little privacy she had throughout her childhood, Carla was deeply respectful of the privacy of other people. There might be messages from X in there, even love letters, ewwww, but they weren't her business.

All morning, Pointers drifted in and out, which was sort of pleasant for Carla, who didn't often interact with them. Manny Singh, the nice man whose cell she had been exploring just before she found Toonie's body, came in full of happy news about his wife, now pregnant with their seventh. Ricky Buzza stopped by to complain that his cell keycard wasn't working, and it took the two of them a half hour to figure out how to open the cell remotely. Ricky asked if Tiffany had the day off, and Carla said, "Sort of." After lunch came Mrs. Colodny, flushed and breathless, asking Carla if she'd heard "the latest."

"Not really."

Mrs. Colodny sat down on the extreme edge of the chair, poised to spring up and run in what Ma would call a New York Minute, and took a breath. "They haven't found the stripper yet, but that Bunting woman, the philosophy professor, got chopped up just like Mrs. Ng. It was just on the news. They found her on the Torrey Pines hiking trails. That's 'trails' with an s. She was all over the place! Where's Dr. Cousins? Where's Tiffany?"

"No idea," said Carla. If she sent Mrs. Colodny to the Rotunda, they might not get it cleaned up today. "Also, what are you talking about?"

"You know about the two missing women, right?"

"The high schoolers? They're okay. They were just partying."

"No, not them, the philosophy professor and the stripper!"

"Simona—"

"Simonetta!"

"Sorry, Simonetta, I hadn't heard about it." Carla, who didn't want to think about the missing kids, jotted down "the philosophy professor and the stripper" on the yellow pad. It was the kind of thing that Chuck would do something with, like a silly poem. Or an improv! *You're a philosophy professor, you're a stripper, and you're stuck in an elevator together. Go!*

"Well," said Mrs. Colodny, "there was this Professor Bunting. She taught at State. She went missing yesterday morning, never showed up for classes, and they just found her body! It was horrible!"

From hours spent as an extra reacting in TV and movie mob scenes, Carla knew there were a hundred different ways to register horrified alarm, and not one of them was displayed by Mrs.

Colodny, who looked like she'd just won the Publishers Clearing House Sweepstakes. "And the stripper?"

"Still missing, I think."

"Wrong." This from a familiar-looking woman in a sweatshirt and jeans, who walked in and said to Carla, "I have a message from John. He says they'll have to finish up tomorrow."

"The heck they will! I have plans!" Carla didn't actually have plans, but so what. "Do I know you?"

"Cindy Stokes," the woman said. "My husband was in that murder workshop."

Carla remembered now. She remembered that Mrs. Stokes tried to boss Marvy, her husband, into "spinning gold" out of the workshop murders. Marvy had been so embarrassed. "I don't want to go public with this stuff," he had whispered to Carla. "She wants us on one of those crime shows." But that had been a couple of years ago. What was Cindy Stokes doing here?

Cindy was filling in Mrs. Colodny on "the latest." Apparently the stripper's body had been found too. "Of course it's just terrible," she was saying, "but at least now people will pay attention to John."

Carla interrupted them. "Cindy, would you please go back down and tell 'John' and Tiffany to get moving?"

Cindy Stokes crossed her arms. "I work for John," she said. "I'll convey your message, but that's all I can do."

"Where did they find the stripper?" asked Mrs. Colodny. "Was she, you know, dismembered?"

"Excuse me," said Carla, standing up and walking past the two women and out the door. *I work for John.* She had to get out of there, because if she stayed she was going to say something really, really rude to Cindy Stokes.

The Rotunda wasn't cleaned up, although they had moved things around. The dollhouse was back in the center of the room, and both cameras were shoved against the wall. Those damn pictures of X and Misha had been taken down but Amy and Edith Sitwell still stood in the corner, and now, surrounding the dollhouse, were four standing quartz lamps. Those things got hot as hell. They were turned off, but how long had they been left on, and why? They could have bubbled the paint! Carla checked the outer walls to make sure this hadn't happened.

X and Tiffany were standing at the window.

"Would you mind explaining this?" Carla said.

"Sorry," said X, who clearly wasn't, "I thought Cindy explained—"

"She conveyed your message, which was not an explanation." Again came that amazing adult vibe. Carla felt six feet tall. Not happy, but still this was kind of remarkable.

"We're pretty sure we can get everything put back just as it was by midday tomorrow."

Tiffany advanced toward Carla, her expression guarded. "Remember now, I told you it would be a big job—"

"What are you doing with these lights?"

X and Tiffany looked at each other and said nothing.

"I said—"

"Carla," said X, beckoning to her, "would you please come sit down? I'd like to talk something over with you. I should have done this earlier, but the right time never—"

"Do I need to call Harry B.?" Siccing her lawyer on X had never before occurred to her. Another adult sign. She wished Chuck were here to see it.

"No, no. I mean, eventually, maybe, but not now. Please sit."

They both ushered her into the largest chair, like it was some bogus throne, and then sat on either side, leaning toward her. "As you know," said X, "I am in the process of filming my Writing Guru webinars—"

"Which has what to do with klieg lights on my dollhouse?"

"They're hardly klieg lights—"

"Let him explain," said Tiffany.

"I'm still working on the series, but the recent local murders have opened up an entirely new area for me. My first plan was to put together a freestanding unsolved murder piece—you know, the likely serial killer angle, and the fact that investigations are ongoing. Two of the most popular streaming true-crime series have expressed a great deal of interest."

"You got a title yet? How about 'The Ill Wind'?"

"Ha ha," said X. "The point is, I've had another idea, and it involves this house. And you, hopefully." He leaned back in his chair for a second to give her a second to process this.

When she saw he was waiting for some response from her, she said, "And?" Because what else was there to say? Whatever his proposal was, she was going to shoot it down, so there was no point in drawing out the explanation.

"I understand," said X, in that deep smoky register that some actors use when they're supposed to be seductive. He was leaning in close. He rested his hand on her actual knee.

Carla flashed on X and Tiffany rolling around in bed doing Hollywood sex, the lighting and the shadows just so, their bodies nude but not naked. Carla's mouth suddenly watered. She wanted to spit.

"Carla, I understand that—"

"Excuse me, would you please back off? I can hear you just fine if you sit up straight."

"Of course," he said. His hand slithered off her knee. "I understand that you and your mother shared this house for some time before Mrs. Massengill's death."

Tiffany had the grace to look down, avoiding Carla's stare. Tiffany had told this creep all about her. Her mother, the Birdhouse, hell, probably her whole miserable Hollywood childhood. Thank god Carla never told Tiffany about the Squirrel Hoving. This betrayal overwhelmed Carla. Tiffany wasn't her best friend, but she was—had been—a friend, a trusted one.

"And your point," Carla asked, "is what?"

"Well, there have been more than one murder involving this house. Dr. Garabedian, of course, but this house was home to a workshop in which two of its members were murdered. One of them in this very room."

Carla closed her eyes and held herself still. She could avoid yelling if she didn't have to look at them. "Continue," she said.

"And I understand that some weeks ago you had what may have been a paranormal experience here."

"Carla," said Tiffany, "I hope you don't mind that I mentioned it to John. You never said not to."

Because it never occurred to me that you would. Carla didn't say this aloud.

"There's a certain—for lack of a better expression—'vibe' about this house," said X. "Everyone senses it."

Carla was taking deep, calming breaths, the sort you took to ward off stage fright. Which she had never experienced, and her concern here wasn't stage fright, it was being overcome by an irresistible impulse to hit somebody.

"You sense it too, Carla. Probably more strongly than anyone—"

"I need you to just be quiet for a minute. Can you do that?"

They shut up.

Finally Carla opened her eyes. "So you want to do some haunted-house spectacular shit show."

"Well, I wouldn't put it that way—"

"Of course *you* would narrate it. You've got the voice. Let's see. Start off with a helicopter shot of La Jolla, the jewel of San Diego, nestled in the blahdeeblah, home to the rich and buff, slo-mo shots of sea lions and beach bodies, and then zoom in on this strange house shaped just like a bird on the wing, and then you'd toss around a lot of snapshots of dead women and my mother and then the workshop people and me, and cheesy music, and then the house again, at night, and then the title *splats* all over it, and—CUT. Got a title yet? 'Workshop of Horror'? 'Birdhouse of Blood'?"

"You're not being fair," said Tiffany.

"You planning an episode or a whole series or what?"

Unlike Tiffany, X seemed encouraged. Carla could see the gears turning: *I could work with this little nutjob.* "I haven't decided," he said. "What do you think?"

You really don't want to know what I think. "I think you still haven't explained why my dollhouse was lit up. I know what those lamps can do."

"Well," said X. He exchanged a look with Tiffany; they appeared to agree on something. "Yesterday, we were looking at the dollhouse. I'd seen it before, of course—everyone has, it's striking—but I really looked inside it, studied it. All that amazing period detail! So many delicate touches! Even a tiny black bug in the basement wall—"

"Yes," said Tiffany, "that bug is so creepy. In a good way! Of course, not nearly as creepy as the, you know, little figures. I'd never really looked at the house before either. It's just amazing, Carla. Who built it? Where did you buy it? You never told me."

Little figures? Tiffany was creeped out by the gopher and the purple martins? Carla didn't understand Tiffany at all.

"I had this idea," said X. "It's nascent now—not fully formed yet—"

"I know what 'nascent' means."

"—but I went ahead and did the preliminaries, just in case it turned out to be a good idea."

"Are we getting to the klieg lights now?"

"Last night, after you called, I started filming."

"We were up all night!" Tiffany looked more energized than exhausted.

"We'd like to show you the footage. Want to see it? I'd appreciate your opinion."

"It's on my iPad," said Tiffany, handing it to Carla. "Just press play."

Carla took the iPad, walked all the way to the opposite wall, and sat down. They wanted to watch her watch this thing; it was bad enough they could see her from a distance. *This is a watchbird watching a watcher.* Her father used to say that. He said it was from some old cartoon. *This is a watchbird watching you.* She pressed play.

First, all around the outside of the house, close-ups of the forsythia bushes under the front porch, the red and orange azaleas along both sides of the house, and the backyard with the purple martin house and the gopher. Up close, the gopher looked fake, painted and shiny. You weren't supposed to see it this close.

Then the front door opened. They must have tied a string or something to the doorknob; you couldn't see anybody's fingertips. Harsh light spilled the length of the front hall. Here was the cherry console table and on it a tiny pewter lamp. He must have ordered it special. For a moment Carla let herself enjoy her father's work. The actual hall table had been shaped just like this one but fake, pine with cherry-colored varnish. This table, Carla's table, was carved from cherrywood. This was the real table.

Somehow the camera angled through the parlor door on the left. X must have attached something to the iPad so he could film around corners. There was the brick fireplace, the oak mantel with family pictures propped on it. Carla had always appreciated that touch, but now, just like with the gopher, the view was too close, you could see the pictures were fake, pasted in from magazines. Carla had never spent much time in the parlor; Ma kept it spiffed up for company that never came.

The camera pulled back into the hall and now to the right, the dining room, another place that held few memories, but her father had done his best with the Ethan Allen table and matching hutch, and at the table's center, just for her, he'd glued a golden bowl piled high with the smallest pearls imaginable. When the dollhouse arrived in Tarzana and Carla opened the crate, which was a huge job in itself since Ma didn't help, those pearls had escaped from their plastic bag and rolled everywhere; it had taken Carla weeks before she was sure she'd found them all.

The tour continued, through kitchen and pantry and bathroom. Tiffany called across the room, "Carla, there's a soundtrack. You should turn it up." They had certainly gone to a lot of trouble, and why? True-crime TV was all about newspaper headlines, blurry corpse photos, and oily narrators droning on about how everyone in the neighborhood knew everybody else and nobody locked their doors until the hideous death of a semi-attractive girl whose smile lit up the room. Carla had begun to relax: She resented the intrusive camera and hated those lights, but the house itself was, as always, her private safe room. Her father was here.

In the kitchen, the door to the cellar opened, and below darkness spread wide as the camera descended. Carla turned up the sound: There were amateur fake footsteps—it sounded like X or Tiffany tapping on a cardboard box—and the cellar light flicked on.

No. Carla closed her eyes at the sound. The cellar was private—the workbench, the centipede, her mother's voice calling down, this belonged to her, not for sharing with anybody but Amy, and right now she hated Tiffany for making all this possible. She waited until the footsteps came back and opened her eyes again. "What do you think?" shouted Tiffany. "Now do you see why we're so excited?" To her credit, she sounded worried. She had known better than to help him do this.

When the camera began to climb the stairs to the second floor, Carla marveled at the stair runner, Oriental just like the real one, frayed in just the same places; he must have spent hours on it. She'd never noticed that before. The camera peeked into her parents' bedroom and the guest room but didn't enter either one; thank god, this would be over in a minute. And here finally was her own room. The door was closed, which was odd. Whenever Carla stopped by the dollhouse, she spent most of her time in this room. On the soundtrack was the sound of breathing, which was both corny and unnerving. Who was doing the heavy breathing? It had to be X. What an idiot.

The door opened, and the room was wrong.

Wrinkled clothes lay on the open closet floor. Her rocking horse was knocked over on its side underneath the windowsill, and the blue and gold bedspread was pulled back, displaying rumpled sheets splashed with streaks of red.

"What have you done?" Carla yelled when she got her breath. Her voice was so loud. "What have you done to my father's house?"

"What's she talking about?" X asked Tiffany, who ran across the room to Carla and knelt down beside her.

"Carla, your father? Did your dad make this? I didn't know that! And all we did was, you know, film it and do the soundtrack, we thought—"

"What did you do to my bedroom? Fix it! PUT IT BACK! PUT IT BACK NOW!"

"Carla, please, lower your voice—"

"Put what back, Carla?" X was standing right there. If he touched her, she would kill him.

"You know what," Carla hissed.

X was quiet for a minute. "Are you telling us," he said, "that the child's bedroom is somehow different?"

Carla stood, handed the iPad to Tiffany, and hurried over to the dollhouse. There was her bedroom, door open, defiled. "Yes," she finally said, "*the child's bedroom is somehow different!* As you perfectly well know. And if you don't put everything back exactly as it was—"

"Carla, listen to me," said Tiffany. "The house *is* exactly as it was. We didn't do anything to it."

"How can you say that? You've seen it a thousand times—"

"Actually, I haven't. I mean I've admired the outside, everybody does, but I spend my time here upstairs and in the wings. I never looked inside until last night and neither did John."

"Which was remiss of me, I know," said X, "but until now my focus was solely on this house—the real house—and how I might use it, this gorgeous room especially, to—"

"I don't believe you."

"Carla," said Tiffany. "Look, you might as well know. We're— John and I are—"

"I've figured that out."

"Okay, and my point is that whenever he is here, he's with me. If the house has changed—"

"If!!"

"He couldn't have done it. Unless you think I let him do it."

Carla looked at Tiffany for a long minute. No, Tiffany wouldn't lie to her, not about this.

X dragged a chair over to the dollhouse and sat down. "Carla, have you ever heard of Frances Glessner Lee?"

Carla was doing her best to straighten out the room, hanging up the dress and coat, righting the rocking horse. She stripped the little bed, handling the sheets with great care, wondering how to get the paint out without disintegrating the delicate cloth. Her eyes filled with tears.

"She's sometimes called the Mother of Forensic Science."

"No shit."

"She studied crime scene analysis before there even was such a thing. She created painstaking dioramas of crime scenes— small rooms fashioned exactly like the rooms in which the crimes had taken place, every detail, every piece of furniture, just so—"

"And this fascinates you why?" Carla kept her back to them both.

"What occurred to me is that here, within the Birdhouse,

which, I'm sorry, *is* a crime scene, is this incredible dollhouse, somehow mimicking—"

"It's not mimicking anything. It has nothing to do with this house. You have no idea what you're talking about. My dollhouse is not a *crime scene*. My dollhouse is a *victim*."

"Of course you see it that way, but you must admit that—"

"I must admit nothing except you need to get all these damn lights and cameras and crap out of here and leave me the hell alone."

"John," said Tiffany. "John, she's right. This was a bad idea. Let's just load up the van now. We don't have to wait till tomorrow."

Carla faced the window while they wrestled with the gear, making trip after trip down to the driveway. Finally she could see, reflected in the window, the uncluttered far wall, the chairs and sofas put back where they belonged. When X and Tiffany returned, Carla told them to hang up the two pictures where they were supposed to be.

"Sure thing," said X.

She watched him. "No," she said, "Amy on the left, Edith Sitwell on the right."

When he was done, he held out his hand to her. His damn hand. "No hard feelings, I hope?"

"Let's go, John," said Tiffany.

"Harry will call you in a few days," said Carla, "to update you on your plans to turn my home into a Halloween funhouse."

"Fair enough. Carla, if you don't mind, I have just one question." He put his damn slimy hand back in his pocket. "If that's all right with you."

"Can't it wait? I'm very tired."

"I'm sure you are. And I'm so very sorry for the grief I have inadvertently caused you. That was never my intention. But I have to know: Why did the bedroom upset you so much, when you were apparently enjoying, or at least not objecting to, what you saw in the basement?"

The basement? "What are you talking about?"

"I'm talking about—well—" X looked baffled. He shrugged, palms up, casting about for words. "You know," he finally said.

"No, I don't. Please go."

"Carla," said Tiffany, "seriously. The basement—"

"Cellar," said Carla.

"The cellar is a lot more disturbing than the bedroom. You have to admit that."

"You have a problem with bugs?"

X cocked his head, narrowed his eyes. "Were you not watching when the camera moved downstairs? Wait—you weren't, were you?" He had stopped being sorry. He was *curious* now. He was looking at her like she was some kind of *subject*.

Carla sat very still while Tiffany fished the iPad out of her bag and handed it to her. "I think you need to see this," she said. "Or else come with me to the dollhouse and I'll show you—"

Carla needed to not see.

She was aware of becoming very cold; her hand shook as she forwarded past the hall and the dining room and the kitchen and then the cellar light came on and she pressed play. At the far end of the cellar, past the centipede, past the furnace, beside the workbench, the crude figure of a woman, poorly fashioned from paraffin, its eyes black dots, its wide mouth red and jagged, its painted gray hair knotted in a bun like Mrs. Bates in the fruit cellar, only this woman was standing, holding an outsized axe over the body of a smaller figure laid out on the workbench, decapitated, splashed with red paint.

"Carla?"

"Tiffany, I need to be alone now."

"I don't think that's a good idea."

"I need for you to go."

"Can we talk about this tomorrow?" Tiffany whispered.

"Just go."

Carla handed the iPad back to Tiffany and then curled up facing the window, her back to them as they left. She felt nothing but cold. After a long while the sun went down, the room went dark, and behind her waited the ruin of her father's house.

CHAPTER NINETEEN

Amy

Wednesday, May 5

Edna's story arrived by FedEx a week after Amy's visit to Chino. Amy tried to put off opening the package but was soon overcome with curiosity. It was just that workshop story; this wasn't a promising sign. Couldn't she have come up with new material? The way Edna had gone on, she was ditching polemics, newly confident, spreading her wings, but instead here she was, walled up and worrying at a failed story that had years ago collapsed at the end into a Hallmark Moment. Already Amy regretted issuing this invitation. She brought a mug of green tea out to the patio and started to read.

THE GOOD WOMAN

Alice locked the twins in the car with the windows cracked, which she knew she shouldn't do, and ran into the Thrifty for just a minute. Here was an everyday gamble: a big bottle of No More Tears on sale for $1.59 vs. your children being snatched and butchered by a roving pervert. She was in line watching the car through the plate glass doors when a tall old woman walked past, stepped off the curb in front of the car, and stood waiting to cross. She wore a blue flannel overshirt and heavy denim workpants rolled at the ankle and black with dirt at the knees and baggy seat. Her pewter gray hair was clipped short, like a man's. She wasn't really mannish, though. There was a spinsterish correctness in her spine, straight as a schoolmarm's pointer, and in the high, alert set of her head. She looked like the grandmother of all schoolteachers and would have looked that in a sarong or stark naked. A no-nonsense old dame. Familiar, too. Alice knew her from somewhere. The old woman turned her head and stared for a long moment into Alice's car, then crossed the street.

As Alice followed her progress, the image of a roadside mailbox popped into her mind, and she knew who the woman was. She lived in the little old green house on the hill, and her name was Hestevold.

Unlocking the car door, Alice was greeted by screams and howls of outrage. Meg, not a bully by nature, was slapping her brother on the arm. "Dougie did something horrible," she said. "He called that lady dirty names! He said the F-word!"

Dougie giggled defiantly, like any kid with his back to the wall. "Poopy-pants," he croaked, flopping around in the backseat, his features reddened and gross. "Old Mrs. Poop Poop Poopie!" Alice smacked him hard and drove home at unsafe speed, with Meg crying, humiliated, as though she had been slapped and Dougie too stunned to make a sound. Her rage had come out of nowhere, it was outsized, but for now could not be helped. She would figure out the reason for it later. The poopy-pants woman was a *neighbor.* When they got home she pulled him into the kitchen and, watching herself from a godlike distance, squirted dishwashing detergent into his mouth and made him rinse and spit. Charlie got home from work and found them like this. "Jesus, Alice," he said, but she turned on him a look so savage that he backed off, while his tiny son spat and spat and spat.

The Hestevold house was the neighborhood castle. This according to Charlie, who wanted the kids to grow their minds by living as long as possible in a magical world. Dougie loved his father's stories; Meg adored her dad but was, like her mother, a born skeptic. "How can it be a castle?" Meg would ask. "Castles are big. The green house isn't any bigger than ours," and Charlie would go on about the turret on the green house, and how turrets meant a castle, no question, which was in Alice's opinion ridiculous. A turret on a small wooden house was just bad design. It squatted on the exact center of the roof like a toad. On weekends in spring and summer Charlie and Alice would sometimes spot the Hestevold woman working her garden. Wide beds of flowering perennials lined the tiered stone walk and the house itself was ringed with creamy white and apricot rhododendron. "The woman's a weeding fanatic," Charlie would say, and "I wish I had half her spirit," and "Shouldn't we have a garden?"

The next morning, Sunday, Alice marched Dougie up the hill to the green house and rang the bell. From the porch you could look out over the whole block. From up here, you could see Alice's house, front and back. From up here, in fact, you had a front-row seat. The door opened; the old woman stepped out onto the porch and regarded them with no expression. Dougie was purring with fear. "Mrs. Hestevold," said Alice.

"Miss Hestevold," said the old woman.

"Miss Hestevold, my son has something he wants to tell you."

Miss Hestevold nodded. Up close she was remarkably ugly. The lower half of her face was long and equine, not exactly deformed but still so extreme that it was hard not to stare, and there was white down on her chin and upper lip. She had the large brown eyes of a once pretty woman, which cruelly heightened her ugliness. She had never been pretty. Alice doubted that she had even been plain. Miss Hestevold regarded Dougie now with a kind of brutal reserve.

Dougie, wide eyes fixed on the old lady's beard, cried sound-lessly, openmouthed. Alice squeezed his hand. He was so young, and he lived so purely in each moment. The immediate and the eternal were one and the same to him and now he twisted in a universe of shame without limit or perspective. Willing him strength, Alice squeezed as softly as she could but said nothing, and neither did Miss Hestevold. Finally he got it out. "I'm sorry, lady," he said. "I didn't mean it." Then he could cry out loud. The tension left his body and he hung his head, and Alice moved be-hind him, her hands gentle on his shoulders. She smiled at Miss Hestevold, who did not smile back.

"Why are you sorry?" Miss Hestevold asked her son.

Dougie looked up. "Because," he said. Miss Hestevold stared. "Because I called you names." Miss Hestevold waited. "Because I called you 'poopy-pants' and—" Dougie started crying again.

"But why," asked Miss Hestevold, "are you sorry for that?"

Why, you vicious old bat. "He's sorry," Alice said, "because he was rude to you and used bad language. He knows better."

Miss Hestevold did not look away from Dougie. "Is that why you're sorry?"

Dougie nodded. "It's wrong to say bad words."

Miss Hestevold nodded too, in his solemn rhythm. "Why is it wrong?"

Alice drew her son back against her body. Dougie twisted his head around and looked up at her in dazed inquiry. "Because it just is," Alice said.

"Because it just is," said Dougie.

Alice opened her mouth to say goodbye, but the old woman sighed and pinned her with disgust, a look that transformed Alice into a powerless child as unworthy as her son. "It's just wrong! What do you want him to say?" She shamed herself with her own whining voice.

Miss Hestevold knelt down then in front of Dougie and smiled at him and took his hands in her own. "Shall I tell you why?" she asked him. Dougie nodded in just the way he would nod to Big Bird on TV. Though she couldn't see his face, Alice could picture it, mesmerized by the old woman's sudden kind attention. "Because when you call people nasty names, even in fun, you often hurt them. Not always. For instance you did not hurt me. But this is the risk you run. Of making someone else feel foolish, ugly, or sad. Of causing pain without meaning to."

Alice had an absurd impulse to raise her hand and yell, "I knew that!" Obviously Miss Hestevold thought she had Alice's number: Alice was yet another shallow young person who didn't know manners from morals. Alice hated to be misunderstood.

"Do you know what 'dignity' means?" asked Miss Hestevold. Dougie shook his head. "Well, you don't have to know. Just remember this: It is always wrong to treat other people as though they were toys. It is always terribly wrong to be cruel. Do you understand now?" Dougie nodded slowly. She stroked back his shiny hair with a strong liver-spotted hand. "It was nice meeting you," she said.

Dougie asked Alice then if he could go and play. He ran half-way down the steps, then turned and called up to Miss Hestevold. "I'm five," he said. "I live in that house there."

"I know," said Miss Hestevold, waving.

"It was nice meeting you," he said, then fled, running flat out and wild, exhilarated by joy and fear, just like the way he ran from Charlie when Charlie was the Jabberwock.

"He likes you," said Alice. Miss Hestevold laughed, and not in a friendly way. Miss Hestevold didn't like her one bit. "Look." Alice backed down one step. "If you had kids, you'd know. He didn't have a clue what you were talking about. Just because a kid nods his head don't think he understands you. Five is too young for a lecture on the foundations of ethics." Behind Miss Hestevold's neutral expression, curled in her long blinkless stare, lay a contempt so plain and so personal that it weakened Alice at the knees. Miss Hestevold didn't just despise Alice's *type;* she despised

Alice. Why? Alice, who had never to her knowledge been despised, raised her voice. "First you get them to behave. When they're older there's plenty of time to explain why. Five is not the age of reason."

Miss Hestevold slouched hip-first into the doorframe with sudden, bizarre informality, expressing her opinion of Alice openly now, with every line of her body. "What is the age of reason, Mrs. Earnshaw?"

Right then Alice saw the New Horizon Cable Company van as clearly as if it were actually reflected in the old brown eyes. Parked across the street smack in front of Alice's door every Thursday from one to one-thirty. She sweated, cold as a dreamer nude in front of school assembly. Her knees almost buckled. She opened her mouth. "Good day to you," she said like somebody in an old play, and turned without waiting, and descended the hill without running, though only with great effort. Almost home, she stopped and whirled around and yelled, "I'm a good mother!" But already Miss Hestevold had disappeared behind her door.

Alice Earnshaw had never imagined wanting any man but Charlie. Besides, adultery was trashy, and only trashy people did trashy things. Besides, if you had kids you had no right to endanger your marriage. Right is right, she once told a confessing friend, wrong is wrong, and that's all there is to it.

Then she got cable. The cable installer had the name, Calvin Frechette, and demeanor of a big dolt, and an extraordinarily cherubic face. As he explained how to operate the unit, each time she interrupted his spiel with a question he had to go back to the beginning and start over. She listened carefully so she could imitate him for Charlie later. Lennie in *Of Mice and Men*, she would tell him. Frechette demonstrated the remote control, flipping through three hundred channels, hypnotizing himself. He got that drugged look Dougie got while watching TV. "You got Spanish, you got Christian, weather, something, Fox, I don't know, here's your all-sports . . ." He stalled at a basketball game, then pressed advance. "Sex," he said. "This lady's weird." A well-groomed woman Alice's age perched on a stool surrounded by enormous potted plants and inclined toward someone hiding, back turned, in a thicket of aralia, expressing with the goosey curve of her long neck and her luminous, protuberant eyes an almost berserk sympathy. "Exactly when," she was saying, "did you first confront the reality of your sexuality?" Alice and Calvin Frechette laughed at the same moment. Alice glanced at him. He had a face absolutely without guile, like Dougie. He was sweet, almost pitiable, and he was very, very large.

The next thing she knew in the sense that requires coherent thought, she was naked and exhausted on the braided living room rug, listening to the van door slam outside. He said into a squawking two-way radio, "Just did Earnshaw." After he drove away she sat up stiffly like a marionette, and stared down at the good old ordinary pink body that had just turned on her like a family dog suddenly rabid, and thought that now she must be capable of anything. Murder, lynching, shoplifting, Buchenwald. She could never again say about any act, however foul, "I would never do that."

In the next days she took to returning to bed after her family was fed and gone, not to sleep but because she seemed to belong there, caffeine-ridden and staring. She was just slipping into bed one day when Frechette called her. He said, "Hi." He didn't identify himself or call her by name. Just "Hi."

Alice gripped the receiver. This had not occurred to her. But then anything was possible now. She said, "Hi."

"So."

"So?"

"So, what do you say?" He was holding the receiver too close to his mouth, but surely not on purpose like a trolling breather. He had no more menace and no less than a toddler who's gotten an adult on the phone and won't hang up. Alice held her breath and listened to him. "What do you think?" he said, his voice further distorted.

She knelt on her bed, head bowed low. His acres of skin were poreless and moist, his body sleek and strong, he was simple, tactile, irresistible, like a golden bath toy, and hers to do with as she wished. "Come here," she said. "Come here to me."

Dougie came home from school with a crayon drawing of Miss Hestevold, with scribbled white hair and a smiling face, standing jaunty on a mountaintop next to a castle half her size. The sky was sketched with blue and held a formal, radiant sun, and at the end of each of her stick arms bloomed a great orange flower. Dougie wanted to give it to Miss Hestevold. "Maybe later," Alice kept telling him. Sometimes, when he was out playing or the family was piling into the car, he would look uphill and wave. Alice could tell, when Dougie started hopping up and down, that the old woman had waved back.

For the first weeks Alice made Calvin park the van on the next street over. On the third Thursday she heard his radio squawk and lifted herself from him, peering through the blinds. "Sorry, I can't just park it anywhere," he told her. "Somebody broke into it last week." While she returned her attention to him, the radio sounded like a police car was out there, its blue light revolving. She had been taken hostage, or she had taken Calvin hostage, and the police and press surrounded her house, rifles trained on her bedroom window, and television cameras, and no matter which channel Miss Fucking Hestevold turned to, there was Alice on the screen with Calvin Frechette. Doing the hell out of Calvin Frechette. The hell with Miss Hestevold. Alice shook apart like an overstressed motor and threw back her head to howl. Frechette clapped his hand over her mouth. "Listen," he said. Charlie's voice. Charlie was outside.

His car was in the driveway and he was standing in the backyard with Miss Hestevold, who gestured in an animated way as the two began to ascend the hill. She was purposely leading him away, she was chatty, she kept touching his arm and pointing out trees and plants and then sections of her tiered garden. At the summit she drew him off the path and over to a big rubbish can overflowing with sticks and leaves. Charlie stooped to get his hands around it. There were three more rubbish cans to be moved to the street. That Miss Hestevold had always carried out this weekly duty herself with no trouble had apparently not occurred to Charlie.

Alice yelled at Calvin Frechette to get his clothes on. There was a sickening scramble, Calvin hopping into his jeans, buttocks jiggling girlishly, Alice begging, while she dressed, "Why were you here? Why were you here?" while Calvin understandably shot her puzzled looks. She grabbed his sweatshirt. "What am I going to tell him? Help me, you moron!" She shook him.

"I'm thinking," he said, then brightened. "You mighta had a horizontal roll," he said. He lifted his hands as though holding a basketball and swept them from left to right. "Sometimes they get this what we call—"

"GET OUT GET OUT GET OUT!"

She pushed hopelessly against his chest, attempting to stuff him outside her door, outside her life. It was like trying to force a party-joke snake back into its can. When she did get him outside, she slammed the door on his big foot. He had turned back to face her, with a worried look. "I didn't bring my tool case in. That's gonna look weird."

"No it won't! Get out!"

"Well." Calvin smiled manfully, assuming a sad look that had some sincerity in it. "You're a special lady, Alice, and I want you to know—"

"Thank you," she said, smiling horribly. "You take care, Calvin."

"I don't think you were, you know, cheap or nothing and what we had was, you know—"

"Goodbye!"

Charlie was closing in, engaged in a staggering, back-leaning descent downhill, his arms full of plants.

"—something special, and I'll never forget it. You're good people."

The hardest physical thing Alice ever did was to reach out then and shake his hand. But if she didn't do this he would never feel he had the right to leave. "Good luck, Calvin," she said.

He made a humble-dumb happy face, then turned and walked to the van. "Need a hand?" he asked Charlie, who puffed past him carrying a long box loaded with zucchini, tomatoes, and newly dug chrysanthemums and Shasta daisies, their roots encased in black balls of wet earth.

"Thanks, man, I got it," Charlie told him, reaching the door just as the cable van cruised away over his right shoulder.

Alice put her fists on her hips. "What," she demanded, "the hell are we supposed to do with all this zucchini?"

"Isn't it funny," said Charlie in a low, wondering voice, "how a person can just open up to you all of a sudden." He stood at the kitchen sink, his back to her.

Alice wanted to go and raise all the bedroom windows and strip the bed and bleach the sheets and then walk off somewhere and die.

"She's such a terrific person," said Charlie. "Ruth." He turned around. "Ruth Hestevold. Isn't she the one that had that thing with Dougie? Look at these daisies, honey!" Charlie, who didn't know a daisy from a dahlia, held up a dripping clump as though it were the lamp of Diogenes. "She says we can just stick them in the ground and they'll grow like weeds!"

Thereafter Miss Hestevold loomed like a thunderhead, casting Alice in permanent shadow, blanketing her with worthlessness and shame. To what end had the woman chosen to shield her from discovery? Whatever her purpose, it had to be malignant. At first Alice was simply terrified. When it became clear that

Miss Hestevold wasn't going to tell on her, Alice grew furious. By then Charlie and the kids had made countless uphill pilgrimages, returning after minutes or hours with treasures—a homemade paper doll collection made from pictures in old Sears, Roebuck catalogs, ancient tin toys, packets of seeds, little red wagonloads of plants. Dougie in particular was enchanted by Miss Hestevold. Alice watched their tiny figures in the tiered garden, squatting close together over some hole in the ground. Sometimes Dougie handed her things, garden shears carefully pointed down, trays of seedlings. Once Alice saw him watering the garden by himself, with the old woman gone around back, and he held the hose steady and swept it across and back with the patience of an old man. Miss Hestevold was stealing her family. Alice burned with jealousy. She wanted to pound on that old woman's door and shake the green castle and bellow GIVE ME BACK MY FAMILY like the vengeful ghost in that old tale about the golden arm.

Her home, her property, her life had become a stage on which she was forced to perform for an audience of one. She took the damn Shastas and stuck them in the ground all around the house so Miss Hestevold could see the flourishing evidence of her defiance. They died. Alice then determined to become a skilled gardener, and through the months right up until the first snowfall, she was outside ripping up hedges, chopping roots, double-digging, mulching, aching. Showing Miss Hestevold. She also tried to show Miss Hestevold that she was again and for all time a faithful wife, but all she could show her was an empty curb each Thursday afternoon, and time did not shoot by.

As she labored, Alice contended with sudden unpredictable bouts of self-disgust. She was clammy with it. Guilt was a tangible thing of a luminescent hue that splashed all over her and the house and the garden. Charlie was blind to it. She felt as if she had crippled him. Worse was the knowledge that she had a permanent secret kept from him. She had damaged her marriage, not ruined it, but the damage was defining. This became for Alice a manageable horror. Something like, but worse than, the horror she had known as a child when trying to imagine hell. And worst of all were the waves of gross carnality that didn't go away with Calvin Frechette. She was afraid, not of giving in, but of enduring it forever. Charlie, who had once been too much, was not enough for her now. There was not enough of anything in the world to fill her up. This was the god's truth. It made her ridiculous. Long ago, before Calvin Frechette, she had thought nothing of telling a rageful child, "You can't get everything you want in life." Now when she had to deny them something, she mourned with them. No matter what you want, she thought, no matter how foolish, how overreaching, it is terrible, tragic, to want and want and want.

On Christmas Day Charlie took the kids to the castle. Alice had planned an elaborate dinner menu so she would have an excuse not to go with them on this special day. She said she'd have to finish brining the turkey, it was an all-day thing, and Charlie gave her a look. He knew she really didn't want to come anyway, she never came with them, and he didn't hold that against her. He was the sweetest, most reasonable man. "Back in a few," he said, kissing her.

When they had been gone two hours, he called. "We're in a bind," he whispered. "She has Christmas cookies and eggnog and presents for the kids. I just peeked into the kitchen and she's prepared some kind of high tea. Little sandwiches. What am I going to do?"

"Stay and eat. We'll do dinner late."

"But you're all by yourself on Christmas."

"It's okay."

"Look, we all love her, but—"

"Whenever you come back is fine," Alice said. "No worries."

She sat alone until nightfall, finally at peace, like someone in a doomed city who has just put her loved ones on a train bound for the provinces. There was something right about all this, as though scales were coming into balance. Miss Hestevold, whatever her antipathies toward her, was good for her family. Alice could live with that.

They returned after dark. The children were fractious and no one but Alice was hungry. Deranged with fatigue, Dougie started wailing as Alice put little portions on his plate. "What's the matter, Sluggo?" He said he didn't want orange potatoes and she was always giving him orange potatoes when she knew he hated them and she was never fair to him and always made him eat food he didn't like and he didn't want eggs for breakfast ever again.

"I think it's time for bed," said Charlie.

Dougie said he never had any fun, Charlie and Alice tried to keep their faces straight, and Meg whispered to her brother, "It's time to go to the Land of Slime."

Dougie smiled as though a smile button had been pushed. *"Yeah,"* he said. *"Wicked Lucinda!"* Both children giggled, though Doug's face went into meltdown during the laugh as he recalled his orange potato grievance. He was easy to distract but only for the short run. Meg prodded him with the Land of Slime line but it didn't work a second time, which made her cross and bossy, and in a moment each furious child was being taken to bed. Charlie had his screaming son in a fireman's carry as they mounted the stairs together, Meg stomping ahead of them in her full-dress Churchillian pout. Charlie turned to Alice and said, "Isn't this laughs?" And it was. They shared a sadistic, sexy laugh, and Alice had a moment of simple joy.

Alice tucked her daughter in. "Tell me," Alice said, "about Wicked Lucinda." She said it in a coaxing way, stroking Meg's thick strawberry hair, but Meg wouldn't look at her. "Tell me," Alice ordered. She wasn't going to turn out the light on a pouting child on Christmas night.

"Wicked Lucinda," Meg said, after a heavy sigh, "was a beautiful princess married to a handsome prince in the Kingdom of the Cornucopia."

"Oh my," said Alice. "What was the prince's name?"

"The prince's name was Charlemagne, and every day he rode out of the castle and went into the countryside to oversee the harvest and make sure everybody in his kingdom was okay."

Alice smiled. "Does Miss Hestevold tell you many stories?"

"Yeah," Meg said, pushing herself up a little in bed. She still wouldn't look at Alice but was sending out signals of possible forgiveness in the distant future. "This is the best one. I told it to Dougie."

"But why is the princess called Wicked Lucinda?"

"See, she's got these two kids, a son and a daughter and their names are Galahad and Primrose. But she doesn't love them. See, she's really a witch." Meg was wholly engaged now. She regarded Alice with shy excitement and spoke rapidly, offering up the story with the touching hope that it would not bore her. It didn't.

"Every day, after Charlemagne rode away, Wicked Lucinda would send her children out to play in the Black Forest. The forest was huge and dark and dangerous because you could get lost and starve to death. But this spirit, the Spirit of the Forest, watched over them and made sure they always got back home safely. Which made Wicked Lucinda mad. What's the matter, Mom?"

"Nothing, honey," Alice said. "Go on."

"Because the only thing Wicked Lucinda wanted to do was go down to the basement, which was really a dungeon, and cast spells and summon up demons and stuff. So one day she fell in love with the ugliest, most disgusting demon of all, and his name"—Meg's eyes shone—"was Barbo, and he was a troll, and he taught Wicked Lucinda how to dance and spin. Barbo's real gross. And together, every day, when Charlemagne was gone and the children were playing in the Black Forest, Wicked Lucinda and Barbo would sing this special song that would let them disappear, and they would fly away on big black wings into the Land of Slime."

"Sleep time," said Alice.

"Don't you want to hear the rest? That's just the beginning."

"Tomorrow." Alice switched off the light. "I love you, Meg," she said, and the warmth of her voice was quite an achievement, considering how cold she was.

Charlie worked the next day but the children were still on holiday, so it was afternoon by the time Alice managed to get them out of the house, to an ice skating party with friends. She had two hours and she didn't waste a minute preparing or counting to ten or doing anything that might diminish her rage. She was buoyant with it. She made it up the hill and up the porch steps in what amounted to a jog, and when she came to the door she had enough breath to blow it down. But Miss Hestevold opened it right away.

"There you are!" said Alice. "How's the weather up here on Olympus? I just want to thank you for giving my family such a lovely Christmas and for being so kind, so benevolent, so caring, so very *good* to my children, and if you ever so much as speak to them again I'm going to call the police."

For a second Miss Hestevold was caught off-guard but she bounced right back. She looked like she was swallowing a laugh. "And what will you say when you call the police?"

"I will say—" What? Shrieked obscenities would just amuse the witch further—and a witch, a *witch,* was exactly what she was. "Wicked Lucinda!" shouted Alice. "Wicked Goddamn Lucinda, and how dare you corrupt my children—"

"Oh, *that,*" said Miss Hestevold. She drew a pack of Marlboros from her shirt pocket and lit a cigarette. She offered the pack to Alice, who, amazed that this woman *smoked,* could only shake her head no. "Fairy tales do not corrupt children. As Chesterton said, fairy tales don't teach children there are monsters. Children already know—"

"—yes, they know about monsters, fairy tales teach them that monsters can be killed, I know that, you're not the only one who knows that, and it was dragons, not monsters, and this was no fairy tale, it was a wicked story you made up for your own rotten amusement. Who the hell do you think you are?"

"A concerned bystander?"

"What?"

"The Neighborhood Watch? The eye in the sky?"

"You think this is funny?"

"Perhaps I'm just performing a public service."

"What service would that be? Are you the morality police?"

"Morality police?" Miss Hestevold blinked. "Hardly."

"Then what makes you think you're a better person than me?"

Miss Hestevold's eyes narrowed to slits and her lips drew back, displaying yellow teeth. She regarded Alice with an outrage so powerful it shook the floor beneath Alice's feet. "A 'better person'? You silly woman, you stupid woman, WHAT MAKES YOU THINK I DO?" The force of her shout knocked Alice back. She pointed a claw toward Alice's house. "Run along home now, Mrs. Earnshaw. I am fatigued. Christmas was enervating."

Alice backed down the steps, afraid to turn away from this crazy woman's naked, malevolent gaze. "Not until you tell me," she said, "tell me one thing first."

"And what one thing would that be?"

"What you want from me! Just tell me what in god's name you want from me!"

Miss Hestevold grinned. "Everything," she said. "Isn't it obvious? Everything you've got."

Halfway down, Alice turned, took a stand. "You can't have them. This is *my* life. Mine!"

Miss Hestevold spread her arms wide like a great bird, a condor with a wingspan that blocked the winter sun. "I'll take what I want," she cried out. "I always do."

Running downhill, Alice stumbled and fell to her knees,

and when she got up and stood and looked back, expecting to see Miss Hestevold laughing at her, the green castle was closed, the monster shut inside.

All around her, around the whole neighborhood, blinding sunlight bounced off the rooftops, every one of them, not just her own, and beneath those rooftops were all those secrets, those coveted lives. *We* are the morality police, Alice thought. God help us all.

Amy called Lottie, picked her up, held her in her lap, and waited on the real sun, which, just as she read the last page, had slyly crept behind a low cloud. "Good one, Edna," she said.

CHAPTER TWENTY

Carla

Friday, May 7

Carla came awake at daybreak, escaping from a dream of her father standing in the cellar with his back to her and repeating, like a metronome, "You know she keeps her promises." He said this dully and would not turn around and her waking face was wet. Carla seldom dreamed. For years she had wished for dreams about him, and finally she had had one, and it was awful. She lay in bed until she felt nothing. She planned her day. *I am growing up,* she thought. *I am in bloom. I am a blooming funeral wreath.*

It was seven o'clock; Chuck would have left for work and Tiffany wouldn't come in for at least an hour. She rose and dressed and, gathering cleaning supplies from the kitchen, she returned to the dollhouse and set about erasing every trace of defilement. She found that as long as she focused on this task she could avoid thinking about how this had happened and what it meant and whether she could tell Chuck about it, which frightened her more than the dollhouse cellar, because how could she tell him about this without telling him everything? She'd told him her father had built the dollhouse, but not why, and she knew that if she started to let him in she'd have to tell him everything, all her secrets, and she had never felt less ready to do that.

She brought with her a small bowl in which to soak the little sheet in hydrogen peroxide. In an hour most of the red lifted out, but to her sorrow the faintest pink remained, and she decided to make her peace with it rather than risk disintegrating the fabric. There was a tiny red dot on the blue and gold bedspread; she blotted most of it away with soapy water; what remained would be noticeable to no one but her. In the cellar she scraped the bloodstains off the workbench with her fingernails. Her father had once told her that the human fingernail was the best tool to use when you needed to scrape something off a scratch-prone surface, and he was right. Unlike the fabrics, the workbench was returned to its rightful state.

Handling the paraffin figures was gross. She could not bring herself to touch them, instead lifting them out with a Kleenex. She put the old woman and the dismembered corpse in a plastic bag, and when she did this she saw that a foot was missing from the corpse. *What fresh hell,* she thought. Amy sometimes said that. It comforted Carla a little to say the words, she felt just a little less frozen, as though Amy were some kind of charm, and god knows she needed one of those. She took the axe too. Unlike the paraffin pieces it looked a lot like the real thing. Whoever did this must have bought it from one of those dollhouse miniature shops but was too much of a slob to insist on the proper scale, so Mother Bates looked like she was wielding a battle-axe.

The foot was nowhere in the cellar. She got a flashlight from Tiffany's desk and rummaged through each room of the dollhouse, the closet in the master bedroom, all the hutch drawers, and when she saw that the lid was down on the toilet, she knew where it was. It was so badly made it looked more like a pink comma than a foot.

She put the thing in the plastic bag and soaked red water out of the toilet with a paper towel, and she was done.

When Carla returned the flashlight to the office, Tiffany was firing up her laptop. "You look like you didn't get any sleep," she said to Carla. "Are you okay? Carla, I am so sorry. *We* are so—"

"Who do you know that makes plexiglass boxes?"

"Well, nobody off the top of my head, but I can track down a guy if you give me a minute."

"Thank you. Find somebody local who can custom-make a box with a lock on it."

"How big? Oh—you're going to put the dollhouse in—"

"Get someone down here today to measure and give me a quote."

"I don't know if I can do that—"

"I also want security cameras in the Rotunda, today if possible, tomorrow at the latest."

Tiffany started to say something, then thought better of it and started a Web search.

"I'm going out," Carla said. "Please call me when you get that quote." Taking a deep breath, she opened the bottom file cabinet drawer, took the lid off the Golden Acorn, and dropped the baggie on top of the ashes. She had planned to bury them deep in the urn but could not bring herself to do that now.

She kicked the drawer shut, went down to her car, and drove to Harry B.'s office in Mira Mesa.

She had been there only once before, when they set up the Point and he made her sign a million pieces of paper. His office was in what he liked to call an upscale strip mall, sandwiched in between a Montessori School and a Bed, Bath & Beyond. Harry always bragged about the money he saved on low rent, used cars, and cheap track suits.

Mrs. Arbogast, Harry's secretary, a dead ringer for Bea Arthur, was on her feet shrugging into a ratty cardigan. "Coffee break," she said. "He's been on the horn since nine. Just knock and wave. He'll want to see you." She was out the door before Carla could ask her why.

Harry B.'s place looked nothing like the *L.A. Law* office. There were a few shelved books—an old *Black's Law Dictionary* and some volumes on California civil statutes—but most of the books were fiction. Carla counted five Grishams, three Turows, and an entire shelf of Stephen King. A saguaro cactus angled menacingly out of a plastic pot on the windowsill, and on the wall a framed poster of *My Cousin Vinny* dwarfed Harry's law school diploma from Cal West. "Have to call you back," he said to someone on the phone, and then motioned her in. "Miriam!" he yelled toward the door. "Forget calling her! Miriam?"

Carla sat down. "Miriam's on break. We have a serious problem with John Cousins."

"No argument there, but never mind that."

"He wants to turn my house into a circus tent. I want a restraining order—"

"The man's a jerk, but here's the thing: He was right about the serial killer. I know, I hate it too, but there it is. That was my guy in the PD on the phone—there's going to be a press conference this morning, and we need to decide—"

"I don't care about stupid serial killers."

Harry sighed. "In the past two months two local women have been murdered and butchered, and their body parts have been left in or near La Jolla. Inspiration Point, which is in La Jolla, was, as you may recall, the site of a third murder."

"Toonie wasn't cut up." Why was he going on about this?

"Yes, but the cops are now saying that whoever killed her may have run out of time. They've called in a profiler and they're going with that possibility."

"Harry, I'm sorry for these women, but right now—"

"DNA evidence has just come in linking the Ng and Bunting crimes."

"Who's Bunting?"

"Don't you watch the news? She was a tenured professor of philosophy at SDSU."

"Oh." *You're a philosophy professor, you're a stripper, and you're stuck in an elevator together. Go!* Oh, the poor woman.

"And again, since Garabedian wasn't sliced and diced there's no DNA on her, but they're thinking she's the third, maybe, because La Jolla and whatever the profiler dreamed up."

Carla could feel herself wilting. She was so tired, so empty. "I don't want to sound dumb, which I am, but what does DNA have to do with the bodies being cut up?"

"Something about axes. Apparently you can sweat a lot and your sweat gets all over everything. Garabedian was strangled from behind. Guy used a garrote made of fancy polyethylene fishing line, and he must have made handles for it and then cut the handles off and taken them with him. You don't work up a sweat if you brace yourself against the victim's back with your knee, and he didn't handle her body after she was dead. A child could do it." As he spoke, Harry pantomimed the garroting and the wielding of the axe.

Now she was light-headed. For the first time in weeks she flashed on Toonie's purple face, popping eyes, protruding tongue. "An axe? How do they know it's an axe?"

"Shape of the bone cuts, plus lots of splintering. You don't get that with a power saw. Carla, are you all right?"

Her ears were ringing, and all she could see was the dollhouse cellar, the old woman, the bloody battle-axe. Harry was beside her with a paper cup half full of water. He was yelling at her to put her head between her legs, which sounded really disgusting and also funny, then she was lying on the floor looking at Harry's cheesy popcorn ceiling zigzagged with cracks that formed an accidental design. "I can see Idaho in your ceiling."

"Hold on," said Harry. "I'm calling 911."

"Don't," said Carla. "I'm all right." She was. She'd never fainted before. She was flat on the floor with an empty stomach, but she felt like herself for the first time since last night. It was like she'd rebooted. "Harry, I have something to tell you. It'll take a while."

Fifteen minutes later they were both seated, and this time Harry looked kind of unwell. "You're not making this up, are you?"

"Why would I do that?"

"Somebody set up an axe murder in your dollhouse? Gotta be Cousins. That sonofabitch."

"Except Tiffany says that's not possible, and I believe her."

He gave her a patronizing look. "Why? Carla, when to your knowledge was the last time you looked at the dollhouse and everything was normal?"

To your knowledge. Harry was cross-examining her like she was a hostile witness or something. "Day before yesterday. Evening of Cinco de Mayo. There was no blood, no axe, nothing. And yesterday they were together in the Rotunda doing their stupid movie, so it had to happen before they got there. Tiffany's not lying. She was right there with him, and she'd never do something like this. You don't know her."

"I know she's a nice girl in love with a con man."

Carla thought for a minute. "Harry, when did you learn about the axe? I mean, that it was an axe that chopped up those women?"

"This morning."

"And you've said Cousins doesn't have an *in* with the PD, so how would he have known about this in time to mess with the dollhouse?"

Harry leaned back in his creaky chair and massaged his eyes. "Look," he finally said, "none of this matters anyway because now we've got proof of whoever did it! Because somebody *made* the scary old bat and the chopped-up body and there's probably DNA and fingerprints all over the wax and the dollhouse, so all we have to do is call the po—"

"I cleaned it all up."

"You *what*?"

"I'm sorry, Harry. I just had to—"

"Well, of course you did. Of *course* you did." Harry rose and paced in front of his cactus. "And then you did what? Ground them up in the garbage disposal? Dissolved them in acid?"

"Of course not, why would I do that? I put them in a baggie."

"And threw the baggie off the Coronado Bridge?"

"Harry, why are you being so mean?"

"Because—" Harry sighed deeply and dropped back into his chair. "You know why I gave up criminal law? The money wasn't great, but I was good at it. There was plenty of work, and it was damn colorful."

"So why did you give it up?"

"I got sick of dealing day after day after day with dumbasses. Most of them were interesting, they had entertaining stories, and lots of these people were funny and likeable, and a few were even innocent, but all their choices were uniformly stupid, and after a while it just got to me. It was depressing. So I hung it up and settled for gray old business law because business may be boring but at least the clients aren't human wrecking balls."

"And?"

"Carla, what am I supposed to do with you?"

Carla's cell rang. It was Tiffany calling about the plexiglass box and the security cameras, both of which could get started tomorrow. Carla gave her the go-ahead and hung up. "Maybe this will help. I'm going to have the whole dollhouse locked up in a plastic box so nobody but me can open it."

"Barn door!"

"Look, I did clean up the red paint, but it's not like I slobbered all over the house. I didn't dust the furniture or scrub the walls, and the bodies could still have somebody else's stuff on them. All they have to do is take my DNA and just, you know, subtract it from any other DNA they find."

"Everybody's a CSI," said Harry, shaking his head. "Okay. Next step, I call Kowalcimi. I'll let you know what he says and when he's coming to look at the house, because for sure he will. Meanwhile DO NOT. TOUCH. ANYTHING. Can you do that? If your plastic box guys get there before he does, DON'T LET THEM TOUCH. ANYTHING. They can measure WITHOUT TOUCHING. Got that?"

"Totally. Now what about my restraining order?"

"What about it?"

"I told you! Cousins is—"

"—a prizewinning dickwad who, if he gets caught violating a restraining order, may be found guilty of a misdemeanor, within thirty days of which time he can file a notice of appeal, which he probably would because he's a prizewinning dickwad, and meanwhile you've got more important things to worry about."

"But—"

"Now, what's the deal with the circus tent?"

Carla collected herself and explained what X said he wanted to do with her house. "And not just the dollhouse, which is bad enough, but the whole house! He wants to tie in the murders, all of them, not just the axe murders, and make a big deal out of my, you know, ghost thing, and turn it into one of those—"

"What ghost thing?"

"It doesn't matter. I thought there was a ghost but there wasn't. And he wants to turn the Birdhouse into one of those stupid Bigfoot spectaculars."

"Bigfoot was in your dollhouse?"

"Not the dollhouse, the Birdhouse and not Bigfoot, but *like* Bigfoot, you know."

"Like Bigfoot." Harry was back to massaging his eyeballs.

"You know. 'Aliens in the Attic!' 'Mothman in the Pantry!' 'My Night with Ogopogo!'"

"Carla, don't take this the wrong way, but are you on something?"

"He wants to feature my house in a show, a *series,* about how the place is haunted and everybody's getting horribly murdered. He wants cameras roaming through my home like buffalo and of course he'd be the star and the voice-over and he's negotiating with Netflix or something and he's going to ruin my life."

Now she had Harry's attention. "And *devalue the Point*! And when your Pointers all start bailing he'll ooze in to lowball it off your hands. *That's* what he's up to!" He slapped his palms on the desk. "Miriam, get in here!"

"Miriam's on break."

"Carla, don't worry about this, there's no way he can force you to let him in. I'm on it. For now, you can go back home and relax. Take a nap. Eat something. I'll let you know what Kowalcimi wants to do about the dollhouse business. Go home, Carla. Will you do that?"

Carla stood. "You're a nice guy, Harry."

"Yes, I am." Harry walked around his desk and cupped her head in his hands. Just like Chuck the first time he kissed her, but this was firmer, like he was saying "Listen carefully." Harry was a really nice guy. This is what nice men did. "Stop worrying. If anything else happens, call me day or night."

"I will!"

On the way out she passed Mrs. Arbogast. When Carla got to her car, Mrs. Arbogast leaned out and called to her. "He says not to touch anything!"

CHAPTER TWENTY-ONE

Amy

Friday, May 7

Amy was debating what to do with Edna's story when a local news alert popped up on her screen and there was Lieutenant Kowalcimi, stalwart in a colorless room flanked by uniformed police officers, being yelled at by reporters. "Yes," he said, "we have evidence that the murders are connected, but I am not at liberty to discuss that evidence at this time." He went on to promise frequent updates and advise that for now women in San Diego, particularly La Jolla, "should not panic but should exercise caution as they go about their daily lives."

Somebody yelled "How are we supposed to do that?" which is what Amy was wondering along with *Why La Jolla?* since the murders she knew about had happened all around the county. She did a quick *U-T* search and learned that two more women had been murdered. One was on the faculty at State; the other had danced at the Bouncy House in Kearny Mesa. The stripper was identified as Cinnamon Bombe. They ran pictures of both women, and Cinnamon Bombe—Why didn't they use her real name? Did they think this was funny?—looked familiar to Amy. She was young, pretty, and clueless in the fashion of murder victims everywhere. Had she taken one of Amy's workshops? Amy stared at the picture. For some reason Tiffany Zuniga's name popped up. Tiffany was blond too, but of course this wasn't her.

Amy had reached the Alzheimer years; like most people her age she had lost the capacity to shrug off the occasional memory lapse, so for peace of mind she needed to remember this girl. After a while she quit staring at the picture and unearthed her old workshop files, and there she was. Tiffany *McGee*. In Amy's final workshop she had shown up for the first class and then dropped. As always, Amy had taken notes on the first-class attendees: She had put Roman numerals next to the names of the two Tiffanies; the surviving Tiffany was II. Tiffany I had apparently said something foolish about "winery ballooning," whatever that meant, and next to her name, encased in asterisks, Amy had all-capped "airhead." And now the poor kid had been slaughtered and turned into a media punch line. Amy could imagine the newsroom hilarity. "Mr. and Mrs. Bombe must be devastated!" "Is the e silent, or is it pronounced 'Bomb bay'?"

She wondered if Kowalcimi should know that she had actually met this person, that there was a tenuous connection here between Tiffany I and Amy, and therefore between Tiffany I and Carla and the Birdhouse, and therefore between Tiffany I and Toonie Garabedian. The question itself made her head pound. It was probably just a coincidence—she reflected that coincidences abound in nature, just not in fiction—but she found she was not sure it was coincidental. Because she was a hermit, and despite her age, Amy had in her lifetime met very few people. Yet here she was, tethered to two murdered women, never mind that the tether had all the substance of dental floss. Maybe she should call Harry B.

For now she returned to Edna's story. If Edna were in an actual workshop, Amy's written critique would have peppered the revised manuscript with *goods* and *greats,* but she would not have presumed to ask the central question: How were you able to resurrect this thing and make it work? The cringeworthy ending of the original story had the warring women magically becoming fast friends on Miss Hestevold's front porch, bonding over the humble admission of their own moral imperfection. It was a classic example of the will doing the work of the imagination. You were supposed to come away realizing that for all their flaws, they were both Good Women.

At the time, Amy had suspected that Edna knew how bad the ending was but had just settled because she couldn't imagine one that worked. Now Amy wondered if Edna, before she began killing people, had actually worried about her own moral shortcomings. As was probably true of most fiction writers, each of whom contained multitudes, Amy's characters were fashioned from bits torn from the clay of her own self, so she now assumed that in creating Hestevold I Edna had intended to explore some aspect of her character. If so, the Edna who came into Amy's last workshop had not known herself at all.

And now she did. Desperate to get published, consumed by resentment of those who did, she had taken two lives and tried to take another. Doing this and facing up to it, even reveling in it, had enabled her to imagine Hestevold II, a creature driven by envy of a supernatural magnitude. *I think I got it right,* she had said. She hadn't been bragging; she worried that she might be deceiving herself; she needed Amy's honest reaction.

On the bottom of the last page, Amy wrote, "If Cousins is serious about having you read something on a TED thing, read this. You got it right." Out of respect for Edna she refrained from festooning the MS with *goods* and *greats;* out of respect for the people Edna murdered, she did not encourage Edna to send her anything else.

When she got Harry on the phone and began to explain about the Tiffanies, he kept repeating, "You are kidding me." When Amy assured him that she wasn't, he spun a deeply alarming tale about Carla's dollhouse.

"We have to do something about this," Amy said.

"We are. The police are dropping by the Birdhouse in an hour, so I gotta take off. Maybe you should come too?"

Amy thought about it. "I don't think so," she said. "I'd just get in the way, and you're looking out for her, aren't you? You and Chuck? Make sure you tell them about Tiffany McGee, though. Will you do that? And ask them to stop calling the poor woman that ridiculous name?"

Harry said he'd let Amy know when there was more news and hung up.

As soon as he did, Amy felt off. Not going to La Jolla was a reasonable decision—these murders were already confusing enough and the police didn't need to be distracted by the Tiffany I connection. Harry would tell them about it. If they thought it was important enough, they'd contact her. But the desecration of Carla's dollhouse was so disturbing. Amy doubted that anyone else knew its history, understood how profound Carla's attachment to it was, and her impulse to see Carla, to comfort her, was strong. It was an ache such as she had not felt for thirty years, when Max needed her. Again she wondered how people could bear bringing children into an unsafe world. She was no longer, in Max's words, wonderfully well-defended. She missed that.

While she was missing it, the phone rang and she picked it up without glancing at the caller ID. There was a brief pause and a beep and then a young man's voice. "Grandma? Grandma, it's me. It's me, and I'm in so much trouble, and I'm so sorry."

Amy didn't hang up. "What's happened, dear? What's wrong?" What was she doing? This was a Carla move. Amy had never called anyone "dear" in her life.

"It was drugs, and I'm so sorry, I wasn't selling them or anything, I was just being stupid, but now I'm in jail in Tijuana and they're saying if I don't pay them a bribe, I'm going to prison for twenty years."

"How much money do they want?"

There was the sound of shuffling paper. Was he working from a script? "Ten thousand dollars! And I know that's a lot! And I'm so sorry, Grandma!"

"Well, I'm sorry too."

"Can you afford the money? I know it's a lot—"

His voice was hoarse. How many of these calls had he made today? What country did he live in? Was he in some prison boiler room? She pictured a pimply redhead with an unfortunate beard; while he talked to her he stared at naked people on his laptop. His mother must be so proud. "You need to call your mother," she told him. "She handles all my money now."

There was a long silence. "Oh," he finally said.

"You take care, son."

"Wait! Grandma, do you know what happens in Mexican prisons?"

"If you don't get the ten thousand dollars? What does happen?"

"They're full of gangsters and rapists. They—"

"Never mind all that. Tell me about the people you work for. They've called me before, so I must be on some list. Are you penalized in some way when you fail with the follow-up?"

"What are you talking about, Grandma?"

"Kid, how did you get to this point in your life?" He was holding the phone close to his mouth; she could hear him breathing. "Are you working from a script? Do they let you improvise? Do you get some sort of commission?"

"Screw you, lady."

"When you look at a mirror, what do you see?"

"Fuck you." He repeated this four times, his voice rising in pitch. He didn't hang up.

"Do you ever imagine the lives of the people you call?"

"Fuck you."

"You know what's funny? I'm beginning to feel guilty about wasting your time."

"Fuck YOU!"

"Call your mother." Amy hung up. She took Lottie out back to play with the ball. While the dog ran up and down Amy could still hear the kid's voice. His echo told her nothing about his worth as a human being yet provided an alarming intimacy, as though he were a brand-new neighbor apt to pop in at any moment. She had deliberately let him in, and she didn't know why. She had given him a piece of herself, a tiny shard, but still.

Lottie's greatest joy was to chase an orange squeaky ball down a blue tube, a long winding polyester tunnel Amy had snaked through her fruit trees. After Lottie brought it to Amy she would turn and face the tunnel, braced to charge through it again. She never looked at Amy to see if the ball might be thrown somewhere else. She would chase the ball until she staggered from fatigue. Lottie was an emotional being, prone to excesses of happiness, outrage, anxiety, and fear. Amy had always loved her dogs but never required them to love her, and she was skeptical about whether they ever truly loved their owners anyway.

But Lottie certainly acted as though she did, following Amy everywhere, and, when left behind, perching on the back of the sofa, waiting for her at the living room window. Amy had never had a small dog before, and the fact that she could pick Lottie up (she had never been able to do this with the basset, whose center of gravity seemed well below the surface of the earth) created in her a frequent desire to do so. This seemed to be instinctive. Sometimes she dreaded losing her to ill health or a rampant coyote, but now she worried about what would happen to Lottie if she died first.

Her own death became less hypothetical with each passing day, and until recently she had been able to contemplate it, to plan for it, in a businesslike manner—like Lucy, the book hoarder in her story. But during the past weeks an emotion, faint, like a steel blue watercolor wash, had begun to color her days and nights, and until right now she had been unable to name it. Right now, loving her happy little dog, she could. It was sorrow. Sorrow of a shape she did not recognize.

She fed Lottie and tried for a story. Nothing came but a list, and the list was pitiful.

Tunnel
Winding blue tube
Obit
Columbarium
Nothing.

She leashed Lottie and left to walk her up the street to bark at the turkeys. Halfway uphill she stopped, turned back, and went to her car, strapping Lottie into her car seat. Out here, in the sunlight, there was no steel blue watercolor wash. The hell with reasonable. She was going to La Jolla.

CHAPTER TWENTY-TWO

Carla

Friday, May 7

When Carla got back home, there was a black Tesla Model 3 in her driveway. She knew this because the license plate frame said "Tesla Model 3." This was a visitor with money to burn—Misha Bernard, maybe? With the echo of Harry's dire warnings ringing in her ears, she dashed inside and was relieved to find the Rotunda unpopulated and her dollhouse apparently untouched. She tore a page from the blank journal she always carried with her, scrawled "HANDS OFF THIS MEANS YOU" on a lined page, and propped it up in front of the doorway, then ran upstairs to Tiffany's office to get the paraffin figures out of the Acorn, and there was Cousins, hunched over Tiffany's desk, the two of them staring at her computer screen.

Carla was not going to open the Acorn in front of Cousins. "What are you looking at?" she asked, and not in a friendly way. When they didn't respond, she said, "There's a Tesla Model 3 in the driveway. Who else is here? If you don't mind my asking?"

X raised his hand without looking up.

"It's *yours*?" How much money did he plan to rake in?

"It's a lease," said Tiffany. "Carla, we're all over the news. Oh my god, look, there we are!"

Against her will, Carla was drawn to the screen, and there was the Birdhouse, bird's-eye view.

"We heard a helicopter about an hour ago but didn't connect it to this story. This is just amazing. You saw the police press conference, right?"

Carla nodded. When X looked up, she said, "You must be so proud of yourself," and the scorn in her voice made her feel sick; this was Ma, coming out of her own mouth for the first time in her life. She did not want to be a hateful person, so before Tiffany could rise to his defense, Carla apologized, pleading fatigue. She started to tell them about her visit with Harry and the prospect of the police coming around at some point to check out the dollhouse.

X smiled at her with what he must have imagined was an expression of fond indulgence. "Carla, I spoke with the Lieutenant this morning. He's coming over this afternoon."

Carla went back outside and called Harry, who had already left; Mrs. Arbogast said he'd be there in plenty of time. In time for what? Carla was frozen with indecision. She had no idea what the police were going to do or what Harry expected of her except NOT TO TOUCH ANYTHING. All she knew for sure was that she needed to get ahold of the baggie with the paraffin evidence, and she didn't want to do that while X was in the room. While she was trying to unstick herself, Amy's old gray Crown Vic pulled into her driveway. "I've got Lottie," Amy called up. "Is it okay for me to bring her in?"

For just a second Carla wondered if she were hallucinating. How could Amy have known to come here, now of all times? "Yes! Meet me in the Rotunda! I'll be there in a sec." She ran back to Tiffany's office and just picked up the Golden Acorn. Tiffany and X stared at her. "What is that?" asked X.

"You don't want to know," said Tiffany. He did want to know, but even if Tiffany told him about Ma and the ashes, Tiffany couldn't know about the baggie. Carla sped downstairs, where Lottie sniffed at the base of the dollhouse while Amy peered inside.

"Some of the little doors are closed now," Amy said. "Are you renovating?"

Carla picked Lottie up and took her to the window to show her the boats out in the harbor. "Not exactly," she said. "Amy, something bad happened, and I made it worse."

"Harry told me all about it."

"About the axe and the wax dolls? About how somebody splashed fake blood all over—"

Carla was tearing up, which she didn't want to do, but it was such a relief to have Amy here.

"Yes, and something rather confusing about Cousins trying to take over the Point. You have a lot on your plate."

"I screwed up and ruined the evidence. Harry's really had it with me."

"Harry works for you; you don't have to please Harry. Carla, you don't have to please anyone."

Carla sat, popped the top off the Acorn, peered inside, and lifted the baggie from the ashes, holding it up for Amy to see. "What should I do with these? Leave them in the baggie or put them back where they were?"

"Harry says there's a video of the dollhouse with the figures in place, right? So you don't have to re-create the scene. Just leave them in the baggie."

"Where?" Carla felt incapable of making the tiniest decision.

Amy took the baggie from her hand and examined it. "You found these in the cellar, right? Let's just do this." Carefully she opened the cellar door, switched on the light, and placed the baggie on the workbench. "Is that all right?"

Carla could only nod.

Amy sat down across from Carla. The two of them watched Lottie patrol the perimeter of the Rotunda.

"I wish I had a dog," said Carla, who hadn't wished for a dog until this very second.

"Where's Chuck?"

"Working. There's a pileup on the 805."

"What does he think about all this, Carla?"

"I haven't been bothering him with it." Why was Amy asking her about Chuck? "He's a great guy, but I can handle this myself."

Amy took off her glasses and massaged her eyeballs with the heel of her left hand, just like Harry.

"I can! Amy, I've changed a lot since Toonie, you know, died."

"In what way?"

"Lots of ways." She wanted to tell about her road trip to Victorville and the Atomic Diner, but then she'd have to tell about Cal Hoving, and she wasn't ready to do that, not to Amy, not even to Chuck. "You should have heard me down here last night—I stood up to X, told him what I thought of him, I made them take away all those stupid cameras. You should have been there! I sounded just like Mrs. Crowley!"

"Who's Mrs. Crowley?"

"She taught second grade. She used to yell at me for making faces in my zeros."

"What is that thing?" Amy was staring at the Acorn.

"It's Ma."

"Oh." Amy examined the fingertips of her right hand, which were lightly dusted with gray. She held up the hand for Carla to see. "Ma?"

Carla was horrified. "I'm so sorry! I didn't think! I'll get a washcloth!"

"No worries," said Amy. She walked to the big window, still fixated on her fingertips. "My parents were cremated; my husband also; but I never looked at the ashes. I just buried them." Amy cupped sunlight in her palm. "Not just ash, is it? There are grains of what looks like sand. Must be particles of bone."

Carla watched Amy watching the ashes.

"If you don't mind my asking," Amy finally said, "why are the ashes still here? Are you trying to decide what to do with them?"

Here it was, finally, the conversation with Amy she had dreamed of, and she didn't have the energy to even start. So many details, about Ma's disappointment and Judy Garland's grave and the Hollywood Forever tomb, and when she tried to turn them over in her mind they felt like moss-covered boulders. She had told herself the story so many times in so many ways that it was completely empty of meaning. As Amy herself would say, it lacked narrative pull.

"Carla?"

"I'm in bloom," she said. "I'm in stupid bloom." She cried without covering her face, without making a sound, the way she had never been able, or willing, to cry on film. Bawling on cue was easy. This was hard. The tears came from her core, like some terrible hydraulic mechanism had started up, it was like the time her appendix burst and she brought up bile, such hard work, such necessary work. The great room was silent, and she could see nothing through her tears. Amy called Lottie; the dog's nails clicked across the marble floor, and then she settled Lottie in Carla's lap. Carla buried her face in the dog's curly coat.

"I find her a great comfort," Amy said.

Carla wrapped her arms around Lottie. It was like hugging Amy.

"Carla, I have an idea. What if we went out right now and found you a dog?"

"Right now? You and me?"

Amy smiled. "Right now." She checked her watch. "There's just time to hit the Humane people."

"Oh, I'd love that so much!"

"You'll have to take care of it. Not just feeding and vet bills, but getting used to the dog, and the dog getting used to you. You'll be developing a relationship. Will you do that?"

"Yes! I love relationships!" And up till now she'd had only two real ones—Amy and Chuck. In her whole life.

Amy studied her for a long minute. "Then let's go."

"But I can't! What about Harry? What about the cops?"

"They can wait."

"I'll have to tell Tiffany. They'll wonder where I am."

"Let them wonder. Wondering is good." She picked Lottie up and started out the door. "Coming?"

As they buckled up, Amy quizzed her about her preferences. Small or big? Short hair or long? Mutt or breed? Briefly she explained that small dogs were easier because you could pick them up, but "You're young, so that's not an issue."

"I can't imagine it until I see it. Do you know what I mean? I need to see the dog. Oh, shit." Two cars, a cop SUV and another car, were pulling up in back of them. "They're here." And there in her doorway was pop-up-John-X. Cousins, poised to greet them like the master of the manor. "I can't stand that man," said Carla.

Lieutenant Kowalcimi stopped by Amy's car and leaned into the driver's-side window. "Sorry if you were leaving, but I could use your input right now."

"And you could use Carla's, too," said Amy. "This place is hers. Just tell her what you need."

"That was my plan." He waited while they got out of the car, Carla holding the little dog close to her, for reasons to which she had no access, except that Lottie seemed to keep her from panicking. Were all dogs therapeutic? The three walked together into the house. Kowalcimi managed to brush past X without a word. Behind them people were milling around the SUV with a lot of equipment. Kowalcimi called back to them: "Leave Myrtle. Crack the window, she'll be fine."

"I hope Myrtle's a dog," said Amy.

Kowalcimi laughed. He really liked Amy, Carla could tell. "We trust her around other dogs, but this one"—he pointed at Lottie—"looks pretty savage."

"She's a killer," said Amy. "She'd make a meal out of Myrtle."

"Seriously, you brought a police dog?" Carla didn't know whether to be alarmed or thrilled. Either way, she was beginning to feel better.

She led everybody to the Rotunda and watched them set up shop. "Shouldn't these guys be in paper slippers and jumpsuits?"

Kowalcimi walked around and around the dollhouse, clearly impressed. "That's how they do it on TV," he said. "Who built this thing? It's incredible."

"My dad."

"This must have taken months. The detail!" He smiled at her. "I built one of these for my own girl, but it wasn't anything like this. He must love you very much."

Carla hugged Lottie tight and just nodded.

"We're going to make a mess, but I promise we'll clean it up. We're just taking pictures and looking for fingerprints and DNA."

"They'll mostly be mine," said Carla. "Sorry about that."

"I understand." He was opening doors, shining his cop MagLite into each room, ending with the cellar. "Those are the dolls, in the baggie? Is that everything?"

"Yes. You can't see the fake blood because I washed it all off."

"No problem." He stepped back so the rest could get to work. "You ladies don't have to stay here for this process. It will take this team a while."

"Cousins made a video of the inside of the house, before I cleaned it up, before I even knew about it. You've seen it, right?"

Kowalcimi sighed. "As a matter of fact, no. I've been told about the video, and I asked him to just shoot it over to us so we could take a look, but he refused. He wants to show it to me in person."

"What was his rationale for that?" Amy looked curious.

"Some deal with copyright. If he sends it out online he's afraid it could leak."

"No he's not," said Amy. "If there's a leak—"

"—it'll come from him," said Kowalcimi. "You said it. We know he's out for himself. Still, if you don't mind, I'd like you both to come with me to watch the video. You've seen it already, Carla. Do have a problem with watching it again?"

"I can stand it." She could stand anything as long as Amy was with her, and the Lieutenant too, and now here came Harry B., who had changed out of his track sweats and was wearing an actual suit, three-piece.

"What's all this?" He was panting; he must have run up the stairs. Harry was so great. "What's the deal with the police dog? Where's Francis X. Bushman?"

"Did Mrs. Arbogast make you wear that? You look like Matlock Junior."

"It's my Mouthpiece Action Costume. What did I miss?"

"You're just in time for the command performance," said Amy.

Tiffany's office had been rearranged: They'd turned her laptop around and put two chairs in front of the screen. X invited them all to sit, asking Tiffany to get chairs for Carla and Amy; god forbid he'd do this himself. At his bidding she set the chairs in a semicircle and adjusted the blinds, darkening the room. X stood in back of the laptop, looming over the screen, and opened his mouth. "What you're about to see—"

"Mr. Cousins," said Kowalcimi, "we all know about the video, we don't need an introduction."

"Popcorn wouldn't be amiss," said Harry.

X snapped his fingers at Tiffany, who began to poke at her iPad. *Snapped at her,* like she was a waiter. Carla studied Tiffany, looking for some sign of offense.

On the small screen John X. Cousins glowered into the camera and began to narrate the tale of "the most disturbing dollhouse in

existence," at which point Kowalcimi did a spiraling hand gesture. "Just the house, please."

"As you wish." X sighed heavily but obliged, and now the
camera panned around and around the house, stopping at the
slowly opening front door (which creaked, which was ridiculous;
he must have used some stupid sound effects app), zooming into
the hallway, and now he had actually added music, some John
Carpenter-y *Halloween*-y piano tune, as his voice pointlessly described what they were actually looking at, and Harry said, "Can
we lose the audio?"

"Shouldn't we be showing them the rough cut anyway?" Tiffany looked mortified.

X gave her a dirty look. "That's what I thought we were doing,"
he said, as though the choice had been hers, which was obviously
not true. Carla was so embarrassed for Tiffany that she couldn't
look at her face.

From the start, the audience, except for Carla, leaned forward,
intent on every frame. Harry was especially excited by the dollhouse furniture. "That hutch is walnut! Did your father make it
himself?" When the bloody bedroom door was opened, they all
gasped; "Good lord, that's awful," said Amy when the cellar light
came on, and Carla looked away because she didn't need to see
that now, or ever again. Amy whispered, "Are you all right?" and
she more or less was, except she was so angry at what had been
done to the house. When the video ended, Kowalcimi asked to
see it once more, pausing before each new scene, freezing the cellar
images, taking notes. "What do you think?" asked Harry.

"Mr. Cousins," said Kowalcimi, "Tell me again when you and
Ms. Zuniga made the original video—which wasn't this one, I
take it."

"Yes, I've been polishing it—"

"The original. What Ms. Zuniga called the rough cut. I hope
it was saved. When was it recorded?"

"We found the dollhouse Wednesday night; we filmed it all that night. So it was essentially made yesterday. And yes, of course, we saved the original."

"What did you touch beside the outside of the house? We're fingerprinting."

Tiffany spoke up. "Very little! We tied string to the doorknobs so we could open them without sticking our hands in front of the camera, so there will be prints on the knobs, but that's about it."

"And Wednesday evening was the first time you came into contact with the dollhouse?"

"Yes," she said.

"And you?" he asked X. "You didn't touch it until the third?"

"I'm having trouble understanding your attitude, Lieutenant."

"Any pertinent information you can give us about these crimes is appreciated, and this dollhouse business opens a new line of inquiry. But it looks like you plan to turn some sort of profit from it, and that's a concern."

"I am a teacher." He said this like *I am a man of the cloth.* "My *plan* is to use this as a teaching aid."

"Teaching what?" asked Harry. "How to make cheesy true-crime docs?"

Kowalcimi stood. "We'll take a copy of the original video," he said.

"As I told you—"

"Put it on a thumb drive. We'll wait."

"That's going to be difficult—"

"No it won't!" Tiffany said. Carla thought *Yay Tiffany!!* and almost said it out loud. "Give me a minute." She smiled at the audience, especially Kowalcimi, and asked X to move so she could get at her laptop. X was not happy about this, which Tiffany either did not notice or didn't mind. In a flash she handed Kowalcimi two thumb drives shaped like open books. "The Point's got tons of these," she told him. "Here's a spare in case you lose one."

"Lieutenant," said Amy, "can you tell us anything about how

or if the dollhouse is connected to these local murders? I'm asking only because I'm concerned for Carla's safety, and Tiffany's too. They're often alone here."

"I wish I could. Fact is, right now either someone connected with the murders has screwed with the dollhouse, or someone unconnected with them is screwing with us. When we know more, you'll know."

"Also," said Harry, "there may be a connection between one of the latest murders and all of us."

Kowalcimi sat back down. "You mean the psych professor?"

"Philosophy," said Amy, "and no, we're talking about the other woman. Tiffany McGee."

"Wrong," said X. "The other woman was Cinnamon Bombe."

"Oh my god," said Tiffany. "I remember Tiffany McGee! She came to first class! She was the one who said she didn't read but she really wanted to be a writer, and she was supposed to bring something in the next week and she dropped. Oh, that's just awful."

"People," said X, rolling his eyes, "pay attention. The other woman was identified as Cinnamon—"

"This is going to be a real shock to you," said Harry, "but Cinnamon Bombe was *not her real name.*"

"Of course it wasn't. I know that. But you're confusing—"

"It's probably nothing," Amy said. "I just thought you should know. We met her only once, during first class a few years ago. One of those small-world things."

"I still don't like it," said Kowalcimi. For the first time, he looked alarmed. "I'm going to arrange for a patrol car to swing by here on a regular basis, and I don't want either of you ladies"—he pointed to Tiffany and Carla—"to hesitate about calling us if you see anything suspicious."

"Carla," said Tiffany, "how about if I stay here at night? I don't want you here by yourself."

"Chuck's staying with me. I'll be fine." Carla liked the idea of

Tiffany's staying too, just so they could maybe be friends again, but she didn't want X oozing around the place any more than he already was.

"I have a question," said Carla. "Do you think there's a connection between the women who got cut up, Donatella Ng and the professor, and all those women who got strangled?"

"Excellent point, Carla," said X. He offered this praise like a generous gift.

"I'm not making a point—I'm asking a question. And only because poor Tiffany was a stripper, and wasn't one of those other women—"

"It's a thought," said Kowalcimi, "although they were prostitutes, not strippers. McGee wasn't a prostitute, and she wasn't dismembered like Ng and Bunting, but she *was* attacked with something big and sharp, could have been an axe or a machete. Not strangled like the prostitutes."

"And Toonie Garabedian."

"And although she worked—and died—in Kearny Mesa, her home was here, in La Jolla. So . . . the answer is, we just don't know. We're sure about Bunting and Ng being related, and that's all we know right now. Except that a lot of women are getting murdered in San Diego County." He got to his feet again, thanking them for their attention. At the door he paused and said, "None of this gets leaked to the press. Not a word." He didn't look at X when he said this; he didn't need to.

Harry B. followed him out of the room, and Carla could hear him asking whether all the Pointers should be warned about the situation and if so, what they should be told. Tiffany joined them, leaving X to clean up the mess, which of course he did not do. Carla watched him: He had been left out, he didn't like it one bit, and he was trying to think what to do about it. He might have had steam shooting out of his ears. Without a word to Carla or Amy, he left down the back stairs. "It's wound-licking time," said Amy.

Carla was suddenly sleepy. Not tired, like she'd felt all day, but ready for bed, even though it wasn't dark out yet. "Can we get the dog another day?"

"We'd have to anyway. I'm sure they're all closed by now, unless you get one from a pet store, and you don't want to do that."

"But soon," said Carla. "Right? Monday maybe?"

"Monday certainly." Amy stood and scooped up Lottie, who'd fallen fast asleep during the matinee, from Carla's lap. "Carla? Are you sure you're all right?"

"I think I really am." She was too sleepy to feel much of anything.

There was a commotion in the hall outside Tiffany's office. They could hear someone, one of the crime techies, talking to the Lieutenant, and the woman sounded excited. They must have discovered something important. Carla got up to go find out what it was, but before she got to the door she heard the techie say, "It's ash of some kind, and it's not cigarette ash! We all think it's from something organic. Could be human cremains!"

"Oh my god," whispered Carla. "What are we going to do?"

"You're not going to do anything," said Amy. "You're going to bed. I'll explain."

"They're going to be so mad!"

"So what? We're not forensic specialists." Amy wandered to the window and looked down. "Here comes Chuck," she said. "Is there some reason why you're keeping him out of the loop? Because you are, aren't you?"

"Sort of."

"Why?"

"There's so much to tell, Amy. I don't know where to begin." This was true.

"It's a story, Carla," Amy said from the doorway. "Pick a scene, any scene. Set it. See what happens. I'll call you Monday."

Carla listened to Amy disappoint the crime scene lady. "My fault," she said. "I didn't think to wipe off the baggie." Nobody yelled at her. Nobody yells at Amy.

She watched Chuck chatting with the cops in the driveway, peering into the SUV. They let Myrtle out so Chuck could see her in action, sniffing at the camellias, following invisible trails up and down the street and driveway. Maybe she should get a German shepherd, Chuck really liked this dog, you could tell, except the dog was awfully big. As she watched, she thought about scenes. Set the scene. There were so many, and most of them were dismal. Chuck looked up, right at her, and waved, so happy to spot her in the high window, and she felt her own smile cross her face before she knew how happy this made her. The scene would just have to wait.

CHAPTER TWENTY-THREE

Amy

Monday, May 10

When Amy called Monday morning, Carla didn't answer. Her voicemail was new, some awful pop song telling everybody to calm down, but Amy was cheered by the sentiment. Something good must have happened to Carla; it was about time. Perhaps she'd gone out with Chuck and gotten her very own dog.

Over the weekend, time Amy should have spent working on new stories had mostly been lavished on imagining the right dog for Carla—she hadn't come up with the answer there—and tracking down online information about the local murders. Until meeting with Kowalcimi and seeing that video, Amy had not been distracted by them. Now she was unable to shake Tiffany McGee from her mind, which was ridiculous given that she'd been all but forgotten until she died, but still.

One of Amy's first stories had been about a middle-aged man whose sister is murdered and who cannot abide the spectacle of her picture in the newspaper. There is his sister's face and, underneath, the caption "Murder Victim." Caption maligns her image, so that everyone who sees it thinks, *Here is the kind of woman who gets herself killed.* Her end becomes inevitable. Every narrative arising from her death makes *sense* of it, and this drives the brother nearly mad. Amy was twenty-five years old when she wrote that story, and most of the others that launched her career. Not all of them wore well in her opinion, but this one did, and Amy wondered now how she had known to write it.

While accidental death was more frightening than murder, not just because it was more common but because it could happen anytime to anyone, murder was supposed to make some kind of sense, except when the murderer's motives were opaque, at which point people got even more outraged. "Senseless murder" was supposed to be the worst kind. Yet "senseless murder" was, like "relative truth," an oxymoron: Murder always happened for a reason, for someone's gratification, instant or otherwise. Accident had causes. Murder had purpose.

Of course there was contingency too, since, if Tiffany I hadn't arrived at the murder site at a certain time, she might be alive now. Unless, rather than being the killer's *type,* interchangeable with a thousand other pole dancers, she had been personally targeted. For her sake Amy found herself hoping the act was personal— that she had not suffered and died at the hands of some stranger to whom she was nothing more substantial than a paper doll with no history, no inner life, no memory.

Though it was like poking at a sore tooth, Amy got back online and searched for updates on "Cinnamon Bombe," hopeful her mourners would come forward and take control of her narrative. The *U-T* ran a story using her real name: Her grandmother, who raised her, praised her high spirits and determination to "better herself." Tiffany I had been dancing to pay her tuition at Concorde Career College; she had planned to be a dental hygienist. "Everybody loved her," said the grandmother.

Everybody but some troglodyte with an axe or a machete. Still, it was somewhat cheering to learn about Tiffany I's career plans, and Amy was about to stop the search when "Breaking News" on the murders popped up on the *U-T* site, and there went the rest of her day, because the news was breaking on all local TV sites. Amy loathed breaking news.

FRANKENSTEIN IN SAN DIEGO
POSSIBLE FRANKENSTEIN KILLER
REAL-LIFE DR. FRANKENSTEIN
POLICE MUM ON FRANKENSTEIN KILLINGS
THE MONSTER OF LA JOLLA

Before subjecting herself to any of the nonsense, Amy focused on "police mum" and knew that Cousins had leaked the story, whatever the story was, to the press. When last spotted on Friday, exiting stage left like a hunched, cloaked villain, Cousins was probably already plotting revenge against his unappreciative audience, and particularly Kowalcimi, whose contempt for him had to be plain even to Cousins.

He had charmed some stooge in the police station into betraying her employers and jeopardizing her own job. The informant had to be a woman, desperate for attention and charmed by this snake. Or maybe not, maybe someone resentful at being passed over for promotion or seduced by promises of Hollywood fame, because this was bound to result in a blockbuster movie and they'd be *in on the ground floor*. Whoever it was didn't matter, since the poor sap would be jobless and abandoned in a heartbeat. And Cousins himself—he had to know he'd be blamed for engineering the leak, and he had to believe that however angry the authorities were, he wouldn't be penalized in any significant way.

When she couldn't put it off any longer, Amy confronted the breaking news.

"It's like something from a horror movie," claims a source close to the police investigation of the murders of Donatella Ng and

Leonora Bunting. "Each of the bodies is missing a part, and it's not the same part." Police have theorized, according to the source, that the killer may be assembling a body out of parts. So far, according to the source, the missing parts are a right foot and a torso. When contacted, police spokesman Lt. Chet Kowalcimi refused to comment.

The story was equal parts horrifying and preposterous. Surely Frankenstein wasn't the only theory being floated at the PD. There were only two sets of body parts so far, hardly enough to replicate Elsa Lanchester, and maybe the torso just hadn't turned up yet and a coyote had run off with the foot.

As Amy stared at the screen, an update wiped it and there was the smirking face of "Dr. J. X. Cousins, local writing teacher and author of the serial killer study *Lightborne Redux*." Cousins praised the "source close to the police investigation" and then divulged that there were not just two dismembered bodies but "as many as six." During the past year the police, he said, had unearthed a number of other body parts, all female, but had not shared this information with the public, "ostensibly because the bodies have not yet been identified. It is my understanding that DNA results have ruled out correspondence with known missing persons, which may be their justification for keeping this under wraps."

"Ostensibly." Cousins was all but asking to be worked over with a telephone book. Did police still do that? Probably not. Also, there were no more telephone books, so how did they work people over without leaving bruises, or was that just a movie thing? Until now Amy had dismissed Cousins as a con artist, more annoyance than threat, even with his designs on the Point, but this was serious. The police must have had a good reason—probably more than one good reason—not to publicize the butchery until they could offer solid advice, and now Cousins had set off a stampede purely for his own benefit.

Amy considered calling Harry B., just to ask him whether Cousins could be arrested for instigating this. Then she thought to call the Birdhouse, to see if Tiffany was all right, but decided against it. Surely Tiffany's behavior last Friday meant she had freed herself of this man's influence. She shut down her computer and called Lottie. It was time to clear her head.

A light mist was falling, unusual for May. Or at least it used to be unusual, back when there was an actual fire season and Southern California weather didn't threaten to rival New England's in unpredictability. The mist was for a time pleasantly moisturizing, as Amy and Lottie ascended the hill, stopping to visit the turkeys and investigate gopher mounds. By the time they got back down, Amy had decided that the police were definitely not calling the murderer Frankenstein. This had to be an office joke that the stooge took seriously and Cousins—whether he believed it or not, and Amy guessed he didn't—ran with.

At home she towel-dried Lottie and herself, brewed a pot of ginger tea, and confronted her latest story, the title of which—"Cremains"—was all she had so far and a poor title at that. She sat still in front of the screen for a full hour trying to divine why the sight of that terrible old woman's remnants on her fingertips had so fascinated her on Friday. There had to be a reason beyond the obvious. But whatever it was, today it was hiding, because today was *Breaking News,* the creation of John X. Cousins, who had crafted a potboiler of epic scope, transforming tens of thousands of complex, living, unknowable human beings into a throng of flat characters, panicked and thrilled by his plot.

And exactly when and how had murder itself turned into a creative endeavor? In the beginning, humans killed in order to survive, or to achieve vengeance. When civilization reached a certain stage—when most people had enough to eat and a degree of physical safety, when leisure became an actual thing—murder's purpose expanded to include enjoyment, and here came Jack the Ripper and DeSalvo and Bundy and all the celebrities who killed for pleasure. "Thrillists," Cousins called them, but they were old hat now: They were now being bumped offstage to make room for the next iteration, the Artists. It wasn't enough to take trophies—you had to do something interesting with them, something original, and if your creation were sufficiently grotesque, you'd be featured in a dozen books, television serials, and movies.

Amy did not believe that the Artists were the killers themselves. No, the Artists were parasites like Cousins, surveying the field of slaughter and gathering it all into grand pulp, creating stories unrecognizable to the actual criminals, who had naively imagined they were just having fun.

She became nostalgic for Lizzie Borden. Lizzie had figured greatly in her own childhood library investigations. She was probably no more than thirteen when she read Pearson's *Trial of Lizzie Borden;* she practically memorized the book, so fascinated was she by the wealthy spinster who took an axe to her father and step-mother one humid August morning. Borden was acquitted, not because her damning inquest testimony was ruled inadmissible, but because while a lady might poison, she would never wield an axe, that was unimaginable. Of course she did wield an axe, and twice, and remained more or less free for the rest of her life.

Whatever Lizzie Borden's purpose, it wasn't aesthetic. She didn't murder for fame, or even notoriety, and the tableaux she left behind that August morning, stunning though they must have been, were not entertainments. The act was private. Lizzie left a mess, and the why of it was, to Amy, much less interesting than the woman herself.

On a whim, she googled Edmund Pearson. He had written a number of books about murder, including one called *Murder at Smutty Nose.* He'd also edited a limited edition of *Frankenstein, or the Modern Prometheus,* which Amy declined to take as evidence of anything but the slapstick of coincidence.

She spent the rest of her day avoiding breaking news, not writing, and tracking down information on the Smutty Nose murders.

If a copy of Pearson's book survived, the Web didn't know about it, but there was plenty about Smutty Nose aka Smuttynose, a tiny island off the coast of New Hampshire and Maine, and when Amy read that it was one of the Isles of Shoals she realized she'd been there as a little kid. Because her childhood memories, like all her memories, were mostly aural, she could not recapture a single sight from that trip, but she did recall her parents whispering about "haunted ground." Her father was laughing, and so was her mother, although she said "Not in front of Amy," which was probably why Amy remembered it at all. "I've never been less haunted in my life," her father said. Now she decided they must have been standing on the site of the murder house, which had burned down in 1908. Two Norwegian women had been axed to death there by a fisherman, who made off with sixteen dollars and, like Lizzie, left a mess.

Amy took Lottie to bed and later awoke in the dark to the afterimage of a frieze shining all around the top of her bedroom wall, a parade of figures dwarfed by their brandished axes, all carved in melting wax. This was, she knew, not real, only a hypno-pompic hallucination. She'd had these since childhood and had taught herself to wait them out. Before tonight it had always been a spider, often blond, always huge, squatting on her nightstand or dangling, writhing, twinkling in front of her face. No matter how detailed the image, no matter how cleverly it nestled among the furnishings of her darkened room, she never panicked, just shrugged it away and returned to sleep.

This was different. In the dark she waited, searching for movement, for the spider that never came, and when at last the wax figures faded out, she was wide awake for good.

CHAPTER TWENTY-FOUR

Carla

Tuesday, May 11

Carla and Chuck lounged on the big sofa in the Rotunda, watching plexiglass get erected around the dollhouse. Chuck was working at home today, taking a break, so now was a good time for Carla to set her first childhood scene for him, as Amy had suggested. It wouldn't be a sad story—pretty funny, in fact—but Carla figured it was a good way in. A gateway story. She'd thought about this last night and decided to start off small, building up slowly, maybe one scene a week. By Christmas she could tell him all about Hoving and Victorville. Or not.

"I was six. No, five. Ma got me doing local commercials in Pennsylvania, New Jersey, New York. We were in this grungy used car lot, Corky Bean's, and they made me wear this Aerosmith T-shirt."

"Why?"

"No clue. This was Jersey City, not Hollywood, so basically amateur hour. Corky Bean, whose real name was Fabian Bermudez—"

"What difference does that make?"

Carla was taken aback. "What do you mean 'what difference does it make?'"

"To the story," said Chuck. "You're telling a story, so I'm wondering about this choice of detail."

"What are you, Amy?"

"Yes! Are we having our first argument?"

"Yes!" Carla laughed.

"Feels kind of good, doesn't it?"

For some reason, it did. "Okay, so scrap Fabian Bermudez."

"May I lie down with my head in your lap? If this is going to be a long story, I need to get comfortable."

"You may." He did, and she caught her breath. The weight of his head. It made her whole body feel light, like she could rise through the ceiling and take him with her.

"And his name was Fabian Bermudez," said Chuck.

"And he was super short with a big nose and a gross mustache and this ugly sports jacket with a checkerboard pattern, and a hat with two red feathers sticking up. I think it must have been a porkpie hat. I liked the feathers." She looked down at him. He was smiling and his eyes were closed. "Are you falling asleep?"

"Just concentrating. I don't want to miss a minute of this."

"He kept calling me Princess. Like, 'Princess, all you gotta do is run back and forth in front of me while I'm talking, and when I say—'"

"Sounds like a jerk."

"He was okay. He was nice. And when he said 'Our sticker prices are INCREDULOUS!' I was supposed to stop right in front him and—"

"He actually said 'incredulous'?"

"Yes, and more than once, because we rehearsed it all afternoon. The bit ended with him picking me up and setting me on his shoulder and I was supposed to yell, 'So motor on down to Corky Bean's WIGHT THIS MINUTE!'"

"Why did it take all afternoon?"

"Because I refused to say 'wight.'"

"You were a principled tot."

"I talked better than that. Every kid I knew, not that I knew very many, knew how to do Rs. 'Wight' was embarrassing. Corky thought I was funny. He got a bang out of my attitude. Nobody else did, especially Ma, but he kept picking me up and I'd say it wrong and he'd just laugh. Finally he said, 'You know what, the kid's right, let's go with the last take.'"

"Good for him!"

"Yeah, only Ma."

"What about her?"

"She had this thing about 'professionalism.' I was a 'professional,' and it was my job to follow directions. To the letter. She actually said that. *To the letter, which means W, not R.* She argued with Corky until he backed down. Because everybody backed down from Ma. Then she made me say 'wight' about a hundred times, in front of everybody. I think he felt bad for me. He must have, because when Ma turned away and told the crew I was ready, I took off running through the lot and he was the only one facing me and he didn't tell her which way I went. I was running down the rows of cars and they were calling out for me, and Ma was furious, she was shrieking, which she never did in public."

Chuck's eyes were open. "You must have been terrified."

"No way! That's just it, I wasn't. I was thrilled! I'd never defied her before. I never did it again, at least not for years, but it was this great discovery, a world without Ma, like an alternate universe or something, and I knew it wouldn't last, but that was okay, because this was now, you know? I was alone and free in this enchanted car lot."

Chuck captured her left hand in both of his, warming it. "How long were you alone and free?"

"Ha! Longer than you'd expect! I found a car with an open trunk full of groceries, and I crawled in and hid behind the bags."

"Carla, somebody could have driven off with you in the trunk!"

"Somebody almost did. The trunk slammed shut and then the driver door, and the car started up, and I could hear these muffled voices from outside the car, and one of them was Ma, she must have been walking close by, so I didn't make a sound. I was off on an adventure!" She leaned back and closed her eyes. "I used to think about that a lot. What would have happened next. I had this fantasy where this huge family with lots of dogs would find me in the trunk and I'd go live with them."

"I'm sorry that didn't happen."

"What did happen was that I was pretty hungry, because we never ate before gigs, Ma had this thing about empty stomachs and top performance, so while I was waiting for the car to get going I rummaged around in one of the bags and got attacked by a lobster."

"Of course you did."

"I did!"

"You're making this up."

"No, it clamped onto my thumb, it was cold and hard and wet and it pinched something awful, and I was screaming my head off because I didn't know what it was. I think I thought it was Ma. So anyway they found me." Chuck squeezed her hand, hard. "The end." He wasn't laughing.

They were quiet for a long while. The plexiglass crew finished up and showed her how to open and lock the box; she asked them to take the key up to Tiffany, and they left. Carla hated the way sunlight coated the plastic, obscuring her view of the house, but at least it was safe now. "I suck at telling stories," she said. "That one was supposed to be funny." She was beginning to cloud up, and then, without asking first, Chuck hugged her tight and kissed her forehead.

"The lobster was funny," he said.

"NOT HERE!" Tiffany's voice emerged from the stairwell at the opposite end of the Rotunda. For a split second Carla thought she and Chuck were being scolded for public displays of affection, but the voice was too far away. Tiffany was in her office yelling at somebody. "I DON'T KNOW HOW ELSE TO SAY IT!"

When they got to her office, a short, stocky woman was leaning over the desk, her fists planted on either side of Tiffany's laptop; Tiffany was standing and backing away, hands outstretched, palms up, showing the woman something that was "NOT HERE." Carla and Chuck rounded the desk and stood on either side of Tiffany.

The woman's posture was aggressive, but her face wasn't. She mostly looked desperate and exhausted, like she hadn't slept once in her whole life. She had a nice face, no meanness in the eyes, no craziness either, she was just a woman at the end of her rope. Forty-plus, Carla decided, and probably pretty once—she looked kind of like Meredith Baxter, if Meredith Baxter had let herself go and taken to leaving home wearing mom jeans and a red T-shirt that said "Read to write! Write to be read! What's your story! Dare to Fail!"

"She's looking for Cousins," said Tiffany.

Carla took a moment to be thrilled. Tiffany had called him "Cousins." Not "John" or even "John Cousins."

"Ma'am," said Carla, "I'm Carla. I'm the owner, and I want to help you. Please sit down so we can figure this out."

The woman dropped into the chair, took a deep breath, and began, her voice trembling. "I want to see him right away," she said. "He's not returning my calls."

Tiffany fiddled with her phone, stared at it for a minute, put it down. "If it's any consolation, he's not returning mine either. So let us help you. Let's start with your name."

The woman took a deep breath. "Paisley. Paisley Shawcross."

"That's a lovely name," said Carla.

"Thank you. Look, I need to know something: You say you're the owner. Is that really true?"

"Sure! I own the house, and Inspiration Point is my company."

"Oh, god." Eyes tight shut, she shook her head back and forth, muttering, "Idiot idiot idiot idiot idiot."

"Let me guess," said Chuck. "He told you the place was his."

She nodded.

"What else did he tell you? That he could get you published?"

"What? No. Well, yes, but that's not it."

Carla decided to wait her out rather than pester her with questions. Eventually Paisley Shawcross opened her eyes, sighed, and began.

"I've been divorced for fifteen years, my kids are out of the house with lives of their own, and yes, I've tried writing romance novels, really just as a time-filler. But I love my job! I *loved* my job." Tears filled her eyes. "I worked for the La Jolla PD for a year, a whole year, the best job I ever had. I was evidence custodian and records clerk. They all liked me. They all trusted me." She started to cry. "They shouldn't have."

Tiffany handed her a box of Kleenex. "He got you to leak all that Frankenstein stuff to the press?"

"No, I would never do that! He got me to leak it to *him*. I leaked it to him because he promised to keep it to himself. He said he would use it later—*much later,* he said. When he writes his book about these killings."

"Of course he did," said Chuck and Carla at the same time.

"And yesterday the news broke, and I called him, and he said not to worry, everything was going to be okay, and he'd see me later last night at our usual place."

Oh, thought Carla. Oh, you poor thing. Nobody asked Paisley Shawcross what their usual place was, or why they had a usual place and what they usually did there, because her broken heart was bleeding right in front of them. Tiffany looked not exactly shocked but sad. Had she really loved him? Carla couldn't fathom it.

"And he never showed up, and he never called, and I actually— listen to this—I actually thought he must have been in an accident, that's what an idiot I am. I've been monitoring traffic reports, I even called three hospitals, not just Scripps. And I came in to work this morning and they fired me."

"How did they know it was you?" Chuck asked.

"Because I told them. The Lieutenant was reading people the riot act, promising to find out who the culprit was, and I couldn't let him keep on grilling the whole office. I just blurted it out in front of everybody and he told me to clear out my desk." She started to rise. "I'm so sorry I came here and carried on like a crazy person." She looked at Tiffany. "Please accept my apologies."

"Don't go," Carla said. "It isn't your fault. You don't deserve any of this."

"Yes, I do. I'm a fool."

Tiffany rose. "I'm going to get you a cup of coffee. Sit right there."

Chuck sat next to Paisley and put a calming hand on her arm. "The man," he said, "is a sociopath. It's not stupid to be conned by a sociopath. It's just human."

Carla saw that his other hand was clenched into a fist. Chuck had never seemed the violent type but she found herself hoping that X would cross his path, and soon. The man needed what Old Sally Gee used to call a clop in the chops. Also, he needed to go to jail. Carla excused herself, went back to the Rotunda, and got Harry B. on the phone.

She reached him right away and told him the whole story. Harry kept saying, "Bastard." Carla started into an impassioned plea for Harry to persuade Kowalcimi to give Paisley Shawcross her job back, which Harry interrupted.

"I'm way ahead of you," he said. "You say she only blabbed to Cousins, right? She didn't tell anybody else? And you believe her?"

"Totally, and so does Chuck, and so does Tiffany."

"I'll see what I can do. I'll get back to you when I know more. Don't make any promises. Meanwhile, if that asshole shows up, sit on him."

"Ewww."

When Carla got back, Tiffany was talking to Paisley in a low, soothing voice, telling her all about how X had fooled her too. She told how she had trusted the man, given him keys and passcards, let him use the Point for his own purposes, which he convinced her were all about promoting creativity and getting book deals. She didn't tell Paisley that she and X had been lovers. That was very kind of her. Carla was so grateful to have her friend back.

"Are you all aware that there's a police cruiser parked across the street?" Misha Bernard stood in the doorway with an armload of what looked like manuscripts. "John has asked me to drop these off."

"Why doesn't he drop them off himself?" asked Chuck.

"Are you also dropping off his passcard and keys?"

Misha cocked her head at Tiffany and smiled. "Sorry, no, but I can arrange for that."

"Please do."

"He was going to bring these in himself, and I talked him out of it. John doesn't always see that not everybody shares his enthusiasms, his degree of commitment to—"

"What not everybody appreciates," said Carla, "is him stampeding all over the feelings and lives of innocent people."

"Which I may have managed to get across to him." Misha seemed amused, not just with Carla and the others, but with the whole situation. Misha was a big-time author, not just a local celeb. Her latest Aztec thing was in the Amazon Top Fifty for a month. Misha, Carla guessed, didn't respect X any more than she did. She was using the user, although how exactly wasn't clear. "John has marked up all the manuscripts and is asking you to get them back to the students."

"What students?" Tiffany asked. "We don't have students here, just clients who use the cells. He knows that. For that matter, so do you."

"Well, apparently over the past year people have asked him to take a look at their writing, which he's done, free of charge, or so he says. I really don't know anything about it—I'm just doing him a favor."

Chuck swiveled around to look at her. "Does he have any idea how much trouble he's in?"

"Because of the press leak? Probably not. He calls it a calculated risk, but I'm not sure how accurate his calculations are. He doesn't have a lawyer." Misha sat down next to Paisley Shawcross, who did not look at her. "He's actually asked to use mine."

"Was that too big a favor?" asked Tiffany.

"Well, yes, and anyway, you don't loan out legal advice. My understanding is that while he's going to be in the doghouse with the police, he hasn't actually broken any laws."

"In the doghouse with Myrtle," said Carla. "I don't think she's going to like that."

"They brought Myrtle?" Paisley looked anxious.

"Nothing to worry about," said Tiffany. "They're just covering all the bases or something."

"Oh. He's such a good man. The Lieutenant." Paisley started to tear up, then stopped and cleared her throat. "I'm wondering about those 'calculations.' What does John—what does *Cousins* gain with this risk? He's infuriated the La Jolla PD and betrayed . . . Oh, forget it."

Misha looked closely at her. "I don't know him that well, but he strikes me as the kind to whom betrayal of trust is a way of life."

"But what for?" Paisley's voice rose. "He'd do all that just to get a book published?"

"He'd do all that, and probably more," said Misha, "to get a book *deal*."

"And he has that?" asked Chuck. "He's already got a book deal on these murders, when nobody knows which ones are connected and who's doing them?"

Misha shook her head. "He claims to have nibbles, and for a guy like this, nibbles are enough to feed the dream. My guess: When they catch the murderer he'll finish the book in a flash, probably won't wait for the trial for fear of getting beaten out by a better-known crime writer, because for sure this will generate books, not to mention TV and movies. One of the nibblers will give him a disappointing advance; if he's lucky, he'll get reviewed somewhere, but not the *NYT*." She stood up and faced Carla. "Another thing: This morning he shared with me his plans to take over your business. I'm telling you this in case you don't know about it—"

"I do," said Carla.

"Good. I thought you might. He tried to interest me in going in with him. I didn't jump at the chance, but I did hear him out. He's thinking of including, in this yet-to-be-written masterpiece, a tell-all exposé—his words—about your teacher, Amy Gallup, and that murder workshop from a few years ago."

"That son of a bitch." Tiffany said this calmly, as though commenting on the weather, but her color was high.

Carla was so angry she couldn't speak.

"That's ridiculous," said Chuck. "There's no connection between then and now. We know who killed our workshop friends, and it wasn't Frankenstein."

"Of course, but you see, his angle is that the Birdhouse is haunted, and the ghost of—"

"Son of a *bitch*."

Carla exploded. "The ghost of *Ma*! He's going to use Ma, right, and me? I'll sue him! He's not going to use Amy, and my house and my family and my private life! This house is my home, and it isn't haunted!"

"Of course it isn't. Harry Blasbalg is your lawyer, correct? Let him deal with this. And tell him I'll be happy to share everything I know about John's plans, which is quite a bit. I can find out more." She handed cards to Carla and Tiffany. "My private number."

"Before you go," said Chuck. "I'm curious, and don't take this the wrong way, but what's in this for you?"

Misha laughed. "No offense. Basically two reasons. First, I like this place. I don't need it, like your other inmates, but I admire what you've done with the Point. It's brilliant. You offer what all writers require: discipline and a plain, simple cell in which to work, with no distractions. The second reason . . . I'm thinking of branching out into nonfiction. The whole Mictlantecihuatl, P.I. thing is boring the crap out of me."

"Huh," said Chuck, who obviously had no idea what she was talking about.

"My Aztec gumshoe," she said. "Carla," she said, at the door, "seriously, have Harry give me a call." She waved to all and disappeared.

The room was quiet for a full minute. "She's branching out into nonfiction," Carla said. "What the heck does that mean? Does anybody understand this?"

"I think maybe I do." For the first time since Carla had met her, Paisley didn't look overwhelmed with self-loathing. She just sat still and focused inward.

"Okay, what is it?" Paisley was turning into kind of an interesting person. Carla decided she was going to offer her a free cell to do her romance writing. It was really the least she could do.

Tiffany said, "So Misha's going to beat him to the punch? Write her own true-crime about the murders?"

"Maybe, but I don't think so. I think she's going to write a book about *him*."

Carla could not imagine who would want to read about such a small-time grifter. X was a crummy human being but hardly a candidate for celebrity. But Chuck and Tiffany both raised hands, waved them like first graders, entered into spirited competition.

"'Portrait of a Grifter'! Paisley, you're brilliant!"

"'Frankenstein Unmasked'!"

"'The Man Who Would Be Something or Other'!"

"'The Man Who Would Be Capote'!"

"You guys are serious? Okay, he's all of those things, but he's hardly Bernie Madoff. It's not like he's conned millions. He just wants to." Carla felt like the only adult in the room. This was a brand-new feeling.

"You're right," said Paisley, "but if it's set against the backdrop of all these killings . . . if it shows him manipulating everybody while people are actually dying . . ." She was transformed with determination. "If that's what she's doing, I want to help. To begin with, I can fill her in on what the man did to my police department. I'll start by writing it all down."

And before Carla could even suggest it, Tiffany handed Paisley Shawcross a keycard. "Cell 5, west wing. First three months on us."

CHAPTER TWENTY-FIVE

Amy

Tuesday, May 11

UNKNOWN CALLER rang while Amy was staring at the solitary word "Cremains" centered at the top of her computer screen. She selected the Sonic Blast Air Horn that Amazon had delivered just last week, donned her special earplugs, blasted the receiver, hung up, and resumed staring. The phone rang again, and again she blew the horn. Maybe it wasn't as deafening to the caller as it was to her, because the phone rang a third time. Amy sighed, picked up, asked, "Is this someone with good news or money?" and a familiar voice chuckled—actually chuckled—and said, *"A Thousand Clowns*! Herb Gardner! You have excellent taste!" Gripping the air horn, Amy regarded the phone with loathing. "Mr. Cousins," she said. "How may I help you?"

"I thought you'd never ask! Apologies for the intrusion, but we happen to be in the area, and we were wondering if we could stop by. There are a couple of matters I'd love to discuss with you. Do you know there's something wrong with your phone?"

By "we" he probably meant Tiffany. Or maybe that Misha

person. By "in the area" he must have meant "down the street," because the bell rang before Amy could fortify herself with green tea. She took her time going to the door, wondering as she did so why she hadn't told him she was busy. Curiosity, maybe, and perhaps she could divine something useful on his nefarious schemes about Inspiration Point!, although surely Harry was on top of all of that.

So it was that Amy ushered into her home John X. Cousins and a ginger-haired fellow in greasy sweatpants and a too-small green T-shirt with the message "KEEP CALM AND YOUR TEXT HERE." The shirt had rolled up at the hem, exposing two inches of pale belly. The stranger had the most guileless gaze Amy had ever seen on an adult; he smiled at Amy as though she were Santa Claus and surveyed her living room with what looked like awe. "This is Eugene Doppler," said Cousins. "I hope you don't mind—he insisted on meeting you."

"Have you read all these books?" Eugene Doppler scanned the shelves and bookcases that lined three walls.

Amy had always wondered why that qualified as a conversation-starter, but Eugene was, she could see, genuinely curious. "Are you a reader?"

"The first time I saw Eugene, he was sitting on the grass near the Zoo reading Flannery O'Connor. Imagine that." Cousins was beaming like a proud parent. He was, of course, the sort to be astounded by the spectacle of an ordinary-looking person behaving unpredictably. Cousins' world was choked with stereotypes.

"I love to read," said Eugene. "I love to read what people throw away."

"You mean thrift shops? The local library here always has an interesting collection for sale. Would you like to know—"

"He means trash cans."

"People throw away Flannery O'Connor?"

"And F. Scott Fitzgerald and Jacqueline Susann and Thomas Berger and Jane Bowles and Marcel Proust and Frank Yerby and

Irving Stone and Kathleen Winsor," said Eugene. "They throw away lots and lots of books."

"In Balboa Park?" He had said "Prowst," but from the reverent look on his face Amy would bet a lot that Eugene Doppler had read more of *Remembrance* than she had.

"He means libraries. Libraries have to weed their collections, and what they can't sell secondhand they throw away."

"I had no idea."

"Neither did I. Eugene has taught me a lot about it."

"The finest dumpster is on Park Boulevard," said Eugene. "That's where I got your book *Monstrous Women*."

"It was probably falling apart from overuse," said Cousins, affecting not to enjoy this information.

"I very much doubt that," said Amy. "Where do you live, Eugene?" She would never dream of asking such a personal question of an adult, but Eugene Doppler was, to her eyes, a middle-aged child.

"Dr. Cousins lets me sleep in his driveway."

Cousins had the grace to look abashed. "Eugene has his own RV."

"I see." Amy didn't see. More baffling than the appearance in her living room of Eugene Doppler was the notion of Cousins extending kindness to him, or to anyone else who could not be of use. Because neither man was in a hurry to explain what they were doing in her house, Amy seated them, excused herself, and made up a pot of tea. When she returned with the tray, Eugene was standing in front of the bookcase devoted to short fiction, hands in pockets, reading the spines intently, as though memorizing the titles. "You're welcome to borrow one," she said. "Or two. I have too many."

"Eugene wants to be a writer."

Of course he did. Everybody did. Amy would have ignored this bizarre gambit (what *was* Cousins up to?) except that the back of Eugene's neck suddenly reddened. He was embarrassed by Cousins' indiscretion.

"Actually I was—we were—wondering if you might help," Cousins said.

"In what way?"

"I've told Eugene that you are a legendary teacher of—"

"I'm nothing of the sort, and I ran my last workshop three years ago. The only thing legendary about it was that two members died at the hands of a third."

"Yes, and I'm glad you brought that up! If you don't mind, I would very much like to discuss that workshop with you."

A very old memory now popped up: Mr. Cleary, the neighborhood insurance salesman, was in the kitchen haranguing Amy's mother about the urgent need to upgrade her husband's policy, and Amy was listening while pretending to color a picture of Tonto perched on a boulder. "I cannot tell you, Mrs. Gallup, how many widows have thanked me for this advice," and her mother, ordinarily the soul of kindness and courtesy, said, "Leave my house." Just three words, uttered with thrilling gravity, and the man slunk off without another oleaginous word. (This was the day she learned the word "oleaginous," from her mother.) Now she opened her mouth to say it, *Leave my house,* and Eugene Doppler turned from the bookcase, faced Cousins, and said, "I want to go now."

Cousins looked as shocked as Amy felt. The expression on Eugene's face was more sad than angry, something in between. What an interesting person. "Do you know about the murders, Eugene?"

"Yes, and I'm sorry," he said.

"You have nothing to apologize for."

"He promised me he wouldn't bring it up."

"Eugene," said Cousins. "Why don't you wait in the car. I won't be long."

Clearly Eugene had gone off-script. Amy wondered why Cousins had ever imagined he wouldn't. The man was a perfect innocent. Was he on the spectrum? What did that mean, anyway? The phrase seemed to spring up overnight. Suddenly people carried on as though they knew what "on the spectrum" meant. Whatever category Eugene fell into, assuming there was one, she had at first thought him intellectually disabled, but he had read Proust, and he was sensitive to the tension between Cousins and herself. Amy was not by nature a trusting person, but instinctively she trusted Eugene Doppler. "Do you like dogs, Eugene?"

"I like them very much." He was smiling down at Lottie sniffing at his shoes and the cuffs of his sweatpants.

"Would you be willing to take Lottie here for a walk? I'd be very grateful. Mr. Cousins and I have a few things to discuss."

Lottie took to Eugene Doppler right away; Amy watched them through the picture window. She waited Cousins out.

After a full minute, he cleared his throat. "As you may know, I've been working on a study of serial killers for some time. The recent unfortunate series of local murders has caused me to rethink the focus of my current work; I'm now committed to narrowing that focus to the murders here, especially those centered in La Jolla. Of course, the crimes and the mystery are ongoing, but in a way that makes for a perfect opportunity—"

"You're good at that, aren't you? Opportunity?"

"What I'd like to run by you—"

"'Run by me'??"

"Look," he said, "I understand you don't approve of my, shall we say, presence in La Jolla, my influence upon Inspiration Point!, and I can imagine that you feel somewhat—"

"Mr. Cousins." Amy turned from the window and sat down across from him. "You are making me do something I never do. You are forcing me to be, *shall we say, confrontational.* I doubt that you can imagine how I feel about your presence in La Jolla, let alone in my house, so let me spell it out. I don't trust you. I don't trust your intentions with respect to Inspiration Point! Carla Karolak came up with a brilliant idea and made it work, she created a successful business, although her objective wasn't to make money, it was to help people achieve their dreams. But it's also a moneymaker, and I think you want it for yourself."

"Perhaps," said Cousins. "I'll admit, it has occurred to me. Still, I'm a writer, a teacher, not a businessman. You of all people should understand that."

As though they were colleagues.

"In furtherance of my new project, I would like to interview you. If not today, then at a time of your own choosing." When she did not respond, he opened a briefcase, took out a silver laptop, and opened it.

"For what purpose?" she asked.

"Nothing from the interview will be used except by your express consent."

"Used for what? I take it you're working on an article. Who is your publisher?" She said this only to twit him—surely he was planning to blog the thing.

Cousins smiled. "Sadly, this won't be in print. It's exciting, though. I'm tasked with creating a docuseries, and that series will, as I mentioned, examine the La Jolla killings."

I was tasked, Amy imagined explaining to the police, *with enduring another minute with this malignant buffoon without resorting to homicidal violence.* "Which is what you were doing with Carla's dollhouse last week, with the Rod Serling nonsense and the spooky tunes. You're planning to include the dollhouse in your series? Imply something supernatural is going on?"

"That I haven't decided. You will admit that the presence of those wax figures is disturbing. Evidence of a certain malevolence."

"A human malevolence, yes. Someone is messing with Carla. She calls what happened a desecration, and that was the intent of it."

"Be that as it may—"

"For the last time. What do you want from me?"

Cousins sighed, appeared to regroup. "I believe that the notorious events in your last workshop have a certain thematic relevance to what is going on now."

For once, the man looked like he really believed what he was saying. The "thematic relevance," whatever that meant, seemed to excite him. Despite herself, Amy was intrigued. "Artistic endeavors have themes. Real life does not."

"True, but listen. Yes, those workshop murders were solved, that's over and done with. But the atmosphere in that workshop, its . . . ethos. It is in the air today, here, and it may well have started with you. You may in fact be its key. I'm sorry, but there it is. And that's why I wanted to interview you."

"I don't know what you mean by 'ethos,' let alone 'key,' but if you really want to know how the workshops were run, interview group members, not me. Many have Inspiration Point accounts, and probably the others would be easy enough to track down."

"Which I have begun to do, and I plan to do more, but in order to process that information, I need to learn more about your method."

"Classic workshops. No lectures, no outside reading, one hundred percent classwork critique. Nothing to see here."

"Now come on," he said, "you know that's not what I'm talking about." He had weirdly assumed a fond frown, the sort you give a child whose face is smeared with stolen chocolate.

"*John.*" She heard herself actually using his first name but couldn't help it, because she was beginning to doubt he was the low-level evil mastermind she had taken him to be. He wasn't here to play her, as he had tried to play Carla and Tiffany and the La Jolla PD and everybody else. He had a *mission.* A stupid mission, but he didn't know that. "Listen to me. I'm too old to waste time playing games. I do not know what 'method' you mean."

He nodded and held up his index finger. "Here is what it is." he said. He cleared his throat. "There were always three exercises, conducted during the first three workshop meetings. Correct?"

"Really? What were they?"

"Exercise One: The Hazing."

"The *what*?"

"Exercise Two. The—"

"What hazing?"

He typed into his laptop, read from the screen. "'In First Class, she would go around the room, first to ask for names, then for our favorite writers, then to tell about our writing experiences so far. And then, when that was done and we were all relaxed, she would ask each of us to tell a true story about ourselves. Something we had never told a living soul. She said this was the most direct tunnel into the heart of the narrative engine.'"

"I don't know where you're getting this, but it's not true. In the first place, I've never shown up drunk at a workshop, which I'd have to be to call anything 'a tunnel into an engine.' More to the point, what this describes is both unethical and goofy. How would pressuring people to publicize their innermost secrets help them write fiction and share it with one another?"

"'She called it a trust-building exercise.'"

Cousins wasn't clever enough to have come up with this bilge, and he'd never give her his "source." Somebody in an earlier group? Carla was the only constant in the earlier groups, the only memorable one. Amy tried to think where she had stored her old group lists. Or maybe she'd chucked them. Tiffany would know. Or ... maybe it was Marvy Stokes' wife, from the final group? Cindy Stokes had helped Cousins with that silly PowerPoint presentation about serial killers and trophies and crampons. She was working with Cousins, so she must like him, and she had, Amy now recalled, yanked Marvy out of the final workshop halfway through the term, blaming Amy for continuing the group after the first death.

"Two," said Cousins. "The Hotseat."

"You're joking."

"Quote: 'During Second Class, we focused on character. One

by one, we'd take a seat at the front of the class, and everybody would give brutally honest first impressions of our character and personality based on our appearance.'"

"Well, that makes sense. *Let's each say six wrenching things about Marlene.*"

"You're claiming this never happened?"

"What would have been the point of it? Beyond satisfying some sadistic impulse? What am I supposed to have said was the purpose of this Hotseat?" *Hotseat.* What a horrible word.

"'She said this would show us how to create characters from the outside in.'"

Amy thought. "That's actually kind of brilliant. If I were a psychopath, I'd definitely use it. Only wouldn't it pretty much counteract all that trust-building? John, think. Does any of this make sense?"

He refused to engage. He was on a roll. "Lastly—"

"Stop."

"Exercise Three."

"Oh for god's sake."

He quieted her with a stern look, took a theatrical pause, and spoke: "The Séance."

Amy's laugh, explosive and unannounced, shocked herself as much as it did Cousins. It erupted at the exact instant she knew who was responsible for The Hazing, The Hotseat, The Séance, the epic pranking of John X. Cousins.

She tried to apologize but couldn't until she got control of herself, which took a while. And she *was* sorry. As much as she disliked the man, he'd been made a fool of, and nobody quite deserved that degree of humiliation. It was odd, really, how disappointment, when revealed in the face of even the most obnoxious person, always evoked pity. At least in Amy. "John," she finally said. He was busying himself with the laptop, snapping it shut, shoving it into his briefcase, acting as though everything were just fine and he had places to go. His color was high. "John. Edna was having fun with you."

He actually snorted. "I don't know what you're talking about." It was Edna, all right, though he'd never admit it. "Anyway, I can see that we won't get any further with this today."

"Ask Tiffany how to get in touch with former class members. Tell her I said it was okay to share the information. Ask *them* about séances and hotseats. See what happens."

He ignored her, stood up, looked out the window.

She had forgotten all about Lottie. "Are they out there?"

"Coming down the street."

"Before you go, tell me what you wanted me to do for Eugene. You must have brought him here for a reason." Amy felt expansive enough, perhaps guilty enough, though why she wasn't sure, to play along with whatever it was.

He fished a sheaf of pages out of his briefcase. "Eugene has talent, but not of the kind I deal with. He writes children's fiction." He shrugged. "Why, I can't imagine, but there it is. I've tried to mentor him, to get him to see how to make his work more marketable, but he writes what he writes, and that's it."

Amy said she was pretty sure that children's fiction sells.

"Yes, but Eugene . . . Eugene wants to write a series. Like *The Hardy Boys* or whatever."

"*Nancy Drew. Honey Bunch. Little House.* They must have made money."

"How about *The Homeless Club*? How's that for a money-maker?"

"*The Homeless Club.*" Brilliant! Eugene had to be some species of savant.

"He's written six books already. Makeshift family of fifteen homeless children, some with no parents, others saddled with adults who are crazy or drug-addicted, scampering through the canyons of Balboa Park. They have 'adventures.'" Based on his curling lip, Eugene Doppler might have been a pornographer.

In the Reagan years, Amy recalled, they had churned out kids' books about the nuclear menace. Instead of allowing their little ones to grow at their own pace into awareness of their mortality, enlightened parents were supposed to introduce them to the world they themselves had helped to make, where every second of their lives they hung by a thread over a boiling cauldron. In contrast, Eugene's impulse, to explore an aspect of the world as it was right now, and as the child could not help but witness it, rather than as it might be in some future over which the child was powerless, was at the very least not foolish, not cruel. "I really don't see a problem," she said.

Cousins laughed mirthlessly. "How are you going to sell it? Who's going to line up to buy a book, let alone a series of books, about children living in cardboard boxes, scrounging for food, dodging the police? Who would want their kids to read that? It's bleak, hopeless, and depressing. It's just not marketable."

Amy was about to make a wisecrack about Charles Dickens and marketability when the front door opened and Lottie bounded inside, followed by Eugene. "Everybody on the street knows your dog," he said. "The turkey lady says she's a celebrity."

"Thank you, Eugene. And I would like to read some of your fiction. May I?" She had to be abrupt, as Cousins was already bundling him out the door.

"You don't have to do that."

"Still, I'd like to take a look. Understand that I'm not particularly good with children's fiction, but I know some people who are. Is it all right if Mr. Cousins leaves it with me?"

It was more than all right with Eugene. Amy watched them drive away in that foolish Tesla and wondered what Cousins would do next. If he had any sense, he'd pay Edna one last visit to tell her that TED Talk was off.

At the end of the day she was back at her desk, staring at "Cremains," trying to find her way into that moment at Carla's when the old woman's dust on her fingertips sparkled in the sunlight and two tiny fragments had been tall enough, just, to throw shadows.

She moused through the Web, looking for images, data, explanations, everything out there about the history and process of cremation, but nothing resonated. She did learn there was something called "water cremation" now, illegal in most states, which involved liquefying the dead. So far it had not caught on. People content to sprinkle ashes at sea, in rose gardens, on mountaintops, apparently drew the line at watching their loved ones circle the drain. This information was not helpful.

She had cremated her parents and Max and buried them in small square cardboard boxes because it seemed sensible. Though she never visited their graves, she knew she could if she wanted to, which was a kind of comfort. They were, as the Brits said, done and dusted. Now she wished she had opened those boxes before interring them, not to confront the sobering reality of the contents, but simply to file those images in memory, to make them her own. Like Lucy the Book Hoarder, Amy was unable to conjure up the faces of the dead, no matter how dear. But she could still recall in sharp detail Max's favorite necktie, her mother's pewter pitcher, her old Nurse Jane doll, one-eyed and stained with tape glue; the sight of a *stranger's* bone dust on her fingertips would, she knew, remain hers for life.

She wondered if in the sad little kingdom of John X. Cousins was a wall with that staple of police procedurals, an enormous corkboard decorated like a molecular structure chart, thumbtacked with little pictures connected here and there by colored string. Pictures of Donatella Ng, Toonie Garabedian, Carla and Tiffany, the Birdhouse, Edna, Tiffany McGee, all the living and all the dead, and at the center Amy herself, strings radiating from her image like starshine.

Today was a day for particles, gathering, colliding, connecting. Cousins was surely wrong that she was the *key,* but she was somehow connected, though understanding the nature of each connection was beyond his pay grade. And hers. Causation? Correlation? Coincidence? Amy wanted not to wonder at it, but now she needed to. Her dreams had turned bad enough to steal her sleep. Something was coming. Something wrong, in which she recognized nothing but countless soulless particles, persisting throughout time, throwing their tiny shadows.

CHAPTER TWENTY-SIX

Carla

Friday, May 14

There's good news and bad news," said Tiffany. "Which do you want first?"

"No news," said Carla. "I need to wake up." She poured herself a mug of coffee and sat down before Tiffany's desk. "Let's start with the bad."

"The Herman Twins, the McPhails, Sophia Rosales, and Manny Singh have all declined to renew their cells. 'For the time being,' they all say. Only Manny gives the honest reason. The rest say they're sidelined by various bogus obligations and they'll probably be re-upping later this summer."

"And the honest reason is what?"

"What do you think? The serial killer!"

"Really? Well, that's only four accounts. How bad is that, really?

"Yes, the four accounts whose three-month period is ending in May. There will be others, unless they catch this guy soon."

Carla thought. "Maybe it's just as well. Chuck and I were talking about this last night, about whether I should close down for a little while. He was saying we should really think about it. It's great that the cops are coming around every day, but it's also kind of scary—plus what if the murderer actually did come here? Or come *back* here? I still don't think Toonie was one of the Frankensteins, but I don't want to get anybody hurt."

"Which brings us to the good news, which is that we've got a new one. Showed up first thing this morning, and he's already in the east wing, beavering away. So maybe closing down isn't the best idea right now."

"What's he like?"

"I actually know him." Tiffany sat still for a moment, her hands folded on the desk. "Carla, I'm just so sorry about everything, about me getting involved with that man and not looking out for you. I just wish I could take it all back. It wasn't like me at all! I let him in and I don't know why." Neither did Carla, and she doubted she ever would. "Just so you know, I broke up with him a week ago. He was blaming me for the dollhouse video 'fiasco,' asked me what was going on in my 'tiny mind' when I handed the video over to the cops. My *tiny mind*. I gave him back his keys and told him to stick them up his tiny ass, which wasn't my finest moment, but I feel like I've been let out of jail."

"Good for you!"

"So that new guy, Eugene Doppler, I met him a couple of weeks ago. He was staying with John in Clairemont. I know, it's weird—even before I realized what John is, I didn't expect him to be so nice to some random homeless guy. Turns out Eugene's a good writer—I've read some of his stuff. John was working with him."

"Why?"

"He said that with the right direction Eugene would be big. Eugene writes for kids, so I don't know what he meant by that, and he never explained. Anyway, he must have given up because here's Eugene with John's check for three months at the Point. His RV's parked outside, so I think he must have moved out of John's driveway. Of course, we can't let him sleep here."

"Why not?"

"Zoning laws."

"I'll call Harry."

"And then there's this," said Tiffany, pointing at a stack of papers. "The student stuff Misha dumped here yesterday. Have you
looked at it?"

"Do we have to? He's marked it all up, right? Otherwise, why
would he give it back? We can just slip them into their cells."
Carla checked out the topmost manuscript. "The Herman Twins
are working together on a sci-fi? Both of their names are on this
'Mobius Freeway' thing."

"Yes, and it's not bad. They've only done three chapters, but a
decent start. But look what he says."

"Well, he says the title is 'intriguing.' And . . ." Carla leafed
through all twenty-five pages. "Here at the end, just 'Nice work
keep going.' That's it! What kind of feedback is that?"

"Exactly! What it is is exactly the same feedback he gives to
Surtees and two of the McPhails, and they're doing better-than-
okay work too. I don't think he even read these, not really. He
read enough to see that there wasn't anything obviously wrong
with them."

"What a jerk. Probably didn't read them at all. Do you think
he charged them for this service? Check this out." Carla hefted an
inch-thick manuscript held together with pink satin ribbon fed
through a single hole punched in the upper left corner. "Behold
Mrs. Colodny's 'JOURNALING ADVENTURE.'"

Simonetta Colodny had apparently chronicled her entire life.
"Look," said Carla. "It says here she's transcribed diary pages from
when she was in kindergarten. That might be kind of interesting."

"Only it's not. Of course he claims to have found it intriguing
and tells her to keep writing."

Still curious, Carla hefted the "Journaling Adventure," which
immediately spiraled out into a thick fan and sent flying to the
carpet loose sheets of paper, which Carla retrieved. One was

Simonetta's movie review of *Operation Dumbo Drop*. "Tiffany, she was sixteen years old and she loved *Operation Dumbo Drop*. I feel bad that I know that. Should we even be looking at these?"

The other sheets weren't Simonetta's but had somehow gotten stuck inside her immense adventure. One was by Cindy Stokes. The corner was ragged, probably torn loose from a staple.

All it said was "Here is my screenplay! Hope you like it! What do you think! Be brutal!"

"Cindy Stokes wrote a screenplay?"

"I heard her say so. Cindy works for John, you know. She brags about it. Stuff like running the projector when he gives his talks. She's his gofer, and he doesn't pay her a cent. Is the thing all about the workshop murders? She was fixated on doing something with that."

"The screenplay? No idea, because this is just a cover sheet, not even a title. Either he threw it away or he's holding on to it in case he can use it himself."

The last sheet of paper was typed, not printed, with no name on it, just the page number 1. "Listen to this."

> This is just a start. There's more but I wanted some feedback on the first part. Is this a story or should it be a poem? If it's a story, does it start well?
>
> The sounds are music but also color. Sometimes deep and the throat is open and the color is dark dark brown. Sometimes higher pitch and staccato, jumping up and down the scale and you can see splashes of red. Or long and rising low to high, soft to loud, pink to burgundy to maroon, the streak widening as it climbs. Early on come words but then they stop and just the music and the dancing colors.

"Well, that's different."

"Also *intriguing*. Although he does say 'Show me more,' which is encouraging, I guess." Carla read it over to herself a few times, wondering what Amy would make of it. "Dancing colors" was good. "Hey, maybe this is about somebody with that thing where you hear colors and see sounds. Synesthesia. I found out about synesthesia when I was trying to figure out what was wrong with me."

"There's nothing wrong with you."

"You sound like Toonie. What I'm pretty sure I have is pseudobulbar affect."

Tiffany laughed. "Did you make that up? Sounds like that guy who mistook his wife for a hat. Hey, there's your book! *The Woman Who Confused Herself with a Fake Tulip*!"

"Very funny." Still, it was nice seeing Tiffany having a good time. "FYI, pseudobulbar affect is emotional incontinence," she said, putting "emotional incontinence" in air quotes. Tiffany spat orange juice all over herself. "Look it up! It's a real thing! It's when you get uncontrollable fits of laughing or crying." Tiffany was holding her stomach. "Apparently you have it too."

It took a full minute for Tiffany to calm down. "I've never seen you uncontrollably doing anything."

"Well, I don't do it in public."

"Then you can control it, right? I mean if it's uncontrollable it can happen at a gas station or a Starbucks. Seriously, when was the last time you—"

"Skip it."

"The best laughs *are* uncontrollable. Aren't they? When they just take over and you're rolling on the floor—"

"When was the last time you rolled on the floor laughing?"

Tiffany blinked. "Fair question. It's been quite a while. It's been too long."

"Maybe you're right." Carla didn't mean it, but Tiffany was still pretty fragile, and she felt bad about arguing with her. She got up and poured herself a half-mug of coffee that she really didn't want. "What's that?" A FedEx box addressed to Tiffany was wedged between the potted fern and the Acorn of Broken Dreams. It looked as though it had been kicked there with some force—one side was dented, and it had come to a stop on edge, leaning against the Acorn.

"Nothing," said Tiffany. "It came yesterday."

"Look, it's addressed to you, not me, not the Point, and . . . oh." The sender was J. X. Cousins. "Don't you want to at least open it?"

"I don't need to. There's only one thing it could be. I'll open it later when I'm in the mood."

"Do you mind if I move it?" The box was precariously balanced, and the last thing Carla needed was Ma's ashes spilling all over the carpet. It was surprisingly heavy. "Wow, what is it, a bowling ball?"

Tiffany sighed. "It's the man's *very favorite dictionary.* The compact edition of the Oxford Unabridged. A steal at five hundred and thirty-eight dollars."

"I hate to admit it, but that's pretty generous."

"It sure was."

Carla set it down beside the desk. "Well, at least you got something good out of the relationship, so it wasn't a total—"

"Carla, he's *returning* the book. Get it? *I* gave *him* the damn thing two months ago."

"Oh."

"Frankly I'm stunned he's been decent enough to give it back."

"I'm sorry."

"Now, did you talk to Chuck about getting more security cameras inside the wings?"

Carla made a mental note not to ever ask Tiffany about anything that could possibly be X-related. "Chuck thinks it's a great idea."

"Good. I wanted to do this two years ago, before people started getting dismembered. Now where, exactly? In the hallways, or in the cells too?"

"I don't like the invasion of privacy, but as long as I'm going to get the security guys out here I might as well put them everywhere. When things calm down, we can decide whether to turn on the ones in the cells, or maybe leave that up to each member. I mean, I don't think I'd want anybody spying on me while I was working. If I ever actually worked."

Then Carla remembered she had to ask Tiffany about one more X-related issue. "There's something else, and I wouldn't bring it up except . . . You remember that thing that happened two months ago, when I freaked out because I thought Ma's ghost had messed with my cell phone?"

"How could I forget? What I remember most clearly," said Tiffany, "is that you stopped freaking out when you decided it was a person, not a ghost, although I never understood why you thought that, or why a person instead of a ghost didn't worry you."

"Which I know didn't make a lot of sense, but you had to be there. That was a spooky night. And I didn't worry about some*one* messing with me because, let's face it, some*one* is less scary than some*thing*. Plus this was before the Frankenstein murders."

"So we're calling them that now?"

"But here's the thing: I want to know who did that nasty thing with my phone. Somebody had to stand right over me, close to me, watching me, while I was in this hypnotic state—I was out for two hours, you know—and deliberately whisper weird crap into my phone. And there had to be a reason for it, and the only one I can come up with is Cousins gaslighting me so that I panic and sell the Point. Is that crazy?"

Tiffany didn't answer right away. "I wish I could say it was."

"This was the afternoon before Toonie's funeral. Do you remember . . . I'm sorry, but do you remember if you were with him that day? All day?"

"Let me check." Tiffany leafed through a calendar on her desk. "Seventh of March. I spent the previous night at his place, left him there, came here, and called up all the Pointers to make sure they knew about the funeral and to sound them out about whether they were concerned about safety—which at the time they mostly weren't. Then you said I didn't need to stay since the cells were all empty. I called John and we met up and spent the day together. The night too, and we went to the funeral in my car."

"Wow, you wrote all that down on your calendar?"

"No. Just 'Marine Room.' We met there for brunch."

"So there's no way he could have . . ."

"No. I remember that day. He was courting me. Dad's expression. That evening I took him home to meet Dad. Later he said, 'Honey, I believe that gentleman is courting you.' He didn't look all that pleased when he said it, but . . . I was just so happy then."

What's it like, Carla wanted to ask, to be courted? Was Chuck courting her? "Okay, so not him. But maybe an accomplice? How about this Eugene person? How long has he been staying—"

"No, they met just a couple of weeks ago, and anyway, Eugene's a sweetheart."

"Then who? If it wasn't somebody doing him a favor, then which of the Pointers could it be? Because nobody else has a keycard."

They went down the list together. Paisley Shawcross had gotten a keycard only last week. Cindy Stokes? She would probably do anything for him. "No," said Carla, "I'm almost positive it was a man. The whisper was pitched low. That's how I knew it wasn't me."

"If we're just looking at males with keycards, then that's Manny Singh, Ken McPhail, Ricky Buzza, Chuck, and Syl Reyes. Cousins, of course, but he hardly uses his cell. Pete Purvis just did one month here in January, and the two docs aren't active members either. I could dig out old names from the early days, people we haven't seen for over a year, but they all turned in their cards."

"Forget it," said Carla. She sat back and closed her eyes. Maybe it was just as well. If she knew who it was, she'd have to do something about it. She hadn't been looking forward to that. "It can't be anybody on that list, we know all those people. Of course, we knew Edna too, but this is different. Hey, did you give me decaf? I'm ready to climb back in bed." When Tiffany didn't respond, Carla sat up. Tiffany was sitting stock still, with a stricken look on her face. "What is it?"

"We left the Marine Room and were going to my house so he could meet my father, and he wanted to stop off here to pick up a copy of his first book, to give to Dad. He keeps copies in his cell. I said I'd wait in the car. He was gone for maybe five minutes, ten at the most. I just now remembered."

"Well, if it was only five or ten minutes—"

"Five or ten minutes in the late afternoon. Tell me: On that tape, when you listened to it, how long did the whispering last?"

"Just, I don't know, a minute or so. It didn't go on and on. But look, how would he have known you'd stay in the car?"

"What if he didn't plan it? What if he just noticed you were here and found you out cold and just . . ."

"Winged it?" Yes, that would work. Tiffany looked like she might start crying any minute. "Look, sure, it's a possibility, but let's not get carried away."

"I waited in the car and listened to this Elton John song about growing old together, it was our song, and I was so happy."

"Hey—"

"And while I was out there swaying to the music he was in here torturing you."

"It's not your fault! Anyway, we don't *know* this. And how could my phone have ended up in the Rotunda with the recording erased?"

"You don't remember, do you? He was with me when we found you on the steps. He went into the house before I did, and he was charging all over the place, checking and double-checking. Or so he said. He had plenty of time to do it all. That bastard. That cold-hearted son of a bitch."

"Oh."

Tiffany grabbed a Kleenex from her desk drawer and blew her nose. "Elton Fucking John. I must have been out of my mind."

Carla watched her friend gather herself together. Tiffany closed her laptop, grabbed her bag, and stood. "I have to go," she said. "Can you stay here for an hour or so until I get back?"

"Sure. Where are you going?"

"Out."

Carla stood at the window watching Tiffany get in her car and back out of the driveway. She wondered whether she should have tried to stop her, or at least insisted she tag along, back her up, because for sure Tiffany had a score to settle. But if she'd needed backup, or wanted it, she would have said. Tiffany could take care of herself.

Carla had a score to settle, too. Could she sue Cousins for what he had done to her? She'd have to ask Harry, but probably not, since they had no actual proof. But if Misha Bernard and that Paisley woman were serious about writing a tell-all thing about Cousins, she could share the story with them. She'd ask Harry about that too—whether she'd need to worry about libel or whatever.

A cop car pulled into Tiffany's space and the Lieutenant emerged, looked up and saw Carla, waved. Carla opened the window.

"Is John Cousins here? I have a few questions for the gentleman."

"I'll just bet you do! Not here, though. He's got an apartment someplace in Clairemont, I don't know the address. Maybe call first? Do you have his number?"

"I absolutely do have his number," he said, and took off.

Everybody who counted now had his number. Carla hoped Tiffany beat the Lieutenant to Clairemont; man was overdue for a clop in the chops. She was about to head out to her cell when a FedEx truck pulled in. She watched as the guy piled armloads of boxes onto a cart. Were they all from X? Had Tiffany given him a romantic keepsake for each magical day they'd had together before she realized what he was? Should Carla be showering Chuck with mementos? Should they, by now, have a song?

After the truck drove off she checked out some of the boxes, and yes, they were addressed to Tiffany. Judging from all the different sizes, some of them might be jewelry, or a watch, or maybe more books, but most of the boxes were bigger. Had Tiffany given the man a Rolex? A microwave oven? What was there about the guy that made him so appealing to Tiffany and Cindy and Paisley and so repellent to everyone else? She decided to shove all the boxes in the far corner of the Rotunda and not mention them to Tiffany, at least for a couple of days, because how embarrassing.

She'd promised to man the office for an hour, but really there was no need. The cells weren't exactly full—the only dweller she knew about was that Doppler person—and she could just take the phone with her in case somebody called. Carla headed down to the tide pools because she needed—no, deserved—at least one hour of grace. The boulevard wasn't jammed with cars, so the pools wouldn't be crowded.

But that was because the tide was coming in, so the few pools she could get to were shallow and peopled only with tiny crabs too shy to dance, or perhaps it was the sunlight that put them off, they probably danced only after dark, under discreet starlight, she knew how they felt, they were creatures of purpose, not spectacles for the amusement of strangers. After a while she decided to leave. If there was a minus tide tonight, she and Chuck would come down and sit and talk, or say nothing at all. They had their best times here.

Halfway back she noticed the black car. It must have been there when she walked down, but now cars on either end were parked so close it was boxed in, which was why she noticed it, somebody was going to be stuck here for hours unless they called the tow police, people could be so thoughtless, and she stopped to commiserate with the sleek caged thing. Which was, she now saw, a Tesla Model 3. No, it couldn't be . . . Why would X park here?? She had convinced herself it was a different black Tesla Model 3, La Jolla was probably crawling with the stupid things, when peering down the car's rear bumper she caught sight of the license plate holder, the top of which said "Your Guru."

Had the creep been stalking her? For how long? Did he know about her favorite tide pools? Carla whirled around but he wasn't in the street or on the sidewalk. She ran back to the pools, scanned the sparse crowd; his bald dome was conspicuously absent.

She would call Harry B., although maybe it would make sense to wait until Tiffany got back, and she was halfway up the hill to the Birdhouse when her phone chirped, which was handy since the cricket chirp was Tiffany's ringtone. "Tiff," she said, "you're not going to believe this." Tiffany said nothing. "Seriously." Nothing. "Hello?" Background noises, then somebody, not Tiffany, a man, said, *"Give me the phone, ma'am."*

"Hello?"

"Miss Karolak?" Not X, thank god, but still, some guy was screwing with Tiffany's phone. *Ma'am?*

"Who am I speaking to? What have you done with Tiffany? Put her on! I'm calling the police!"

"This *is* the police. Your friend is safe. Miss Karolak, where are you right now, exactly?"

"I'm in La Jolla. What do you mean *'safe'*? Lieutenant, is that you?"

"Yes. Where exactly in La Jolla?"

"What the heck—okay, I'm walking up Prospect. I'm two blocks from my house. Now put her on the phone."

More background sounds, then Tiffany. Her voice was so small. "Carla? Carla? It's worse than we thought."

"Where are you?"

"Monster."

"What?"

"He's a monster."

"That's a news flash? What's the deal with the cops? Talk to me. Where are you?"

A long silence, and then just "His place."

So she was at his apartment in Clairemont and she was with the police. This was turning into a guessing game like Botticelli, which she used to play with Holman Bellavance at Universal when they were supposed to be running lines. Carla hated Botticelli. "What has he done now?"

The Lieutenant was back on the phone. "Do you know where John Cousins is?"

"As a matter of fact, I do! But I'm not telling until somebody explains—"

"This is no time for games."

"Which is my point exactly! Lieutenant, is Tiffany okay? What's going on?"

In the background she could hear Tiffany yelling. *Is he there? Is he with her?* "Listen to me," said the Lieutenant. "We have a situation. Is he with you right now?"

"No! But he *is* in La Jolla, unless there are two Model 3s with '*Your Guru*' on the plates—"

"Get out of the house."

"I'm not in the house."

"Then stay out of it."

"Look," she said, "I'm standing in my driveway now. There's only one car, an RV, in the driveway. He can't be in the house unless I let him in, and I didn't. His car is *not up here*. Get it? It's down on Coast Boulevard, and it's not going anywhere, because it's—"

"If he's not in the car, he might still be in the house or nearby. Walk back down to Roslyn. Now! Just stand there on the corner where people can see you. I'm sending a car for you now. Do you understand? Remain visible at all times."

"I always am! I'm visible right now!" she shouted, but he'd clicked off.

What with all the monster talk and visibility baloney she knew she should be frightened, even frantic, but she was too angry to manage it. Whatever the heck was freaking everybody out had to be some trail of evidence, like incriminating stuff on his laptop, like he'd figured out who Frankenstein was and was blackmailing the guy, or maybe Frankenstein had contacted him and they were working on a book deal. Yes, that was probably it! Which was gross, but not exactly terrifying. John X. Cousins was a huge jerk but not a scary guy. She liked the Lieutenant well enough, but she hated being ordered around. *We have a situation.*

All she knew for sure was her friend was in some kind of trouble and nobody trusted her enough to tell her what it was. Only that *It's worse than we thought.*

CHAPTER TWENTY-SEVEN

Carla

Friday, May 14

The cop looked a lot like Fred Savage and called her ma'am and asked her if she would prefer to sit up front like she was some kind of ride-along fiend, and she said thanks but no thanks and slid into the back. Literally slid because the seat, which looked upholstered, was actually molded plastic, and not molded to the human butt. When she asked what the deal was, the cop said the plastic was so it could be hosed off. Ewww.

In two minutes she was scrambling out into her driveway. As before, the only vehicle there was the RV. "Are you coming in with me or what?"

"I'm going to ask you to remain here until we get the go-ahead."

Do they teach you to talk like that? she didn't say. "Well, I'm going to go around back and check out the garage to make sure—"

"I'm going to ask you not to do that."

"—that NOBODY SWIPED MY CAR." Carla wasn't worried about her car, she was just sick of being told what to do. "How about you go with me?"

"How about if we just wait here."

Over his shoulder she saw the side door of the RV open, and a schlubby barefoot guy in gray sweats and a green T-shirt that said "KEEP CALM AND YOUR TEXT HERE" emerged eating a torpedo sandwich. He walked toward the entryway of the Birdhouse, ignoring or maybe not noticing the cop car, or Carla, or the cop. This must be the famous Doppler person. The cop didn't hear him because Doppler wasn't wearing shoes. Carla wanted to let him go ahead into the house just to piss off Fred Savage, but then the poor man might end up in a chokehold or something. "Hello there!" she called out. He turned and blinked in her direction.

When the cop demanded Doppler's ID, it took the man fifteen minutes to extract his driver's license from the jumbled interior of the RV. "I'm methodical," he said, "about where I put important objects; I never use the same place twice." He was allowed to rummage for it only when he'd handed his keys over to Savage, who was concerned that otherwise Doppler might peel out down the drive in a trailer so ancient and decrepit the back end was held on with bungee cords.

Savage stared skeptically at the license and back up at Doppler. "What is your name, sir?"

Doppler cocked his head like a shaggy owl, swallowed the last of his sandwich, and said nothing. What a strange person, but kind of lovable. There was something soothing about his presence, like he was some kind of mystic.

"When were you born, sir?"

"This is Eugene Doppler," said Carla.

"Ma'am, let him answer for himself."

"He is a very good friend of mine."

"No I'm not," said Eugene Doppler.

The cop turned to her and got in her actual face. "Ma'am," he said, "I don't know what your problem is, but I have a job to do," and he went on about his super-important job but Carla was distracted by Eugene, now staring beyond the two of them, with blue lights flashing in his wide pale eyes. How did he make them do that? And of course here came the patrol cars, a parade of them, no sirens but a carnival of blue lights. Only four could fit in her driveway, but they kept coming anyway.

Tiffany was in the lead car with the Lieutenant. They didn't come out right away: He was saying something to her, and she was nodding slowly, as though she were in a trance, and when they got out he led her up to Carla, supporting her steps like she was a frail old lady. "She's had a shock," he said. He sat the two of them down on the front steps and directed a small army of cops into the house. "Who is this?"

Eugene, unfazed by the procession of armed men passing by on either side, introduced himself. "I am Eugene Doppler. When can I go back inside?"

"Not for a while," said the Lieutenant. "I understand you're living with John Cousins?"

"No I'm not."

"This guy's a loony tune," whispered Savage.

"I need to get back to my book."

Carla had to speak up before Eugene was hauled off for being a loony tune. "He *was* living with Cousins, but he's not anymore. He has a right to be here. He's got his own cell."

Savage snorted. Carla was pleased to see the Lieutenant shoot him an annoyed look, but then he told Eugene that he was welcome to wait in the RV, but he was going to have to come down to the station later to answer a few questions. This was in Carla's opinion wholly unfair. "Look, he's a client. He just came out here to eat a sandwich. He hasn't done anything wrong." Eugene shuffled back into the RV and closed the door. "Also, as I may have mentioned before, *Cousins isn't in my house,* and even if he is, in what universe would it take a SWAT team to bring him out? He's a con man, not a desperado." She would have gone on, she was just getting started, except Tiffany suddenly sagged against her, weeping.

"Take care of your friend," ordered the Lieutenant. And disappeared into her house.

Carla had comforted countless distraught pals in scenes and improvs and once in a Baby Alive commercial, but she had never tended to a real one before. She held Tiffany, not too tight, but close, and said nothing. At first this was awkward but then she relaxed into it and recognized something there, something old and warm. She closed her eyes and listened and felt and marveled at her own ability to perform this simple service. Someone must have done the same for me once, she thought. A long time ago.

"It could have been me," Tiffany said.

"Uh-huh."

"It could have been you."

"Well, whatever it was, it wasn't us."

"It was somebody," said Tiffany. "Carla," she whispered, "it was *somebody*."

Carla had been so enjoying not thinking about what awful thing Tiffany had just experienced, but apparently it had to be faced. "Do you want to tell me what happened?"

Tiffany pulled away and began to pace back and forth in front of her, hugging her shoulders as though she were freezing. "The door was open. His car wasn't there, but he had to be home because the door was open; he'd never leave it that way. I had it all planned, what I was going to say to him, the disgusting way he treated you, the disgusting way he treats everybody. But the place was empty and there was a smell. A coppery smell, copper and something else, and it was so still I knew he wasn't home. Nobody was there. Nothing was there. Carla, that silence, it was huge, pressing in on me like I was deep underwater. I went into the bedroom anyway. I wish I hadn't done that. I'd give anything. Blood everywhere."

"Blood." *Blood*. This was hard to imagine, X being such a bloodless guy.

Much later, when she recalled this moment, Carla understood that right here she had slipped into character. Or maybe she'd done that earlier, when the Lieutenant called her, or when she mouthed off to Fred Stupid Savage. She had stopped acting like herself and become Carla the Gum-Chewing Wiseass, surrounded by fools, wearily cleaning up the messes they had made. Like *His Girl Friday* Roz Russell, only flat-out obnoxious. And she had done this before, too, and not just with Old Sally Gee. She had done this in a funhouse in Victorville.

"Everywhere," said Tiffany. "The bed, the walls, the floor. Long red smear into the bathroom." The way she shuddered when she said *"smear,"* the word contorting her mouth, like it made her sick just to say it. "He dragged her in there. The bathtub was cracked in pieces. A pool of blood. Nothing but blood."

"Who? Dragged who?"

"Oh, we'll find out soon enough." Tiffany sighed a ragged sigh. "They just haven't found his *display* yet. They will." She looked at Carla. "It could have been you."

"And you! It could have been you!"

"It *should* have been me."

"He's not here." Lieutenant Kowalcimi stood in the doorway and said something into his phone about an APB.

"See? Tiffany needs to go home now."

"And we'll see she gets there but right now I have some questions."

"Of course you do. Who doesn't? I have a few questions myself! Can we at least go inside?"

"Not yet. What can you tell me about the packages?"

"What packages? The ones in the Rotunda? They came today. That's it! That's all I know about them, and if you won't let me go into my own house, I'm going to call my lawyer because I have totally had it." Carla couldn't believe she had actually said "call my lawyer." She was in fucking bloom. "Now, let Tiffany go home to her dad, she doesn't know about the packages anyway, they came after she left. Except for the one in her office. That came when, Tiff? Yesterday?"

Tiffany nodded.

"Was the one in her office addressed to her too?" asked Kowalcimi.

"'Too'? There were more? From him?" The color was coming back into Tiffany's cheeks. "That bastard! That sick bastard!"

"It's nothing," Carla said. "Just some packages." When she said this, the Lieutenant gave her a really strange look. He seemed about to speak but then this large woman in a helmet and body armor ran past with a German shepherd. He spoke to her and she disappeared behind him. "Was that Myrtle?"

"No. Did they all come in a FedEx truck?"

"Yeah, FedEx. It says 'FedEx' right there on the labels. The guy left them on the steps and I just put them in the Rotunda because there wasn't room in the office. Who is that dog? What's with the body armor?"

The Lieutenant was staring at her. "Were you in a particularly . . . playful mood at the time?"

"'Playful mood'?? I just dumped them in the corner. What was I supposed to do?"

He went back into the house without answering.

"You said the house was safe!" she yelled after him. Fifteen minutes later he came back, this time with the armored woman and the dog, who both ran off. The dog was wearing a harness that said "ATF."

"That's not Myrtle. Is it a bomb-sniffing dog? It is, right? There's a bomb in my house. Oh my god."

"No, there isn't, but we had to check."

"Because of the stupid packages?"

"Because of the crime scene in Clairemont and the packages, yes. I'm going to ask you one more time, and please understand that we're just concerned for your safety and the safety of everyone here. I know this has been difficult for both of you. About those packages: You just dumped them in the corner. In no particular order. Right? And the person in the house when you got back here was . . ." He pointed toward the RV.

"Eugene Doppler? Yes. And so what? All you have to do is look at him, he's just a sweet guy who wants to write a book and eat a sandwich."

The Lieutenant called Eugene out and told him it was time to go down to the station. "It won't take long," the Lieutenant said. "We just want to ask you some questions."

Carla was more upset about this than Eugene, who asked if he could bring his notebook with him, and the Lieutenant let him back into the house so he could retrieve writing stuff from his cell in the west wing. He was accompanied by a triumphant Savage, who actually looked back at Carla and smirked.

"Now I need to show you something," the Lieutenant said, at last ushering Carla and Tiffany into the house and across the hall into the Rotunda.

The whole room was yellow with midday sun. Carla could see right away that the packages were not where she had left them. She couldn't see them at all until she rounded the plexiglassed doll-house, and there were all the boxes laid out in front of the long curved window. "This is how we found them," the Lieutenant said.

From where she stood, with the sun in her eyes, they might have been ordered in two, no three, long straight lines, but when he led her farther in so that she stood facing down those lines, they widened into a symmetrical design, the two biggest packages end to end in the middle, the long and narrow ones, four of them, arrayed top and bottom on either side, and at the end of each a series of smaller boxes. Who had done this? It looked like a huge robot action figure, only missing a part. "No head," said Carla, and behind her Tiffany whispered, "I know where it is," and then Carla knew too, the box in Tiffany's office. *Is that a bowling ball?*

A phone rang, a guitar riff coming from one of the small square boxes, and then Elton John singing *Please please let me grow old with you,* and Tiffany threw up.

Everyone, the Lieutenant and Carla and the three other cops and Tiffany when she stopped retching, stood and listened to the telephone until the singing stopped. Then it sang again. "Isn't anybody," Carla asked, "going to answer that?" and behind her, Tiffany began to giggle. Carla turned and was going to grab her and shush her or something but the laughter was so infectious that she couldn't help herself, because she had been so wrong about everything. The ugly sound they made together echoed around the room, bounced off the window, the plexiglass, must have snaked out through the wings because here came Fred Savage and Eugene Doppler. Eugene stood between Carla and Tiffany looking with mild curiosity at the robot action figure, and his presence had an instant calming effect, shutting them down.

"Mr. Doppler," said the Lieutenant, pointing toward the packages, "what do you know about this?"

Eugene gazed palely, considered for a full silent minute, shrugged. "Needs a head," he said.

"Thank you. And what do you know about John Cousins?"

"I know he's a bad man," said Eugene.

In the end it was the Lieutenant who pulled on a pair of purple latex gloves and opened the small square package, which was not a Rolex or a set of platinum cuff links but a human hand crusted in blood, and in the hand was an iPhone.

The Lieutenant read out a ten-digit phone number and asked if it was familiar to Carla or Tiffany.

"That's Amy," Carla said, once she could speak. "That's Amy's number."

CHAPTER TWENTY-EIGHT

Amy

Friday, May 14

Eugene Doppler was a fine writer. Midmorning, having put off attending to his manuscript, Amy began with the intention of scanning the first few pages for evidence of talent and ended up reading the whole thing for pleasure. Like all gifted children's writers, he did not write down to his readers but fully inhabited the world he created.

Although the setting wasn't Camelot, *The Homeless Club at Paramount Keep* had the heart and scope of *The Once and Future King.* Also no lessons. The oldest child in the club was twelve, the youngest four, and none were encumbered by parents or backstories. What Cousins had dismissed as "adventures" were formal quests, some humorous, some frightening, some doomed, all determined by council vote; formal council meetings took place at a dented metal picnic table spirited away from a local playground. The table was round. The ultimate goal of the club was simply to prevail. The grail was survival.

Adults milled about in the background, never named, referred to casually as Zoms, Fams, Creeps, and Authorities. Reading between the lines, which children can do as well as adults, the Zoms were addicts and the mentally ill, Fams were families of one sort or another, Creeps were monsters, likely pedophiles, and Authorities were police, social workers, and teachers. Some meant well; all were avoided, by both children and author. The only magical element was Faustina, a talking coyote: She was not very nice (they had to protect their pets from her, often unsuccessfully), but a reliable source of information, particularly about Creeps and The Authorities. Dumpsters played an important role in the narrative and were nicknamed and described in detail and took on more personality than the adults.

The main quest of this book was the creation of an enormous castle in a secluded canyon near the 163, initiated when they chanced upon huge corrugated boxes outside a Paramount Plumbing Supply store. An amused Faustina showed them how to dig a moat in anticipation of winter rains, and they scoured dumpsters for discarded pallets and tarps. Three chapters covered the planning of Paramount Keep and five its haphazard construction. Ramparts collapsed twice under the weight of even the littlest human sentries; rebuilt a third time, they were manned by the smaller dogs. The story ended at nightfall, with all inside, safe for now, deafened by the clattering October rain.

In the last pages of the manuscript Eugene had included blueprints showing how, with the dogged accumulation of cardboard, duct tape, and fabric scraps, and the willingness to insert tab A into slot B, readers could construct their own Keep, complete with turrets, ramparts, moat, and drawbridge. Cousins had scribbled *No publisher would agree to this too much $$$* in pencil on one of the turrets; Amy struck through the scribble and printed, in large letters, *Do not back down about these blueprints.*

It was almost lunchtime when Amy finished reading. She was now faced with a quandary. She could ship it off to her agent Robin Something, who would certainly know where to direct it if she wasn't interested in it herself. But Amy didn't feel comfortable contacting any agent without the writer's permission, and she had no idea how to get in touch with Doppler. Except through Cousins, in whose driveway Doppler resided, and who had thoughtfully scribbled *thx for looking this over any ideas?* followed by a ten-digit number that had to be his own.

She put off calling him as long as possible. Lottie distracted her for a while, as did a late lunch of cheese and mandarins from her tiny backyard tree and a writerly hour staring dutifully at a blank screen, wondering what it would be like to be able to write for children, which she knew she couldn't do, having barely ever been one herself. But she had loved fairy tales, especially the unexpurgated Grimms, and T. H. White, whose work had carried her over the threshold of adulthood. Eugene Doppler was the real deal. The blueprints, the darkness, the ineffectual saviors, the constant danger that defined the children's lives, all these things would argue against publication for just the reasons Cousins alluded to. *Who would want their kids to read that? It's bleak, hopeless, and depressing.* No it's not, Amy thought, and if I had children, I would want them to read that.

She had to dial three times; the first two times it rang forever with no ending message, which was odd. Third time was the charm.

"Ms. Gallup?" Cousins didn't sound like himself, and he'd never called her that. Nobody ever called her that.

"Amy Gallup, yes, and I would like to get in touch with Eugene Doppler." In the background she could hear some woman yelling her name; it sounded strangely like Carla.

"This is Lieutenant Kowalcimi. We have a situation."

Again the Birdhouse was garlanded with crime scene tape, inside and out. Again Carla slumped on her front steps looking catatonic, only this time Chuck was beside her, holding her tight. As she passed them, Amy offered Lottie, whom she had brought along for just this purpose. Chuck nestled Lottie in Carla's lap and Carla clutched her and began to sob. Chuck looked up at Amy. "It's crazy in there," he said.

The Rotunda was jammed with people in uniforms and paper jumpsuits, so she couldn't have gotten in there even if Kowalcimi hadn't appeared in the doorway to usher her upstairs. "You don't want to see that anyway," he said.

"You're opening the boxes here?" Amy could not imagine why. Wouldn't it make more sense to take them to a morgue?

"Some of them, yes. Right now, with Ms. Zuniga and Mr. Doppler on-site, we might be able to get an ID right way."

Amy stopped halfway up the stairs and touched his elbow. "You expect her to look at body parts? That's a bit brutal, isn't it?" A paper-suited woman gingerly carrying a cube-shaped FedEx box brushed by them on her way down.

"We hope it won't come to that." They entered Tiffany's office. "Ms. Shawcross!" he said. "What are you doing here?"

Amy had heard all about Paisley Shawcross from Harry B. A nervous, diffident woman, she was bustling about, attending to Tiffany, smoothing her hair, freshening her untouched tea. She neither answered Kowalcimi nor looked up at him; her lowered face blushed a mottled pink. Harry had said he was trying to get the woman her job back. Evidently this hadn't worked out.

Misha Bernard was here too, attending to no one but herself. She reminded Amy of a hawk, soaring above the scene, scouring it for prey. Amy liked hawks and could appreciate the woman's intense curiosity about unfolding events and the behavior of motley characters—she was a writer, after all, and probably more skilled than her Aztec books indicated, but Amy didn't like her. Like X, Misha Bernard was a user, only smoother at it.

"Paisley and I were working together in the west wing," said Misha Bernard. "It's so quiet out there we didn't know about all the festivities until we took a break just now—"

"According to Karolak," said Kowalcimi, "the only person in the wings today was Eugene Doppler. Was she wrong about that?"

"Yes." Tiffany's voice was faint—she had to clear her throat to make herself heard. "I knew Misha and Paisley were here. I just didn't think to mention it. We had . . . other matters to discuss."

"Still, when we arrived, the only vehicle in the driveway was Doppler's RV."

"I live two streets over," said Misha Bernard. "Paisley and I walked in together this morning."

Kowalcimi quizzed her on the particulars—exactly when had they arrived, did either of them take bathroom breaks or for any other reason leave that west wing cell, did either of them hear or see anything or anyone out of the ordinary. She assured him that they hadn't budged until fifteen minutes ago. Paisley said nothing. She met his eyes with an expression so hangdog it hurt to witness. The woman looked like she'd been cornered committing some unspeakably shameful act. Which, in a way, she had. Clearly she would never forgive herself for betraying the PD, and it looked like Kowalcimi wouldn't either.

"I have some questions for you, Tiffany. And since you're here, Ms. Shawcross, for you too. We could do this at the station, but there's no real need for that provided we can have some privacy here, right now."

Amy and Misha Bernard exchanged glances and quickly left the room. Outside, Carla was doing much better. Chuck had located a dropped tangerine and he and Carla were taking turns throwing it for Lottie to fetch. Amy sat down next to them. "Have you thought any more about getting a dog? They're a great comfort."

"I've thought about it a lot. We were talking about it last night. We'll start small, though. A chameleon. I'll start with that."

"She told me about Boffo," Chuck said, tossing the tangerine deep into a thicket of Salvia. "Her mother was a real piece of work."

Amy wondered if Carla was being more forthcoming with Chuck about her childhood horrors than she had with her. Amy hoped so. As long as she'd known Carla—which was at least ten years by now—Carla's mantra had consistently been No Big Deal. Yes, her mother had never said a kind word to her, had used her for money, had ripped her away from the parent who loved her, had murdered her only pet when she was just a little kid, but it was all No Big Deal because Everybody Has Problems.

Amy watched her wipe her eyes, clap for Lottie, laugh when Lottie leaped like a salmon for Chuck's airborne tangerine, and, minute by minute, will the latest grotesque violation of her sanctuary into No Big Deal. Amy deeply admired the strength of Carla's will, and she'd never been sold on the value of therapy for people who were already functional, but Carla's behavior was concerning. Perhaps, Amy thought, bouncing back was not what you should always do.

"I'm thinking," said Misha Bernard, "that the good Lieutenant probably doesn't need me right now, so I'll be taking off."

"Before you go: You said you were working with this Paisley person? Would you mind telling me more about that? I'm always curious about collaborating writers." Amy wasn't remotely curious—most writers were spiders, not ants—but she did want to know what Bernard had been up to, collaborating with such a sad sack.

"The idea was a tell-all podcast, maybe a book but probably not, about Cousins. Man never did pass the smell test, and Paisley knows him a lot better than I do, and she's been a lot more motivated than me, what with the nasty way he treated her—I assume you've heard about that? Anyway, that was the idea, but now Paisley's getting cold feet. I just spent three hours trying to get her to open up, give me some juicy anecdotes, and she started making excuses for him. *He's a wonderful teacher!* No, he's not. *I learned so much from him!* Yeah, you learned how to file for unemployment. *Really, I was too old for John.* How pathetic is that!

The woman's a human doormat." She lit a cigarette. "What are the odds she'll keep defending him now? I'm thinking fifty-fifty. *He can't be Frankenstein! Deep down he's a snugglebunny!*"

The door opened and Tiffany, pale as paper, eyes unfocused, descended the steps like a sleepwalker.

"Tiff?" Carla said. "How are you doing? Let's Chuck and I drive you home. You need to go—"

Amy held her hand up to quiet Carla. "Tiffany, perhaps you should sit for a minute."

"Perhaps I should," she said, but she stood still. After a long minute she seemed to collect herself, at least in the sense that her eyes weren't so hollow. She stared, hard, at Amy, shook her head slowly back and forth, shrugged, palms up, as if to show she had nothing left to give. "It's not," she said.

"It's not what?"

"It's not a woman."

"What?" Carla was on her feet. "What's not a woman?"

"In the boxes. It's not a woman."

"Oh. Well . . . in a way, that's good, isn't it? I mean, unless it's somebody's dog—that would be awful. What is it?"

"Carla, for god's sake," said Amy.

"She means it's a man," said Misha Bernard.

Tiffany looked at Carla. "I couldn't do it. They wanted me to but I couldn't look. What does that say about me?"

Chuck and Carla got on either side of her and sat her down between them.

"He's killed a man this time," said Misha Bernard, who almost seemed to be enjoying herself. "How very interesting."

"Or maybe not," said Tiffany. "Maybe I had it wrong."

"Wanted her to what?" Carla whispered at Chuck. "ID the body parts? Are they nuts? How's she supposed to identify some random guy?"

Tiffany whispered, "Paisley said she'd do it."

From behind the half-open front door emanated a series of

sharp screams, rising in pitch and volume. The screams were far enough away so they weren't terribly loud, but somehow that was worse. They were the lonesome cries of some small doomed animal.

"She's done it," said Misha Bernard.

CHAPTER TWENTY-NINE

Amy

Though screaming was a staple in movies, Amy had rarely heard anyone really do it. She herself had yet to scream and was unlikely to do so in the years left to her. Screaming was not a universally instinctive and purely involuntary response. You had to learn how and when to make such a noise; in an odd way it was like dancing, that mysterious ease with the dimensions and possibilities of one's own body that so many people had and she did not. You had to grow up witnessing it and doing it, and of course she hadn't because her people did not scream when frightened, or, for that matter, ululate when in the throes of grief. Listening to Paisley Shawcross, she wondered if it helped. It didn't seem to. The screams would start to die down and then start up again, more ragged and wrenching than before; the sound was awful. Maybe screaming was a delaying tactic, a way to postpone thought about the terrible thing.

Amy knew that instead of pondering the phenomenon she ought to do something about it, or somebody should, someone should stop it somehow, comfort the poor woman, but armchair analysis was her own delaying tactic.

So it was Misha Bernard, of all people, who broke the spell. "I guess we can assume whose body has just been identified," she said, "R.I.P. John X. C. And with that, I'm off. If the cops ask about me, I'm at home." She sauntered down the crowded driveway.

"That is one cold-blooded human," said Chuck.

The screams began again. "I'm going in," said Carla, and she'd disappeared into the house before anyone could stop her. *I'm in fucking bloom,* she had once said, and right then Amy understood what she had meant. Carla was growing up.

"What the hell is going on?" Harry B., out of breath, emerged from behind the row of cop cars. "I had to park at the bottom of the damn hill. Where's Carla? What's this about FedEx? Who's that screaming?"

While Amy wrestled with the age-old problem of the exposition—where to start? with the packages? with the blood-soaked bathtub? with Eugene Doppler?—Tiffany spoke up. Her face was tearstained, but her voice was strong and clear. She explained about the FedEx delivery, her trip to Cousins' house, her discovery there, her assumption that Cousins himself was the murderer, the arrival of Paisley and Misha and the police, the headless robot, Eugene Doppler calling Cousins a bad man, and the bloody chopped-off hand with the ringing cell phone. "They called Paisley and me into the Rotunda to see if we could identify the body. I said I'm sorry but I will not look at a disembodied head, can't you just do fingerprints, and they said there were no finger*tips* and there was no *head,* and I said what do you mean, didn't you get the box out of my office, and they said that wasn't a head it was an unabridged dictionary, and I said what makes you think I could identify this woman, and they said it wasn't a woman. And I said how do you know? Because I wasn't thinking clearly at that point, and Paisley said can't you do DNA, and they said yes but that would take hours. And Paisley said what makes you think I'd know who the man is, there's only one man I could identify this way, I mean without a head, and it can't be him, it just *can't be John,* and they said how would you do it, and she said well he has a group of moles on his inner left thigh that looks exactly like the Dog Constellation, but you're making a terrible mistake, there's no way it's him, and I just walked away before it got any worse. Because I had had enough. I really have. I have had enough."

"There's a dog constellation?" Chuck began to fiddle with his phone. "Canis Major? Or Minor?"

"Actually she said 'puppy.' Puppy Constellation."

"Well, this has been fun," said Harry. "Carla called me, so I'd better get in there."

"Harry," said Amy. "Have you stopped doing criminal law altogether? Are you still licensed for it, or whatever you have to be? Because if he called Cousins a bad man, I think Eugene Doppler's going to need a lawyer. Can you check in on him?"

"I can try, but if there's a conflict with the Point I can't represent him—I'm Carla's lawyer. But I'll look into it, sure," and he sped inside.

"Was it 'Puppis the Poop'?" asked Chuck.

Amy wondered how people ever dealt with not having arcane facts at their fingertips 24-7.

"Right," said Tiffany, "she said 'puppis.' I just assumed that meant 'puppy.' There's a dogshit constellation? How appropriate. I shouldn't say that."

"No, it's the poop of a ship. The stern."

"It was the Argonaut ship," said Amy, "Jason and the quest for the Golden Fleece. Where's my dog?" She never worried about Lottie disappearing, since the dog followed her like a shadow, and even now she could hear her stabbing at something in the Salvia bushes, but Amy needed a sighting. At the sound of her voice, Lottie ran to her with the soil-caked remains of the tangerine in her mouth. "Tiffany, exactly when did Eugene call him a bad man?"

"Just before you called and the phone rang. In the little package. In the hand. The cops asked him what he knew about Cousins, and that's when Eugene said that thing. And he was right, of course.

Look, I'm sorry he got murdered, but he *was* a bad man, and I'm not just saying that because, you know—"

"We know," said Chuck. "The question is, why did Doppler say it? Wasn't Cousins kind of nice to him? Didn't he let the guy stay at his house?"

Amy had been puzzling over this too. Even though he'd dismissed the Homeless Club as unmarketable, Cousins had been uncharacteristically generous with attention, as well as real estate, to Eugene Doppler. In her opinion this was a greater mystery than the one facing them right now.

The only murderer Amy had ever met—to her knowledge, at least—*was* an intriguing mystery. Edna was a bad woman, but she had been driven by malice and fury, not appetite. Whoever was doing these disgusting things—taking lives, reveling in gore—was engaged in sport. He was beneath contempt, yet, when caught, he would generate an industry of books, novels, movies, documentaries, and podcasts. His victims would be reduced to interchangeable cutouts while the minutest of his biographical details would be scoured for clues to the mystery of his character.

But there was no mystery, because there was no character. People often used the word "human" in silly ways, as though it meant "decent"; as though it were synonymous with "humane"; they'd describe a person as "inhuman" because he behaved cruelly. But cruelty was all too human, as were selfishness, altruism, narcissism, stupidity, vanity, integrity. What *was* literally "inhuman" was the absolute lack of fellow feeling. To be human was to be a social animal. Even extreme introverts, like Amy, were part of a larger group. Like everyone else, Amy had read way too much about Bundy and Gacy and Jack the Ripper and all the other creatures of legend, and she always came away certain of only one thing—that they were simply not like us, and just as fascinating as well-built machinery, if you were interested in that sort of thing, which she was not. If fate had treated Edna fairly, she never would have killed anybody, and that made her interesting. Rotten, but human. So was Cousins. The humanoid playing with the body parts of human beings was not the product of bad luck, of circumstance. He was an error of evolution.

So what *had* Cousins wanted with Doppler? Clearly he had recognized Doppler's talent, perhaps Doppler had been the most talented writer he'd ever come into contact with, but so what? Cousins was—had been—entirely devoted to his own ends, had treated his "students" with disguised contempt, had made heartless use of two women in order to make himself famous. Had even tried to make use of Edna. So he must have had some use in mind for Doppler. And was Doppler now a suspect? Why did the police want to question him?

The door opened and Paisley Shawcross, flanked by Carla and Lieutenant Kowalcimi, slowly descended the steps. She was trembling, her face swollen and shining. Distraught because she loved the man, or because she'd been forced to look at a severed leg? Or both?

"Where's the Bernard woman?" Kowalcimi looked pretty wiped out himself. It had been a long day. "Ms. Shawcross needs some help here."

"We'll take care of her," said Carla. "We'll get her home." She had trouble disengaging Paisley from the Lieutenant—the woman seemed loath to relinquish his arm, as though it were some sort of safety harness, which was a little surprising seeing as how he had just forced her to endure a gross ordeal. She moved a few steps away, then turned back and threw herself against him, weeping like a child. Plainly discomfited, he held her close to his chest, although he didn't exactly throw himself into the gesture; maybe after years of delivering terrible news to loved ones, cops got compassion fatigue. "I'm so sorry," she was saying, "you know I'm so, so sorry." And he said yes, he knew she was sorry, and after a while he sighed deeply and told her, "Paisley, let these people take care of you now. And later, when you're more yourself, come see me and we'll talk about reinstatement. Would you like to do that?"

"Oh, yes," she said, sobbing anew. "Oh, thank you so much!" and Chuck and Carla gently pried her loose and led her away.

Harry came out and joined Amy, Lottie, and Lieutenant Kowalcimi, and they all watched the procession. "I'm going to represent him," he said. "There's no conflict with the Point, and even if there were, you know Carla, she'd want me to do it."

The Lieutenant perked up. "You're Doppler's lawyer? Good. He's going to need one. We're taking him down to the station now."

Was he a suspect, Amy wondered, or a person of interest? And what was the difference? "I don't suppose there's any chance I could talk to him?"

The Lieutenant shook his head, and Harry explained that eventually she could, but probably not today.

In the end, Eugene Doppler, carrying a beat-up military duffel bag and looking serene, was escorted into the backseat of the Lieutenant's car. Amy guessed he had his writing materials with him, and that that was really all he needed. The Lieutenant treated him courteously, asked if he was comfortable and if he understood where he was going. In England, Amy thought, Eugene Doppler would be assigned an "appropriate adult." Here, his adult was Harry, which, she thought, was a pretty good thing. Together they watched Kowalcimi drive off.

"Really," Harry told her, "besides the fact that he's an oddball, all they have at this point is opportunity. He was on the premises between the time the packages were dropped off and the time we got here, which means he had the means to rearrange them. They don't even know yet if he has an alibi for the murder itself, let alone the other murders. And all they have for motive is that thing he said about Cousins being a bad guy. So they'll question him, and I'll be there. I have no idea what they have for weaponry.

Anybody can wield an axe. I'm assuming they didn't find one in his RV."

"Why are you assuming that?"

"They don't look nearly excited enough. You like this guy?" He looked at Amy curiously.

"I don't know him. I like his writing very much."

"Norman Mailer stabbed his wife."

"I was never crazy about Norman Mailer."

"William Burroughs—"

"Ditto."

Harry smiled and started downhill. Just before he got out of sight he turned and shouted up to her. "I'll call you," he said.

Tiffany excused herself, ran inside, and came out with a tennis ball. "Never once used," she said, lobbing it into the bushes for Lottie. "John said he loved tennis and why don't we go play in Balboa Park, which of course we never did, but I bought six of these so I'd be all ready. I don't know what's happened to me."

"You trusted the wrong person."

"I don't mean that. I mean . . ." She threw the ball again. "I mean that I've gotten over it. What happened to him was a big shock, but I'm over it now. Just like that. Want to know something really awful?"

Amy loved questions like this, had loved them ever since she was a kid. *Wanna see something horrible? Want to hear the most disgusting part of all?* The answer was always yes, of course you did. How could you not? "Tell me," she said.

"I'm relieved. I'm beginning, already, right now, to feel better. A man I thought I loved, a man I slept with, shared with, the man of my daydreams, he got butchered and FedExed and turned into some joke art installation, and I'm feeling better by the minute. I'm free. It's almost like he never existed, or at least never came into my life at all. What is wrong with me?"

Amy thought. "When the spell is lifted, you come to yourself, good as new. Maybe even better than new, because cleansed in some way, or at least grateful to be free."

"You're saying he was some kind of enchanter? Hardly. You didn't like him. Neither did Carla."

"That's exactly what he was. Just because some of us didn't find him enchanting doesn't mean he wasn't. Enchanters, users, they're very good at recognizing vulnerability. You were vulnerable in some way he could detect. So you were charmed, and now the charm is lifted."

"Like in a fairy tale."

"Yes."

Tiffany stood and got out her car keys. "I'm going home. Dad doesn't know about any of this. He'll be happy too. He only met John once and tried to warn me off. Thanks, Amy." She smiled and ruffled Lottie's head and left.

After some time, Amy did too. She drove north thinking about enchantment, wondering all the way if some serial killers were particularly skilled enchanters. If they charmed everybody rather than just the few weakened by need and circumstance. How did they manage that without fellow feeling? Were humans like lab mice to them, and did they learn how to charm through experimentation? She had never met one. Or perhaps she had.

That evening she walked Lottie up the longest hill in the neighborhood. Coyotes were bolder after dark, but tonight, after such an ugly day, she required the stars. She had been, off and on, learning to recognize them through a mildly helpful constellation app on her phone. Unfortunately the app included Steele Savage–style images superimposed on the star clusters, which she did not find particularly illuminating. The ancients looked at the Lupus constellation and saw a wolf; Amy did not. Only the Big Dipper looked like its name, except its real name wasn't the Big Dipper, it was supposed to be a bear. She was having more luck with the planets—Mars, Jupiter, and Saturn anyway. Mars really was red. And tonight Sirius gleamed proudly from the face of the Great Dog, Canis Major. "That's the dog star, Lottie," she said. She lifted her up and pointed her at the sky. "And there's Lepus. Dog's been chasing that rabbit for billions and billions of years."

Lottie's eyes mirrored the sky, until she turned from the spectacle and gazed at Amy with absolute trust. Amy set her down and walked her back home, all the way, because she was in a mythological mood, recounting to Lottie the tale of Argos, faithful dog of Odysseus, and then the story of Beaumont, Master Twyti's hunting dog who gave his life bringing down a grimly boar in *The Once and Future King*. "You must never give your life for me," she said. "You are not a hunting hound. You are my faithful companion."

She unearthed her dog-eared paperback T. H. White and took it to bed with her. She was planning to visit the part about King Pellinore and the Questing Beast, the Beast Glatisant, which was so funny, but on her way there she stumbled upon the noble death of Beaumont. It rendered her as tearful now, at seventy-two, as it had when she was ten. *What does this mean about me?* Tiffany had asked, and what did it mean about Amy that she could cry for Beaumont and had not shed a tear for her husband since the day of his death? She had loved only him. He was the one person she had ever let in. And he was entirely gone now, while Alphonse the Basset and all her other dogs endured fully in memory, their howls and colors and scents and the texture of their fur as immediate as ever. Maybe they kept her in the world. Maybe that was it.

"I really have no idea," she said to Lottie, who moved up from the foot of her bed to nestle under her arm. She read her to sleep.

He stroked Beaumont's head, and said, "Hark to Beaumont. Softly, Beaumont, mon amy. Oyez à Beaumont the valiant. Swef, le douce Beaumont, swef, swef." Beaumont licked his hand but could not wag his tail. The huntsman nodded to Robin, who was standing behind, and held the hound's eyes with his own. He said, "Good dog, Beaumont the valiant, sleep now, old friend Beaumont, good old dog." Then Robin's falchion let Beaumont out of this world, to run free with Orion and roll among the stars.

CHAPTER THIRTY

Carla

J eez."

"No kidding."

"That's the most depressing thing I've ever seen, and that's saying a lot. Now I feel like a huge snob." Carla looked back as they drove away from Paisley Shawcross, who stood in front of her trailer doing that wave where you just flutter your fingers.

"You're not," said Chuck. "My first home was a trailer, it was all we could afford when we got married, but it looked like a house, with a porch and garden and a couple of small trees. Paisley's place could be the job office in a construction site." They exited the Excelsior Mobile Home Park, heading west out of La Mesa. "Sonofabitch had to know the woman didn't have two cents and he screwed her over anyway."

"Do you think we were right to leave her alone?"

"She'd settled down pretty well. She didn't come off like she was in danger of harming herself. Right? And if she'd wanted us to stay, I think she'd have said so."

They talked for a while about Paisley and her troubles, and how at least she might be getting her job back, now that she was free of Snidely Whiplash. "Which," said Carla, "she's sad about now, but she's bound to figure out is a good thing. Why are you smiling?"

"You. You always give people the benefit of the doubt. I don't, so I'm glad you do."

"Why?"

"Means we're a good fit," he said.

A good fit. Sometimes, like now, Chuck made her feel like she was a teenager, or what she assumed a teenager must feel like, given that she had never actually been a teenager. "Do we have a song?"

He laughed, hard. He understood her ridiculous question. That was the thing: Sometimes she could just say two or three words and he'd be like he'd read the whole damn novel. "No. Suggestions?"

She thought. "It would have to be jazz, right?"

"Jazz would be nice, but I can compromise."

All the way to the coast, she tried to figure out a compromise. How do you compromise with jazz? "Maybe 'Blackbird'?" She remembered sort of liking that one at one of their jazz club dates.

"McCartney or 'Bye Bye'?"

"I don't know. *Nuts.*" When they pulled into her driveway, the place was still clogged with cop cars. "How long are they going to be here?" Chuck ran into the house and came back with the news that they might not be able to move back in until tomorrow because they were fingerprinting everywhere.

So they drove down to the boulevard and parked where that Your Guru Tesla Model 3 had been—the cops must have hauled it away for evidence—and walked down to the tide pools to catch the sunset. A squad of schoolchildren were squatting around her favorite pool, getting lectured about its inhabitants by some old guy in a safari hat.

They settled instead on a flat rock far from the water's edge, and sat for a while in silence. Carla loved how they could do that.

As it always did, the dark came quickly. The children left, the sun rolled out a golden carpet on the water, they stayed where they were.

"You choose," she said.

"Choose what?"

"Our song."

"We don't need a song."

"Yes we do."

"'Be Kind to Your Web-Footed Friends.'"

"I'm serious."

"So am I. A duck may be somebody's mother."

"Did you and Charmaine have a song? I'm sorry. I shouldn't ask about that."

"Ask about anything. As a matter of fact, we did. We had to have a song for the wedding. We let the band pick it."

Carla waited him out.

"'You Had Me from Hello.'"

A large gull touched down on a nearby rock and, noting that they had no food, eyed them with contempt. "Maybe we don't need a song." She had almost made a wisecrack about "You Had Me from Hello," which must have been some country-western thing, but then she pictured the sad little wedding reception, Chuck and Charmaine and the baby who died and the marriage that failed, and there was so much she didn't know about him. Or about herself. Or about what they were supposed to do. "I don't know," she said.

"A Randy Newman song, I think."

"I don't know what I'm doing."

He rested his hand over hers, on the warm rock. He always knew when not to say anything.

"There's a lot you don't know about me."

"Let's see," he finally said. "I know that the first time I met you was in Amy's class, and you read a suicide poem. It started *The rope must be new, or all bets are off*. I know you had a mother from

hell and a father who loved you but for some reason didn't protect
you from her. I know you're smart and funny and you have the
most generous heart."

"And a legible face."

"Not always."

"It wasn't his fault."

"If you say so."

"You would have liked him."

"I like his dollhouse. I like his daughter."

"What *is* this?"

For the first time since she'd known him, he looked at her in
a guarded way.

"I mean," she said, "what are we doing?"

"Okay. I'm going to assume you don't mean we're sitting on a
rock on the beach and watching—"

"Are we dating? Is that what we're doing?"

"Yes, Carla. We're dating. We've been dating for a couple of
months."

"Because I don't know what dating is."

He looked baffled. "What about when you were in school?"

"I missed school, most of it anyway."

"What about—Okay, I have to confess something. I looked
you up once. You're a mild internet sensation, you know. There are
a couple of fan sites, and you're in Wikipedia and IMDb."

She had withdrawn her hand and now crossed her arms and lowered her head, which she knew was a defensive gesture, and while she
was really feeling extremely defensive, she was also acting it. Carla
wondered if she could ever stop acting.

"And now I've pissed you off, and I'm sorry, but Carla, you
rarely tell me anything. And that's your privilege! You don't have
to. I just . . . I'm just waiting. Waiting isn't always easy. You know?"

"Go on," said Carla.

"So I looked you up, and there was stuff here and there about
actors you were going out with—"

"Like Holman Bellavance?"

"Yes. And you even *told* me about him. That's another thing: You almost married the guy. How could you almost marry somebody without dating?"

"I lied. I lied! HB and I were just foxhole buddies. And Ma came up with that showbiz romance crap and fed it to my agent. By that time she was really desperate since I was eating myself out of work."

"So you're saying that in your whole life . . . Carla, in your whole life, you never—"

"I ate my way out of show business. I ate my way out of romance. I ate my way out of sex." She raised her head and faced him squarely. "And I don't regret it. I would do it again." He reached for her face, to caress her, and he stopped. He was afraid, she could see, of doing the wrong thing. This was exactly what she didn't want to happen. "I'm what they call a damaged person. I'm okay with it though. It's not really all that—"

"Hey, I see damage every day. I see cars mangled on the freeway, T-boned at intersections—I know damage. I look at you and I don't see damage. I see you. When you tell me you have no regrets about the past, I believe you. Because here you are, and you are wonderful. But right now, right this minute, you are not okay, and that may not be a big deal to you, but it's a big deal to me. So." He cupped her face in his hands. "So. When you are ready, we'll figure out what we're doing."

A pair of black skimmers drew a long X on the surface of the water, never landing, scooping up little fish with their bills. A squadron of pelicans sailed past in a perfect V formation under the full moon. Was she ready right now? She didn't know. How could you know a thing like that? "I wish we could sleep here," she said.

Chuck had just sublet his place, so that was out, and in the end they settled on the Artemis Hotel, which was within walking distance. Suddenly famished, they ate in the courtyard grill and fell into a discussion of the day's events, which, however terrible, were safer to talk about than where their relationship was going.

"Are we still," Carla wondered, "supposed to think that whoever killed Donatella Ng and that Bunting woman and Cousins also killed those prostitutes? And Toonie? Does that make any sense at all? Nobody's even mentioned those poor girls, it's like they don't count because they weren't chopped up and packaged. And because of who they were and who they weren't. And isn't it weird that he killed a man?"

Chuck guessed there was a lot the police weren't saying and that some of it might help to make sense of it all.

"Well," said Carla, "if Paisley gets her job back she could maybe fill us in."

"And get fired again."

"You are so very right."

They talked without looking at each other, but for the occasional nanoglance. They had eaten out tons of times before but only at places like Jersey Mike's. Carla, having choked down a plate of carbonara, toyed with her salad—she always toyed with salad—and stared at Chuck's octopus ceviche, trying to decide if she could ever bring herself to nibble a raw tentacle, or even a cooked one. They were definitely dating now, if dating meant being so self-conscious that you found yourself rehearsing a sentence in your head before saying it. Like "You are so very right." What a stupid thing to say.

They'd booked a room with two beds. They had fallen asleep together plenty of times but never in a room with beds. Except that first time at Amy's, and that was different.

"Come here often?" Misha Stupid Bernard, drink in one hand, waving to a waiter with the other, slid a chair to one side of their little table, sat down, and ordered "what he's having. And drinks all around."

"Diet Coke for me," Carla said, and Chuck said, "Me, too." Chuck hated soda.

If Misha Bernard sensed they weren't thrilled to see her, it didn't show. She probably didn't give a rat's. "So," she said. "Poor pitiful Paisley Shawcross. What's going on with her?"

"What's going on," Carla said, "is that we took her home. To her trailer." She stopped herself from adding that Paisley was getting her job back, because that was none of Misha Bernard's beeswax.

"Poor kid," said Misha. "I'll have to back off for a little while, give her some room."

"Room for what?" Chuck, usually the most affable of men, didn't bother to mask his skepticism. "You're not still planning to do that tell-all thing about Cousins. What would be the point?"

"You're joking." She downed her drink, a neat jigger of bourbon or scotch, and started on the next one. She wasn't drunk, but she wasn't sober either, and Carla wondered if this was habitual with her, or if the day's events had rattled her. She didn't look rattled. "The book will practically write itself. I just got off the phone with my agent, who's over the moon."

"Well," said Carla, "it's an ill wind," remembering as she spoke that she'd given Cousins such a hard time about the whole "ill wind" thing when they were all in Amy's backyard and he was babbling about meta-metaphors, and she could see that Chuck was remembering it too. He kept a poker face but there was laughter in his eyes.

"I mean," said Misha Bernard, "even before his spectacular demise he would have made a workable subject for a trendy con-man study, Svengali Lite against the sun-drenched backdrop of outlandish gore. Hotcakes. But this! *Frankenstein Meets the Profiler! Guess Who Wins!*"

"I don't think he was a profiler," said Carla.

"Honey, in his own mind he was. Paisley said he had the whole profile worked out. I haven't seen it yet, and I can't wait, it'll be gold, particularly after they nab Frankenstein, who probably bears a closer resemblance to Mister Rogers than to the Master's profile. Or—hey, if by some miracle the profile is accurate, that will work just as well. Either way, it'll sell in the millions. *The Corpse Came FedEx!*"

Carla was actually beginning to feel sorry for John X. Cousins. Hadn't he trusted this woman as an ally? She could see Chuck was thinking the same thing. As one they shut down Misha Bernard by saying nothing, and after a minute of pointed silence, she rose. "Toodles, kids. Miles to go, and all that." She swanned off, pausing to chuck the bartender under his chin on her way out the door.

"Apparently she's a regular," said Chuck.

"Yeah, a regular snake in the grass. Miles to go where, I wonder."

Misha Bernard had been such a distraction that Carla made it all the way up to the third floor of the Artemis without getting nervous, and then there they were outside of Room 310. Chuck opened it with a card. "After you," he said.

"No, after *you*."

"I insist."

"You first."

"I won't hear of it."

They did this cornball routine a bunch of times until they were both laughing—at themselves, at dating, at the whole situation—and then he picked her up and carried her in.

"You are carrying me across the threshold," she said.

"Yes, I am doing that very thing."

He stood between two enormous beds, holding her, saying nothing. His face was illegible.

"What is it?" she asked.

"Well, I have to put you down and I don't want to."

"Then don't."

"I could do this forever. You are wisp-light."

"And yet you're grimacing and I can see the veins in your forehead."

"Sorry." He sat down, with her in his lap. "I need to work out."

Carla was sitting in a man's lap on a hotel bed. For so many years—how many? . . . since she was twelve years old in the Victorville funhouse: twenty-four years—she had imagined moments like this with Anybody But Cal Hoving. She had daydreamed and night-dreamed the scenes, trying to find her way in, and they all went ugly. It wasn't the *sight* of Cal Hoving, because her eyes had been closed, and it wasn't his *touch,* because her body had magically frosted over, so even in her worst dreams *that* memory was missing, never there. But the *sounds.* The sound of that scratchy laughing funhouse record and the sound of him murmuring all over her, not the high-pitched Nutty Squirrel Hiya Kids voice, the husky smoky purr coating her ears and face and throat and spiraling deep into her body, taking up residence there. And then Chuck, Chuck was such a miracle that all she ever wanted from him, all she asked for, was that one day, when it was time, she would do the Big Reveal. She would tell him about the funhouse and what came after, about how she ran to Ma, of all people, looking for sanctuary, of all things, and *Did he put his thing in you?* and *No, Ma, he didn't, but he* and Ma handed Carla an old yellow book called *The Story of Life* and told her to watch herself and said she'd have a word with that S.O.B. and she must have, because Carla was promoted to Nutty's Joint Head Squirrel Pup the very next day, and he never bothered her again. *My mother pimped me out to a perv in a squirrel suit,* she'd say, and Chuck would wipe away her tears and swear eternal vengeance and promise to protect her forever, and that would be enough.

But now she listened and listened and there was no murmuring, no ugly. All she could hear was the two of them breathing, and they were breathing fast, and she was suddenly on fire and she popped off the top two buttons of his shirt and he said "Really?" and then his pants and her pants and he said "Are you sure?" and she was laughing and then they were naked and then she was shaking apart and hearing the most amazing noise, and it was coming from her. The sound was her own. And then they were quiet together, skin to skin.

The bedside phone rang. Chuck picked it up and listened and said, "Sorry. We're fine. She just stubbed her toe on a—on a thing—I don't know what it was, but she's . . . Sure, just a minute." He covered the receiver with his hand. "It's the front desk. They want to talk to you."

"Why?"

"They think I murdered you."

She grabbed the phone. "Yes, my poor toe! I stubbed it on a thing. I have an abnormally low pain threshold. What? You're very kind, but it won't be necessary." She hung up.

"What won't be necessary?"

"A bucket of ice for my toe. He sounded kind of sarcastic. What's so funny?"

"Your abnormally low pain threshold."

"Shut up."

They did it again, slower and better although quieter, and again later on. "You're killing me," he told her. And again.

In the morning, when Carla looked back what she remembered most was touch. The feel of his skin on her own, the stubble of his beard, the sensation of him inside her, beside her, beneath her, all around her, the caress of his hands. Her body had returned to her good as new. She watched him sleep. He was smiling. Someday, she thought, she will tell him the story, but it won't be important. Significant, yes, it will explain a lot, but they had emerged into this sweet morning without that explanation, that Big Stupid Reveal.

He opened his eyes. "I love you," he said.

"I know," she said.

CHAPTER THIRTY-ONE

Amy

Monday, May 17

Amy, Harry, and Eugene Doppler sat in her backyard watching Lottie try to wrestle her squeaky ball from the depths of a rampant plumbago. Blue petals and dried stem bits rained down to decorate her face, back, and paws. Eugene offered to help her, but Amy explained that for Lottie the hunt was the best part.

Harry had called her that morning to explain that his client wanted to visit her. "Frankly," he said, "this is the only way I can get him to talk at all. You can be my interpreter."

She had begun interpreting by praising *The Homeless Club at Paramount Keep* and giving him back his manuscript, inviting him to let her know if any of her markups were unclear. "Honestly," she said, "I couldn't find a thing wrong with it. Reading it was a real treat for me."

If he found this news encouraging, it didn't show. From the moment they arrived, he had regarded her with hypervigilance, as though scanning her face for evidence—of what she couldn't imagine, except that it had to do with trust. This was interesting. During his first visit, when Cousins had brought him here, he had not armed himself against her. Reading his book had now rendered her suspect. This must, she thought, have been Cousins' doing. "Mr. Doppler," she said, "when I say I couldn't find a thing wrong with it, I mean exactly that. If there are parts that you want to work on, for whatever reason, I'm willing to hear you out, but as far as I can see, it's publishable. Whether you can actually get it published is a different—"

"Backstories," he said.

"I beg your pardon?"

"Do the children need backstories?"

"Why do you ask?"

"Do you want to know more about the Creeps?"

"Certainly not."

"Does it need a through line?"

"I don't even know what that is."

"A through line"—he closed his eyes—"begins with a hook and inexorably pulls the reader through to the last page."

John X. Cousins, Writing Guru. "While I loathe the metaphorical hook, which treats your reader like a wriggling fish, what this describes is narrative pull, and you don't *need* that because you already have it."

"Why is 'pull' less insulting than 'hook'?"

He had a point. "Perhaps it isn't. My point is that there already is a 'through line.' The children have an overarching quest—to build that wonderful castle—and that carries the reader through to the last scene, in which they are all safe within its battlements. For the time being."

This made him notably less vigilant, but he was still wary. Eugene Doppler had the most interesting stare, unblinking yet not discomfiting. You could see you were being assessed and at the same time you were utterly safe. Amy could not imagine this man killing a fly.

"Thank you," he said. "But what about character? The characters of the children? He said . . . he said I needed to explain how they got to be homeless, and especially who had treated them badly, and how. Why they didn't have families." He paused. "Especially Rose and Zachary." Rose and Zachary were the oldest children—they shared club leadership.

Amy thought. "I suppose you could have added that, but I don't think it's necessary. It's the sort of thing you, the author, should probably know—knowing your characters helps greatly with dialogue and behavior, makes each character distinct—but I can't say I needed to know these things as a reader. Also, including that information would lengthen the book, and I'm not sure you want to do that. Short books seem to be in these days."

He leaned in suddenly, his face no more than three feet from her own, which for Eugene Doppler was close quarters. "He wanted me to say what had been done *to* them. He wanted some of the Creeps to have been the ones who did it to them. A *ring of Creeps*. He wanted me to flash back."

Oh lord. Of course he wanted that. No better hook barb than a pedophile ring.

"He wanted that to be the quest. To exact vengeance on—"

"In a children's book? What kind of vengeance? No, don't tell me."

"He didn't want a children's book."

"Excuse me, Eugene, but I think we may be zeroing in," said Harry, "on why my client called Cousins a bad man. Is that it, Eugene?" When Eugene didn't respond—he was fixated inward, unmoving—Harry turned to Amy. "This is exactly why we're here. I couldn't get him to open up—"

"He said, *pedophile payback thriller with kid protagonists.* He said I should stop writing *kid stuff* and do this because . . ." He closed his eyes and stopped.

"Because it would sell like crazy. Right?" Whatever sympathy Cousins' horrific death had aroused in her was ebbing.

"No. Yes, it would sell, but no. It was because *a good writer writes what he knows* and *you don't know about round tables and cardboard castles, you're just making those up, but you do know about pedophiles and you do know about kids."*

After a long silence, Amy asked, "And did he have some reason, some . . . excuse for saying that?" Harry shot her a look, but how could she not ask?

Eugene's eyes opened wide, and for the first time since they'd arrived he looked almost happy. "That's what I asked him! *Why would you say this to me?* And he said, *Eugene, look at how you live. Look at how much you know about homeless children. Eugene, they are your whole world.* I said I live in my car, and I know how homeless people live, and some of them are children, but they are not my whole world. This"—he held up the manuscript—"this is my whole world."

Amy was beginning to understand. It would never have occurred to Cousins that Eugene could write so well unless he were either ripping someone off or transcribing personal experiences. "Making things up," she said as gently as possible, "is what we do. You and I. He didn't know that."

"But he was a writing expert!"

"No, he wasn't."

"He was a sonofabitch, pardon my French. Eugene," said Harry. "Is this why he kicked you out of his driveway? Because you wouldn't change your book?"

Eugene blinked. "He didn't kick me out. I left."

"Why?"

"I explained that all I knew about homeless people, including children, was what I'd seen and overheard in passing, usually after nightfall. I know more details about San Diego dumpsters than I do about other people. I explained that I keep to myself and always have. Then he stopped telling me to change my books. I thought he understood."

Lottie ran up with the squeaky ball, not to Amy but to Eugene. She jumped in his lap and showered him with plumbago petals. "I have never had a dog," he said. "I should have a dog."

"Where are you living now?" asked Amy. He should have a dog, but not in a broken-down RV in the middle of god knows where.

"I have places," he said.

He was silent for a while, just smiling at her dog. Harry started to speak up and Amy put out her hand. Eugene would speak when he was ready.

"He wanted me to use them," he said.

"Use who?"

"On the night I met you, when we got back to his house he ordered pineapple curry, because he knew I liked pineapple curry, and he sat with me out on the front lawn, and I trusted him, and he got me to tell a story about one of the children, a story I overheard. It was a terrible story. I should not have told it and will never tell it again. And he clapped his hands and said, *There it is! Use it, Eugene! There's your story!* And I said it doesn't belong to me. And he said, *It belongs to anyone who wants to use it. Of course it belongs to you. And if you don't use it, I'll find someone who will.*"

"Well, in all fairness," said Harry, "that makes him an asshole, but not an out-and-out villain."

"Why?" asked Amy.

"It's a property dispute. I'd have to read up on intellectual property law, but—"

"It's about right and wrong. Never mind the law."

"And he could not see that," said Eugene. "He wanted a different series, *not a kiddy series,* one about children murdering the people that hurt them. *Butchering,* he said. *No hook like revenge, Eugene! Now, tell me about the Creeps.*" He lowered Lottie to the ground and threw the ball across the yard. "So I left."

Harry's phone rang. He looked at it and then went into the house.

"Eugene," said Amy, "did you explain this to the Lieutenant?"

He shook his head.

"I think you should."

Harry came back out. "They want to see you again," he said to Eugene.

"Okay."

Over Eugene's head, Harry shot Amy an unhappy look. "They won't say why, and that's not great. I'll keep you posted."

"Thank you," said Eugene, on his way out the front door. "You were very helpful."

Amy, who never did anything on impulse, grabbed her dog and her house keys, locked the door, and followed them. "I'm coming with you," she said.

She was surprised by the pleasant, uncluttered interior of the La Jolla police station. All the police stations in movies and TV shows were crowded, shabby offices strewn with piles of paper and out-dated computers. This place, except for the security measures, looked like an upscale doctor's waiting room, with upholstery and magazines. Even the archway metal detector was a tasteful shade of muted gold. She expected someone would give her a hard time about Lottie and was prepared to lie about her being a service dog, but apparently no one minded. After Harry promised to get back to her, he and Eugene disappeared into a room, which she assumed must be for interrogations.

Hoping not to hear muffled curses and thuds, she distracted herself thumbing through a nearby magazine collection, which featured current issues of *Smithsonian, Forbes, Bon Appétit,* and *Sports Illustrated,* and was gazing at a caramelized plantain recipe when the door opened and the Lieutenant beckoned her inside. "Understand," he said, "that you're here strictly as emotional support for Mr. Doppler. I'm sorry, but you cannot participate in the conversation."

"Of course not," she said. "I'll just be an appropriate adult." She hadn't been trying to be funny but was gratified to startle him into a laugh.

"You crack me up," he said.

In the room was a long table at which Harry and Eugene sat together. On the wall opposite them was what looked like a wide-screen TV. The Lieutenant sat down with his back to the screen, while a younger man, leaning against the closed door, fiddled with some sort of tablet.

"As I mentioned," said the Lieutenant, "we've found the FedEx location from which those packages were sent. Luckily for us, they had not erased their CCTV footage. As you can see . . ." He signaled to the guy with the tablet, and on the TV screen appeared impressively nongrainy footage of a FedEx counter, upon which someone in sweatpants and a hoodie walked up and deposited an armload of packages—the smaller ones. These must have been Cousins' hands and feet. He—Amy was sure it was a man—said something to the guy behind the counter, then walked off-camera and in a few minutes returned with more packages. He had to do this six times.

"Well, this is riveting," said Harry, "but his back is to the camera, which is angled down from up near the ceiling, so I don't see the point—"

"Wait for it."

When the man turned from dropping off the last package he faced the camera and stretched out his arms wide, as though loosening his muscles, and the oversized hood still shadowed his face, but you could now see the T-shirt he wore underneath the hoodie. It said "KEEP CALM AND YOUR TEXT HERE."

"That's my T-shirt!" said Eugene. For the first time since she'd met him, he looked ecstatic. "Have you found it?"

"I suppose you're going to tell me it's gone missing," said the Lieutenant.

"Yes! I haven't been able to find it since I left, which is bad because I always know where every—"

"And you will notice that the general size and shape of this individual, and the other clothes he is wearing, are quite similar to your own size, shape, and clothing style."

"Yes!" said Eugene.

Harry massaged his eyeballs.

"Except the hoodie," said Eugene.

"And why is that?"

"I don't like hoodies. I never wear those."

"Why not?"

"When you wear them, people are afraid of you. Bad people wear them. Good people wear them too, but when they do they make other people nervous. It's safer to wear a hat."

"Really? What hat do you wear?"

"White bucket hat from the Zoo dumpster."

The Lieutenant sat back and studied Eugene. Amy watched him closely. *He likes Eugene,* she thought. *He doesn't think he did this.* She hoped she was right.

"There must be a million of those T-shirts," said Harry. He monkeyed with his phone. "Look here, you can order them online."

"I got it from the Old Town dumpster."

"You're not helping, Eugene."

"Can I have my T-shirt back?"

The Lieutenant's phone rang. He listened for a while, said, "No kidding," promised to be back in a minute, and left, bringing the tablet cop with him.

Amy decided that the main reason she enjoyed Eugene Doppler's company was that he didn't have a phone to stare at, talk to, and fiddle with. Eugene was always fully wherever he was. "Harry, how bad is this?" Harry was staring at the screen, which remained frozen on the T-shirt display. The shirt rode up on the man's slack belly, just as Eugene's had the day she first met him, but there had to be other shirts like this, and for sure there were other bellies. "Harry, I mean it, should we be worried?"

He pointed at the screen. "It's a billboard," he said. "It's a big honking billboard. Look at him stretch out his arms, like he's posing—it's fake. He didn't have to do that. He chose to do that. He wanted us to see it. And not see his face."

"So what are you saying? He framed Eugene?"

"And he stole my shirt."

"Eugene," said Harry. "I want you to think. Do you know of anyone who wishes you harm?"

Eugene blinked. "I knew John X. Cousins. I know you. I know Amy. I don't know anyone else."

"Oh, come on, you must know other people."

"No, he doesn't," said Amy. "You heard him, back at my house. Eugene keeps his own company."

The door opened and the Lieutenant stuck his head in. "We're finished for today," he said. "Thanks for your cooperation."

"What does that mean?" asked Amy.

"It means we're finished for today."

Harry got up and followed him into the next room.

"Eugene," said Amy, "this may be good news." He didn't look particularly interested—he was probably still thinking about his shirt—so Amy handed Lottie to him, and they went out to the waiting room. Through the front window she could see Harry and the Lieutenant standing on the sidewalk, arguing about something, though not very contentiously.

"Eugene! Eugene Doppler, what are you doing here? Is anything the matter?" Paisley Shawcross emerged from behind the reception desk, her arms outstretched. She stopped short of hugging him, though she clearly wanted to. Exactly when had Cousins thrown her over for Tiffany, and where did Eugene fit into that time line? Amy loathed time lines.

"You've got your job back," said Amy. "Congratulations."

"Not exactly, not yet. It'll be a while before I can work with evidence custody, but yes, I'm back, and I'm so grateful. I file and run errands and make a mean cappuccino!" She lowered her voice.

"What's with—" She nodded toward Eugene, who was focused on Lottie.

"Nothing important. Just some questions."

"They don't suspect him of anything, do they?" She said this in a whisper that was pointless, given that Eugene was standing right there.

Amy shook her head no, which wasn't exactly true. Though Paisley was likeable enough, she had not proved herself a model of discretion. "How are you doing? Are you feeling better?"

Paisley smiled. "You know," she said, "once I got over it . . . The funny thing is that I'm kind of . . ."

"Bouncing back?"

"Yes! Isn't that odd?"

"Not at all. That's good news indeed." Apparently John X. Cousins had not been entirely without virtue: Women bounced off him like Super Balls. She almost told Paisley to keep in touch, then realized that she didn't particularly want her to. More than enough people were keeping in touch already. She and Eugene Doppler had a lot in common.

"Something's going on," said Harry, as they sped onto the 163 North ramp en route to Escondido. "Something really weird."

"Weird in a good way?"

"If I had to bet, I'd bet big that it's very good for Eugene. But I couldn't get him to spill. All he said was I'd hear from him."

"You're six inches in back of that semi."

"Six feet. It's the free ride zone! Reduces the hell out of drag."

Eugene piped up from the backseat. "At six feet the drag re-duction can be ninety percent. That doubles your gas mileage."

"My man!" yelled Harry.

"At this distance, if the truck brakes, we'll be decapitated." Eu-gene did not sound concerned, just informed.

Sighing theatrically, Harry tapped the brakes and they retreated to a manageable distance.

"Harry, did you ever consider a career in the clergy?" Amy's mother always claimed that the world's most reckless drivers were nuns and men of the cloth.

"Funny you should ask! No."

"If you had to bet, what do you think Kowalcimi is up to?"

"I'm pretty sure that call was from someone in San Ysidro, because that's where he told his sergeant he was heading. Which is a weird hike from La Jolla, in more ways than one. Right in the middle of an interrogation he quits and schleps all the way to the border. And whatever it was didn't have him make Eugene wait at the station or even tell him not to leave town."

"I never leave town," said Eugene.

They dropped Amy and Lottie back home and drove off. She had been considering inviting Eugene to stay at her place—this would have been a difficult sacrifice of privacy; still, she didn't care for the idea of him going back to those "places," wherever they were—but before she could suggest it, Harry said he was taking Eugene home with him. "I have a fabulous driveway," he said. Harry was a very good man.

That evening, after she had walked Lottie, who was already pretty exhausted by the rigors of the day, Amy sat down to work. She hadn't completed anything since "Leaving a Mess." Surely a day like this, with chic police stations and CCTV and driveways and a mysterious T-shirt theft, should kick something loose in her brain, but nothing happened, and after a dutiful hour staring at the white screen, she opened her blog. She hadn't checked in since February, a month before the Garabedian murder, and she had nothing to report now, but every now and then someone responded to a post, so she thought to take a look at her blog lists. Amy liked lists, in moderation.

She knew of writers who built their characters from them, first listing what a character likes and dislikes, where he was born, how he dresses on his days off, what his religious persuasion, sexual history, and favorite jokes are. Amy had never been drawn to this practice—to her it seemed a cold-blooded approach, as though details were Legos, creating the person instead of the other way around. In her own experience, characters arrived first, shimmering out of her subconscious, magnetically drawing properties to themselves until they came into focus.

On the other hand, when enlivening a face or dialogue or a static scene or series of events you often need a list of possible properties, details to bring it all, or at least enough of it, into sharp relief. Lists of fifties American cars, stone fruit, old lady perfumes, Polish names, hyphenated townships, silent film comics, window coverings, shades of orange. Keeping those lists was one way of spending time creatively.

Most of what she had posted in recent years had been in the form of other kinds of lists, lists of curiosities rather than of use, lists devoted to *wasting* time creatively, a process she had found calming because it was pointless.

Amy had learned some time ago to live in the moment, the moment being all one has, but she had never subscribed to the belief that every moment should count. That philosophy worked for gusto-grabbers, to whom it was a kind of religion, but gusto was as alien to her as social anxiety and the need for speed. Living in the moment meant just that and only that: The only culpable waste of time was time spent worrying about the future. Life had taught her this.

Her blog lists had been her most efficient time-wasters. She liked it when people added to them. Looking forward to hearing from one or two anonymous readers, she opened her site.

Apparently her exhaustive list of newspaper headlines featuring naked people running around in public no longer interested anyone but her. She did a quick search of recent news headlines, and there were at least fifteen from the last month alone, so she spent a good ten minutes pasting them into her blog list. She had no idea why so many men (and virtually no women) enjoyed sunbathing on park benches, clog-dancing in traffic, and jogging through supermarkets in the nude, but thought someone should be keeping track. On a whim, she set up a Google alert for Naked News, then moved on to the next list.

She had posted a list of words she found aesthetically repellent not because of what they meant but because of what the words looked like on the page or sounded like to the ear. She'd started with just one word—*besom*—and been delighted during the ensuing years by readers' additions, which included *louche, fecund, sebum, Clamato,* and *smegma,* but no one had visited this list of late.

Some time ago they had added *scissors, thanks, tongs, dregs,* and *gallows* to her list of nouns that could only be plural, which she had started off with *heebie-jeebies, fantods, congratulations, oodles, fisticuffs,* and *suds.* But again, nothing new. To her list of words that were not repulsive, just funny-looking, which included *crabapple, loblolly, kumquat, bomb, blowtorch, botfly, lardoon, galoot, spittoon, onus, yurt, larb,* and *disembosomee,* the last reader contribution—*catawampus*—was eight months old.

At last she came to the oldest list, which had started off as hybrid novel and play titles, like *Call of the Wild Duck*, but eventually morphed into hybrid titles of novels, movies, TV series, and what have you. This was her favorite time-wasting list and had drawn many contributions in the old days. Happily, today there were actually new ones, posted within the past month. She hadn't done much this year with the list herself, adding only *Funny Girl with the Dragon Tattoo*, in which an androgynous motorcyclist eviscerates Flo Ziegfeld, *Raiders of the Lost Horizon* (a Tibetan paradise is looted by thrill-crazed archeologists), and *CSI: Harper Valley PTA*, a title so lame she hadn't bothered to come up with a plot. Amy wondered if she had gotten too old for this silliness. She might no longer have time to waste.

Still it was pleasant to behold the column of new messages, as usual from apparent strangers. All but one had suggested only titles, which was too bad but understandable. Plots were the hard part. The titles included *Ghostbusters in the Darkness, Groundhog Day of the Triffids, Bleak House of Wax, In the Heat of the Night Kitchen, King Kong and I, The Invisible Music Man,* and *Long Day's Journey into Night at the Opera*. All but one of these had been posted in early April. They struck her as probably the work of one person, or maybe a group. Their names—jennyjobob, hollygonuts, letticealone—were quite similar, uncluttered with numbers, and they all used the same email provider. She wondered if this was a former student, like Ricky B. or Pete Purvis; sometimes they clocked in here.

The username of the most recent one did contain a number. Jxc4sooth was the author of *The Princess Bride of Frankenstein*. The title was amusing enough; the plot, *A handsome sculptor is tortured to death and resurrected on the third day to create a new species out of human body parts,* was not. Amy wasted a minute trying to convince herself that this was just a clueless attempt at wit. The original *Princess Bride* had involved torture and resurrection, and Mary Shelley's monster was made of body parts.

But this thing had been posted a few hours ago. Someone had sat down and thought about it and typed it and shipped it out to her while she was in La Jolla with Harry and Eugene. This was just wrong.

She stared at jxc4sooth until she recognized and understood the jxc and then she shut off her computer without closing out first, which she never did; she'd have to baby it on start-up tomorrow, but she needed to disconnect. She locked and double-locked her doors, checked her windows, took the last Halcion from a ten-year-old prescription, and for the first time in her adult life went to bed with the lights on.

CHAPTER THIRTY-TWO

Carla

Wednesday, May 19

"Misha Bernard's missing."

Carla opened her eyes and stared at Chuck, who was sitting up in bed and holding her phone to his ear. "What time is it?"

"Time to talk to Tiffany." He handed her the phone. "She's worried. Also, she says the cops have cleared out, so we can go back home."

Carla looked around the hotel room, which they hadn't left since Monday night. "That's good, I guess. Hey, we don't need a song, but we do need this room. Room 310 will always be our room."

Chuck handed her the phone. "Yes, we'll have it bronzed. But right now—"

"I know. What's up, Tiff? What's the deal with Misha Bernard?"

"The deal is she's missing. Paisley just called here looking for her, and I told her Misha's Lexus wasn't in the driveway and her cell was empty, and she said she and Misha were supposed to meet at the Artemis for brunch but she was an hour late and not answering her phone."

"Hey, Paisley Shawcross is downstairs having brunch!" Carla whispered to Chuck.

"No she's not," said Tiffany. "So that's where you guys went, eh? Anyway, she's not there now, because she called me back fifteen minutes later hyperventilating because she'd gotten to Misha's house and the Lexus was there but the door was locked and she kept ringing the bell and there was no answer, and then she tried calling Misha's phone again, and she could hear it ringing inside the house."

"That's kind of creepy."

"No kidding. I told her to call the cops, but she was hysterical, so I thought I should let you know first. Should we call Harry? Or just the cops?"

"Maybe the Lieutenant? Do you have his number?"

She did, and she hung up.

"This is getting serious," Carla said.

"I can't take another day off," said Chuck, "and I don't want you hanging around the Birdhouse by yourself. Maybe you should stay right here."

"And leave Tiffany all alone? Gotta go back."

By the time Chuck dropped Carla off at the Birdhouse, Tiffany had called the police and Harry and was now FaceTiming with Paisley. It sounded like she was trying to talk her off a ledge. "This has nothing to do with you," she was saying in a super-calm voice, "if something has happened to Misha, it's not your fault, and she's probably fine anyway." Tiffany locked eyes with Carla and made a crazy face. She whispered, "Flashing back to Cousins all chopped up and freaking out about being a walking broken mirror, whatever that means. The cops aren't there yet."

"Is anybody in the cells?" asked Carla. "Because if the place is empty, why don't we just lock it up and go to Misha's."

Misha Bernard lived a couple of streets west of the Birdhouse in a million-dollar beach cottage near Windansea. When Carla and Tiffany pulled up, Paisley was standing on an overturned barrel planter, peering through a side window. She seemed to have calmed down. "The kitchen looks okay," she said. "Except . . ."

"You better get down from there," Tiffany said. "Except what?"

She jumped down. "Well, except it's messy. I can see on the table half a pizza and salad and an empty wine bottle. I'm going to go around to the other side."

Tiffany spoke up. "Maybe we should wait. You don't want to contaminate the crime scene. Not that it's a crime scene! But, you know, just in case . . ." Paisley was clouding up again.

Carla suggested the three of them go around the house together, to make sure they didn't actually touch anything when they looked in. How that would work was anybody's guess, so it was a relief when the police pulled up before they could get started. Paisley brightened then—she called both officers by name and asked if the Lieutenant was coming. When they told her Kowalcimi was busy, she was disappointed but managed to rally when they banged on Misha's front door, and, at Paisley's suggestion, smashed open the kitchen window and entered that way. "Why not bust the door down?" asked Carla, who had been looking forward to that simply because she'd never seen it done in real life, and the older cop said, "Do you have any idea what a door like this costs? We break it, we own it." The wrought-iron door had to have been made special for Misha: In the center was a wavy green serpent with big gnashing teeth. Then the front door opened and he disappeared inside, closing it behind him. "Why does she have this ugly snake on her door?" Carla asked Paisley.

"It's a symbol of the Feathered Serpent god, Quetzalcoatl. In back there's a fountain shaped like an Aztec birthing figure. It's incredible! Want to see?"

"Not right now. So, you've been working with Misha, huh?" Carla wasn't all that curious, but she wanted to distract her. "What on?"

"Well, originally we were going to collaborate on an exposé of John. About how he used people, like me—and of course you, Tiffany—for what Misha calls self-aggrandizement."

"You stopped doing that?"

"Well, yes, because when I showed her John's profile she—"

"Of his face?"

"No, John worked out a profile of Frankenstein, like an FBI profile, and it was really pretty impressive. Misha said so." She walked up to the front door and peered through the dark green glass. "What's taking so long?"

The door opened and one of the cops showed Paisley a slip of paper. "Is that your phone number?"

"Yes!"

"You were calling her landline, not her cell phone, that's why you heard it ringing."

"Oh." Paisley regrouped. "Well, she's still missing, and I know there's something wrong, because her car—"

"Maybe she's on a date. She's been 'missing' for what, two hours? She missed *brunch*?"

"But her kitchen's a mess!"

"You should see mine. Go home."

Carla could understand why he was so cross; he probably had to fill out a million forms about the broken window, plus Paisley might still be pretty unpopular with the troops. She felt bad for her. "I guess we were just jumpy," she said, as though all three women were jumpy, which wasn't exactly true. "Please tell the Lieutenant we're sorry."

As both cops filed past them on the way to their car, the pissy one said the Lieutenant was "kinda busy at the moment, ladies," as though any idiot would know that, and Paisley yelled, "Busy how?" and they drove off without answering. She stamped her foot. "BUSY HOW YOU SONS OF BEES!"

Stamping your foot to signal indignation was always a no-no with Old Sally Gee. She called it the Shirley Temple Stamp and claimed that nobody ever actually did that, but apparently she was wrong. Carla was beginning to tire of Paisley Shawcross, who seemed to live in a perpetual state of high need, a thought so uncharitable that Carla suggested the three of them do brunch, which was the last thing she wanted to do.

So it was that they ended up at a Torrey Pines bar and grill ordering huevos and pancakes which they never ate because suddenly, on the TV over the bar, there was Lieutenant Kowalcimi talking to a crowd of reporters on the front steps of the police station. ". . . Specifically the murders of Patrisse Robinson, Marisol Jimenez, Martha Jensen, and Tiffany McGee," he was saying, and when somebody asked for more information on the suspect, he said, "As I said, Mr. Furness is a pharmacist from Rancho Bernardo, and that's all I'm prepared to say at the moment." Then he turned to go back into the police station and somebody yelled, "How does it connect with Frankenstein?" which he ignored as he disappeared into the station.

"No, no, that's wrong," said Paisley. "He's getting it wrong! It can't be a pharmacist!" She fished a crumpled document out of her handbag. "Look at this." She handed it to Carla.

Together, Carla and Tiffany read through John Cousins' "Profile of San Diego's Frankenstein Killer," dated March 12.

Frankenstein is

1. A white male between 30 and 40.
2. A hedonistic thrill-seeking serial killer who receives non-eroticized pleasure from torturing, mutilating, and killing his victims.

3. Highly intelligent.
4. Unemployed or low-level employed.
5. The product of an unstable, abusive mother, probably a sex worker. *Mother may have been his first kill.*
6. Unmarried.
7. Asocial.
8. *Unusually for a serial killer* kind to animals; also no history of fire-starting.
9. Creative.
10. Possibly on the spectrum.

Carla was instantly outraged. "'Spectrum'? This is bullshit!"

"It's worse than bullshit," said Tiffany. "Autism doesn't make people dangerous. Cousins had to know that. He did this on purpose."

"Yeah, he profiled Eugene Doppler, this sweet little guy he was supposed to be helping out, who isn't on any spectrum anyway, he's just Eugene. What a jerk!"

Paisley put a calming hand on her shoulder. "Carla, look at the date. He did this two months ago, right after they found Professor Bunting. This was weeks before he even met Eugene. Eugene didn't start living on his property until the beginning of April."

"Then the date's phony."

"It can't be. On my laptop you could see that he sent this to me on the twelfth."

"Of *March*? So you've had it all this time? Why didn't you say anything about it—"

"Because I didn't even look at that email account until a couple of days ago. John was really finicky about privacy, he always worried about his work leaking—"

"Well, that's rich, considering what he did to you!"

"I know! But he had me set up two email accounts—"

"For him?"

"No, for me. One was the one we used, you know, to just talk back and forth, personal stuff. The other was a backup address. Like the Cloud, only private, just me. He uploaded all his papers to the Cloud too but he didn't trust it, so he also uploaded to that backup address, and he made me promise not to look at it until later. He called it a dedicated safe place. So of course I never looked at it, not even after he dumped me and screwed me over with the PD. But last Sunday, when I started feeling better, I was going to clean house, get rid of both email accounts, you know?, wipe it all off the face of the earth, start fresh, wash that man right out of my hair, and I did wipe out the personal one, with all our private letters, but then I thought . . . Why not look. I had a perfect right to look. Nuts to him! So I did, and there it was, the profile. And not that much other stuff, by the way. I don't know why he bothered with all the coat-and-dagger, there was just this profile and some cv's and an old *Lightborne* draft."

"'Cloak,'" murmured Tiffany.

"Why didn't he want you to look at it?"

"I don't know! I never figured that out. I was better than him with computer stuff, but he had this idea that I could accidentally screw something up. He was really paranoid about it."

On the TV screen a squat guy in khakis, flanked by six cops, was propelled up the steps. His feet barely touched the ground, and his head was wrapped in a Bada Bing windbreaker. "Why do they do that?" Tiffany wondered. "It's not like we're never going to see his face." She poked at her phone. "Look, there's his face. He looks like Ned Beatty."

"Paisley, I don't care when he wrote it," Carla said. "I just don't believe this stupid profile. Unless there's another creative animal-loving spectrum guy running around chopping people up, it's wrong. Eugene Doppler didn't do this."

"I totally understand where you're coming from. I like Eugene too!"

"Everybody does," said Carla. "That's my point."

"How many people actually know him, though?" This from Tiffany, who was still looking at the profile. "He's not exactly chatty. He doesn't volunteer much about himself, and you have to admit he's pretty strange."

"Yeah, but not creepy-strange. And we don't know anything about his family, so why assume his mother was a prostitute? He writes books and keeps to himself. He lives in an RV. If he's a crazed thrill-seeker, he's awfully good at hiding it."

"Well, he would be, wouldn't he?" Tiffany pushed away her uneaten pancakes. Nobody was hungry today. "And really, how well do you know Eugene? Have you ever had a conversation with him that lasted more than thirty seconds?"

"Right!" said Paisley. "Nobody really knows him. We just take him at face value."

"Wrong! Harry knows him," said Carla. "And so does Amy. And they both like him. A lot." This was a guess on her part, but an educated one. Harry was his lawyer, so he must have spent time with him, plus he told her that Amy really liked what Eugene was writing and wanted to work with him. Now Tiffany and Paisley exchanged knowing glances right in front of her, not bothering to hide their skepticism, which seriously ticked her off. "And you say Misha Bernard thought this profile was impressive?"

"Not just impressive. Brilliant. That's what she said."

"Are you sure she wasn't being sarcastic?"

"Carla!" Tiffany had joined Team Paisley and was staring at Carla in shocked reproach.

"That's all right," Paisley said. "I understand. Misha can be pretty high-handed. But not this time. She meant it."

"What do you plan to do with this profile?" Carla asked.

"Well, I was going to discuss that with Misha, but now I can't, I need to show it to the Lieutenant before this poor pharmacy guy's life is totally ruined. Even if it's not Eugene, it's definitely not a pharmacist. Do you mind? I need a ride to my car at Misha's place."

After they drove away from Aztec Manor—Paisley was again standing on the front steps, banging on the door in forlorn hope—Carla and Tiffany returned to the Birdhouse. Tiffany went back to her office and Carla to the Rotunda, and their parting was wordless because they were annoyed with each other. It was kind of nice, actually, to have a real friendship, where you could be mad without making a big deal out of it. Tiffany was wrong about Eugene, but Carla understood why. Like Paisley, she'd been badly burned by someone she trusted. This had never happened to Carla. She'd never fully trusted anyone but Amy and Chuck, and she would trust both with her life.

She was standing at the big curved window, looking out at the water, trying to decide whether to call Harry about the profile thing, when Tiffany came in.

"You're right," she said. "It's not Eugene."

"Hey, forget it. I understand why you—"

"Here's why." She handed Carla a single sheet of paper, which Carla recognized as one of those student pieces Misha had dumped on Tiffany a few days ago, the ones Cousins had pretended to critique.

"I've seen this already," Carla said. "It's just this unsigned page. And I saw the other stuff too, Colodny's 'Journaling Adventure,' and he had a lot of nerve passing himself off as a teacher, he just scribbled a word here and there—"

"I've returned all the hard copies to their authors: the McPhails, the Hermans, Doc Surtees, Kurt, Manny Singh, and Simonetta. And I also sent out a scan of this one to everybody, asking whose it was, and nobody's claimed it. Read it again," said Tiffany.

"Why? Okay. *The sounds are music but also color. Sometimes deep and the throat is open and the color is dark dark brown. Some-*

times higher pitch and staccato, jumping up and down the scale and you can see splashes of red." Carla sighed. "Tiff, what are we doing? It's interesting and kind of weird, but so what? *Or long and rising low to high, soft to loud, pink to burgundy to maroon, the streak widening as it climbs. Early on come words but then they stop and just the music and the dancing colors.* And see, the bastard just scribbles 'Show me more,' no feedback at all."

"Sometimes deep," said Tiffany, "and the throat is open."

"So? It's a description of somebody singing. It's like a poem. Artsy, but it's not bad. If somebody wrote this for Amy she'd find something nice to say about bringing together the sounds and the colors. Of course, Cousins didn't bother."

"Dark dark brown. Splashes of red. Pink to burgundy to maroon."

"So?"

"No blues or greens. And why do you think it's about somebody singing?"

"Well, what else would it be? Why else would you open your throat and—"

"Early on come words but then they stop and just the music—"

"Tiffany, you're kind of freaking me out." Carla sat down. She was beginning to feel light-headed. *Early on come words and they stop.*

"I didn't see it either, but Kurt Robetussien did. He sent it back just now, and he says *Not mine, but whoever this is I wouldn't want to meet him in a dark alley.* Carla, it's not singing. It's—"

"Oh god."

"You can see it now, right?"

Screaming. Early on come words and then they stop. "Someone we know wrote this. Tiffany, somebody we know—"

"The only one we can ask about that is Misha; she's the one who dumped it on us. Maybe Cousins told her something about it? We have no idea who else he was working with—he claimed people were always asking his opinion about their stuff. Maybe there's information about it on his laptop, but I don't know where that is. The police must have it.

"Anyway, this isn't Eugene. I've read Eugene's pages, most of them, and he could never write this. His stories are packed with detail, with what Amy calls 'concreta,' he doesn't do metaphors, he just comes right out and tells you what's happening. Of course Amy likes it—he relies mostly on verbs and nouns and always the right ones. Remember how she used to go on about 'clean sentences'? All his sentences are squeaky clean. These . . . these are not."

Carla tried to take comfort in this, but it wasn't working. Of course this wasn't Eugene, but it was *somebody*. Probably somebody she knew.

"Look, we're overreacting," said Tiffany. "Maybe he's just some guy with a wild imagination."

"Yeah! Working on some stupid horror novel!"

"Right. Psycho tortures people to death because he loves the music they make!"

"Right!"

They were silent for a full minute.

"That didn't help, did it?" said Tiffany.

"No."

Tiffany went up to the office and came back with a bottle of merlot and two glasses. Between them they drained the bottle in thirty minutes, not saying a word. Carla got more wine from the kitchen, Tiffany brought down her laptop, and they took turns reading aloud from Tiffany's saved copy of Simonetta Colodny's "Journaling Adventure."

From what Carla could later remember about that afternoon, which wasn't much, this was the most hilarious two hours of her entire life. When Chuck came home, they had gotten as far as the

Colodnys' honeymoon flight to Oahu and Carla was dramatizing the part where Simonetta's beautiful wedding ring was "tragically lost while toileting."

"'Toilet'!" yelled Tiffany. "There's a verb for you! Hi, Chuck!"

Chuck gazed down at them. "Why are you two on the floor?"

They said "Don't ask" in unison.

Chuck disappeared for a while and came back with a giant pizza and cans of iced tea. It was dark by the time they sobered up. At one point, Carla was sick in the office bathroom and Tiffany was holding her hair back, which was so sweet of her, and then she did the same for Tiffany. Like they were real girlfriends. Which they were! What a great day this would have been if only the music hadn't streaked into dancing maroon. Tiffany said she couldn't go home like this, and Carla said she could stay in the guest room and she'd give Tiffany some pajamas and they could have a pajama party. Which is what happened. The three of them ate cold pizza and watched twenty minutes of *Aliens* and went to bed. Tiffany yelled from the hallway, "I love you guys."

In bed Carla and Chuck held each other and talked about the profile and Misha and the pharmacist and the scary paragraph, and Paisley Shawcross, whose argument about the pre-Doppler profile was as confusing to Chuck as it was headachy to Carla, whose head didn't feel good to begin with. Chuck said either her story about the dedicated email was true or she was making it up for some reason, and it wasn't obvious which, and Carla said one minute Paisley was bad-mouthing Cousins and the next she was treasuring his every word, like she couldn't let go of him. Carla said that Paisley was one of those people who was really complicated without being interesting and she was getting tired of her and did that make Carla a terrible person, and Chuck said it made her a spectacularly complicated and uncommonly interesting person, and then he fell asleep, and she, expecting to worry the night away, followed soon after, cradled as she was.

CHAPTER THIRTY-THREE

Amy

Thursday, May 20

Yesterday some Health-Aid pharmacist had been arrested for the murders of Tiffany McGee and three other women. Wherever Amy looked online for information she encountered one of two images of Jackson Furness: a color photo of an affable fellow posed arms akimbo like Peter Pan and wearing a white coat with "WELLNESS YOU CAN TRUST" on the lapel, and a video of him getting bum-rushed up a familiar flight of stairs by a squadron of police. The squadron formed a flying wedge, as though intent on using his jacket-swaddled head as a battering ram.

His arrest was the end product of a multi-city taskforce headed by Lieutenant Kowalcimi, which was why he had been bum-rushed to La Jolla rather than National City, Jamul, Kearny Mesa, or Rancho Bernardo, the four murder sites. Tiffany McGee hadn't died in La Jolla, but she lived there, so La Jolla got the honors. This was Amy's guess.

She could also guess at how they zeroed in on Jackson Furness.

Police declined to provide the press with details, but his home address was a matter of public record, as was the fact that the Rancho Bernardo victim had been his next-door neighbor. Had he confined his predations to strippers and prostitutes, he might still be at large. His neighbors liked him; his family were active members of their local Presbyterian church; they had two kids in high school; his wife was a Scripps endocrinologist.

Ah. There it was.

Already his narrative was taking shape all over San Diego (possibly the country, though that was doubtful given his anemic kill count): Soon would come speculation about how humiliated he must have been, a lowly pharmacist married to a big-shot physician, how emasculated he was in his Health-Aid jacket, how that resentment festered and drove him to places where women were reduced to pliable objects, how in time this objectification was not enough. They would *make sense* of Jackson Furness.

In time, after conviction and years of incarceration, when interviewed for some documentary, he'll have made the story his own: *When I killed them, I felt like a man.* Or maybe he'll bring Satan and the passive voice into the mix: *I was tempted and I fell.* Or maybe, just maybe, he'll honor the truth: *I felt like it.*

No mention was made of Toonie Garabedian, Donatella Ng, Leonora Bunting, or John Cousins. Amy doubted that anybody besides Cousins himself and his followers had ever believed all the local murders were the work of the same man. Frankenstein was still on the loose.

Earlier in the afternoon, Amy had called Tiffany Zuniga to ask if she would mind taking a look at Amy's Web page, specifically those recent entries in her list of hybrids. She was embarrassed but could see no way around it: If she was going to obsess about *The Princess Bride of Frankenstein,* which she'd done most of last night, she needed to make sure it wasn't the innocent work of one of her old students. Because she was hoping for a callback setting her mind at ease, she picked up the phone the next time it rang without checking the caller ID, and it was her grandson again, calling from a Mazatlán hellhole.

She reached for the air horn and of course it wasn't under the desk because last night, at 3 A.M., after she and Lottie had risen and prowled the house in search of some way to set her mind at rest, she'd taken the damn thing and put it on her bedstand. If you didn't want a gun, and she didn't, a 130-decibel Sonic Blast Air Horn was better than nothing. She hung up the phone, which immediately rang again, and she picked it up. "For god's sake, kid, don't you people keep records?"

"I have a secretary who does that for me. Miriam Arbogast, worth her weight in platinum."

"Harry, is there some way I can sue the so-called National Do Not Call Registry? I am at the end of my wit."

"No, but I thought you might like to know that Eugene is officially off the Frankenstein Suspect Registry."

"Can you tell me how this happened? It's the first good news I've had in quite a while."

Harry could and did, but first he informed her, "Calling from the road on our way back to the office from the PD."

"Hang up and drive. I'm not kidding, Harry." This was a fatal I-5 pileup waiting to happen.

"I'm not driving. Eugene, you'll be happy to know, is a human cruise control. We're right lane all the way." They were on their way from the PD because Kowalcimi had invited them there to share what Harry called bombshell news. "Turns out Eugene was definitely set up to take the fall for the Frankenstein murders."

"Did he literally say 'take the fall'? Also, why did he share this with you? Are the police obligated to do that?"

"Chet's a good cop and a decent guy."

"Who's Chet?"

"The Lieutenant. He had put out a countywide call to be on the lookout for a guy in a 'Keep Calm' T-shirt—he'd caught the same grandstanding act as I did on the video, and figured whoever was wearing it was making sure we got an eyeful. San Ysidro called and told him they had a DOA wearing a 'Keep Calm' shirt, and that's why he took off on us last Monday. Get this: The dead guy, Marty Balew, was a local addict, just a kid, sad case. Somebody had slit his throat and left the body in back of a Motel 6. Probably the kill site. When they found him, he was wearing a Padres sweatshirt, not a hoodie. But when they got him on the table, there, underneath the sweatshirt, was Eugene's famous T-shirt, the shirt he had deliberately worn at the FedEx drop. Chet says whoever killed him must have told him to dump the T-shirt someplace. Probably promised money or drugs, then met up with the poor kid and killed him."

"Killed him why?"

"Because he'd served his purpose and might run his mouth. Which he probably wouldn't have done anyway, poor bastard."

"So . . . Harry, I have no head for these things. Are they saying that Frankenstein got this kid to FedEx the packages?"

"He never says 'Frankenstein,' but yeah, that's the idea."

"But how do they know the shirt was Eugene's?"

"DNA. It's got two sets, Eugene's and the dead guy. So that's that. They'll have to hang on to the T-shirt for a while, but Eugene's dealing pretty well with that. Right, Eugene?"

Amy thought. "So, on the basis of a murdered addict's wearing his shirt, Eugene's completely in the clear?"

"Well, this, plus the phony profile. Frankenstein's still out there, and Chet says he's screwing up. Devolving. Whatever the hell that means. Eugene's staying with me until they chase him down. Carla needs to watch her back too. Anyway, thought you'd like to know. Talk later."

"Wait," Amy said, "what profile?" but he'd hung up. She vaguely recalled hearing that an FBI profiler had been brought in but could not imagine how a profile would clear anyone, even Eugene, or why the FBI would come up with a phony profile.

Still, this was good news, and she tried to enjoy it, to let it lighten her mood. To apply it like a balm to her jangled nerves. She had gotten at most two hours of sleep the previous night, neither of them unbroken; she had come awake more than once to lurid, silly afterimages—FedEx spiders, animated axes, mirrors of blood. She needed to sleep.

And write. She opened a new Word file and waited. After an hour staring at the blank screen, which was all the "writing" she'd accomplished since finishing the Lucy story, Amy wandered through the house, cruising her bookshelves, desperate for inspiration—which sometimes came from the sight of an old forgotten book spine—and on a bottom shelf in a corner of her guest room she spied an old notebook from 1967, when she had, for no particular reason, taken a creative writing class at Colby and been assigned to keep a "writer's journal."

Amy didn't like keeping journals. As a child she had kept a child's diary, and much later she had used yellow legal pads to jot down lists, but the jotting down was itself a mnemonic device, so she rarely looked at them. She hadn't looked at this notebook for over fifty years. It was an old-fashioned composition notebook with a black-and-white marbled cover, ninety-six sheets, wide-ruled. She wondered if they still made these. She took it back to her office and opened it.

The notebook contained at most twenty-five pages of desultory scribbles, beginning with titles:

A Hostage Situation
Looney Tunes
God from a Machine
N-O Spells "No"
Lather, Rinse, Repeat
U.S. Pat. Pending
Tell Me Something Old
Tell Me What I Did with My Keys
Larger Than Life

She had no idea why these titles had ever appealed or even occurred to her, though apparently the last one had generated a first line: "Nothing about her was larger than life." This was a wiseass list.

Beyond the page of titles were a couple of pages of "story ideas." These were interesting only because utterly mysterious, having been thought up and written down by a total stranger:

Creole manatees, dark-skinned, bald, large beautiful eyes, long lashes, full pursed lips, bodies pale and dolphin-size, cluster at dockside, heads together at water's surface, tails fanning out like goldfish? A little girl (Vanessa, white, daughter of Clara, they are lost) is welcomed, they are fed ripe melons. Vanessa climbs onto the back of a manatee—another rears up behind her, head back, mouth open with lion teeth, body like serpent, amused eyes never leave Clara's face. IDEA! CLARA HAS NO DAUGHTER

"P.O.V." Title for first-person story in which narrator tells about events he can't possibly know ("This is from my point of view, so I can't possibly know what X is thinking. Here is what X is thinking.")

Workshop Story! Entire story through comments on stories in workshop

Child named Enola Gay Maldonado

Scene: Mother and little girl going to mother-daughter banquet in identical inappropriate clothes

Man's p.o.v. shopping at Food Land with wife and children, gets separated from them, fantasizes about showing Food Land to Mozart (Mark Twain? Lincoln?)—at end fantasizes about losing his family and his car

Church of the Famous Maker
    Character name: Sidecar
St. Vitus School of the Dance

A rapist is terrorized by phone calls from a female stranger, "I'm going to stab you in places you never knew existed"

These lists smacked of anxiety leavened with condescension— she had been forced to keep the journal, so she made fun of it with "ideas" like turning a set of workshop comments into a narrative, which was pointless unless you were just showing off for an A. What was the deal with Clara's daughter, and how did it rate ALL CAPS? Had she ever been this young? Apparently. The "I'm going to stab you" line was funny, but with no recollection of having written it, or, indeed, of who she was when she wrote it, she couldn't be absolutely sure it was funny on purpose.

At the end of this foolishness, in the last six populated notebook pages, came the seeds of what turned into her first book, *Monstrous Women,* a short story collection that came out in 1971 and did not, thank god, include a story about Creole manatees or anyone named Sidecar or Enola Gay Maldonado. She'd forgotten this—that the journal had begun a career to which she had not aspired when she took that class.

Amy typed "P.O.V." at the top of the blank Word document.

She had begun writing fiction as a philosophy major; she was attracted to both disciplines—if fiction writing could be described as a discipline—because neither involved much in the way of research. Whatever was in your head either filled the page or didn't, and you never had to cite your sources. The more she worked with stories, the more fascinated she became by the concept of *point of view*, and how the setting, circumstances, and events of a story changed radically depending upon which character was telling it. P.O.V., she came to understand, was the most fictional aspect of fiction.

Outlandish plots could and did play out in real life, but never would one human being escape the confines of her own head and inhabit the mind of another. She had never seen the world through Max's eyes; she could never see it through Edna's, or Carla's. Real people were unknowable, even to themselves. Especially to themselves. The most brilliantly complex fictional character was a cartoon compared with a real live one, no matter how ordinary that real live one seemed to be. Fictional creations could be known. Fictional characters made sense.

When Frankenstein was brought to ground, spurious sense would be made of him. She made a list of obvious Frankenstein attributes—patience, envy, malice, energy, lust for power. Arrogance, too, heightened by an inability to empathize that prevented him from knowing that a homeless kid, a complex human being with an inner life, might elect not to toss a perfectly good T-shirt. If this was how profilers worked, she was not impressed. She could imagine Frankenstein backstories running the gamut from victim of severe childhood abuse to cynosure of parental adoration, and any and all of them could be made to fit if one assumed Frankenstein made sense, but he didn't, any more than Jackson Furness made sense.

An audio alert from Amy's email program rescued her from this fruitless quest, and there was an email from Tiffany. "Pete P. copped to the Ghostbusters and King Kong hybrids, and Ricky claimed all the others except for that dumb Bride of Frankenstein one. Nobody's claiming that one. We're too classy! Also, what do you think of the attached page? It was in a pile of papers some

Pointers showed Cousins to review, but nobody at the Point, present or past, is claiming it. Chuck and Carla and I would like your thoughts. Sorry it's an image file."

Amy opened the file. There was Cousins' lazy scribble across the top of the page, then the writer's eager questions—"This is just a start. There's more but I wanted some feedback on the first part. Is this a story or should it be a poem? If it's a story, does it start well?" Of course Cousins had answered none of these questions.

Amy read the paragraph once, twice, three times.

In her Word file, beneath "P.O.V." she typed

> This is from my point of view, so I couldn't possibly know what Frankenstein is thinking.
>
> Unless I'm Frankenstein.
>
> The sounds are music but also color. Sometimes deep and the throat is open and the color is dark dark brown. Sometimes higher pitch and staccato, jumping up and down the scale and you can see splashes of red. Or long and rising low to high, soft to loud, pink to burgundy to maroon, the streak widening as it climbs. Early on come words but then they stop and just the music and the dancing colors.

She stared at the screen until the room darkened. Dinnertime came and went. She was not hungry.

She stared, trying to imagine someone handing this thing in during one of her old workshops, in another, kinder world, one unpopulated by free-roaming, butchering sadists. Someone—someone likeable, a bit diffident, understandably anxious about sharing it with a critical stranger—comes up to her at the end of class, hands her this paragraph, says, "This is just a start. There's more but I wanted some feedback on the first part." She doesn't get to it for a couple of days. She reads it in her backyard on a sunny morning, her little dog at her feet. What is she reading, exactly?

Can anything but *blood* streak wide and splash red? And the open throat and the high pitch and the rest of it. Pulpy, but really, not bad. She will tell the writer that it's a story, first person, the narrator as killer, and so far this is energetic, imaginative work. The challenge, she will tell him, is to stay fully within this P.O.V. She will encourage him to keep going and see what happens.

Amy rose and fixed Lottie her dinner. Stewed dark-meat chicken, yams, green beans, and rice, on a bed of chow.

They were almost out the door when her computer chimed again. Amy was sick to death of rings, chimes, and alerts. This was the Google "Naked News" alert she'd made the mistake of setting up yesterday, and this was the third time it had chimed today, which was obnoxious. She sat down, checked out the story. It was a Naked *Woman* story, which was rare. It was also local. Naked Man news headlines were almost always amusing; Naked Woman news, not so much. Women didn't get naked in public for fun, and headlines about them were usually just disturbing. This one, for instance, which had been filed overnight. "Naked woman, incoherent and injured, found on Palomar Mountain." Not one for the list. Which, she decided, had run its course.

Amy disabled the damn chime, shut down the damn news and the damn Word file, leashed her dog, and headed out. She needed a marathon stroll with nothing in her P.O.V. but Lottie and stars and planets and coyotes and rabbits and a great big full moon. If she walked until midnight, she could sleep.

CHAPTER THIRTY-FOUR

Carla

Thursday, May 20

By lunchtime, Chuck was working in a vacant cell, and Carla and Tiffany were lounging in the Rotunda, finally feeling almost human and talking about going on a sushi run, when Paisley Shawcross slouched in. Worked up, as usual. "I'm not going to keep apologizing," she said, by way of hello.

"How do you feel about sushi?" Carla asked. Tiffany gave her an eyebrow raise, but really Carla was so not interested in what Paisley's problem was today, and maybe she could distract her with a yellowtail roll. Then again, Paisley was probably more of a burrito girl, and with this thought Carla felt bad about being such a snot. Paisley just had this effect on her. "What's the matter?" she asked.

"The matter is I'm fired again," she said, slamming herself down in a chair with such force that it slid backward and made contact with the plexiglass. "I'm sorry," she said, meaning the plexiglass.

Tiffany went up to the office and came back with a mug of tea for Paisley.

Together, Carla and Tiffany waited, while Paisley sipped. After a full minute of sullen sipping, Carla asked the question she was supposed to ask. "Why were you fired?" They were never going to get the sushi.

"Why? Well, that depends, really, on who you ask. If you ask the *Lieutenant,* he'll say it's because I looked at some files I wasn't technically supposed to have access to, although I did have access to them when I was Evidence Custodian, so it's not like I was running license plate numbers for the mob, I was just trying to find out if they had entered John's profile yet."

Of his face? Carla remembered saying the last time Paisley had gone on about "John's profile," and this time she had to swallow a laugh, which again was mean, but the profile again?

"Which they hadn't, even though I'd left it on his desk yesterday with a note explaining about when John sent it to me and why they needed to look at it, and it never even left his fucking desk, that's how highly they think of John. And me."

"So he fired you, just like that?"

"Just like that. I gave him a piece of my mind, and also about Misha, who is still missing, but nobody gives a shit. It's like they think I'm stupid or pathetic or something. And now I'm out of a job, and I'm so sick of San Diego, I can't wait to move on."

"Move on where?"

"Anywhere. I don't care. Anywhere but here."

"Well," said Carla. Should she be polite and urge her to stay? "Well, at least you've got a mobile home—you can live wherever you want, so that's good."

"Damn right." Paisley rose. "I'm going to go clean up my cell. Get my stuff together. I'll see you before I leave."

They waited in silence until they heard the door close to the east wing. "She lives in a trailer?" Tiffany whispered.

"In La Mesa."

"Look at all the damage he did! That's twice he cost her that job. Even dead he's messing with her."

"That's one way of looking at it," Carla said. "I mean, yes, he was a creep, but she could have seen him for what he was, like you did, and she still hasn't. Not really."

Tiffany sighed, shook her head. "It was easier for me. She was a lot more invested in him. It's heartbreaking. Pregnant at sixteen, two kids, husband who beat her up, no support from her family. Hasn't heard from her kids since they took off. Both of them on drugs. It just gets worse and worse."

"How do you know all this?"

"She told me about it the day she first showed up here. Don't you remember what a mess she was? She'd lost her job, and Cousins, who'd lied to her about owning the Point, wasn't returning her calls. I think what hurt her the most wasn't that he was cheating on her with me. He had made her feel good about herself, like she was a special, worthwhile person. Nobody had ever done that for her before, and he picked up on that and used it, and when she'd served her purpose, he dumped her. Oh, hi!"

Paisley standing in the doorway. "I have to get into Misha's cell," she said.

Tiffany frowned. "Paisley, nobody can go in there except Misha. Hey, I hope you understand that what I was just saying didn't mean—"

"But you have a skeleton card or something, don't you?"

"I do, but I can't use it, so neither can you. We have a contract with all Pointers, including Misha, and yourself, ensuring the privacy of the cells. I can only violate that if there's an emergency safety issue, like a fire."

"Well, this is an *emergency safety issue,* Tiffany. Misha's gone missing and it's been two full days and nobody's looking for her, nobody cares about her, except me."

"Let's just calm down for a minute," said Carla. Paisley was headed for a meltdown. "Why do you need to get into—"

"Because there has to be something on her laptop, or her notes, she keeps tons of notes, there might be some clue."

"But Tiffany's correct. We can't just barge into—"

"You own this place, right? So can't you just change the rule?"

Carla thought *Harry wouldn't go for that,* and then realized a way out. "What we'll do," she said, "is we'll ask Harry. Harry's our lawyer."

"I know who Harry is."

"We'll go upstairs and call him."

"But why can't you just—"

"Because Harry scares me. Not physically, but . . . you have no idea what he's like. Right, Tiff?" Going into an improv by yourself was tricky, but Carla trusted Tiffany not to mess it up.

Paisley looked confused. "Scares you how?"

"It's complicated," said Tiffany. "You'd have to know him. He comes across as such a sweetheart, and he *is,* fundamentally, but he's such a . . ." She fluttered her hands expressively. Tiffany was so great.

"Stickler!" said Carla.

"Yes! A real stickler!"

"He sure is, he's a maniac for the fine print, and he's the one in charge of the setup for my business, like . . ."

"Like contracts, insurance, and taxes! He does all the tax work; if he ever quit on us we'd be in serious bandini."

Bandini? "So," said Carla, "Tiffany can just go up to the office and—"

"As a matter of fact," said Paisley, "I ran into him at the PD. I was on my way out, big-time, and he was coming in. With Eugene Doppler. So he's your lawyer and he's also Doppler's lawyer? That's interesting."

"No it's not," said Carla. She wished Chuck were here. He was really good at calming people down. Paisley was working up a head of steam. "He's Eugene's lawyer because I asked him to be and he said there was no conflict."

"Huh. Everybody loves Eugene."

What was Harry doing with Eugene and the police? Now Carla really wanted to call him, but not with Paisley right there.

Tiffany tried getting Paisley to wait in the Rotunda while she ran up to the office, but Paisley was having none of it, so all three went. Tiffany began by firing up her laptop, sitting Paisley down at her desk, and showing all the contracts and everything, page after page of small print. Carla was seriously impressed—she had no idea the Point had "bylaws," whatever that was—but Paisley was not.

Tiffany called Harry's office; Miriam Arbogast said he was still out and she wasn't sure when he'd be back, but she'd let Harry know she'd called. Paisley wanted them to call his cell, and Tiffany refused, as nicely as possible, because "Harry always leaves it off when he's driving or working," which was probably not true but could be.

"While we're waiting," Carla said, "why don't we all run downtown and grab a burrito, and then when we come back we can—" The phone rang; it was Harry. Nuts.

Tiffany asked him if he had time for a theoretical question, and apparently he did, because she handed the phone to Carla.

"Shoot," said Harry. He sounded like he was in a great mood. Was he still at the PD?

Carla thought it best not to ask. "Yes, well, one of our Pointers—Paisley Shawcross; I think you've met her—wants access to the cell of another Pointer, and we've been telling her it's a violation of something or other in the, you know, bylaws, and we just wanted to run this by you first. We really want to help her but we don't want to screw up the fine print or anything."

"She's right there, isn't she?"

"Yes."

"And you really don't want to help her, do you?"

"No."

"Just a sec."

She heard a muffled conversation with someone, maybe the Lieutenant; whoever it was was laughing. Poor Paisley.

"Absolutely NOT!" Harry's yell was so loud he might as well have been on speakerphone. If Carla ever did that improv class at the Point, she would definitely use Tiffany and Harry. They were naturals. "You have NO IDEA the liability issues you'd be letting yourself in for. Do this and you can go ahead and GET YOURSELF ANOTHER LAWYER." He hung up.

"Paisley," Carla said, "I don't know if you heard, but it looks like we can't do it. I'm so sorry! So, why don't we all go grab a bite. I'm famished."

Paisley looked frankly skeptical. The fact that she'd fallen for Cousins' bullshit didn't necessarily mean she'd fall for Carla's.

"Okay," said Carla. "I'm not sorry, and I'll tell you why. I'm not a big fan of Misha Bernard, but she's our most important client—everybody knows who she is. Her being here attracts other writers. She's been missing for what? A couple of days? She isn't here every day. She's never in La Jolla nonstop."

"She travels all the time," Tiffany chimed in. "Sometimes we don't see her for weeks. She doesn't tell anybody, at least not anyone here, about her travel plans, because why should she?"

"Also she can be a kind of a bitch, frankly. She's god's gift, and she wouldn't like us rummaging through her private stuff, and I could lose her, and I don't want to. She likes it here, but I need her more than she needs the Point. Especially now. I don't know if you've noticed, but what with all the Frankensteining, most Pointers are staying away, and that's a worry, so the last thing I need is for Misha to quit. Which probably makes me selfish, but that's the way it is." Carla heard herself saying this and realized it was true. She did care about the success of the Point. What an adult she was. "But I promise you that if she hasn't turned up by Monday, then the hell with Harry, I'll let you in. Okay?"

Paisley smiled. "I appreciate that so much," she said. "Thank you. I love burritos!"

So they wound up eating at Banditos Bar & Burrito just down the street, which Carla had never tried before, but the food wasn't half bad, and best of all they weren't arguing. They chatted like three friends, about La Jolla, and the Point, and then more personal things. Carla asked Tiffany what "bandini" was and Tiffany said that's what her dad always said instead of "shit," and Paisley explained to both of them that Bandini was a brand of fertilizer. Carla opened up a tiny bit about her showbiz career—just light, super-expurgated, non-Ma stuff about filming commercials and working with future TV stars. And Paisley talked about her younger daughter, Serena, who had just gotten back in touch and seemed to be doing better. When Paisley left town, she was thinking about driving to Prescott, Arizona, where Serena was living. "She's done rehab, and she wants to make amends, and so do I."

A lull followed this glad news, and then Paisley brought up Cousins. But this time she seemed almost reasonable. "I know," she said, "everybody thinks I was an idiot to believe in him. No, I know you do, don't feel bad about it. But he had this dynamite enthusiasm, he was so excited about Inspiration Point and what he could do with it, and so happy to have a place he could connect with people, *like-minded people,* he would say. And I know you won't believe this, but there was a sweetness to him."

What a steaming pile of bandini. Carla knew Tiffany was thinking the same, but they let her go on.

"He did bad things. Really bad. I know. But he loved teaching, and he loved writing, and he had hopes. He didn't just want to be a celebrity. He wanted to be a real guru."

To end this particular discussion without ruining the mood, Carla said, "Well, and we have to admit he added to the Point. He did bring in some people. Not as many as Misha, but—"

"Yes, he did!"

"So let's raise a glass!" Good old Tiffany, who had social smarts, held up her stein and the three of them clinked, and that was that about John X. Cousins, thank god.

They chatted for a while about the Point and how Carla was going to attract more Pointers with Cousins gone and Misha off who-knew-where, and Tiffany said, "Well, how about we get Amy?" Carla, though gladdened by just hearing Amy's name, said, "No, she'd never go back to teaching," and Tiffany said she thought Carla was wrong about that. She couldn't explain why, but she had a feeling they might be able to get her back in some capacity or other. "She likes us," Tiffany said. "Especially you. She cares about you, I can tell." Paisley said she had met Amy but really didn't know about her, except that she was a fan of Eugene Doppler, and of course *John* thought highly of her, which Carla seriously doubted but didn't say.

So they told her all about Amy and the murder workshop, their final workshop, and the train wreck the next year, and Alphonse, Amy's famous basset hound, and Lottie. They told her about the radio play and the scary walk down Moonlight Beach, and Edna, and most of all how much they learned in Amy's classes. Outside the window the streetlights came on, and Carla realized she'd been babbling nonstop about Amy for at least an hour. "Sorry, we must be boring the heck out of you," but Paisley smiled warmly and said absolutely not, she only wished she had gotten to know Amy better.

Carla was thinking about Chuck and how she would describe this day to him, how it turned out so well. She figured he must be through with work by now and wondering where she was. "Here's an idea," she said. "Why don't we all go back to the Birdhouse and see what Chuck is up to. Maybe we can watch a movie or something. What do you think?"

Tiffany looked up for it, but Paisley didn't answer. She was staring in Carla's direction but not at Carla, and she had this sudden odd expression. She'd been laughing and happy and now her face was pale.

Carla turned her head, and on the TV over the bar a reporter was standing in front of a green screen with the Palomar Observatory slapped up on it. "I've been there," said Carla. "It's cool, but they don't let you look through the telescope, you just get this guided tour." The reporter was saying something about a mystery, but you couldn't hear much since it was apparently happy hour at Banditos Bar & Burrito. "Hey, are you okay?"

Paisley was practically white, and it wasn't a trick of the light. "I've been there, too," she said, "with John. It was such a special day. I'm sorry." After a beat—no, three beats—she blinked, as though she'd been somewhere and had just come back to the table and refocused. "I'm okay," she said. "Just crashing, just sad. And I've never been so tired. It's been a day." She stood up. "I'll check back in with you in a couple of days. About Misha." In the doorway, she turned and waved. "Thanks for everything!" she said. "Carla, I want you to know how much this has meant to me! So very, very much." And then she was gone.

"What the hell was that?" said Carla.

"No clue, but I don't think it had anything to do with us. She's still carrying a torch for the bastard."

"We gave her a good time, didn't we?"

"A very, very, very good time."

They waited for five minutes, giving Paisley enough time to get back to her car and take off, and then they returned to the Birdhouse.

A cop car was in the driveway, and there was good old Fred Savage ringing the doorbell. Carla and Tiffany reached him just as Chuck opened the door. "The Lieutenant sent me," he said, addressing Chuck, ignoring Carla, which she could sort of understand given how snippy she'd been to him the other day, but still.

Carla cleared her throat. "For what purpose?"

"Just to make sure you're safe."

"Well, that's nice, and thank him for me, I mean it, but as you can see we're perfectly—"

"May I come in, ma'am?" This time he was looking at her. *Ma'am.* So she said yes.

Tiffany asked if it was all right if she left, because she needed to go home and fix supper for her dad. Fred Savage, whose name tag, now that Carla bothered to look at it, said "Jerry Lamott," held up an index finger in Tiffany's face, walked away, and made a phone call. The conversation went on for at least a minute, after which he returned and said she could leave. He made a point of escorting her to her car.

"Power-trip much?" Carla whispered to Chuck, and he said maybe, but he didn't think so. He looked kind of worried.

The three sat down in the Rotunda. "So we need to bring you up to speed," said Jerry Lamott. "You probably heard about the Mount Palomar woman."

Carla and Chuck looked at each other. "What Mount Palomar woman?"

"Found wandering around the mountain last night, stark naked, bleeding, four fingers cut off of one hand, couldn't say what had happened to her or who she was. Just totally out of it."

Oh. That was the Observatory thing on the news. "Well, that's horrible. But what does that have to do with—"

"We think we know who she is. She's been sedated, but we've done an image search; her face isn't beat up too bad. It looks like she might be this Bernard lady, the author. There's lots of pictures of her online because she's famous, but she doesn't have family around here. We need a positive ID. Do you think you could recognize her from this?" He got a picture up on his phone and handed it to Carla.

Someone had chopped off her hair in chunks and poured oil or mud or worse on it so it clung to her scalp in streaks, and her jaw was swollen, her eyes were wild, and there were deep ugly scratches across her forehead and cheeks, but it was Misha all right. She looked like a caged animal. When Carla could speak, she asked, "Who did this?"

"We're not sure, and we won't be until she comes to, but the Lieutenant says whoever did this did the others."

"The others? Meaning who?" asked Chuck.

"Ng, Bunting, Cousins, and a bunch of bones that we don't know who they are."

Carla just stared at Misha's picture. She had no idea what he meant by "a bunch of bones" and didn't want to know. But Chuck asked.

So Jerry told them about bloodhounds following Misha's trail through the Mount Palomar woods. Misha had wandered for miles, out of her head and terrified, sometimes looping back where she'd been before, and the dogs had to follow that crazy looping trail, so it wasn't until early morning that they'd found the cabin. "I wasn't there," Jerry said, "and I'm glad I missed it. I've seen the pictures."

There was going to be more, but Carla needed to stop, just stop for a little bit. She stood and looked out the window at the dark bay. Chuck said let's have some coffee, and the two men left to take care of that.

Except for that night when Cousins messed up her phone with his stupid whispering, she hadn't been afraid about any of this Frankenstein stuff, and she wasn't afraid now. She was outraged. Nobody but Paisley liked Misha, but what had been done to her, the cruelty of it, sickened her, enraged her. Somewhere out there was a human being whose idea of fun this was, and Carla, who had never in her life hated anyone, not even Ma, hated him. Behind her, Chuck and Jerry came back with the coffee, and she sat down and heard the rest of it, about the *foot* and the *torso* and the *head,* and the stench, and then all the bones, not clean, probably enough flesh left for DNA, but lots older than the remnants of Ng and Bunting and Cousins.

And the filthy stained cot with the four zip-ties, all chewed through. Misha'd been left alone for a while and chewed her way out. "Imagine," said Jerry Lamott, who looked stricken, as though he were doing just that. Carla started to like Jerry Lamott.

"Do you think we can go see her? In the hospital, when she's better?"

Jerry said he didn't know, but right now Carla needed to stay here. "The Lieutenant's going to send a cop to Miss Zuniga's place, he's probably there already, and there's another one with Doppler and his lawyer. We're staying close until they get the perp."

Why Eugene? Carla wondered. But Jerry didn't know, so after they finished coffee she called Harry B.

"You okay, kid?" asked Harry. And they talked for a while about how terrible this was, and poor Misha, and then Carla asked why the cops were guarding him and Eugene. "Because Frankenstein already targeted him. Twice. Set him up with the FedEx delivery and then the profile."

"Profile? You mean the Cousins thing that Paisley was trying to—"

"Exactly."

"Harry, are you saying that Cousins was setting Eugene up? That profile was obviously bogus, but it was set up before he even knew Eugene."

"And you believe that?"

Carla's headache had returned. "I don't know. But Paisley believes it, I know that much."

"She still there?"

"No, she went home. Thanks for helping with that. Oh, god, Harry, she doesn't know any of this! When she hears the news about Misha she'll lose her mind, I should call her—"

"No need," said Harry. "Chet's sent somebody out there."

"To La Mesa? Oh! She could be in terrible danger! She was just here an hour ago. Harry, this is so bad."

"But it won't last much longer. The cops know who it is."

"Who?"

"They won't share, but they're on it. Misha and the cabin broke it wide open. Just stay safe, kid, and hang on."

"Keep calm!" yelled Eugene Doppler, not directly into Harry's phone, because he'd never do anything that rude, but in the background, and he sounded happy. "Keep calm and your text here!"

Chuck heated up mac and cheese and Carla made a salad, and the three sat down and picked at supper, because they were all just waiting. "Something is going to happen," said Carla. Jerry's phone rang. He excused himself and left the room.

Chuck got up and kissed her on the top of her head, his hands warm on her shoulders.

Jerry came back and handed Carla his phone. "The Lieutenant wants to talk to you."

Lieutenant Kowalcimi wanted to know when she had last seen Paisley. Carla told him and he asked where she might have gone, and she said home, La Mesa. "She's not there," the Lieutenant said, "and the trailer door is hanging open, and her car is gone. So I need you to think. Is there anywhere else she might be? Any friends?"

"Besides Misha, I don't think so. I mean, we're sort of friends with her, Tiffany and me, especially after today. She's a lonely person." Why was he asking her? He'd worked with Paisley, for god's sake, weren't cops supposed to be super-observers? He shouldn't need to ask her this stuff. "And for your information she was pretty upset about being fired. Again. We cheered her up, but she was really dragging when she left. Wait! Her daughter! She said one of her daughters had contacted her, which was a huge deal, she hadn't seen either of her kids for years. She said she was going to go visit her. But I don't think she meant right way. Lieutenant, she wouldn't have left the door open—"

"Are you sure?"

"Yes! Nobody's going to drive away and leave a place wide open—"

"Are you sure about the daughter?"

"Yes, I'm sure. She was so glad to hear from her. Maybe you could contact the daughter? Her name is Serena. She lives in Prescott, Arizona."

He didn't answer.

Maybe they'd lost connection. "Lieutenant, are you there? Hello?"

"Let me speak to Officer Lamott."

Carla handed him the phone and asked Chuck if he'd finished eating, which he sort of had, so she picked up the plates and scraped most of the food into the trash and did the dishes. Chuck dried. "When this is over," she said, "we have to go someplace, just the two of us. Maybe a train trip. Maybe take that Trans Canada thing through the Rockies, I've always wanted to do that."

"We'll do that," he said. He held her until she stopped crying.

Jerry Lamott stood in the kitchen doorway. "The Lieutenant says if you hear from her, you need to tell me right away. I'm staying in the big room with the dollhouse; just get me if she calls."

"Well, of course. He's going to contact her daughter, right? I told him where she lives."

"She has a daughter?"

"Yes, she has two of them, and one of them lives in Prescott, Arizona, which isn't all that far away, she could probably get there by morning."

"Huh." He started away, then turned back. "Little bit of a coincidence," he said. "Prescott. Happens a lot on the job. One week I arrested three unrelated guys named Maurice."

"Why is Prescott a coincidence?" asked Chuck.

"Name of the owner of that Palomar cabin. I mean, it's a person, not a place, but still. Serena Prescott. Small world. 'Night, folks."

She listened to his footsteps down the hall and didn't call out to him; behind her, Chuck was putting the dishes away, and she didn't want to say anything until she could think straight. She stood still and put herself back in Banditos Bar & Burrito, listening to Paisley. Had she misremembered? Had Paisley said *Prescott*? Maybe it was *Scottsdale*. Maybe it wasn't Serena. Sabrina, maybe. Carla went up to the office and called Tiffany. She was watching *SVU* with her dad and Officer Gomez, you could hear Mariska Hargitay yelling, "Sex is not abuse." Carla asked her what the name of Paisley's daughter was, and she said Serena. From Prescott, Arizona, and isn't it terrible about that woman on Palomar Mountain, and Carla said it sure was, and see you tomorrow.

So it was what Jerry said, a coincidence. Had to be.

Now, without understanding why, Carla got the cell passkey card out of Tiffany's desk and went downstairs to the east wing. Misha's cell was at the very end of the wing, just as Toonie's had been on the west wing. She stood outside the door and recalled that Bing Crosby song, that meeting song, and she hesitated before swiping her way in because now she was afraid. Of what? Toonie wasn't in there, dead and smelling bad; Misha was alive in Scripps. She opened the door.

Misha Bernard had decorated her cell with Aztecky tchotchkes—a bronze skull next to her laptop, a snake paperweight, a framed print of some Mayan god with his tongue sticking out. Carla thumbed through the pile of papers under the snake paperweight; Paisley had said Misha kept lots of notes. She had, but they were notes about business, her agent, some bills, a mani-pedi appointment card. Carla opened the desk drawer and there was nothing in it but this gold banana, not solid gold, it wasn't heavy enough, but definitely gold-plated, must have cost a fortune, and she turned it over and it started vibrating, and she slammed the drawer shut and almost left the cell because she had no business in here, snooping around in Misha's private life. Did everybody have sex in their cells? Not that there was a rule against it, but ewww. Poor Toonie with the penis, and now Misha and her vibrating banana, which was still buzzing, so she had to open the drawer again to shut it off.

She had come down here like a robot on autopilot; now she had a purpose: to get the hell out and go find Chuck and try to get a decent night's sleep, but first she had to look at the laptop, just take a brief look, not because she had a right to—she had no right to be in here at all—but because if she didn't she'd lie awake driving herself crazy wondering what was in it.

The screen was super tidy. It looked like Misha kept all her files in the Cloud, which Carla couldn't access without a password, which was just fine with her. She was about to shut the thing down and leave when she wondered about Misha's search history, maybe a clue would be there, probably not, but it was worth a look.

The browser was not so tidy. Carla counted fifteen tabs, starting with the Scottish Tartans Authority, the Ascot Emporium, and the Grand Shawls of Kashmir, so maybe she was getting sick of the Aztecs and going in another direction, but a *Bank Dick* YouTube video didn't exactly fit with that. On a whim, Carla clicked on it and there was W. C. Fields going on about beer flowing through the estate over his grandmother's paisley shawl. Carla's dad had loved W. C. Fields. One wonderful afternoon when Ma had the flu they'd watched *Never Give a Sucker an Even Break* and *It's a Gift* and *The Bank Dick* on the TV.

The next tab was a site with the lyrics to an old song.

When your true love comes to claim you
Wear this dear, old Paisley Shawl
With my blessing I bequeath it
May there always be a faithful heart beneath it
Never wear it for another
But the dearest one of all
Leave the mem'ry of your one true love
In your grandmother's Paisley Shawl

So this was what W. C. Fields was making fun of in *The Bank Dick*.

Carla paused rummaging through the tabs because Misha Bernard's search focus was staring her in the face. Even the tartans and the Kashmirs were paisley-related sites. Carla opened up

Misha's search history, and there was only one search, at 9:14 on Tuesday, May 18.

PAISLEY SHAWCROSS—Google Search

Why had she done that?

The last five tabs were sites about a man named Arthur Shawcross. Who had died in prison after killing eleven women in upstate New York. Was Paisley related to this man?

No. Following Misha's history trail, Carla saw that she was too young to be his child and too old to be his grandchild. A distant relative, or another coincidence, like the three Maurices? She shut down the laptop and fled the cell, because she just couldn't think anymore.

Chuck was standing at the entry to the east wing, red-faced, furious. "Where the hell have you been? We've been looking all over the house, Jerry's about to call you in as a missing person, Jesus, do you have any idea—"

She had never seen him angry. For some reason, this comforted her. She opened her mouth to apologize and said, "Come with me. I need you to see something."

After he let Jerry know she was okay, he went to Misha's cell with her, and she opened the laptop. She didn't say a word; she just let him look through Misha's history at his own methodical pace. She leaned against him, closed her eyes, slept like somebody had slipped her a Mickey, and there was W. C. Fields bellying up to the Banditos Bar & Burrito, drawling, "Has Michael Finn been in here today?"

Sometime later, maybe five minutes, maybe fifteen, Chuck brought her back with a question. "First," he said, "I need to know why you came in here."

"I'm not sure, but I think it was because *Paisley* wanted to so badly. She said maybe Misha would have left a note or something, a clue about where she might have gone."

"But you didn't let her in?"

"No. I probably would have, but Tiffany was here, and Tiff's all about office procedure and doing things right, so I got out of it by calling Harry . . ."

"So instead you came here yourself."

"Yes, I was looking for . . ." What? She couldn't have been looking for clues about where Misha had gone, because Misha was already horribly *found*. "Look, this is why I need you here. I don't know what I was looking for. I'm a mess. You're an incredibly sane person, an orderly person, you can reconstruct freeway pileups. Tell me."

"Okay, for starters: Do you like Paisley?"

"Not a lot, but I'm beginning to. Today the three of us went out to lunch." She told him about the afternoon, and how they'd all gotten closer, sharing.

"And then she left," he said, "and fell off the face of the earth with her door open and the place ransacked and blood on the walls."

"*What?* What blood on the walls?"

"Jerry didn't want to freak you out. Not a lot of blood, he says, but a few smears."

"Then—he's got her now! Oh my god!"

"Maybe," Chuck said.

"Blood on the walls!"

"Carla, why did you come here?"

"Stop asking me that!"

"How about because you didn't trust her."

"How about you stop interrogating me! How about my ass!"

Chuck, who had been glowering at her, looming like the Witchfinder General, cracked up laughing. "Yeah, how about that ass!"

And she was laughing too and like magic the windowless cell brightened, and never mind the blood on the walls, she saw Paisley staring up at the TV in the Banditos Bar & Burrito, the sight of the Palomar Observatory draining all the color from her face. "She knew!" Carla cried. "She knew about Palomar Mountain, which means she . . . knew about Misha and the cabin! And before that, before she knew Misha had gotten loose, she wanted to get in *here*, because . . . Misha must have gotten suspicious and Paisley thought she could have found evidence or something and she needed to make it disappear. Okay, now I'm getting confused again."

"How about her name isn't Paisley Shawcross. How about she took the name of Shawcross on a whim. A private joke. How about maybe she's used other names, like Bundy and Ramirez? How about Misha was starting to figure that out and that's how she ended up in that cabin."

"How about she has no daughters and her name is Serena Prescott!"

"Or maybe Serena was her mother or her grandmother. Or another victim. Doesn't matter."

Together they climbed the stairs. "So we're saying," said Carla, "that someone we know, a woman we know, chopped up those people? That she killed Cousins? Are we really saying that?"

They caught up with Jerry in the Rotunda—he was standing at the window, working on his third Red Bull—and really said all that to him. Jerry was impressed. "The Lieutenant didn't want to worry you about it, but yeah, he thinks it's her. He's had his eye on her for a while, ever since Cousins. Not that he told me either, before today. Anyway, there's an APB out. This time tomorrow, we'll have her, bank on it."

Fifteen minutes later they were in bed. All doors were double-double-checked, double-double-locked, and Jerry Lamott was standing guard, wired like a Christmas tree. Carla thought she'd fall asleep right away, like she had in Misha's cell, but she was a bit wired herself.

She wasn't thinking about Paisley—in a perfect world, she would never think about Paisley Shawcross again—but she marveled at her subconscious, how it had chugged along today, silent in the background, nudging her into that cell, poking at the laptop keys, enlisting Chuck's help to draw out into the light what she already secretly knew but didn't. How cool was that! This must be what Amy always called the little man in the projection booth, who Amy trusted to guide her dreams and her fiction and otherwise leave her daylight self alone. When you write, she said, you must respect that little man. He's a sneak, but he tells a good story. You can't make sense out of chaos without him.

And with this thought, the thought of Amy, of sense and chaos, Carla saw Paisley standing in the doorway of the Banditos Bar & Burrito, waving, smiling sweetly, saying, "Carla, I want you to know this has meant so very, very much to me."

Carla sat up. "We have to go."

"Go where?"

"Amy's house," she said. "She's going for Amy."

CHAPTER THIRTY-FIVE

Amy

Thursday, May 20

Amy and Lottie walked up the longest hill in their neighborhood and stayed perched on a flat rock at the summit for over an hour, gazing up at meteor showers in a cloudless sky of darkest blue. They lingered just long enough to catch the rising of Jupiter and Saturn. The view made Amy's world small and inconsequential, which was a kind of comfort. "We are accidents of stardust," she said to Lottie as they rose and strolled back home. Pausing at her front door, she said, "I have no idea what I'm talking about. It's just a thought."

She set Lottie down and locked the door behind her. When she turned around, instead of staying by her side Lottie was sniffing her way into the bedroom, which would have been alarming had Amy not been preoccupied with stardust and metaphysics, so that she took her time following her in.

In the dark room, silhouetted against the far window, was the shape of something perched on her bed. Had she been waking from a deep sleep, she'd have dismissed it as a hypnopompic hallucination, a spider of ridiculous size. The lamp beside her bed clicked on. The creature, clad in an undersized "Read to write!" T-shirt and cutoffs, sat holding Lottie in her lap. Arrayed around her on the bedspread were gleaming objects of various shapes, and an axe was propped up against Amy's cherrywood dresser. In the creature's right hand was a straight razor. "I love your dog," it said.

Amy had always had a bum denial mechanism, which was now for the first time in her life an advantage. She did not waste precious seconds resisting the truth of her circumstances. This creature had to be responsible for the Frankenstein killings and meant now to kill Amy and her dog. It had brought along implements of prolonged torture. There was really nothing to think about now, time only to act. Everything was immediate.

Amy walked toward Paisley Shawcross, arms outstretched toward Lottie. "Give me my dog," she said.

It held the razor against Lottie's face. Lottie looked at Amy without fear; with absolute trust. "Back off or I'll kill her."

"Hurt her," Amy said, inches away, "and I will kill *you*."

It laughed a stage laugh; Amy had surprised it. "And how will you manage that?"

"No idea. We'll just see." Amy reached out to her dog, cupping her hand around Lottie's neck, shielding it from the razor. "Give me my dog," she said again.

"What the hell is the deal with the goddamn dog?" The thing, the creature, inched back on the bed.

"The deal is that if you hurt my dog the rest of the evening will not go as planned. I don't know what will happen, and neither do you, but I can promise it will be quick, messy, and uncinematic. You don't want that, do you?"

It shoved Lottie off her lap onto the floor.

Amy picked her up. "Excuse me," she said.

"Where do you think you're going?"

"I am going to put her in the backyard."

Another stage laugh. "You do realize that later—*much later*—I'll go out there and kill her. If the coyotes haven't gotten to her already."

Amy held Lottie close, breathing in her scent, her warmth, and walked to the open French doors. She must have left them unlocked. Would it have mattered? She set Lottie down on the top step and closed the door against her.

Of course Lottie did not run but sat still, coated in porchlight, gazing at her through the glass. Amy knew she would be right there when the door opened again. Behind Amy, the creature's throat cleared. Amy turned to face it.

It gaped at her. "You're crying? You're crying for a dog?"

Amy brushed past her and grabbed a Kleenex.

"You keep turning your back on me. Not a smart move."

Amy blew her nose, wiped her eyes.

It reached into its sweater pocket and held up a bouquet of plastic loops; Amy guessed they were what she used to tie people down. "Let's go back to the bedroom."

"No."

"It's not a request."

Amy ignored this, sank down in a living room chair, one she rarely used, a platform rocking chair she'd inherited from Max's Aunt Phoebe. She felt the firm curve against the small of her back; her fingertips caressed the worn yellow velvet arms. When Max died she had railed against the dumb persistence of inanimate objects; now was different. This rocker, the warm night air around her, the room cluttered with books, tables, sofa and chairs, all marvelously detailed. Wondrous, really. The thingness of things in the eternal now. "I'm not sure we are," she said.

"Get up," it said, and when she didn't, "You're not sure we are *what*?"

"Accidents of stardust."

A disgusted sigh. "Get the hell up!"

"I'm having a moment," Amy said.

It loomed down at her. "I promise you lots and lots and lots of moments."

"Let me guess: You're going to stab me in places I never knew existed."

It moved in back of the chair, reached around, held the razor to Amy's throat. "Get. Up. Now."

In the daytime, Lottie always perched on top of the sofa so she could keep an eye on passersby. Now in the dim light her nose-prints stretched in a perfect straight line from edge to edge of the dark picture window. The world was a wonderful place. *Now. Let it happen now.* But all that came was the sting of a tiny slice, a nick, an accident. The creature's hand was shaking. Probably with rage. Or maybe it was as exhausted as Amy. "You've never killed an old one before, have you?"

"You have no idea what I've done."

"You reach a certain point in your life and death becomes thinkable. You begin to wonder, to prepare. You trip and fall and hit your head and afterward you think, *Whoa, it could have happened then.* You lie in bed shaking with fever and again, *Maybe like this.*

"You are probably used to dealing with people who haven't already come to terms with it. Makes them more pliable."

"Makes them desperate!" It moved around, sat on the sofa facing Amy, Lottie's noseprints balanced like a seesaw on its head. "Makes them offer you anything at all if you'll just stop. Little lady in . . . Iowa, I think it was . . . kept screaming *You can both have sex on me! You can do anything!* She kept yelling this even with her feet lopped off. We showed them to her! Shook them in front of her face like maracas!" It leaned back, grinning. The smile, unlike its laugh, was genuine. It was relaxing into unforeseen territory. Winging it. So what if it couldn't terrify Amy with knives and axes, it would do it like this, with a horror story.

"That's what you need, isn't it? Their desperate hope." Why she was bothering to argue wasn't entirely clear to Amy. She was not physically afraid—that would come later and would, with any luck, not last long—but the idea of this thing laying hands on her, the intimacy of it, was deeply nauseating. Maybe she was trying to provoke a quick kill. She didn't know.

" 'Need'? I don't *need* anything. We're talking about *pleasure*! You don't know what pleasure is. You cannot imagine it. I took their lives!"

"You did no such thing. Their lives were their own. You took their deaths."

"What the hell are you talking about? The look in their eyes! Each and every one of them! They were mine!"

"You horn in on their dying. Their lives are ending and they cannot attend to that final task because you're whining at them like a mosquito."

"Crucifying! Torturing!"

"Doesn't matter what you call it. You're not Torquemada. You're a gate-crasher."

Again the false laugh. "Shows how much you know. I am a power-seeker. A power-control killer, that's what they call it, and I have to tell you, there's nothing like it—"

"You seek power and control in order to get what you need—the attention, the coerced focus of actual human beings with complex inner lives. Without us, you are twisting in a void. Without us, you are *nothing*." From the outraged expression on the creature's face, Amy saw she had wounded it. But instead of springing forward, it leaned back, eyes unfocused, thinking.

"You said 'both,'" Amy said. "You said 'we.' You and who else?"

Amy was profoundly incurious about the details of its brilliant career; yet it had a story to tell, during which she could affect interest and meanwhile continue to appreciate the now. Lottie might be tunneling under the back fence to find refuge. It could happen. There was a small section in the northeast corner where rains had washed away a crescent of earth. Amy pictured it now, saw Lottie sniffing at it, pondering escape. Still she guarded against the rising up of hope, which would only feed the beast.

"His name was Henry. Henry something. My third partner. Total retard, strong as hell. We had some fun times."

"How many?"

"Times?"

"Partners."

"Four. And a half."

"And you killed them all?"

"Except Henry. He was too dumb to be a threat to me. Henry's on death row in Florida for doing some little kid after we split. He probably doesn't remember my real name anyway. Barely knows his own."

"Well, unless his last name was 'Something,' you barely knew his."

"Fair enough," it said. "It was Da Something. Da Rocha, Da Rosa . . . Something Italian."

"Perhaps Portuguese."

"What's the difference?"

"Four and a half . . . Was Cousins the 'half'?"

"Don't you want to know about the others?"

"Not particularly." Amy found she really was a little curious about Cousins. Had he "partnered" with the creature in her murders? This was hard to believe.

It had set aside the bouquet of zip-ties and was now playing with the straight razor, opening and closing it with its thumb. Not for show, though. More of an idle gesture. Like Max, when he got bored and impatient in company, would flip his Zippo lighter open and shut. She now recalled, enjoyed, the sound of it, the bright clink. The memory echoing deep inside her ears.

"I thought he was the real deal. He had the makings. Of course he wasn't a street thug, like Henry and the rest, he hadn't got his hands dirty yet, but he was a big step up, potentially. A con man with a long game; he was going to take over the company, the Point, he said it was a moneymaker's wet dream, he said—"

"Did he actually say 'wet dream'?"

"Okay, no, I added the 'wet,' but that's what he meant. Hey, you're awfully snobby for somebody who's gonna be dead in a minute."

"I'm a writer. I can't help myself."

The creature goggled at her and laughed a real laugh. "Play your cards right, old woman, and you might be partner material yourself. Like whositz, Watson. You could write my story. What do you think?"

"So he told you his plans, right from the beginning?"

"Took a little prodding, but yeah. I thought he recognized what my mom used to call a kindred spirit. He conned everybody else, especially Miss *Tiffany,* but not me. By the way, I didn't care who he fucked. That was not what we had." She said this as though "what we had" was something epic.

Amy, momentarily distracted by the news that the creature had a "mom," tried to piece together the chronology of the murders. "The first murder . . . the Ng woman. That was in early March, wasn't it? Did he know what you had done?"

It got up and went to the kitchen and could be heard rummaging in the refrigerator, which was oddly annoying. It took its time. The nearest phone was in Amy's office, between living room and kitchen, and there was no point in running for the door, even assuming that with her bad knees she could run anywhere.

It returned with a Diet Coke, sat back down. Apparently, for the near future, Amy really was Watson to the creature's Holmes. "Of course he didn't know. You can't just say, 'Hey, I chopped up a lady, wanna play?' You have to ease them in. He'd been trying to find a way to take over the Point. I suggested doing something witchy, as Charlie would say, so he scared the hell out of Karolak, whispered a bunch of creepy stuff into the dumb bitch's phone while she was asleep—"

With the mention of Carla's name, Amy had a horrible thought. "Have you hurt her?"

"Who?"

"Carla! Have you hurt Carla?"

"I wish. Good old Lieutenant K. sent cops to watch over her. Miss Tiffany too. So no. I was going to do them both. *Bastard.*" It pointed at Amy. "No cops for *you*," she said. "Bitch thinks the sun shines out of your ass."

They were safe, thank god. "And that's why you're here, is it? Because she thinks I'm a human flashlight."

"You're a riot."

"About Cousins. You were saying?"

"Yeah, so when he'd done the whispering bit, he was so proud of himself, so the next day I did Ng. She was my first gift to him. He didn't know she was mine, of course, but he loved it. Now he had two ways in, he could freak out Karolak *and* amp up the serial killer angle, get everybody worked up. It was perfect. You should have seen his face when the news broke about the foot in the Aquarium. *I knew it! It's a Serial! Right here in San Diego!* He was like a little kid on Christmas morning."

"Who's Charlie?'"

"You've got to be kidding me. *Manson,* Charlie *Manson.* Everybody knows that! So, Ng was tough because I didn't have a place to do it, it was quick and dirty and I had to save the other foot in Styrofoam with ice, which sucked. Then I had to find a place of my own and make sure it was secure."

"You don't have a home?"

"You can't do this stuff in a trailer park. The walls aren't exactly soundproof. I found the Palomar cabin in April, it was perfect, nobody around for miles, and it wasn't like the owner was gonna show up." She giggled like a child. "Did Bunting in the cabin. Did Misha Fucking Bernard . . ." Its face clouded up, reddened.

"*What?* You killed Misha Bernard?"

"No, idiot, I didn't *kill Misha Bernard.* Where have you been?"

Walking my dog, she didn't say. No need to remind it about Lottie. Also no need to know what exactly had been done to Misha Bernard, but now she heard about it anyway, how Misha had started acting "hinky," seemed weirdly suspicious, how she was lured to the cabin, terrorized, mutilated, left there alone to wait for the creature's inevitable return. "Which was my first and last mistake ever! I still don't know how she got loose."

It stopped, shaking its head, perhaps waiting for some response from Amy, some acknowledgment of fate's caprice. Amy was too busy stringing events together, understanding that Misha's escape had ruined everything for the creature, who was now on the run, who had stopped off here for a fix.

"So, like I was saying, I didn't do Bunting until May, but meanwhile working with John every day, dropping hints, asking questions. We spent hours on the phone talking about Serials—whether Frankenstein was a Gacy or a Nilsen, who was a kind of Gacy/Dahmer hybrid. He knew more about these guys than anybody. Except me." It shook its head in fond remembrance. "Told me all about Arthur Shawcross! *I'll bet you don't know there's a Serial with your last name!* and I said, *You've got to be kidding! Do tell!*"

Would it ever shut up? This must be how therapists felt; Amy wondered how they could stand it. The creature thought herself a storyteller, and all she had was a shapeless cluster of foul deeds.

"Screwing with the dollhouse was my idea. I made the wax figures, but I couldn't put them in myself because I wasn't in the club; he didn't get around to sticking them in there until I did Bunting. He should have screwed with the dollhouse much earlier but he was worried about getting caught. And then Bunting, and it was *Sky's the limit*!"

To the extent the creature was capable of it, it had apparently cared for the man. It was silent for a long moment, its expression shifting from moony nostalgia to fury, with a brief stopover at regret. "Then the asshole turns on me. Sells me out to the press. Wants it all for himself. Doesn't give a shit about my job, which was, which would have been, a gold mine for us, I had access to everything they knew. Dumbass."

"So you killed him."

"You think I wanted to? He could have had—We could have been—" It shrugged, grandly, shook its head. Amy didn't doubt its anguish, but there was theater in these gestures. Amy wondered what Carla would think of the performance. And with this thought, the thought of Carla, of leaving her behind, came sorrow, which was the last thing she needed. How to end this? "I gave him every single murder," the creature was saying. "Went to his house when Miss Tiffany was prancing around someplace else, pretended like I wasn't royally pissed off about being fucked over and fired. Gave him all the murders, made a story out of it, just to ease him in—you know, fiction, like, *I know this girl and she's offed twenty-nine people in eight states and nobody's even heard of her*—and he kept asking for details, more and more details, and of course I could give him every one of those but he wanted names and dates, and finally I gave him the truth. Which he thought was bullshit, he was even laughing. But then he stopped laughing. And the look on his face. Like I was a bug. Like I wasn't even human." It stared down at the straight razor, flipped it open and shut. "Took it slow with him. In his own bathtub. Taped his mouth so he couldn't scream."

Enough.

Amy rose to her feet. "It's time."

"Don't you want to know why I—"

"No."

"Hey, we're not finished! What's the rush?"

"I'm tired." Lottie had begun to scrabble patiently at the back door; Amy could not bear the sound or, indeed, another minute with Paisley Shawcross. "What's your name, by the way?"

Reluctantly, it stood. "If I told you, would you believe me?"

"No."

"Bedroom," it said, flourishing the zip-ties.

"You can forget about those," said Amy. "I won't be tied down."

The axe still rested against the dresser, and on her quilt bedspread were a hatchet, a butcher knife, a hacksaw, and some electric-looking thing, maybe a Taser? Amy slipped it beneath the quilt, since whatever happened she did not want to be knocked out first, because then she could be zip-tied. Behind her, it entered the room, flicking its razor, this time for effect. Amy turned to face it. "I should probably warn you: I have a bad heart," she lied. "You're not likely to get many dancing colors from me."

It stopped flicking, its eyes widened. "You read it! You read my story!" Its face lit up like (as it would say) a little kid on Christmas morning.

"I read your *paragraph*." For god's sake the creature wanted feedback.

"That one about the screams? There was lots more, a whole short story, but he never got back to me about it. In the story—"

"Paisley, there's something you need to understand. You are not the first murderer who has attacked me in my home while simulta-neously seeking inspirational writing tips. I am not in the mood." For an insane half-second she had actually considered assuring the creature that its paragraph had imaginatively conveyed Franken-stein's P.O.V.

She emptied her mind and sat down on the bed.

A warm breeze wafted in behind her, caressed her neck, bringing with it the vanilla scent of evening primrose outside her window. She closed her eyes, inhaled, declining to wait or hold her breath or brace herself, no point in any of that, just let go. In her room the creature paced, muttered, sighed, neared. "Let's go with the axe," the creature said.

Now. This is how it ends.

The phone rang.

The creature dropped the axe. Amy couldn't blame it—the ring of the phone was, in context, as shrill as a burgundy scream. It bent to pick up the axe, shouting, "Don't you answer that!"

Amy held the phone to her ear.

"Amy? Sorry it's late but listen, Chuck and I are on the way to your house, we were just going to stake it out but I'm really scared! It's *Paisley*, you have to watch out for *Paisley*, I know it sounds nuts, but if the doorbell rings don't answer—"

Damn, this changed everything. She would have to rally.

To her astonishment she had the appetite for it.

"For the last time," Amy said, "I have no children, so I have no grandson, and whoever you are, you aren't within a thousand miles of a Mexican prison, which is a damn shame. Listen, son, you must change your life!"

Carla whispered, "Is she there already? She is, isn't she?"

"You said it."

"Oh my god!"

"Where are you calling from, son?"

"We're a block from your house!"

The creature yanked the phone from her hand and threw it across the room. "You old bitch, everything's a big fucking joke to you!" It opened the razor and wielded it, probably aiming for Amy's neck but instead slicing down the side of her head, a scalp slice that didn't hurt at all. Warm blood gushed down her shirt-front. Time somehow both sped up and fragmented.

It lifted the razor again but before it could bring it down, Amy had managed to grab the 130-decibel Sonic Blast Air Horn that had been hiding behind the phone and blasted it in the creature's face.

This sound, ricocheting off the bedroom walls, was so ear-shattering both women screamed in pain and it took all Amy's will to keep the button depressed. With the axe it tried to bat the canister out of Amy's hand and Amy blocked it with her left arm, which hurt like crazy, and the axe dropped and Amy closed in, blasting away, pressed the plastic bell of the shrieking horn against the creature's ear and followed the creature out of the bedroom, attached to its ear like a limpet, through the house, almost to the back door, but she couldn't let it out there with Lottie, had to do something to stop it, and then the horn ran out of air and they faced each other in clanging silence and the razor came out and up and the door was open and a magic hand, Chuck's hand, gripped its wrist, stopped it cold, and Carla wrapped her arms around the creature's midriff, and a vaguely familiar young cop knocked out Paisley Shawcross with a punch to the jaw.

A great deal happened afterward, but Amy's attention to it was scattered, dimmed by profound deafness and the throb of her shattered arm, and by her joy at the safe return of her dog, who tactfully ignored the blood on her shirt and licked her face as though it were an ice-cream cone. Lottie did this from the floor where Amy lay. Whether Amy had fallen or just settled there was lost to memory and hardly mattered anyway. At some point Chuck lifted them together, Amy and Lottie, and set them down on the sofa. Chuck and Carla sat on either side of her and talked to her from very far away; she could make out "hospital" and "only when you're ready." Outside her window red and blue lights twinkled festively. She wanted to stay there forever with these two lovely people, but it was time. Carla's face was shining. Amy took her hand and squeezed. "I'm think I'm ready," she said.

CHAPTER THIRTY-SIX

Amy and Carla

Summer

They kept Amy in the hospital for only one full day and night, which was one full day and night too long. The stitching of her head and the splinting of her fractured arm were accomplished in the ER, but they kept her all day and overnight anyway. She assumed it was because of her age, couldn't fault them for that, but when it came time to leave she was confronted by a psychologist. Must she pass some sort of test? Perhaps it wasn't a requirement, but the large dimpled man who came to her room as she was gathering herself together evidently imagined himself authorized to ask her a series of personal questions. He smiled in a practiced way, called her by her first name, sat down beside her bed as though invited to do so, and produced a PTSD checklist on a clipboard from which he read in a pseudo-soothing monotone. There were twenty questions, all about her response to her recent "stressful experience."

"Have you experienced repeated, disturbing dreams of the stressful experience?"

"The stressful experience happened thirty-six hours ago, so no."

"So sorry, but as I explained, you must answer *not at all, a little bit, moderately, quite a bit,* or *extremely.*"

"Not at all." She had had a disturbing dream, but it was none of this person's business.

"Do you have trouble remembering parts of the stressful experience?"

"Not at all." Perhaps if she had semaphored at the outset that she was still deaf, he would have gone away. Deafness had passed, leaving behind just a mildly annoying intermittent tinnitus.

"Do you have strong physical reactions when something reminds you of the stressful experience?"

"Well, right now I'm having a strong physical reaction to—"

"Not at all, a little bit, moderately, quite a bit, or *extremely?"*

This went on for minutes. She was asked if she ever felt like the stressful experience was happening again, if she got upset if somebody reminded her of the stressful experience (!), if she was excessively alert or excessively somnolent, if she had trouble falling asleep. The interrogation then veered from PTSD symptoms to a direct assault on her personality. Did she have strong negative feelings such as fear, horror, anger, guilt, or shame? Did she feel distant from other people? Did she find herself behaving irritably? If Chuck had not arrived when he did, Amy might have given the dimpled man cause to prescribe an extended stay with restraints.

Carla didn't want to leave Amy alone at her house because she was on pain meds, plus the place was haunted by Paisley Shawcross. They had slept in her guest room with Lottie while Amy was in the hospital, and Carla had come awake more than once, not to a ghost exactly, since after all Paisley wasn't dead, but to an awful feeling, what Amy might call a malignancy, as though Paisley's spirit was somehow gathering in filthy clouds in the four corners of each room. Chuck was kind enough not to say this was the work of her imagination, but she knew he thought so, because he had slept like a baby.

So when they brought Amy back home, Carla suggested they stay with her for a few days. "Because," she said, "your poor arm, and you're on pain meds and you might, you know . . ."

"Fall? I do that all the time. I have great bones and a hard head."

She waved at them from her front door as they pulled away. Chuck asked Carla what the matter was.

"She looks so small."

He was quiet most of the way home, and then he asked if they should get a dog or a chameleon. He always knew what to say.

"Basset hound," said Carla, wiping her eyes.

"Basset hound it is."

"And a chameleon."

Amy fired up her computer and confronted a blank Word screen. She typed in "Stardust." After an hour or so, "Accidents of Stardust." Nothing.

She had been sure that a story would come. What was the point of that *stressful experience* if it did not generate a narrative? In the middle of that *stressful experience* had come the onset of a great epiphany about accidents and stardust. She remembered the sensation of it, that tiny burst of light that always arrives as you grasp a startling and elusive truth.

The epiphany had been occasioned by her gratitude for that wealth of detail that had surrounded her while the creature preened and crowed and celebrated its tedious wickedness. She had understood she was about to die and in those moments she had bathed in stardust and known that it had a purpose.

But what purpose was that? Now she could not remember. She recalled only certainty. Perhaps if she had died, it would have come to her at the very end. For the moment it was gone, and although she did not doubt the truth of it, she knew better than to wait for enlightenment that would come, if it ever did, in its own sweet time. She shut down the computer and took Lottie for a walk.

She hadn't walked her in the daytime for months and was surprised that some of her neighbors were out and about, standing in small groups, chatting. Not until coming abreast of Eugene's turkey lady, Mrs. Bradstreet, did she see they were chatting about her. They glanced discreetly at her bandaged head and sling and asked her how she was doing and if she needed any help, and they did not ask her what had happened, which meant they already knew. Amy considered for the first time the effect the stressful incident must have had on the whole neighborhood. Had the sonic blast of her air horn through the open window in her bedroom echoed up here at the top of the hill? Had the police and ambulance arrived at two in the morning with sirens blaring? And of course the whole thing must have been in the news. Touched by their discretion, she apologized for the fuss. Both the Bradstreets and the Blaines, her next-door neighbors, assured her that the fuss had been terrifically exciting.

When she came back home she realized that the phone hadn't rung since she'd returned from the hospital, which wasn't at all like it, and then pictured the creature throwing her bedside handset across the room, and now there it was, on the floor beneath the tall bureau. She put it back and within a minute it rang. The caller ID read *San Diego Union-Tribune*. She blocked it, and continued to block every number that called that day that wasn't recognizably Carla or someone else she wouldn't mind talking to, which was basically Carla. Eventually she'd have to deal with the press, but not in an interview, and not right now.

Right now she needed to think about that bad dream.

Amy almost never remembered dreams, and when she did, never in detail. There had been a mirror and an ugly mask, but as usual she had not hung on to the images, just the words, *mirror, mask*. She had been shown something, and even though she could not call it up it directly she could remember all too well coming awake with a terrible smile on her face. The stretch of muscles beneath it felt anchored deep, immobile, and she knew not to look at it in a mirror. The muscles relaxed right away but the memory did not. It had been a *risus sardonicus,* that "rictus" that had so often featured in the murder mysteries she'd read in her teens. As a kid she had thrilled to the word "rictus," which sounded so deliciously awful. It was supposed to be a hallmark of strychnine poisoning. Now she saw it was the hallmark of something far worse, the ecstasy of doing something dreadful.

In daylight she forced herself to acknowledge that ecstasy. To relive her assault on Paisley Shawcross, the alacrity with which she had chased her through the house, rejoicing all the way in the damage she was doing, in the agony she was causing. If Chuck and Carla had not arrived when they did, she might have killed the creature with her bare hands. And loved it.

She herself had been, for those moments, a creature.

Had she shared her dream with the dimpled man, he'd have said this was perfectly natural. As though that would have been a comfort. She would never share it. She would never make a story out of it. She would just have to take it in and live with it.

Within one day of the arrest of Paisley Shawcross her exploits were a feature of the twenty-four-hour worldwide news cycle. Paisley's face, joined by the faces of Cousins, Leonora Bunting, and Donatella Ng, and a homeless addict named Marty Balew, became recognizable to Americans, Brazilians, Ukrainians, and Finns. Within a month there was buzz about three movies and an HBO series. Carla knew this because Harriet Cogwell, daughter of Carla's old agent, called her daily trying to get her to join in the fun. Chuck asked if she had really said "join in the fun," and Carla said no, just a load of BS about lemons and lemonade and jump-starting. "As if," she said.

Tiffany had become obsessed with the unacknowledged, unsolved murder of Toonie Garabedian. Who had strangled her? Why wasn't she ever listed among Paisley's victims? "It's like she never even existed," Tiffany said. "It's not right." Carla had come around to thinking that Toonie's killer was probably Paisley and they just didn't have enough evidence yet. Chuck said no, it had to be Jackson Furness. The three had this conversation often, and it was always Tiffany who brought the subject up, and every time Carla felt guilty because Tiffany cared so much and she cared so little. "It's not that I liked her," Tiffany said. "Let's face it, she wasn't all that likeable. Still. It's like a sore tooth." Except for the tooth, Tiffany was coming out of the funk left by John X. Cousins. In July she started dating Jerry Lamott, who turned out to be a nice guy and very good for her. Her father approved.

They named their tricolor basset puppy Gaston. This was Chuck's idea. Carla figured he meant the *Beauty and the Beast* guy, but when Chuck showed her the old comic strip she was enchanted. "Amy will totally get that!" *You first, my dear Gaston! After you, my dear Alphonse!*

Chuck created a beautiful net cage next to the dollhouse for Boffo II, their pygmy chameleon. Inside it he fashioned a jungle filled with leafy branches and ficus trees. Except for the netting, it looked wonderful next to the dollhouse, or would have if the house hadn't been shielded by plexiglass, so they got rid of the plexiglass, which she hated anyway. Occasionally Boffo got loose, but he always went right next door, and almost always to the basement. Sometimes they found him sleeping on Carla's father's workbench. Chuck took the netting away and arranged little trees and plants all around the dollhouse. Boffo sometimes freaked out the Pointers, but, as Carla said, that was their problem.

The Pointers—all of whom returned after the arrest of Frankenstein—were spending quite a bit of time in the Rotunda, watching Carla discuss and perform improvs and trying to do them with her and with one another. For a couple of weeks that's all they did, because though Carla had no trouble coming up with situations, she couldn't figure out how to explain using the exercises to develop their characters and polish their dialogue. She called Amy and asked her for advice, and to her amazement Amy volunteered to come down and help out.

Amy suggested beginning by asking the Pointers to improvise a troublesome scene from their own pages. The first evening, assigned to resurrect *Womb to Tomb*, one of his old anti-HMO novels, Dr. Surtees performed woodenly as a bedside physician droning on at length to a dying patient that he could not perform a lifesaving procedure because his government-sponsored insurance had run out. After Amy suggested that instead he play the dying patient, he surprised both himself and his audience with dialogue and behavior driven by circumstance rather than agenda. At the end of the improv he told the physician, Manny Singh, to go fuck himself.

There followed, on that night and many others, game and sometimes useful exercises. Simonetta Colodny's "Journaling Adventure" re-creation of her honeymoon arrival at Oahu (not, thank god, of the tragic toileting mishap), which had featured her husband's violent allergic reaction to a tuberose in his lei, became instructively hilarious when she improvised the lei greeter's sarcastic, eye-rolling response. Soon they were ready for more imaginative work. They jotted down situations from their own pages, put them in a hat, then drew from the hat and improvised. Often the experience of watching the improv helped with rewrites, and even when it didn't, everyone had fun. Carla's classes resulted in the longest waiting list ever, so long that Carla and Harry B. began to explore the possibility of purchasing neighboring property and expanding the Point.

And Amy was enjoying herself, Carla could tell. One night in August, at the end of a particularly wild session, Amy put her hand on Carla's shoulder and said, "You are teaching, and you are brilliant at it. Do you see that?" And Carla realized she did.

And when Amy asked her if she still missed writing, Carla saw that she did not, and that she was, for the moment, doing exactly what she should be doing.

Paisley Shawcross's real name was Joy Rose Sheppard. This fact did not come out until late summer, when Florida death row inmate Henry DaSilva tried to trade her real name for a commutation; when that didn't work he gave it up anyway. Much was made of the irony of her real name, none of it worth making.

Worn down by tireless interview attempts, by phone and internet and more than once by doorbell, Amy gave a videoed one to the *U-T* with the express assurance that they would promote it as an exclusive, because that was what it literally was. She also stipulated that they not ask her how she *felt* about anything that had happened to her, since feelings were not news. And since she might at some point be called upon to testify against her, she was also disinclined to describe her interactions with Joy Rose Sheppard, in case doing so would risk a defense claim that she couldn't get a fair trial in San Diego.

This made for a brief interview. They moved quickly from the topic of Sheppard to that of what society should do with people like her. Amy said they should be denied the opportunity to indulge their appetites and then ignored for all time. When asked if they should be put to death, Amy said not in her opinion. When asked if certain acts weren't so heinous that the people committing them gave up the right to life, she said yes, but that meant only that society had the option of killing, not the duty. "When we kill them," she said, "we degrade ourselves." When asked what should be done, she said, "Declare them anathema and put them away." When asked how that would work, she said, "We could start by not writing about them."

The interview garnered a wealth of comments, one of which described Amy as "pompous." She had to agree, although she also felt it was hard to come across otherwise when answering such questions. While "What Should We Do with a Joy Rose Sheppard?" was an excellent debate topic, it was an inappropriate one for an interview.

She tried explaining this to Carla, who was outraged by the "pompous" comment. "Everyone's got an opinion," Amy said. "Why ask for mine?" "Because they might learn something!" said Carla. "They'd learn a lot more if they asked themselves," Amy said.

One evening Harry B. dropped by to enjoy an improv class and then a drink with Carla, Chuck, Amy, Tiffany, and Jerry at the Artemis bar. Eugene was back to living in one of his "places"— Harry guessed it was in Balboa Park. Everybody but Harry wanted to rescue him in some way. Carla and Chuck would have housed him rent-free; even Amy considered, for a second, giving the man her guest room. "He's fine," said Harry. "Eugene's got a publisher and a contract you wouldn't believe, and when the money comes through he's going to buy an Airstream. He's where he wants to be." Harry assured them that he would help Eugene manage his money.

Tiffany wondered aloud what was wrong with his family and why they had just let him go off by himself. "They didn't," said Harry. "They spent thousands to track him down and bring him home. They've done everything short of kidnapping. He says they actually sent a deprogrammer, as if his lifestyle made him a one-man cult. He was their only child, and without him there was nobody to inherit their vast fortune." Eugene, he said, wanted no part of the family firm. "We're disclaiming the inheritance. New one on me, but it's a real thing." And Eugene was keeping his cell at the Point, so they'd see him from time to time. Chuck wanted to know what the family firm was. "Lady Isabella Dolls," said Harry. "Company's worth a crapload. Eugene says they gave him the creeps when he was a kid. Apparently the eyes follow you around the room."

"Hi, kids!" Here was Misha Bernard. Over her left hand was what looked like a liquid silver glove, a prosthetic device so impressive that Carla couldn't tell which fingers were missing. She drew up a chair and ordered drinks all around. Clearly she had been drinking for a while. They welcomed her, told her about Eugene, and Carla's classes, and they asked how she was. She talked about her newest book deal, a "captor-survivor quickie." Apparently there was a niche for that. "It's just for the publicity," she said. "So when the real book comes out, I'll be set for life."

In preparation for the real book, her agent was deep in preliminary discussions with the agent for Joy Rose Sheppard. Nobody made a crack about niches or expressed horror at the thought of Joy Rose Sheppard having a literary agent. Nobody, including Misha, mentioned the hand or alluded specifically to what she had endured. When she rose to leave, Amy spoke. "I hope you are well," she said, locking eyes with Misha, who stared back, expressionless. Then smiled, though not with her eyes. "Never better," she said, and waved goodbye with her silver hand, and she was gone. Nobody said anything for a long time. "She's tough," said Harry B. "She'll be all right."

"I wouldn't bet on it," said Amy.

"Who killed Toonie Garabedian?"

"Give it a rest, Tiff."

"I will not give it a rest. Harry, you're friends with Kowalcimi, right? Do you know?"

"Not exactly, and no. Why ask me? You're sitting right next to somebody who works for him."

"Jerry won't tell me."

"Actually," said Jerry Lamott.

"Actually what?"

"There's going to be an arrest." Jerry smiled mysteriously and did a Groucho Marx eyebrow wiggle. "Tomorrow morning."

"I can't believe you didn't tell me!"

"If I told you, I'd have to kill you."

"But if it's tomorrow morning—"

"You realize I'd lose my job if you told anyone—"

As one, the rest swore themselves to eternal secrecy. Jerry Lamott sighed. He was crazy about Tiff, you could tell.

"Okay," said Carla, "tell us if we're getting warm. Was it Paisley?"

"Nope."

"See?" said Chuck to Carla. "It was the druggist."

"Not the druggist," said Jerry.

"Well, that's just great," said Tiffany. "We have another random maniac running around—"

"No we don't."

Harry raised his stein, grinned, pointed to Jerry. "Ex-husband," he said.

"Bingo."

"What?" yelled Carla and Tiffany.

"It's always the ex," said Harry B.

At summer's end, Amy and Carla took a road trip to the Hollywood Forever Cemetery on Santa Monica Boulevard. They brought along Ma's Acorn of Broken Dreams, anchored in Lottie's car seat. Carla's plan was to scatter the ashes around Judy Garland's grave, which to Amy wasn't much of a plan unless they were going to drop furtive handfuls here and there like breadcrumbs and hope they weren't spotted and thrown out. In order to carry the Acorn onto the grounds they bought a spray of white glads so they could explain that the Acorn was really a vase, but the uniformed man at the gate didn't even ask.

Judy Garland's grave was in a crypt within a pavilion, the Judy Garland Pavilion. "Ma would have loved this," Carla said. Before them was a polished marble wall that read, "I'll come to you smiling through the years."

"Your mother never saw it?" Amy had thought the woman practically lived here, so adamant had she been about mingling her remains with those of the greatest of child stars.

"Judy Garland used to be buried in New York. They moved her body out here a few years ago. Ma died before they finished building the crypt. She missed the big unveiling by six months."

"She must have loved Judy Garland."

"Not really."

"Then why—"

"Ma didn't love anything." Carla traced the etched words with her fingertips. *Smiling through the years.* "She made me promise to do this so she could stick it to me from the grave."

"Is it working? Because if it is, we should leave. You don't owe your mother anything."

"I know." Carla laid the gladiolas beneath the marble wall. They would be swept away as rubbish by nightfall, she was sure. "Toto's grave is over there." She pointed north. "I wanted to bring the dogs."

Carla looked so forlorn. She had seemed hopeful, almost excited, when they set out this morning. Now disappointment shrouded her. What had she thought would happen? Was it a ceremony that she needed? Amy was bad at those. "I have an idea," she said. Carla looked up. "There must be a view around here somewhere. Where's that Hollywood sign? It's real place, isn't it? Perhaps we could scatter the ashes there."

Instantly Carla brightened. "It's a real place! There's an overlook a few miles away. I had to do photo shoots there. Ma always carried on like that stupid sign was Mount Rushmore."

"So, bad memories? Is there another place?"

"No, the overlook's perfect!"

✳ ✳ ✳

Carla, Amy, and the Acorn had the overlook all to themselves. There was a curved stone wall and a telescope, which they didn't need in order to see the white Hollywood sign across the valley. There was also a nasty Santa Ana gusting westward in arrhythmic bursts through the tall pines at their backs. Facing the sign they risked facing the buffeting wind.

Amy said, "If we don't time this just right . . ."

"I know." Carla pried the top off the Acorn, glared down at the ashes. "It never ends with you!"

"It ends today," said Amy. Carla's mother would never vanish completely, might still function as an object lesson, but not as a burden. This was Amy's hope.

"It ends today," said Carla. She rested the Acorn on the railing and waited for the wind to die down. "Should we have some kind of ceremony?"

"Up to you."

"Let's not."

"Excellent."

Carla sighed, smiled. "There's so much I'd like to tell you. But not today. Today is just for this."

"I look forward to it."

"She should never have had children."

"Then she never would have had you."

"Did you ever—"

"Did I ever what?"

"Sorry," said Carla. "Not my business."

"Maybe it is."

"Want children? Did you ever?"

"Yes, but only after it was too late."

"Does that make you sad?"

"Sometimes. But I have my dog, and I have my books."

"And you have me," said Carla.

"And I have you."

Into this moment swept a gust so strong it whipped their hair and stung their eyes. Carla turned to steady the Acorn and before she could get there a pine cone the size of a football slammed into it, shattering the Acorn, and its contents clung together midair just beyond the railing and stretched upward, spindled by quarreling winds into a pencil-thin tornado, a dust devil, and the dust was Ma, stretching higher and higher and then, still holding together, spiraling and twisting out and away and down into the valley and gone.

"Wow," said Carla, "That was really . . . What's so funny?"

"Stardust," said Amy.

ACKNOWLEDGMENTS

Thanks to all who slogged through my draft, including:
   Tess Link
   M. J. Andersen
   Kristin Nielsen
   Alisa Willett
   Batya MacAdam-Somer
   Ed Kornhauser
   Asa Baker-Rouse
   And special lifetime acknowledgment to Thomas L. Dunne, without whose friendship, encouragement, and support I'd never have written a word.